"Miss Malone, the only protection that can be given to you on this post is the appearance of being in a man's care, having a man living with you in this cabin."

The warm color seeped from her features, leaving them the color of ashes. Her hands gripped each other until the knuckles whitened. "What man?" she whispered.

"I'm making the offer." He watched her terror, and rage welled up within his breast. "All men aren't villains. And I'm not suggesting what you think. I mean to make up another bed, and all I'll do is stay under the same roof. In no manner will I give you cause for alarm. If you wish, I'll swear on a Bible!"

"Forgive me. It's only that men . . . they have been terrible to me. With the exception of Father Martin, I've never met a man I felt trust in."

"Will you trust me?" Laurie asked.

By the same author:

HAWTHORN HILL   23261 $1.95

CAIN'S DAUGHTERS   23961 $2.25

DORIS SHANNON

BEYOND THE SHINING MOUNTAINS

FAWCETT CREST • NEW YORK

THIS BOOK IS FOR ANN FOXALL
AND IN MEMORY OF LEWIS FOXALL,
WHO WAS A TRUE SAHIB-*BAHADUR*

BEYOND THE SHINING MOUNTAINS

THIS BOOK CONTAINS THE COMPLETE TEXT OF
THE ORIGINAL HARDCOVER EDITION.

Published by Fawcett Crest Books, a unit of CBS Publications,
the Consumer Publishing Division of CBS Inc., by arrangement with St. Martin's Press, Inc.

Printed in the United States of America

First Fawcett Crest printing: July 1980

10 9 8 7 6 5 4 3 2 1

1

Historical mileposts, works of art and literature richly studded the year 1812. The first two cantos of *Childe Harold* tripped off the pen of Byron; two German brothers with the misleading surname Grimm published a collection of fairy tales; a Spanish artist, Goya, completed a superb portrait of Doña Antonia Zarapata; and on the river Clyde a steamship, the *Comet*, signaled the radical beginning of a newer, faster method of transportation. In Russia the army of Napoleon Bonaparte left the field of Borodino and, not even dreaming it was doomed, entered Moscow in triumph. Far across the Atlantic Ocean the young United States of America added a new state, Louisiana, to its growing territory. Then, with magnificent confidence, the new nation turned its attention northward to the British colony in Upper Canada. The War of 1812, between the United States and Britain, was declared. Far in the west of the continent, in a territory that would in time be called British Columbia, a fur trading post, Fort Thompson, was sold by the American Fur Company to the North West Company.

None of these events made the slightest difference to Laurence Woodbyne. Indeed, if he had heard of any of them he had conveniently erased them from his mind. As he relaxed in the rented carriage bearing him from London to his father's small estate in Essex, his mind was occupied with thoughts of his favorite pastimes—gambling tables, the theater, and the lovely ladies who made the theater such a pleasure. One lady in particular, Lila Lansom, the toast of London, and his mistress for a few short months, entranced him. As he mentally traced the voluptuous lines of her body, he sighed with pleasure. He had thought nothing could tear him from her bed, but then his father's summons had arrived; Laurie had kissed Lila one last time and, like a dutiful son, made his way north.

He shook himself, dispelling the memory of Lila's supple waist and extravagant bosom. What could Sir Christopher want? he wondered. Although the affection between them was warm and genuine, Christopher Woodbyne rarely bothered his son. Each quarter a letter and his allowance would arrive. Laurie usually managed to get home for Christmas, and once in a long time his father would visit him in London, but never before had he summoned his son to his side.

Leaning forward, Laurie pushed aside the panel and called to the coachman, "Whip them up a bit, man, you're dawdling."

The man muttered and then called back, "Case you haven't noticed, sir, we're here."

Laurie glanced out the window. They were indeed there. The horses were trotting under the brick arch, and the driveway, lined on either side with lime trees, curved away toward the house. He was glad his older brother wasn't with him. Ashbury always had some asinine remark to make about the age of the place and the Woodbyne claim to fame and history. But then Ashbury was, always had been, a thorough ass—though the ass had managed to marry shrewdly, Laurie conceded. Ashbury had plucked off a girl with a good dowry. Laurie chuckled. All the money in England couldn't have forced him to marry Mildred. She had the build of a plank and the face of a lemon. Thank God they were on their marriage trip and he wouldn't have to see them.

As the carriage rumbled up to the house, signs of neglect became apparent. The place had been running down for years, but now it looked even worse. The grounds were unkempt and, without being able to put a finger on the cause, Laurie felt that the house looked seedy, down at the heels. Then all thoughts of his surroundings vanished. His father was standing at the top of the steps.

With genuine pleasure Laurie threw open the door and, hardly waiting for the carriage to draw to a stop, sprang down and ran up the steps. Ignoring his father's outstretched hand, Laurie threw his arms around the slender shoulders and embraced the older man.

"God's teeth, but it's good to see you. I've missed you, father."

Sir Christopher smiled. "And weren't aware of it until this minute. Come in, Laurie, come in."

Jarvis was waiting a few paces behind his master, his angular face set in the sour lines of disapproval that were reserved for the younger son. Now, if it had been Ashbury, Laurie thought, the old man would be beaming. As he handed the butler his caped greatcoat he shivered, and his eyes flew to the huge fireplace at the far end of the great paneled hall. No cheery fire burned on its hearth.

Sir Christopher followed his gaze. "Conserving on fuel. Come into the study. There's a good fire going there."

"But it's November. You should have fires all over the house. This place is icy."

"Conserving on fuel," his father repeated. "Watch that loose tile."

His warning came too late. Laurie tripped and nearly went sprawling. "What's going on here? The grounds look wretched, and this house is starting to look like a tenement."

"That's one of the reasons you're here. But sit down close to the fire and warm up. Jarvis, bring a bottle of brandy."

"Only two left, sir," Jarvis grumbled.

"Damn it all, man, do as I say!"

Selecting one of the big shabby chairs near the fire, Laurie looked around with pleasure. Of all the rooms in the house this one was his favorite. When he thought of his father, he always pictured him here, surrounded by hunting trophies, books, family portraits, and all the small

7

treasures he had picked up through the years. On the mantelpiece were miniatures of Ashbury and himself, and on the wall behind them hung a full-length painting of his mother. She was young and pretty, exactly as he remembered her. His mother had never lived long enough to lose either youth or beauty.

"Ah, the brandy." Sir Christopher met Jarvis at the door, took the tray of bottles and glasses, and pushed the door shut with his foot. Carefully he poured a few ounces in both glasses and handed one to his son.

Over the rim Laurie grinned at his father. "I think the old devil is trying to save the decent brandy for Ashbury. When are he and his blushing bride due back?"

"Next week."

"Should have him use some of Mildred's money on repairs."

"He's only too willing, can hardly wait to start; but he'll have to be patient. Ashbury will have his turn soon enough."

"What do you mean?"

Ignoring the question, his father asked abruptly, "And how is your life going?"

"Frantic but fine."

"Yes, I should say it probably is. And what of your debts?"

"One can't live without debts."

Leaning over, Christopher Woodbyne plucked a sheaf of papers from his desk. "Hmm, yes, but these are a bit excessive, aren't they?"

His son's brows drew together. "Have they been harrying you, father?"

The older man shuffled through the papers. "Gambling debts, tailors', three months' rent on your flat. Women's bills here too, milliners'—"

"In my last letter I told you about Lila."

Without glancing up, Christopher continued, "Shoemakers', dressmakers', rent for her rooms. Some expensive trinkets." He slapped them back on the desk. "A

8

sizable amount, and no possible way I can pay even a portion of them."

"Don't worry about them, sir. I'll stave the blood-suckers off until my next allowance."

Leaning his head back, Christopher sighed and reached for his brandy. Laurie studied his father's face in the fire-light. It was like looking into a mirror and seeing himself in thirty-odd years. Christopher bore his years lightly. His hair, like Laurie's, was that shade of silver gilt that merely silvers more with age, and it was as thick and silky as his son's. The planes of his face, from the rounded brow through the thin nose and down to a beautifully modeled mouth, were Laurie's—fastidious, sensitive, touches of humor near the eyes, around the mouth. Against the background of light hair and fair skin, his eyes and brows were startling. He had dark brown eyes framed in dark, girlishly long lashes, with dark brows arching above them. Much as he disliked the word *beautiful*, Laurie used it under his breath. A beautiful man, beautiful rather than handsome. And yet there was no touch of effeminacy in either his face or his thin, elegant body. That's what Lila had said when she'd accepted Laurie's overtures. "You're prettier than most girls, but you're all man. And that's why I'm picking you, love, instead of some of the gents with more cash who'd like to buy me." Let's not knock the Woodbyne looks, Laurie told himself; at least they gain the delectable females.

His father sighed again, this time heavily. "There won't be a next allowance. No matter how I try, how much I try to cut costs here . . . there's no way."

Laurie's conscience hit him with a jolt. "That's the reason this house is falling down around your ears, why you haven't even fires lit. I've always known your income was limited, but—"

"We've been living off capital for years, son. Now it's gone. Your brother is all right; he married well. But you—you're exactly like me. How can you earn your keep?"

"There must be a way. I've had a fair education."

9

"And what has it fitted you for? A lawyer, a doctor, even a clerk? Out of the question. You had no wish to become a career soldier or apprentice in the navy. Like me, you're doing what you do best. We're both suited only as dilettantes."

Laurie couldn't deny the truth of that statement. He was qualified for absolutely nothing. For three years, since his twentieth birthday, he'd lived the life of a young man about town, with no thought of anything but pleasure. He grasped at a straw.

"Ashbury. Surely he'll agree to continue my allowance."

His father chuckled. "Do you really believe that? Anyway, Mildred only brought a dowry, not a fortune. Ashbury, even if he wished, couldn't afford you."

Reaching for the bottle, Laurie splashed more brandy in his father's glass and then in his own. "I'll have to find something. Maybe tutoring, something of that sort. I've numerous friends who will help."

"Soon enough you'll learn that today's friends melt like snow under a spring sun when misfortune comes. No, there's only one answer to our problem. You must marry money."

"Emulate my dear brother? Find the plain fourth daughter of an earl, another Mildred, and bed her?"

His father tried to turn a chuckle into a cough. He cared no more for his elder son than Laurie did. The thought of plump, serious Ashbury laboring over his new wife's long, scrawny body tickled his own humor. "At least the boy had sense enough to marry for money, not love."

Looking up at his mother's pretty painted face, Laurie raised his glass in salute. "You give good advice, but you married for love yourself."

Christopher studied his wife's features. "And never once regretted it. But after all, that's what has us in this difficulty, isn't it?"

Laurie forced himself to be serious. "Have you already selected the plain fourth daughter, sir?"

"I wish I could say yes. I'll admit I've looked the

market over, but the only eligible girls of your class are looking as hard for a moneyed husband as you must for a moneyed wife."

"So?"

"So we must bring our sights down, be realistic. There's a new class with ready money these days, a growing number of merchants and traders who've made fortunes."

Moodily, the younger man looked into the depths of the glowing coals. "And I'm to wed the daughter of some tradesman, probably a cow of a woman with thick wrists and ankles and the manners of a coal heaver."

His father extended a thin hand and patted the boy's shoulder. "Not as bad as that." As he moved he caught his breath sharply, and one hand grasped and pressed against his stomach.

Laurie jumped to his feet. Only then did he see changes in the face that so resembled his own. Lines of pain as well as humor indented the lips, stitched bitter creases beside the fine eyes.

"Are you ill, father?"

"I'll be better in a moment . . . . Sit down, Laurie. This will pass."

Laurie stood over the other man's chair. "How long has this been going on?"

"Long enough." Christopher took a deep breath, and his hand dropped away from his stomach. "Do sit down, boy. Don't hover over me like that."

Obediently, Laurie returned to his chair. "Have you consulted a doctor?"

A ghost of a smile twitched the other man's lips. "Several."

"What do they say?"

"They haven't the faintest idea. They've bled me and physicked me and purged me, and done not the slightest bit of good. But this is one more reason to get you settled. My instinct tells me not to dally."

Bending his head, Laurie muttered, "You were speaking of me settling with a tradesman's daughter."

11

"On the contrary, what I am speaking of is a young and attractive heiress. Small, but with a good figure, big brown eyes, and a mouth that will probably put your Lila's to shame. As you would say, a nice little piece."

"May I know her name?"

"Esmeralda Hatch."

"Is this nice little piece any relation to Charlie Hatch?"

His father avoided Laurie's eyes. "His daughter, his only child."

"*The* Charlie Hatch?"

"One is quite enough of him, isn't it?"

"Too much. I thought you were speaking of a humbly born but honest merchant. Charlie Hatch is a monster. Started as a dustman—"

"Peddler, I believe."

"Well, he didn't make his money from peddling. He's rumored to be involved in much of the crime in London. I know for a fact he's the owner of bawdyhouses, of low gambling dens. Hatch has his slimy fingers in every piece of dirty—"

"Calm down, son. What you say is true as far as it goes. But Charlie now has an urge for respectability, and he's converted his . . . ah, unsavory gains into legitimate businesses. And he's a man of substance now, with a huge amount of money and power at his fingertips."

"Which doesn't take the filth from those fingers!"

Christopher poked the fire, and flames shot up, their red glow for an instant making his face ruddy, creating a fleeting illusion of health. "Where do you think the financial foundations for the present aristocracy came from? Some from piracy, others from sharp business practices. Many of our ancestors were moneylenders and such. Don't look too far back into your own heritage. I know for a fact one of our ancestors was a pirate off the Barbary Coast. All Hatch is trying to do is found a dynasty. When he took a wife rather late in life, he left all the fancy ladies like your Lila alone and selected an aging spinster, the daughter of a country parson. It's a wonder

12

she ever gave him even one child. Searching years ago for what Hatch would call gentility."

"You sound as though you sympathize with the man."

"Understand him, yes. Sympathize with him, no. He's absolutely ruthless, knows exactly what he wants, and is going to get it."

Suspicion crossed Laurie's features. "Have you met him?"

His father bent his head. "Mr. Hatch took the liberty of paying me a call. As an inducement he brought these." His head jerked toward the papers on his desk.

"The brass of the man! Sneaking around gathering up my debts, things none of his infernal business. I hope you showed him the door."

"On the contrary, I listened closely. It would seem our man of iron has one vulnerable point—his daughter. He worships her. He led me to understand she has seen you and yearns for you."

"Did you believe him?"

"In spite of your obvious assets in the physical sense, Laurie, no. I would imagine Hatch tried a couple of titles first, was thrown out on his ear, and now is eyeing you."

Laurie laughed. "Too bad he didn't catch Ashbury while he was available. He'll have the title, the estate, everything that promises gentility."

"And would be more willing to listen to reason," his father said drily. "Are you?"

"How far has this gone?"

"Hatch talked and I listened. He's prepared to be most generous."

"I'd never live under the same roof with Charlie Hatch."

"You wouldn't be expected to. I insisted, and he finally agreed, that you would have your own home, one of your choosing."

His son thought of Lila, and as he did he felt heat in his loins. Her warm silky curves, those jutting breasts . . . He said miserably, "I'd have to give up Lila."

"Naturally, and any other little doxy you're considering. But come now, a couple of children, the relaxing of Hatch's vigilance, and with a little discretion—" Breaking off, his father lowered an eyelid in a wink. "I've never asked, but what exactly does your Lila do?"

"She acts."

"Well?"

"Hardly at all. But she doesn't have to. What porportions, what a body! At present she's appearing in a play where she's Aphrodite, popping out of a huge seashell—"

"Aphrodite and a *seashell?*"

"When Lila rises from that seashell bathed in pink light, with her skin showing through a few scraps of pink tulle, no one questions the authenticity of her act. They're too busy staring."

"She sounds delectable. It will be a sacrifice giving this girl up, but there'll be other Lilas."

"Not like this one."

"All Lilas are much the same, son, and to have them, you have to afford them. This marriage could put you in that position for life. What are you thinking?"

"I'm confused. I don't believe I could stomach being Charlie Hatch's son-in-law."

Christopher studied the younger man's face. "Take your time. Think about it for a few days."

As Laurie opened his mouth to say he had thought about it and wouldn't do it, a tap sounded on the door. It swung open, and Jarvis said, "Dinner is served, Sir Christopher."

With an obvious effort Christopher Woodbyne struggled to his feet, and for a moment he caught at the back of his chair for support. Jarvis's face was anguished as he watched his master, and then his eyes slid over Laurie with open resentment and contempt. For an instant Laurie saw himself through the old man's eyes, slumped before a fire his father could ill afford, drinking one of his last bottles of good brandy, a ne'er-do-well, a wastrel, living on his parent's bounty and giving nothing in return. At that moment Laurie came to a decision. This was the first time his father had asked anything from him; if it would bring the ailing man peace of mind, this at least he could do.

He took his father's arm. "I'll do it, sir. Go ahead and make the arrangements."

Sir Christopher's face relaxed, and he smiled. "I already have. We return to London tomorrow, and shortly you will meet Miss Esmeralda Hatch."

Laurie smiled back at him. "I keep forgetting how wily you can be."

Christopher patted the hand on his arm. "I was hoping, son. And don't worry, this will be fast and painless."

Under his breath, Laurie muttered. "A life sentence. Charlie Hatch and a girl with an awful name like Esmeralda."

2

The union of the Woodbyne and Hatch families was not only fast and relatively painless but also cold-bloodedly businesslike. Miss Esmeralda Hatch became Mrs. Laurence Woodbyne on Christmas Day, barely a month after their introduction.

Sir Christopher allowed his son little time for second thoughts; the night they returned from Essex found them presenting themselves at the Hatch home. Laurie had two shocks in store for him. He'd expected Charlie Hatch's house to be garish and tasteless, reflecting a man jumped up in a comparatively short time from peddler and crime tsar to the ranks of the nouveau riche. Instead the house, situated on a quiet street in a fairly fashionable district, was solid, substantial, and unostentatiously luxurious. Inside the massive door were warm well-tended hearths, graceful vases of hothouse flowers, and what appeared to be an army of silent, attentive servants. The master of the house was as much of a shock as his background. Braced for grossness, Laurie found himself exchanging pleasantries with a short, compact, well-tailored man possessing a soft, rather stilted diction and the coldest eyes he'd ever seen.

In the drawing room the ladies waited, three of them perched in a line on the sofa close to the fireplace. Two tall women in dark clothes flanked Miss Hatch, and at first glance the girl looked like a well-behaved child between two adults. Christopher had said she was small, and she was, barely reaching Laurie's shoulder. He had said she had a good figure, and she certainly had, with a swelling bosom and rounded hips outlined in a chaste pink gown that was high-necked and touched with white at the throat and wrists.

Taking his place opposite her, Laurie studied the girl with covert interest. Ash-blond hair clustered in short, childish curls around a plump face. She had skin like peaches and cream, bright brown eyes, and one entrancing dimple in her left cheek. But it was her mouth that riveted his eyes. Mobile, thick lips drew back in frequent smiles from tiny, perfect teeth. It was a mouth that didn't hint at sexuality but fairly shrieked it. She had a devastating habit of darting a red tongue out to lick those thick pink lips. Watching her, Laurie was conscious of a tightening through his groin and forced himself to look away, to pay some attention to her companions.

Miss Grace—Laurie wasn't sure whether Grace was her first name or her surname—had been Esmeralda's governess and was now her companion. She was a tall, strongly built, handsome woman with a high-pitched voice and a strident laugh. Deep color mantled her cheekbones, and Laurie had a hunch she resented him. Although the woman on Esmeralda's other side was as tall as Miss Grace, there the resemblance ceased. Charlie Hatch's wife was a slender, drooping woman with a tired face and anxious eyes. Judith Hatch didn't care any more for her daughter's companion than Miss Grace cared for him, Laurie surmised. As she neatly attended to the tray of tea before her, Mrs. Hatch darted sidelong looks at the others—faint fear when she glanced at her husband, flaring dislike for Miss Grace, and a veiled pity for Laurie.

Silently, Laurie accepted the pity and echoed it. Nothing like being set up on display and having Charlie Hatch regarding his every move, weighing his every word, appraising him as one would look over a new investment. Shifting his attention from the women to the master of the house, Laurie caught Hatch's eyes and wondered what the verdict would be. Arrogantly, he stared back until Hatch colored faintly and turned to speak to Sir Christopher. The man had made a valiant effort to become a gentleman, Laurie conceded, but perching on that spindly gilt chair, holding his cup daintily, and speaking in his slow, careful way wouldn't fool anyone. Just the presence of Sir Christopher in the same room underlined their difference, an intangible but very real gulf that no tailor, no shoemaker, no elocution teacher could ever bridge. You could take the man from the gutter, Laurie decided disdainfully, but there was no way to take the gutter out of the man. He wondered if Hatch was aware of this, and decided he probably was. Hatch would have few illusions; he had been shrewd enough to get where he was, and he was shrewd enough to know how far he could go.

Between her two chaperons, Hatch's daughter was giggling, and the sound brought Laurie's attention back to her. Spoiled, he thought. Nothing too good for young Miss Hatch. Pretty clothes and jewelry, her own governess, probably a pony cart as a child, the best of food and attention. A spoiled, cherished, empty-headed little girl. And now daddy was going to buy her a husband, the best his money could get.

Mrs. Hatch was valiantly trying to make conversation, and Laurie politely answered her questions. Yes, he made his home in London. Yes, the family estate was in Essex. No, it wasn't large, a very small one, really. Yes, his brother had been recently married, and he and his bride would be back shortly from their wedding trip. Yes, the weather was dreadful. It was a relief when Hatch put down his cup and rose to his feet.

He addressed Laurie. "The ladies will entertain you, Mr. Woodbyne, while I show Sir Christopher my study. Few pieces of bric-a-brac he may enjoy seeing."

This excuse didn't fool any of them. Mrs. Hatch's thin fingers closed around the handle of the silver creamer, Miss Grace darted a steely stare after the two men, and Miss Hatch began to eat an iced cake. What would the verdict be? Laurie wondered. Had he passed inspection? A wave of fury swept over him. Bartered like a horse! Then his sense of humor came to the rescue. Beggars

18

can't choose, and Esmeralda certainly was a tasty little baggage. She had finished the cake, and instead of wiping her hands on a napkin, she put her fingers to her mouth and licked them clean like a kitten. It should have been crude, but it wasn't. The red tongue making a full circuit of pink lips and leaving them wet and glossy, the red tongue licking at the short, plump fingers, was as stimulating to Laurie as if she'd suddenly whipped up her skirts and displayed her legs.

During this performance her mother sat like a statue, and it was Miss Grace who took the girl's hand away from her mouth and dried it on her own napkin while she beamed indulgently at her charge. The eyes in the statue moved sideways and threw venom at Miss Grace, and it seemed to Laurie that she regarded her daughter with the same emotion. Then Mrs. Hatch turned to Laurie and began feverishly discussing the weather again. In the midst of details of a recent shopping trip that had been spoiled by continuous rain, the two men returned. Neither of them made any effort to seat himself, and after a moment Laurie slowly got to his feet.

Portentously, as though he were addressing a large audience, Charlie Hatch announced, "My beloved daughter, Esmeralda, is now formally engaged to Mr. Laurence Woodbyne."

Pushing Miss Grace's ministering hands aside, Esmeralda jumped to her feet and ran with quick little steps to her father. "Oh, daddy!" she cried, and buried her face against his waistcoat.

Any doubt about whether Hatch had a weak point was at that moment dispelled. As he held his daughter close to his breast with one hand, the other gently stroking her fair curls, his whole face softened, and the small cold eyes radiated affection. Beside them Sir Christopher stood quietly, regarding the father and the daughter.

"May I ask if you have set the wedding day?" Mrs. Hatch murmured.

"On Christmas Day," Hatch replied. Gently he disengaged his daughter's clasp and held her away from him, looking down fondly at her flushed face. "And what does daddy's Christmas angel think of that?"

"Oh, lovely, daddy. And a house, we'll have a house all our own?"

"You certainly will! As soon as your fiancé makes his choice you can get started with decorators and pick the furniture yourself."

"No." Leaving her father, Esmeralda ran back to her companion. She clasped the woman's hand. "Miss Grace, she'll have to help me. I can't do it alone."

"Whatever you want, Esmie." Turning to Laurie, Hatch stuck out his hand. "Can you be ready to house-hunt tomorrow?"

Taking the hand, Laurie avoided his father's eyes. "I think so, sir."

Mrs. Hatch was on her feet, and in a flurry of movement the bargain was sealed. She pecked at Laurie's cheek, pecked at her daughter's cheek, and had her hand kissed by Sir Christopher. Laurie endured a thump over his shoulder from his future father-in-law and a surprisingly strong handclasp from Miss Grace, and bent gallantly over his fiancée's hand.

Wine was produced, and after suitable toasts the two Woodbyne men made their escape. In the corner of the carriage Laurie leaned back and closed his eyes, trying to blank out everything but the swaying movement of the carriage and the clip-clop of the horses' hooves. It proved to be impossible. He was churning inside.

"A Christmas present," he told his father furiously. "A china doll wrapped up and delivered for darling little Esmie."

"Think of it this way, son—you'll never have to put up with this again."

Opening one eye, Laurie squinted and saw his father's thin hand patting the shabby seat. "What?"

"No more rented carriages. You'll have your own house fully furnished, your own carriage. All the household expenses will be taken care of, and there'll be an allowance for your wife and a generous sum quarterly for you."

"You drive a hard bargain." Laurie asked with mild interest, "Will the house be in my name?"

"It will be transferred to you on the birth of your first child."

"Hatch thinks of everything, doesn't he?"

Christopher laughed. "He's taking no chance on you selling and clearing out in a hurry. At least not until he has his heir and you've a child to pin you down." He sobered. "Don't ever play games with that man, Laurie. Don't ever fight him."

Opening both eyes, Laurie turned to look at his father. "You seem to have a healthy respect for him."

"A healthy fear. As long as you're of use . . . fine. If he finds you aren't, he'll crush you like a fly."

"Not as long as little Esmie is my wife." Laurie drew his caped greatcoat closer. "Mama Hatch is a bit of an enigma."

Christopher's brows arched a little higher. "She seems merely a gentle woman whose spirit has been crushed."

"Still something left. She's afraid of her husband—"

"With good reason."

"And she nourishes a loathing for Miss Grace."

"Understandable. Her daughter seems to have transferred her affection to her companion."

"Then why does she hate her daughter?"

"Does she?"

"I caught a couple of glances she tossed Esmie's way. If looks could kill, the dear child would be colder than a mackerel."

Christopher shrugged, and as he did, the carriage lumbered to a halt. He made no move to get out. After a moment he said quietly, "Something about this doesn't seem quite right, Laurie. It's not too late; you can still call it off."

Laurie was tempted to do just that. Then he gave the other man a wry grin. "If I was a strong character I'd never have considered it in the first place. But the price is

21

right, and we'll deliver the goods on Christmas Day."
Opening the door, he stepped down and held his father's
arm while he got out. In the lamplight he could see worried lines on the older man's face. Laurie squeezed the
thin arm he was holding and managed a genuine smile.
"Do you suppose Mildred and Ashbury will attend the
wedding?"

"They'll be there."

"I can't see Ashbury being delighted, and I can imagine
what Mildred's reaction will be to welcoming Charlie
Hatch as a member of the family."

"Mildred is my daughter-in-law." Christopher repeated
grimly, "They'll both be there."

And whatever he said to them had his son and his
daughter-in-law at Laurie's wedding. Once again Laurie
was surprised at Charlie Hatch's good sense. Hatch took
no chances on rebuffs to his invitations to the nuptials. Instead of having a large event with hundreds of guests, he
held the ceremony and reception at his home, and the
guest list was a small one. If Hatch had any relatives, he
certainly didn't produce them, but Mrs. Hatch's brother
and his wife were there. The brother was a country parson who conducted the service fighting a pronounced
stammer, and his wife was a dowdy, awestricken little
woman. Whether Sir Christopher had pressed any of their
numerous relatives to attend, Laurie didn't know, but except for Ashbury and Mildred, the Woodbynes were
represented only by an aged female cousin who had doted
on Laurie when he was a small boy.

In the largest reception room, banked with Yule green-
ery and massed with fragrant blossoms, the ceremony was
performed. A string quartet and a soprano with a magnificent bosom and a voice to match provided the music
appropriate to the occasion. Laurie, attended by his
brother, waited at the improvised altar for the bride. She
eventually made her entrance amid "ohs" and "ahs" from
the small gathering. Clad in white tulle poised over satin
and studded with seed pearls, her hair and face hidden
under more tulle, seed pearls, and orange blossoms, lean-

22

ing on her proud father's arm, Esmeralda tripped to her place beside the groom. Miss Grace, striking in blue brocade and chiffon, was her attendant, and throughout the entire ceremony Esmeralda clung to her tall companion.

"What's wrong with the girl?" Ashbury hissed in his brother's ear. "Can't she stand by herself?"

Accepting the ring, Laurie whispered back, "She's very young and shy."

The parson drew out the ceremony to improbable lengths, but eventually he stuttered through the last prayer, heads were raised, and Laurie carefully lifted the bride's veil, folded it back from her flushed face, and kissed her cheek.

A lavish dinner followed, and it was clear that even if the wedding was small Charlie Hatch was making it a memorable one. In the dining room, banked with flowers and lighted by hundreds of candles, the long table was almost literally groaning with food. Course followed delicious course, and the music provided by the quartet almost masked the fact that it was a subdued gathering. After the initial chatter about the beauty of the house, of the flowers, and of the bride had subsided, no one appeared to have much to say. Mrs. Hatch's country relatives bent bashfully over their plates, Laurie's elderly cousin was grimly intent on hers, and although Sir Christopher tried to make conversation he received little response. It was Ashbury who came to the rescue and proceeded to question Charlie Hatch about one of his businesses. Laurie wasn't even faintly interested, but he attempted to feign polite attention.

"I understand, sir," Ashbury said, "that you have wide interests in the Canadian fur trade. I was wondering if you were connected with the Hudson's Bay Company—"

Laurie nearly laughed aloud at the abrupt way his brother broke off his sentence. Ashbury had really put his foot into it this time. The idea that the "Company for Gentlemen Adventurers" would welcome shady Charlie Hatch to their illustrious circle was ludicrous. Christopher

23

was opening his mouth to bridge the awkward silence when Hatch himself came to the rescue.

He chuckled, leaned back in his chair, and raised his wine goblet. "Come now, Mr. Woodbyne, do you think the Hudson's Bay would have any use for Charlie Hatch? No, I'm afraid I was forced to go into direct competition with those gentlemen."

"In what way? Did you take a partnership in the North West Company?"

Now more interested, Laurie stared at his plump brother. How did Ashbury know so much about fur trading? Of course, Ashbury always had had a good business head.

"What I did," Hatch explained genially, "was found my own company, taking in a few junior partners."

"An independent?"

"Exactly. I now have four posts in Canada and soon hope to have a fifth." Hatch took a sip of wine, dabbed at his lips with a napkin, and continued. "My latest post is now being erected at the confluence of the Nechako and Fraser rivers, not far from the Nor'westers' post at Fort George." He chuckled again. "We hope not only to give them competition but to use some of their own tactics against them. The Hudson's Bay Company really is composed of gentlemen, and because of that hasn't flourished. But the Nor'westers—now, they're men after my own heart. Do anything, including stirring up troubles with the natives, to beat down competition."

Ashbury's expression was attentive. "Fraser River . . . isn't that west of the mountains?"

"The natives have a romantic name for it. They call it 'the land beyond the Shining Mountains.' A beautiful area, I understand, but wild and fraught with danger."

"Others call it *le pays sauvage*," Ashbury said.

Hatch raised heavy brows. "You appear to be well informed on this subject, Mr. Woodbyne. Are you interested in investing in the fur trade?"

"I've toyed with the idea," Ashbury admitted, and added cautiously, "Only a modest amount, of course."

24

"In that case, if you wish more information, come down to my office, or even better, we'll have dinner together."

Ashbury nodded and changed the subject. Conversation was now more general, and Laurie directed his attention to his bride. Esmeralda hadn't even glanced at him throughout the meal. She concentrated on the food, the wine, and whispered asides to Miss Grace. She had a hearty appetite, Laurie observed. If she ate this way habitually, by the time she was thirty the pleasing plumpness would have disappeared beneath a mass of blubber. Her mother merely picked at her food, but Charlie ate stolidly, taking large helpings of each course and demolishing them without haste or apparent relish. Laurie had a hunch the man would take his women in the same methodical way, to appease an appetite and nothing else. And there must be women in his life. He looked a full-blooded man, and poor faded Mrs. Hatch had probably served her purpose when she bore him a daughter. Laurie liked Judith and felt sorry for her. Throughout the last month she'd been unfailingly kind and tactful, and he appreciated it. He shuddered at the thought of her life with the flinty-eyed, implacable man opposite him.

The flinty eyes lifted from the dessert plate and roamed around the table. "We'll excuse the ladies now. Coffee will be served in the parlor for them." Hatch's gaze rested fondly on his daughter. "But first you'll be wanting to go to your own home, Esmie."

"Yes, daddy." She yawned and moved one chubby hand to cover her mouth. "I'm very tired."

Smiles greeted this ingenuous remark, and Ashbury smothered a laugh with a cough. Esmeralda's hand crept out and gripped Miss Grace's. "Can't Miss Grace come with us? We've never been parted, and she's been with me—" Breaking off, she asked the other woman, "How long is it since you came here as my governess?"

Miss Grace flashed a brilliant smile. "Long ago, dear. You were a very small girl."

"No," her father answered firmly. "Miss Grace and the

25

rest of the staff will arrive tomorrow morning. Tonight is yours—" Apparently as an afterthought, he waved at Laurie. "—and your bridegroom's." He rose and helped his daughter from her chair. "We'll see you to your carriage."

In a flurry of chairs being pushed back, raised voices, and repeated good wishes, the bride and groom prepared to depart. In the hall there was more confusion—the bride being draped in a long fur cape, the wife of the parson producing a bag of rice, the parson stammering blessings, and then laughter as Laurie and Esmeralda made their way down the carriage while rice was tossed over their heads.

Laurie extended an arm to assist his bride into the carriage, but his father-in-law shouldered him aside and helped his daughter. Carefully, Hatch caught up the billowing skirts and fur cloak and tucked them around her. Then he turned to Laurie. "Be good to my little girl," he said, and it wasn't a plea or a request but an order.

Not trusting himself to reply, Laurie merely inclined his head and sprang in beside Esmeralda. There was a final flurry of farewell, and then the coachman whipped up the four matched horses and drove smartly off.

Sinking back against the tufted seat covering, Laurie glanced at his bride. Her head was bent, and short fingers were worrying at a cluster of pearls on her skirt.

"Happy?" he asked her.

"I would be if Miss Grace was here. She's been with me since I was—"

"A very small girl. She'll be with you tomorrow, Esmie, but it's time to realize you're no longer a small girl. Miss Grace was part of your childhood, and now you're a married woman. You must let your childhood go."

"I'll never let Miss Grace go."

For the last month he'd been vainly trying to guess the girl's age. Again he wondered how old she was. Eighteen, perhaps only seventeen? Reaching over, he captured her hand and held it. "How old are you, Esmie?"

She lifted round brown eyes. "Twenty-four."

He caught his breath. Twenty-four! She was a year older than he was. The childish curls, childish ruffles, childish mannerisms had completely fooled him. No wonder Hatch had been so generous in his settlement. His little girl was old enough to be well on the way to spinsterhood.

She asked gaily, "How do you like the way I'm fixing up the house?"

"You're doing a wonderful job."

"I still can't see why you insisted on moving all that old stuff into your bedroom and study."

"I'm accustomed to it. I brought it to London when I took my flat. Anyway, that's only two rooms. You have the rest of the house to do what you wish with."

She darted a glance at him. "Why did you pick *that* house?"

"It's much like the townhouse my grandfather once had, same size and style and in the same neighborhood. I used to visit my grandfather when I was a boy, and I've always remembered it."

"What happened to it?"

"My father sold it years ago," he said shortly.

She squeezed his hand. "The Woodbynes used to be one of the great families, didn't they? I suppose they go back to William the Conqueror."

He fought back a feeling of resentment at her tone. "At least to the Crusades."

"And my daddy doesn't even know who his own grand-daddy was."

Silently Laurie decided that Charlie Hatch was lucky if he knew who his own father was. As though she had read his mind, her hand slid away from his and her full mouth set in sullen lines. "At least daddy is rich. Maybe he didn't visit his grand-daddy in a house in Mayfair, but he can *buy* one there."

Laurie lapsed into silence. A feeling of depression and futility gripped him. Bitterly he looked back over the last month; a month he'd spent despising Charlie Hatch, and he wondered whether Hatch was the despicable one or whether he himself was. All the gains he'd made with this marriage—the house in Mayfair, the fine carriage he was riding in, the substantial funds at his disposal—seemed a hollow victory. He hadn't been forced to marry this shallow, petulant girl. At any time he could have said to hell with it and walked away, found some way to support himself. The easy way out, that was the way he always took, and he had a hunch that life with little Esmie might not be so easy.

His mood persisted for the rest of the drive, and even when he opened the massive door of the three-story house on the fashionable square he felt depressed. It was a far cry from Woodbyne Hall in Essex, he thought despondently, looking around at gleaming floors, graceful new furniture, rich carpeting. The staff his wife had engaged must have worked before they left. Flowers banked the hall and parlor, and before a leaping fire a cold meal and wine waited on a low table.

"Would you care for wine?" he asked Esmeralda.

"No, I'm going to bed," she told him, and ran up the staircase.

Wandering into the parlor, he stood before the fire warming his legs. He lifted covers from the dishes and found cold chicken, sliced ham and beef, rolls, cheese, a basket of fruit, and a huge platter of sweets. He slammed the last cover down, strode into the dining room, and located a bottle of brandy in the sideboard. Taking a glass and some soda, he made his way slowly up the stairs. The door of Esmeralda's room was closed, and he passed on to the door of the adjoining room. Here he found a fire kindled on the hearth, and he stood gazing around at the familiar highboy, the old bed with the high carved headboard, the bookcase, the shabby, comfortable chairs. He thumped the tray down on the table before the fireplace, slowly undressed, hesitated over a nightshirt, and finally slipped a robe over his naked body. Sprawling in a chair, he reached for the brandy and held his bare feet out to the warmth. After a few sips he found he was feeling better. His thoughts turned to the girl in the next room. He

28

imagined her tucked in the big ruffled bed, a nightgown swathing her body, securely buttoned to her throat. He felt a remote pity for Esmeralda. She might not be the child he'd taken her for, but in many ways she still seemed very young—and here she was, for the first time wrenched from her father and Miss Grace, waiting nervously for a man she didn't even know to enter her room, enter her bed.

The fears that plague all virgins, he thought compassionately, the terror of hard male flesh pressed to their soft curves, of hard male flesh invading their helpless bodies. He chuckled. Little did Esmie realize that she had nothing to fear from him this night. The final day of bachelorhood had left him an exhausted man. His friends had taken him to the club for a riotous stag dinner and, after much wine and brandy and many toasts, had delivered him to Lila's door. They thumped on the panel, leered at him, and then lurched away. Lila must have known about their plan, because she showed no surprise when she opened the door and found her lover weaving about.

She grasped his arm and pulled him into her room. "Fine shape those hellrakes have you in, love. I hope they haven't got you so sodden you can't enjoy, 'cause Lila has a present for you." Putting warm lips to his ear, she whispered, "I'm going to waste you, boy. When I'm done, there won't be much left for your bride."

He stared owlishly at her. She was wearing no more than she did when she rose in full splendor from the seashell. He spread his arms. "Waste me!" he cried joyously.

Grinning, Laurie spilled more brandy into his glass. Lila was a girl of her word. By the time he'd crawled out of her bed that morning, he'd been a spent, sober man. Esmie was lucky. He was in no shape to rush in and commit rape on her while she screamed for daddy and Miss Grace. In a few minutes he'd go in, give her a tickle and a few kisses, and then make his way back to his own bed for a much-needed sleep.

29

A voice broke through his reverie. "Well?" it asked.

He nearly dropped the glass. In the doorway Esmie stood, the light from behind her turning her fair curls into a halo, her body draped in a delicate dressing gown fluttering with pale blue ribbons.

"Well?" she repeated. "Are you going to drink all night?" Turning on her heel, she threw words over her shoulder. "Get in here."

Putting down the glass, Laurie followed her into the ornate room. It was richly decorated with white furniture picked out with gilt, blue and green brocade masking the windows and covering the chairs, a huge bed spread with more brocade and turned back to show silk sheets. He had no time to admire the room. Esmie had discarded her dressing gown, simply dropping it in a heap on the carpet, and she was standing with her back to him. His eyes followed the indentation of a neat waist down to the sweet curves of a delicious behind and short but shapely legs. She whirled around, and he glimpsed outthrust, ripe breasts, nipples already hardening into tight pink buds, a rounded belly, and a V of fair hair.

"God's teeth!" he grunted.

She flung herself on him, her mouth seizing his, a sharp hot tongue thrusting past his lips and avidly exploring his mouth. With one hand he tore at the belt of his robe, with the other he seized a quivering pink buttock.

Laurie had already learned that this virginal child bride was not a child. In a very short time he made his second discovery. Daddy's little girl was no virgin.

3

Fog was creeping against the nursery window so thickly that even now, in the evening, it wasn't much darker than it had been earlier in the day. Since morning, lamps had been lit all over the house, and it was still cold enough in April to keep fires going in most of the rooms.

Oblivious to the weather, Laurie relaxed with his eyes fixed on his son's face as he rocked the boy to sleep. As always, he admired the baby, large and lusty at not quite four months, skin like a rose, and a perfect skull covered with silver-gilt ringlets. Christopher Charles Woodbyne, he thought—much too large a name for such a small boy, and so he was called Chris. Chris's brown eyes were clouding with drowsiness, and as his father watched, long lashes quivered and fell in the dark crescents on flushed cheeks. Gently, Laurie lifted one hand, spread the fingers, and caressed the tiny little finger. It was slightly crooked, exactly like the finger on his own left hand. The Wood-byne finger—there had never been a Woodbyne male without the family inheritance of a crooked little finger.

Laurie sighed. Only slightly over a year, one Woodbyne male born, another laid to his final rest. Sir Christopher had lived barely long enough to see his grandson and then had died quite peacefully as he slept. It had been a mercy, because during the last few months of his life he had wasted away at an alarming pace. But the finality of the event had shocked Laurie, and the grief that tore at him at the time of his father's death had been overwhelming. The funeral had been at the house in Essex, and after

31

the service his father was carried to the mausoleum where generations of Woodbynes waited.

As he thought of the funeral, Laurie closed his eyes. It had been well attended, as Christopher had inspired affection in all his relatives and friends. Laurie's wife and Mr. and Mrs. Hatch were there, and even through the grief numbing him, Laurie could see that his wife's parents were far from welcome. The other mourners made no effort to disguise their disdain, and after the internment, when they returned to the manor house for the funeral dinner, it could have been awkward.

Laurie made no attempt to pierce the solid front against the Hatches. Strangely enough, it was Sir Ashbury and Lady Woodbyne who made the effort. With tact and determination they led Charlie and Judith Hatch from group to group, forcing recognition of them upon friends and relatives. Laurie hadn't even wondered why they bothered. Leaving the room, he sought sanctuary in his father's study, sitting morosely before the cold hearth, his head buried in his hands. After a time he felt a gentle touch on his shoulder and looked up into Judith's weary, kind face.

She gestured at the portrait over the mantel. "Is that your mother?"

Laurie nodded. "She died young. I barely remember her." He added dully, "I've just discovered that in my entire life I've loved only one person, and he's dead."

Sinking to her knees, she clasped him in her thin arms. "You have Chris now."

"Yes, I have Chris."

She drew his head to her meager breast, and finally he was able to weep. Afterwards he dried his eyes and took her hand. "And I have you too, Judith."

In the nursery Laurie's eyes snapped open, and his arms tightened around the baby. A son and a mother-in-law, he admitted, were the only people in the entire world whom he loved, possibly the only ones who loved him. He was conscious of the silence in the room, the fog muffling the street noises; the only sounds that disturbed the silence were the steady tick of the clock and the tiny hisses of coal as it burned on the hearth. He inhaled deeply. He liked the smell of his son's room—powder and warm milk and the healthy odor of a clean baby.

The door opened softly, and Nurse Leland put her head around it. Her hair was covered with a neat cap, and her full skirts rustled crisply as she moved. "His nibs gone off yet?" she whispered.

"Sound asleep."

He handed her the precious bundle, and she carried the baby to the cradle and competently tucked him in. A good nurse, Laurie decided. He'd selected her himself and had summoned an elderly coachman from Woodbyne Hall to drive the nurse and child on their outings. Esmie had fought both decisions, but Charlie Hatch had solidly backed his son-in-law. "Laurie's right," he'd told his furious daughter. "Both Graves and Nurse Leland are responsible people, and I'll not put my trust for Chris' safety in some ragtag you pick."

Smoothing the coverlet into place, the nurse touched the baby's cheek tenderly. "A bonny boy, Mr. Woodbyne."

Laurie was anxious for praise. "You really think so?"

"Finest baby I've ever nursed, and I've nursed a number. Good baby too; he's off for the night now. Not a minute's trouble from young Chris."

Pleased, Laurie beamed at her. "I'll say good night now, nurse."

"And good night to you, sir. Sleep well."

She watched him leave and then shook her head so violently the ribbons on her cap bounced. "Finest father I've ever seen too," she told the sleeping baby. "But what a mother you had wished on you, you poor lamb!"

As Laurie made his way to his bedchamber, he was thinking of Esmeralda too. He slumped down in his favorite chair and looked resentfully at the door to her room. He knew it was locked, securely locked, as it had been for most of their marriage. Esmie was an enigma. He'd be the first to admit he had no idea what she was. For the first

33

five months of their marriage she had been virtually insatiable, and he had been hard pressed to measure up to her demands. Each night, as soon as dinner was finished and their guests, if they were entertaining, had departed, the same charade would be enacted. Esmie would open her bedroom door, jerk her head toward the bed, and practically rape him. When her appetite was sated she would roll away, turn her back to him, and make it quite clear he could leave her bed. In a way, he hadn't minded this life. Esmie, although far from tender, was an accomplished lover, and no one could complain about her passion or dexterity. Then the end had come with an abruptness that still amazed him.

One night the door remained closed. After a time he tried to open it, but it appeared to be locked. Stepping into the hall, he knocked at her door and, without waiting for an answer, swung it open. In the big bed Esmie was comfortably propped up on a heap of silk pillows, eating chocolate creams. Beside the bed Miss Grace, her florid face glowing in the lamplight, sat reading a novel aloud.

"What do you want?" Esmie asked ungraciously.

"Well . . . to speak with you, I suppose."

Looking the box over, she selected a candy. "Well, talk."

Miss Grace made no effort to rise, so Laurie jerked his head toward the door. "Please leave us."

The woman hesitated, and then she marked her page with a finger and arrogantly pushed past Laurie. He nearly slammed the door behind her but caught himself and closed it softly.

"What's going on?" he demanded.

His wife raised wide, innocent eyes. "I've no idea what you're talking about."

"Why did you lock your door?"

"It's my door. I can lock it if I wish." She nibbled delicately at the candy. "Oh, sit down. I may as well tell you."

He remained standing. "Tell me what?"

A red tongue made a circuit of her lips, catching bits of chocolate. "I'm going to have a baby."

Laurie's knees buckled, and he sat down suddenly. "When?"

"About seven months from now."

"But that's unreasonable. The last few months . . . yes, I can see that. But not yet. There's no reason we can't live as man and wife."

She picked another chocolate. "That's what the doctor said." Biting into the candy, she made a face and threw it back in the box. "Lemon. I hate lemon! Daddy is so pleased, said he'd see to a nursery right away."

"So you told your father first. And I suppose Miss Grace is in on the secret."

"Of course. Why are you looking so gloomy?"

"Everyone told but the father. Esmie, have you no feeling for me?"

"Don't be so sensitive. Daddy is hoping for a boy."

"Naturally," her husband said bitterly.

"What would you like?"

"At this moment I really couldn't care less."

He got to his feet and stalked out. Miss Grace was waiting in the hall. She stepped into Esmie's room and with cool deliberation shut the door in his face.

That had been the last time he'd entered his wife's room. With grim determination he endured the months of Esmie's pregnancy, suffering physical agony from lack of sex, waiting for the baby to arrive and his wait to be over. He thought frequently of Lila, but he managed to fight off her image and remain faithful to his wife. From feast to famine, he told himself glumly, from insatiable Esmie to a cold and lonely bed.

On Christmas Eve Esmie went into labor and was attended by her doctor, two nurses, and a midwife. Charlie Hatch brought the midwife himself, not quite trusting the good doctor. He waited with Laurie in his study, pacing the floor, smoking cigar after cigar, resorting often to the brandy decanter, and scowling fiercely every time even a whimper could be heard from his daughter's room. It was far from a quiet birth. Esmie's howls could be heard from the kitchens to the servants' quarters.

At one particularly shrill cry, Hatch whirled on Laurie. "My God! What is that bungling idiot of a Herfit doing? Maybe I should have brought another doctor."

"They're tripping over each other up there now."

Seizing the decanter, Hatch splashed more brandy in his glass. "It's been too long."

Laurie stretched long legs toward the fire. "Only a bit over two hours."

His father-in-law glared at him. "You're very cool."

Laurie attempted to soothe him. "Look, Esmie's young and healthy, and she's in excellent hands. Dr. Herfit's one of the best doctors in London, and he said there shouldn't be any problem."

Grunting, Hatch resumed his pacing. At ten minutes to four on Christmas morning another sound issued from Esmie's room—the sharp cry of a baby. Running to the foot of the staircase, Hatch gazed impatiently up. When the doctor appeared at the top of the stairs, Hatch called impatiently, "Are they all right?"

"Fine, sir. Your daughter's fine and so is the baby. A boy, Mr. Hatch, a big strong boy."

Hatch bounded up the stairs. "I must see them."

The doctor caught at his arm. "Mrs. Woodbyne is resting, sir."

The other man immediately paused and then tiptoed toward his daughter's door. With Laurie at his heels he entered the room. Esmie was sleeping, and close beside the bed one of the nurses stood with the baby in her arms. With trembling hands Hatch lifted the blanket and gazed down at the baby. "My grandson," he murmured, "my grandson, Charles Christopher Woodbyne."

Laurie glanced from the red, wrinkled face of the child to his father-in-law. I do believe there're tears in the old shark's eyes, he thought; now that's a sight I never expected to see. Carefully, Laurie lifted one of the fists and spread the fingers apart. He caressed the tiny, crooked little finger. Spreading his own left hand so Hatch could see his crooked finger, Laurie said firmly, "*Christopher Charles Woodbyne.*"

"As you wish," Hatch conceded.

"We'll call him Chris."

"As you wish," Hatch repeated.

For two months after his son's birth, Laurie continued the role of devoted family man. He spent much of his time with his son and tried, unsuccessfully, to establish some type of relationship with his wife. Esmie recovered rapidly from the ordeal of pregnancy and birth. She had gained some weight, her lush curves were even lusher, her skin was bright and glowing, and her habit of licking at her full lips nearly drove her husband to distraction. After a reassuring talk with the doctor about his wife's health, Laurie finally knocked at the locked door. There was no answer. Laurie threw open his own door, stalked down the hall, and tapped at the other entrance to his wife's room. The door opened a few inches, and Miss Grace peered out through the crack.

Ignoring the woman, he called, "Esmie, I want to see you."

"I've a headache," she snapped. "Go away and leave me alone."

Wild with rage, he stormed out of the house and went down to his club. He found a friend whose little mistress was appearing in the same play as Lila Lansom. Laurie had guessed that lovely Lila wouldn't be long without a protector, and she did have one, but as his friend explained, Lila was unhappy with the arrangement.

"Try her," the young man advised. "Go down to the theater and see her, Laurie. I'm sure she'll welcome you back."

The welcome was far from warm. When Laurie, grasping a huge bouquet of her favorite flowers, nudged open the door of her dressing room, he found Lila, wrapped in a warm robe trimmed with feathers, seated at her dressing table removing her makeup. She regarded his mirrored image grimly. Without turning her head, she said harshly, "I didn't hear you knock, stranger."

37

He bent over and put the roses in her lap. Impatiently she knocked them to the floor and spun around. "What do you want?"

"You."

"You drop me cold for some thin-blooded chit of a girl, don't even drop by to say hello for over a year, and then think you can walk right back and pick up. I've got another man now. I don't need you!"

For a moment he was tempted to argue, but he'd had enough rejections that night. Shrugging, he bent and picked up the flowers. "If that's the way you want it . . . fine. I hear Carla is looking for someone new, and she's a pretty little piece."

"Wait." Lila's expression softened, and she gazed up at him. "What are you offering?"

"More than I could before. A nice new set of rooms, anywhere you like, bigger than that little hole you have now."

"And?"

"Clothes, jewelry, a carriage if you want it."

"And?"

He touched the front of his trousers. "This."

She patted the bulge in his trousers, plucked the roses from his hands, and buried her face in their cool fragrance. "You don't drive a very shrewd bargain, love. I'd have taken you back just for what you have in your pants. But you've offered the rest, so I'll take that too."

Grabbing the girl, he pressed her to him. He could feel the warmth of her body through her robe. Groping under the hem of the robe, he ran a hand up one silken leg.

"Whoa, love, let's get out of here first."

He pushed her back toward the shabby sofa. "Now. Right now."

Later he lay with her cuddled against him, avidly breathing in the musk from the old sofa, the scents of powder and cologne, the warm odor of female flesh, and he sighed with pleasure. She shivered, groped for her discarded robe, and pulled it over both of them. Her hand

38

moved over his chest to his groin and patted the firmness she found there. "Again, love?"

Closing her lips with his own, he rolled over on top of her. Much later she fumbled for the robe again and said firmly, "That's about enough of that, at least until we get back to my rooms."

He smacked her firm rump. "What about your protector?"

She giggled, and her breath tickled his ear. "I was about to get rid of him anyway, Laurie. He's old and has a breath like a slop jar, and he's also a clutch-purse. But forget about him. You act as though you'd never had a woman in your life."

"I feel as though I'd never had one." His hand groped for and found her round breast. "I can't get enough of you."

She batted his hand away. "What about your bride? And I hear you're a new papa. Must be something going on there."

Laurie fought against his principles. He wouldn't have discussed his wife with a male friend, but Lila . . . she was a woman too. Perhaps she could fathom Esmie's odd behavior. Hesitantly, he told Lila about his married life. She listened intently, her eyes widening.

"And you mean that after months of chasing you around she locked her door and hasn't let you touch her since?" she asked.

"Right. Being pregnant—do you think that could explain why she's turned so cold?"

Sliding out from under the wool robe, Lila walked over to the dressing table, picked up a comb, and ran it through her thick, corn-colored hair. "A woman hot as that doesn't cool off, love. Not so fast. You better start showing a little interest in what she's up to in her spare time."

Laurie was on his feet, a tide of rage sweeping through him. "You mean—"

"I mean this." Slapping down the comb, she put both

39

hands to her brow and waggled her thumbs. "You're wearing horns, boy."

All the way home, Laurie mulled it over. Lila was right, he decided. He'd been a blind fool. Remembering Esmie's flaring passion, he knew it must be finding an outlet. Forcing himself to think cooly, he went over the months of his marriage. Who could his wife's lover be? he wondered. Where could he be? Esmie wasn't that active. She attended church, she visited her parents' home, she saw some female friends, once in a while she'd attend the theatre, but if he wasn't escorting her, Miss Grace was. Could Esmie's companion be in on the plot? Could the tall, handsome Miss Grace be abetting his wife in this treachery?

For over a week he followed Esmie and Miss Grace, dogging their footsteps, shadowing them as they shopped, lunched, entered the Hatch house, went to teas and to the theater. Not a sign of another man. That locked door, he mulled—could Esmie be smuggling a man into her room at night? If that was the case, her lover must be right in the house. A servant? Feeling shabby and soiled, he went to Lila and discussed his thoughts. Lila agreed that it had to be a man already in or near the house, someone whose presence wouldn't excite suspicion.

"Think," she urged. "The footmen, grooms, the coachman—any of them fit the bill?"

"They're two footmen, young and not bad-looking. And there's Esmie's new coachman. Now, he could be the one! Coates is big and brawny and has a head of coal-black hair."

"Find out, love."

"I will," he said grimly. "If she has taken a servant, some damn clod sweating over her every night in my house, I'm going to kill him! I'm going to kill both of them!"

Maddened by his obsession, he lunged out of her flat. He didn't realize how ludicrous it was to leave his mistress's warm arms to pursue his wife's phantom lover with murder in his heart. Briefly he thought of his father.

Sir Christopher would have felt the same. A man's indiscretions, so long as they left his family untouched, were his own affair. But his wife . . . the mother of his son. This woman must be above reproach. Laurie writhed with humiliation as he pictured the expressions of his brother, his friends, if his wife's name was ever sullied.

Cannily, he plotted his campaign. The next evening found him on the roof of his house, a rope knotted around his waist, cautiously lowering himself to the line of tiles that gave access to the garret windows of the servants' quarters. It was a cold, wind-swept night, and he shivered as he crept along the narrow ledge. The first window was the butler's, and he could see a single candle beside the old man's bed shedding flickering light over his sleeping face and gaping, toothless mouth. A gust of wind caught Laurie, and he clawed at the rough brick for support.

Swearing under his breath, he inched toward the next window. Ah, the second footman, the plump fair one, and he had a woman in his bed. Laurie caught a glimpse of short, pumping legs and a tumbled mass of blond curls. Esmie? No, the scullery maid. His foot slipped on the wet tile, and for an instant he hung over the edge, held only by the rope tied to one of the chimney pots. His desperately groping foot searched, for a moment only hit empty air, and then found the ledge again. He was more careful now and got to the window of the first footman in record time. This one—confound it, he couldn't even remember the dratted fellow's name—was as busy as the other footman was. The identity of his partner was not in doubt. She straddled the chap, heavy buttocks bouncing up and down. Laurie eyed her with amazement. It was the new parlormaid. Her flat, plain face under the lace cap hadn't caught his interest previously, but now, as he watched her chubby body, sweat running between heavy breasts, he admired her energy.

"Nice little piece right under my nose, and I didn't notice her," he muttered. "But God's teeth, they're turning the place into a bawdyhouse." He started to edge his way back. "Better get down to the coach house and see what that oaf of a Coates has snaggled off. If it's Esmie, he's a dead man!"

By the time he reached the coach house it had started to rain. Drenched and shaking with cold, Laurie crept silently up to the lighted window. We stood on tiptoes and tried to peer under the lowered blind, but he could see nothing. But figures were blackly silhouetted, and he could see Coates's massive form reaching long arms toward a woman's shadow. Was she too tall for Esmie? The only thing to do was wait and hope she'd eventually leave. He crouched under the window, rain trickling down his collar, wind buffeting him, thoroughly miserable. His long wait was finally rewarded. The door opened, and as a tall woman wrapped in a cloak passed him, he caught a glimpse of her face. She was the wife of a neighbor, a quiet, dignified matron with three grown children. Another husband with horns, Laurie told himself grimly.

He started back to the house and then checked himself and returned to his post. What if Coates hadn't finished? The oaf looked as though he had juice enough in him for several women. Perhaps he would now sneak into the house and into his mistress's room. Grimly, Laurie continued his cold vigil.

Time dragged by, and then the blind flew up and so did the window sash. Coates, looking even larger, leaned out of the window, idly scratching his hairy bare stomach. Laurie cowered, praying the coachman wouldn't look in his direction. But Coates, in the middle of an immense yawn, did glance down, and his eyes narrowed. "Bleedin' Peepin' Tom," he bellowed. "Be off or I'll set the dogs on ye!"

Hoping fervently that in the darkness he hadn't been recognized, Laurie took to his heels. And that was the end of his midnight prowling. From then on he haunted the upper hall or sat in his bedroom, his eyes glaring at his wife's locked door.

Laurie was a changed man. His appetite failed, and he lost weight. No longer did he attend the races, lean avidly over gambling tables, or appear, beautifully groomed, at the theatre and parties. Even his delight in Lila's expert ministrations waned. His only hours of peace were spent in the nursery with his son in his arms. As soon as he left his son, visions of Esmie and her unknown lover returned to plague him as they had this night.

Seated now before the blazing fire in his own room, he sighed and reached for the bottle again. Then he shoved it away and leaped to his feet. This was driving him mad. There was only one course open to him. He'd have to face his wife, tell her of his suspicions, and force a confession from her.

Swinging open his door, he took the few steps to hers and knocked. There was no answer. After a moment he turned the knob and was surprised to find the door unlocked. On the chiffonier a lamp burned; the bed was neatly turned down, but the room was empty. He prowled through the dressing room, glanced into her bathing room, and then went to the nursery. In the cradle Chris slept, chubby arms thrown over his head. Near him on a cot Nurse Leland stirred and lifted her head. "His nibs is fine, sir."

Bending over her, Laurie whispered, "Has Mrs. Woodbyne been in this evening?"

Her nightcap shook, and she muttered something. Laurie bent closer. "I didn't hear you, nurse."

"Said she'd probably be with Miss Grace, sir."

Laurie whispered another good night, bent over the cradle, and then made his way downstairs. In the parlor one of the maids was kneeling before the hearth, banking the fire. She raised her head and gave him a broad smile. It was the new parlormaid, the one he'd seen gyrating over the first footman's long form. Laurie smiled back at her and then returned to the hall. The butler, a lamp in one hand, was putting the chain on the door.

"Has the mistress gone out?" Laurie asked.

"No, sir, everyone in. I'm just locking up, sir."

Laurie nodded at the old man and stood indecisively at the foot of the stairs. Esmie had to be somewhere in the

43

house, but where? Then he remembered not only Nurse Leland's words but the sound of her voice as she'd said them. His hands knotted into fists. That was it! Esmie was meeting her lover in Miss Grace's room. He raced up the stairs and ran down the hall to the staircase leading to the third floor. At the head of the stairs was the room allotted to his wife's companion.

Without knocking, he flung the door open. The room was brightly lit with the pitiless light of candles and lamps.

Finally he discovered the truth about Esmeralda Hatch Woodbyne.

4

The bedchamber was as prim and spartan as Miss Grace herself. Crisp white curtains covered the windowpanes; a plain, white, painted chest of drawers reared toward the sloping ceiling; and both the chairs were straight wooden ones. On the floor were handmade rugs, and the narrow bed was chastely covered with a white cotton spread.

These surroundings served to emphasize the lewdness and debauchery of the two figures entangled on that chaste white bed. They sprawled in the same positions they had been in when Laurie swung open the door, as if they had been frozen into marble statues. The man, staring horror-stricken at them, was as motionless.

Esmie lay across the bed, her head dangling over the edge, the tendons of her neck taut with ecstasy, the thick pink lips drawn back to expose small white teeth. Across her plump body Miss Grace's naked, angular form sprawled. Her dark hair was loose, her face hidden between the girl's legs.

In one stride Laurie was beside them. Grasping the older woman by the leather belt around her waist, he lifted her bodily from his wife and flung her to the floor. She was on her feet in one bound, her features contorted and ugly, her hair flying in witch locks around her flushed face. She leaped at him, her nails curved like talons, clawing for his eyes.

Laurie took one look at the object the strap around her waist supported, and then he closed his fist and struck her with all his strength on the point of her jaw. She flew

45

backwards, struck a corner of the chest, and collapsed on her back. The long, ugly dildo fastened to her waist pointed obscenely upward.

With a sob, Esmie rolled off the bed and ran to the woman on the floor. Kneeling beside her, Esmie sobbed, "You bloody brute! You've killed her."

"I only wish I had! If she wants to act like a man, she should learn to fight like one."

Ripping the spread from the bed, he hauled his wife to her feet and wrapped it around her. With one arm around her waist and a hand clasped over her mouth, he pulled her out of the room. She fought like a tigress. At the top of the staircase she sunk her teeth into his palm and managed to pull loose. She shoved Laurie, and he tripped and nearly fell down the staircase. With a muttered oath, he caught himself, and grabbing her arm, twisted it brutally behind her back.

"Make one sound and I swear I'll break your arm," he grunted in her ear.

She gasped with pain, but she kept quiet as he urged her down the stairs, past the nursery, and to the door of her own room. Kicking it open, he pulled her in and flung her across the bed. Then he closed the door and leaned against it. The spread had fallen away from her body, and she sprawled across the bed in much the same position she'd been in on the bed in Miss Grace's room. Her head dangled over the edge, and her upthrust breasts heaved with her sobs.

Kicking the spread away, he stood over her. "Get up and get yourself covered," he grated.

He went into the bathing room and bent over the slop jar. The bile he'd been fighting back rose in a sour tide in his throat, and he vomited until he was dry-retching. He pulled himself up and stumbled to the commode. Grabbing the pitcher of water, he took a gulp and rinsed his mouth. Then he poured the rest of the water over his wrists and hands. Absently he noticed that the knuckles of his right hand were swelling. He grabbed a towel and dried his hands, wiped at his mouth, and then returned to the bedroom.

Esmie had donned a dressing gown and was crouching on the edge of the bed, her face hidden in her hands. Taking a chair, Laurie pulled it as far away from the bed as he could and then sank down on it. Dispassionately he regarded the woman he had married. No longer was she an enigma. He could even guess where she'd lost her virginity and how. Not with a man, but with that damnable thing strapped to her lover's waist.

After a time he felt a stirring of pity. That monster of a governess had taken charge when Esmie was a small child, had probably corrupted her with threats and fear. Was there anything left for him and his wife? Could any future life be possible together? Chris . . . he had to think of his son. Whatever Esmie was, she was still his wife, still the mother of his child.

"Esmie," he said softly, "look at me."

Fair curls trembled as she shook her head. Laurie continued, "We have to talk this out. We must think of Chris. I'm willing to forgive—"

"I don't want your forgiveness," she muttered.

"All right. I'm willing to try to understand, to make a fresh start. Once that . . . that monster is out of this house, we'll—"

"Miss Grace will never leave this house," she said more clearly. "If anyone goes, it will be you."

"Hush, just listen for a minute. I know this whole business probably wasn't your fault. She must have forced you to . . ." His voice trailed off. Esmie's shoulders were shaking. He thought she was weeping tears of despair. "Don't cry," he whispered.

She finally lifted her head. Her round eyes were bright and dry, her cheeks stained with rich color. "You fool! I was laughing. You poor, stupid fool. Miss Grace's fault! Forcing me! If anyone was forced, it was her. Oh, she had the inclination, but she was scared stiff of daddy, of what he'd do if he found out. *I* was the one who forced. We've been lovers since I was fifteen." Her thick lips twisted. "You want to talk it out? Very well. She's all I want. I love her. Daddy kept insisting I marry, give him his damned grandson, but I managed to wheedle him out of it for a long time. Then he forced me to marry you, and Miss Grace and I made our plans. I'd get pregnant as soon as I could, and that would be the end of you. We'd go back to what we'd always had, all we've ever wanted." Her eyes spat hate at him. "What do you care anyway? You've got what *you* want. Daddy gave you the money, I gave you the son. What I do is my own business."

"No, this is my business."

Drawing herself further back on the bed, she sat cross-legged. "You don't care. What do you know about me? Have you ever tried to get to know me? When we were first married . . . the first few nights, I thought maybe, just maybe, we could really be married. But I was only an object, a way to pry Charlie Hatch's money loose. Oh, you were willing to accept my body, you enjoyed using me, but you didn't care *about* me. Go ahead and deny it!"

Laurie was frowning. There was an element of truth in what she said, enough truth to make him uncomfortable. "After the baby was born, I tried. I tried to talk to you and—"

"Talk!" She mimicked his voice. "How was your day? Have you seen your mother lately? Did you enjoy the theater last night?" The polite, disinterested voice changed and became savage. "That was your conversation, and it came too late. A Woodbyne condescending to an empty-headed Hatch!"

He raised a hand. "I'll admit it; don't go on. But that can be changed. For our son's sake we have to find some answer."

"There is one. We can continue exactly as we were. Live in the same house, appear at friends' houses and in public together, and in private lives go our own way. I'll have Miss Grace, and you can continue with that tawdry strumpet you've been keeping. Oh yes, I know all about Lila Lansom—"

"You drove me back to her. I'd given her up."

48

"Rubbish! You were only waiting for daddy to take his eyes off you. You *gentlemen* always have a fancy lady, don't you? But your wives, the mothers of your children—oh, no. They must be pure as driven snow. Well, I'm not!" She lowered her voice until she purred like a kitten. "Think, Laurie, you'll have everything you want, everything you married me to get. The house, the servants, the money. And your own life to lead as you wish."

"What about Chris?"

Airily she waved a plump hand. "He's yours. You can do anything you want about him. He's a boy; in time he'll be another man. I don't care. Raise him as you want, send him away to school. I won't interfere."

For moments he sat slumped in his chair, his brow furrowed. Then he straightened and said heavily, "I can't do it. I can't live under this roof knowing what you and that . . . no!"

Her eyes blazed. "Then get out! Go and make your own living. But I swear you'll never have your precious son."

Rage came flooding back, and he was on his feet. "We'll see what daddy has to say about that." He watched fear touch her face. "Ah, yes, for once daddy will see my side. Chris is precious to him too. Do you think he'll agree to you and your woman lover having control of his grandson?"

Her supple body came off the bed. Beneath the ruffled gown her breasts were heaving. "You wouldn't dare!"

"Watch and see."

He headed toward the door, but she was there before him. She pulled her gown wide, baring her body. Her face tilted up, a red tongue making a lazy circuit of full pink lips. "You liked me well enough before, Laurie," she said in a husky whisper. "Want to take Miss Grace's leavings?"

Her hands caught at one of his, and she forced it down into the hollow between her legs. A warm, moist hollow. Still moist, Laurie thought, from Miss Grace's mouth, from Miss Grace's wet mouth and eager, questing tongue.

Sickness caught at his throat again, and he raised a hand and slapped Esmie across the face. Taking her shoulder, he spun her away from the door. She flew across the room and fell heavily against the wall. He took a step toward her. The crumpled way she lay—had he hurt her badly?

Lifting a hand, Esmie rubbed at her shoulder. Then she gingerly touched her mouth, her cheek. "Lovely," she said, and she was laughing. "Nice bruises, nice swelling. Thank you, dear husband."

"I shouldn't have hit you, but this doesn't change anything. I'm going to pack and go to my club. Tomorrow I'll see your father."

"Go," she said, and she was still laughing. "Now you can go."

He closed the door on the sound of her laughter.

5

Laurie didn't see Charlie Hatch the following day. For two days and three nights he lay sick and feverish in his room at the club. He slept a great deal and tossed restlessly in a tangle of damp bedclothes, in the throes of nightmares where his wife and her companion coupled in obscene poses. On the morning of the third day he forced himself to rise, washed, and dressed. The porter brought him a tray and a pot of coffee, and he ate a little and drank a cup of coffee before he started on the drive to his father-in-law's place of business.

Climbing unsteadily from his carriage, he braced himself against its door and grimly surveyed the building. Charlie Hatch hadn't taken the pains with his offices that he had with his living quarters. He conducted his various businesses from a corner of an old warehouse in the dock area. Years of soot and grime fouled the bricks, and the windows looked as though the only water that had ever touched them had fallen from the sky. A cool breeze, herding strands of murky yellow fog, drifted up from the Thames, and under the soles of Laurie's trim boots was an accumulation of refuse and running filth. Gingerly he picked his way across the gushing gutter and the wet cobblestones to the unpainted door.

He shivered as he pushed the door open, hoping for a welcoming blast of warmth, but the room he entered was as chill as and more cheerless than the wretched street he'd just left. It was big, high-ceilinged, dank, filled with high desks and tall stools. On the stools perched clerks, huddled in sweaters, chilled blue fingers pushing quills across ledger pages. Over each desk a lamp hung, casting a circle of yellow light over their misery. In one corner a sullen fire smoldered, producing more smoke than heat.

As Laurie entered, a wizened figure climbed down from a stool at the nearest desk. He scuttled toward Laurie, his eyeshade casting a green unhealthy light on the pinched features. On his hands the chief clerk wore fingerless mittens, and his fingers scrabbled as though he were still pushing his quill. In the greenish shadow his bright eyes inspected the visitor, noting the tall brushed hat, the opulent overcoat trimmed with a fur collar, the gleaming boots.

"Yes, sir," he murmured. "Can I help you, sir?"

"Would you be good enough to tell Mr. Hatch that Laurence Woodbyne is here to see him?"

The bright eyes signaled "the master's son-in-law," and he spoke even more obsequiously. "Yes, sir. This way, sir." Then he paused and seemed to reconsider. "Perhaps I had better announce you, sir."

"Do that," Laurie agreed. Silently he was thinking, The slaves, the poor ruddy slaves. As the chief clerk scuttled away, he considered the miserable office. Many of the clerks had stopped working and were gazing with open curiosity at him. One of them, only a boy, was blowing on his cold, stiff fingers. As the chief clerk tapped at the other door, Laurie noticed that they all lowered their heads, hunched over their ledgers, and started to work diligently. He noted their gauntness—they all looked half-starved—and he smelled their fear. That bloody ogre of a Hatch, Laurie thought furiously, wouldn't even give them fuel enough to warm them as they worked.

The chief clerk was back, bowing low. "This way, sir. Mr. Hatch says to come right in, sir."

Skirting the desks, Laurie followed him to the door of the inner office. It had a glass pane with small gilt letters announcing that these premises belonged to Charles Hatch, Esquire, and from the doorway came a blast of heat. Behind a deal table used as a desk, his father-in-law was rising to greet him.

"Come in, m'boy, do come in. This is a surprise. First time you've honored me with your presence here. Take off your coat." One big hand gestured at the roaring fire. "You may have noticed I don't worry too much about the outer office. Found if you get the lazy devils too warm they tend to slack off."

"If that is your objective, I'd say you'd made it." Laurie perched on a chair across from Hatch, loosened his coat, and removing his hat, placed it on his knees. "From what I saw of your clerks, I'd wager if they stop working they'll freeze solid."

Hatch shot him a shrewd look. "As you'll notice, I don't pamper myself either." Hatch waved at the cramped office, and Laurie silently admitted he spoke the truth. The deal table was battered and scarred, and file cabinets were equally shabby, the two chairs were straight and wooden and uncomfortable. "This is a place of commerce," Hatch was saying, "and is treated as such. However, I do have a few of the amenities. Would you care for a drink? Too early? Coffee, perhaps?"

"Coffee will be fine."

His father-in-law bustled around, stirring the leaping fire, getting down cups and sugar and cream. Placing a steaming cup in front of Laurie, he pushed the cream closer and said, "I must admit I'm curious. Here you've been married to little Esmie for a year and a half—"

"One year and four months."

"One year and four months, then. And this is the first time you've decided to visit me here. Are you thinking of entering the business?"

"Hardly."

Hatch gave his sharklike smile. "Exactly. Well, if your interest isn't commercial, just what is your reason for coming here?"

"A personal one. One involving my household and family."

"Ah." Leaning back in his chair, Hatch cocked his

head wisely. "The first tumultuous years of marriage. How well I remember them. You may not believe it, Laurie, but my wife and I had our differences once. I know you look favorably on Judith, and she all but worships you, but she did prove somewhat difficult for a time. Now, out with it. What is troubling you?"

Miserably, Laurie wondered how to tell a man so devoted to his daughter the sordid details of that cherished daughter's sexual proclivity. He found he was speechless, and it was Charlie Hatch who answered his own question.

"I know why you're here," the man said, a peculiar flatness in his voice. "Your wife anticipated you. Esmie came to my house in the middle of the night—now, exactly when was it? Oh yes, three nights ago. She was half out of her mind with fright and grief. During all these months of marriage, she courageously hid this from me, but your last attack on her was so brutal she was forced to tell me the truth."

"And what is the truth?" Laurie enquired. It was evident that wily Esmie had barely waited for him to leave for his club that night before fleeing to her father, complete with swellings and bruises. No wonder she had laughed. When he struck her he'd played right into her hands. He found his respect for her cunning was increasing.

"The truth, you ask? The truth is that you're a swine, a swine who should never have been entrusted with the care of a tender, gently nourished child—"

"Child?"

Hatch threw him a look of flagrant dislike. "Maybe not in years but in experience. I warned you to be good to her, and what did you do but take her from her parents' care and ravish her in her bridal gown. She locked her door against your brutality in fear of her unborn babe, but three nights ago you stormed her room by force. Did you know you broke Miss Grace's jaw?"

"Good."

"The reaction I would expect from a brute. When she tried to protect her mistress, you set on the poor woman and broke her jaw. Then you turned your attention to your wife. I could see the swelling on Esmie's face, but then she bared her shoulders, and there were bruises there and on her wrists. Finally, in her agony, she showed me her breasts, and they were mottled with ugly purple marks. Have you anything to say in your own defense?"

Laurie took a sip of coffee and, leaning forward, put his hat on the table. "I slapped her face with an open hand, and I twisted her wrist. Those bruises are mine. The bruises on her shoulders . . . possibly that was done when I threw her against the wall. But the marks on her breasts—no, those I had nothing to do with." Silently, he considered where those marks had come from. Miss Grace, no doubt, and her lovemaking. But Esmie had used them for her own purpose.

"Is that all you have to say?" Hatch asked heavily.

"Esmie has had her say." Laurie stretched long legs toward the blazing fire. "She's cut the ground out from under me. I doubt you would listen to the truth."

Hatch's face was livid. "Esmie warned me," he raved. "She warned me you had threatened to come to me with terrible stories you had made up for revenge. If you think for one minute I'd believe any disgusting tales about my daughter and Miss Grace . . ." His voice trailed off, and his anger seemed to dissipate. Mutely, Charlie Hatch stared at the man across from him.

Laurie took his time. He shrugged off his greatcoat and put the cup on the table. Then he said softly, "That was a good act. You really *are* little Esmie's father. But you put your foot in your mouth. I never mentioned Miss Grace's name in connection with my wife. Not in that sense. And I know Esmie's too shrewd to have." He studied the other man's face. "How long have *you* known about them?"

"I know nothing about them," Hatch blustered.

"Suspected, then."

"I don't know what you're getting at."

"Oh, but you do." Laurie sighed. "I thought it was your daughter's age that made you so eager to marry her off and inspired such a generous settlement, but it was

55

more than that. You wanted her married and settled, and also married to a man so gutless that he wouldn't even squeak when he eventually found out his wife's companion was her lover. You chose me, but your choice wasn't good." Laurie's voice became bitter with self-disgust. "I'll admit I could have accepted almost anything else. If I'd found out Esmie's lover was another man, I probably wouldn't have done much about it. But even I have my limits, and this I can't and won't stand."

For moments both men sat in silence, a deep, brooding silence. Then Hatch rose, fumbled for a decanter, and poured a drink. He sank back down on his chair. "Judith told me about this years ago," he mumbled. "She's never liked Miss Grace, and I don't think she cares much for Esmie. I thought at the time she was lying." He lifted his head. "What do you propose to do?"

"I take it Esmie has come home to stay and that she brought Miss Grace with her."

"That is correct."

"In that case I'll stay on in my house and see to rearing my son."

"Your son is also in my home. I had him brought home in care of his nurse. Miss Leland raised some objections, claimed she had to have your permission to move the child. It was only when I pointed out that she'd be parted from him if she persisted that she agreed to come."

Laurie tensed. "I'll take my son back to my house—"

"*Your* house?"

"It was deeded to me, sir. It was agreed that the house would be mine on the birth of my child."

Hatch bared his teeth in what might have been a smile. He managed to look even more like a hungry shark. "In the pressure of business, this I overlooked. And it would seem to be well I did. The house is still in my name."

"Then what do you propose?"

"That you join your wife and son in my house. Apart from Esmie, of course, but under the same roof."

Laurie shook his head. "If you look to me to give a

screen of respectability to this unholy union, you're mistaken. I'll never live under your roof."

"Your quarterly allowance will be cut off. What will you live on?"

Laurie managed a smile. "In this particular case I believe my brother will assist me."

Hatch's grin broadened and became a laugh. "I've never considered you unintelligent. Didn't you notice your brother and his lady at your father's funeral? How Ashbury and Mildred were stumbling over their own feet to make my wife and me welcome among that snooty bunch of bastards."

"Say it."

"I have your brother right there." He ground his thumb into the table. "Ashbury hungers for money, and he's invested his wife's entire dowry with me. In a short time he's seen profits that he would never have dreamt possible, and it's made him even greedier. I'll give him this—not just for money. He wants to return the Woodbyne family to their former position, to buy back the parcels of land your father sold from the estate, to purchase a townhouse, to be again a noble scion of a noble family. Believe me, Ashbury will do exactly as I tell him!"

Morosely, Laurie considered his words. He believed the other man. Money for money's sake wouldn't tempt his brother, but the family heritage . . . no, Ashbury wouldn't lift a finger to help him against his benefactor's wishes. Laurie considered his own position—stripped of house, allowance, probably coach, most certainly servants. He remembered his father's words. Never try to fight this man, Sir Christopher had warned. He'd read Hatch correctly.

Laurie spoke slowly. "You want me to act as cloak for your daughter's reputation. If I live apart from her there'll be ugly questions asked, speculation, servants' gossip."

"The servants," Hatch asked quickly. "Do you think any of them suspect?"

"One does, the nurse. You'd better handle Miss Leland carefully."

"Will she talk?"

"I doubt it. She's devoted to her little charge and to me. I chose her because she's a fine, closemouthed woman."

"Good! I'll see she has no complaints." Hatch refilled his glass, and on the decanter his fingers trembled. "Don't you realize, Laurie, we're both striving for the same ends? I'm not only trying to protect my daughter, I'm trying to protect Chris's mother, and Chris himself."

"Not even for Chris can I force myself to do this."

"What is left for you? To wander around London, live from your friends' charity? Soon enough they'll learn you're no longer connected with me. You'll find little charity then. Your creditors will hound you. You'll be in worse shape than you were at the time of your marriage."

Laurie lifted his head, and his fine nostrils flared. "And how will that look? Esmie's husband, your son-in-law, cut adrift. A vagrant. A man who has given up all you have to offer for a life like that. Then questions will really be asked, and the truth may very well come out."

Hatch worried at his lower lip with his teeth. "True. Which is why we must strike a bargain. You can't possibly stay in London, or even in England. I'll give you this assurance about Chris and his welfare. Esmie has no feeling for the boy, so she'll present no problem. Through his infancy Chris will be totally in the care of his nurse and my wife. I think you'll approve of both of these women. Regardless of Judith's shortcomings, I've never denied that she is well qualified to raise a child. Perhaps I should have allowed her more say in her daughter's raising. However, that is past."

"Eventually Chris will have to be released from women's care."

"Granted," Hatch agreed eagerly. "When that time comes your brother will take over as the boy's guardian. Sir Ashbury can select proper schools, see the boy knows the right type of people. Chris can spend his vacations at Woodbyne Hall. After all, someday he'll bear the title—"

"Have you forbidden my brother and his wife to have children?" Laurie asked sarcastically.

"Lady Woodbyne appears to be barren."

"You know more about my family than I."

"I've made it my business to. This vitally affects my grandson. To continue, the boy will be my heir; he'll be one of the richest young men in England. Now, does this meet with your approval?"

"Ashbury as a surrogate father," Laurie said reflectively. "He'll probably make a better father than I would. Yes, this seems a wholesome arrangement. As long as I've proof that Chris will never be under his mother's care."

"You have my word," the older man blurted. Then his mouth twisted. "I forget I'm no gentleman. Very well, you'll have your brother's word."

"Ashbury's word I'll take. Now, your plans for getting me out from underfoot."

Hatch beamed. "Simple. A reason no one would question. You'll be sent to learn my business abroad."

"Exactly where?"

"The New World."

"Canada," Laurie said as though he'd known all along.

Hatch rubbed his lips. "In part. But not Upper or Lower Canada. I'll be sending you to the area disputed by many nations, principally the United States and Britain."

Words spoken at his wedding drifted back into Laurie's mind. "Beyond the Shining Mountains?"

"Yes. The post last established by my company, near Fort George."

When Laurie shook a baffled head, Hatch came to his feet. "I've some maps here that may give you some idea." He rummaged through a filing box and took out several rolls of yellowed parchment. "Incomplete, of course. Most of this territory is unknown and hasn't been properly mapped as yet." He spread them out and picked up a ruler. The ends of the parchment curled stubbornly, and it took him a few moments to pin them into place. Laurie came to stand at Hatch's shoulder and gazed down at the spidery lines.

"Now," Hatch said, "here we have Upper and Lower Canada. Here is Montreal, and the long river it's located on is called the St. Lawrence. I've an agent in Montreal who will take charge of you. M. Charloux will see you're properly outfitted and on your way."

"Which direction?"

The ruler moved down a network of lakes and rivers. "You'll travel by canoe, of course. Here is Montreal. Now, you go up the Ottawa River to Lake Nipissing and across Georgian Bay to Grande Portage. Here it is on the western shore of Lake Superior. Thus far you'll travel by a large canoe in the company of the *mangeurs de lard*—"

"Pork eaters?"

Hatch grinned. "That's what the paddlers are called. I suppose because the country is still civilized enough where they travel that they can eat fresh meat. But the settlement of Grande Portage is the jumping-off place for the wilds, and neither the large canoes nor their paddlers will go farther. At Grande Portage my agent will see you get a place on a canoe flotilla traveling west. The men who man these canoes are a much different breed from the pork eaters. They're French-Canadians, and many of them have Indian blood. They're the true voyageurs. They're also called winterers, and they're wild, savage men." His grin widened. "They have to be in order to challenge the land you'll be heading into. You must make every effort to win the voyageurs' respect. Oh, they'll take you safely through, but if they doubt your courage they'll make your life a hell. Think you're man enough?"

There was no doubt that Hatch was enjoying himself, Laurie decided, and found his lips forming a defiant *yes*. He reconsidered. There was no point in making useless gestures of bravado. "I won't know until I get there, will I? As you know, I'm born and bred a city man." He made a sweeping gesture over the maps. "Those distances are terrifying to a man used to small distances, a small country." His gaze moved from the maps to his father-in-law's amused face. "You seem to know a great deal about the land and various terms. Have you ever been there?"

"Never. But it's my business, and I've made every effort to understand as much as possible about it. I've demanded full reports from my agents and factors."

Laurie took a deep breath. "From Grande Portage where do I go in the charming company of your wild and savage winterers?"

"Into the *pays d'en haut*, a grassland that stretches for hundreds of miles. A land of twisting rivers and prairie where buffalo and hostile Indians abound. Then to the Shining Mountains and through the passes that cut through them. In time you'll arrive at Fort Purline and come to the end of your journey. You'll travel the width of a continent, from the Atlantic almost to the Pacific Ocean. As I said a few minutes ago, this land west of the mountains is disputed territory. The Americans claim it and so do the British, and even the Russians gather furs along the Pacific coast. The country around Fort Astoria at the mouth of the Columbia River is called by the Americans Oregon country. The English, Scots, and French fur traders call their portion New Caledonia, but they infringe on one another continuously. It's a no-man's-land, and the only law governing it is guns and courage. That land kills quickly through intense cold, starvation, hostile savages, and even warring fur traders."

"You're very plainspoken."

"I am. I never want you to say I didn't give you the facts." Hatch's cold eyes raked the length of the young man's body. "You've some assets. You're young and strong, you ride well, and you shoot well. Whether you have the courage, the tenacity, only time will tell."

"Sounds as though you might well lose a son-in-law." Leaving Hatch's side, Laurie slid back onto the uncomfortable chair. "I'll admit you've scared hell out of me. Now, to come to terms. To make this suicidal trip I'll have to have other inducements besides shielding my son's good name."

"And you'll have them. At the most, if you work out well, there'll be a full partnership in the firm. Aside from that, you'll be second in command to the factor at Fort

61

Purline on arrival and eventually will take his place. This will mean you'll not only be on salary but also share in the profits—"

"It will have to be a firm agreement, drawn up legally. This time I won't take the chance I did with my house—pardon me, *your* house."

Chuckling, Hatch rubbed his hands together. "You drive a harder bargain than your father. Never mind, I can understand that, would do the same in your place. I assure you before you take ship from London you will have proper legal forms in your hands. Of course, the partnership will depend on your performance of your duties. A great deal will depend on the reports I receive from my factor, General Purline—"

"Purline?" Laurie's brow furrowed.

"Is the name familiar?"

"Of course. It's an illustrious name, one famed in military history. But I hardly thought there would be a General Purline young enough to be your factor."

"You're thinking of this man's father and grandfather, both of whom enjoyed the title of general. My Ezra Purline was merely a lieutenant when he was cashiered from the army—"

"A Purline cashiered? It doesn't seem possible."

Amusement touched the corners of Hatch's mouth again. "I can understand your surprise. Generations of officers and gentlemen, each Purline son forced to enter the army whether he had the inclination or not. With Ezra they made a grievous mistake. Because of his background the details of his court-martial were kept secret. When he first sought me out, looking for employment as far from England as possible, I dubbed him 'general' as a joke." The amusement deepened, and Laurie sensed it was sadistic. A cruel joke, he thought as his father-in-law continued. "Ezra Purline deeply resented my little joke, but he was in no position to protest. Oddly enough, when he arrived in the colonies he took for himself the rank of general and has been called that ever since. Would you like to know why he was expelled from the army in disgrace?"

"No," Laurie said, and he heard the distaste in his own voice. Hatch's whole demeanor spoke of sharing an off-color joke, and Laurie winced at the familiarity.

The older man was hardly insensitive to the rebuff. His face became a blank, and his cold eyes narrowed. "Well," he said abruptly, "do we have a bargain?"

Getting up, Laurie shrugged on his overcoat. "Provided you attend to the legal matters, we do. I'll await further instructions from you. You can reach me at my club."

Hatch rose too. "I'll attend to everything. You'll want to see your son before you leave."

"Yes. And not in the company of his mother. I have no wish to see her again."

Hatch hesitated and then thrust his hand out. "Shall we shake on it?"

Laurie was about to take the hand; then, with cool deliberation, he reached past Hatch and picked up his hat. "No. Your proposition I accept and will do my best to fulfill my duties, but your hand I can't shake."

The other man pulled his arm back, and his expression became ugly. "Because I'm not a gentleman. You *gentlemen*," he grated, the hate naked in his voice, "how I despise you. I buy and sell you. You're not too proud to take my money, but your pride won't allow you to take my hand." All the polish the man had laboriously acquired fell away from him, and with it he lost the slow, careful diction. His next words came out in a rush. "You and your father and your brother. Oh, I know how Sir Christopher felt about me. Sold me his bloody son and at the same time looked at me as if I was a horse turd his shoe had touched in a gutter—"

"My father wasn't like that!" Laurie protested hotly.

"What do the likes of you with your white hands and smooth faces know about men like me?" Hatch raved on. "Know where I was born? In the hall of a tenement in the lowest, most filthy slum in this city. Torn from the belly of a slut who couldn't even tell me who my father was. 'Some sailor,' she'd say, 'don't rightly remember which one.' A poor little bastard out on the streets at less than six, fighting and cheating and surviving." He spread the hand that Laurie had scorned and stared down at it. "The things that hand has done. Nothing too dirty for it to touch. And in the end I'm a better man than all the lordly snobs like you! I can buy and sell Purlines, Woodbynes. I'm better than any of you!"

"Are you really?" Laurie drew himself to his full height, set his tall hat on thick silver-gilt hair, tapped it into a jaunty angle, and stood aloofly, elegantly, staring down at the other man. Under the curled brim of his hat his expression, all the fine lines of his face, were touched with a remote cruelty. "If you hate us so much, why have you tried so desperately to join us, aped our speech and dress and deportment? But you have no need to worry. You'll never live long enough to be a despised gentleman. You may have left the gutters, the slums, the tenements, but you are and always will be a bastard torn from a slut's belly." He added softly, "You carry the stench and can never lose it."

Hatch raised a ravaged face. "If I was younger . . . by God, I'd challenge you to a duel!"

Flinging the door wide, Laurie threw a few words over his shoulder. "If you were a gentleman, I'd be tempted to accept!"

He strode across the outer office, hardly noticing the pallid, frightened faces of the clerks staring up at him. Behind him Hatch slammed the door so hard it rocked on its hinges. The old chief clerk scrabbled to the street door and held it open, bowing his master's son-in-law out. Once on the filthy cobblestones, Laurie jumped into his carriage and called directions to his coachman. He found he was panting as though he'd been running. He wondered if he should regret his loss of control in Hatch's office. No, the man had asked for it. Rather hopefully he wondered if this would change Hatch's mind, if he would cancel the deal they'd just made. Then Laurie grunted. No such luck. Charlie Hatch wouldn't let a few insults sway him from his plans. He was much too interested in getting rid of his unwanted son-in-law.

Even in his heavy coat Laurie found he was shuddering with cold. Better get used to it, he told himself grimly. If what he'd been told about the land he was being exiled to was even partly true, the land beyond the Shining Mountains would not only be cold but full of hazards. That was the name someone had mentioned—who was it? Ashbury? Well, anyway, a romantic-sounding name. But the other name, *le pays sauvage*, probably fitted better.

A land called savage, Laurie Woodbyne said to himself. He found he liked the sound of the words.

6

The land beyond the Shining Mountains was not only wild and savage but also incredibly beautiful, with a beauty that was as capable of inspiring fear as awe. The western range of mountains guarded the approach to this land, standing in lofty grandeur, its lower slopes draped with jade-green pine and fir and hemlock. Those hoping for gentler terrain beyond found to their dismay a sea of unexplored mountain peaks, craggy gulches of prickly sagebrush, and impenetrable fir jungle. Fear grew, and so did loneliness as the journey into its depths continued. The only roads were rivers, lakes, and streams, at times calm and placid, and then abruptly erupting into foaming falls, stretches of wild, white-tipped rapids, and swirling whirlpools.

The long birch canoe and its ten occupants breasting the waves of the Nechako River only emphasized the emptiness of that land. The eight voyageurs, bending over their paddles, clad in red worsted caps, fringed buckskin coats, and bright sashes, made a flash of color against the browns, greens, and blue foamy water. The two people in the middle of the canoe were dressed in soberer clothes. The woman was dressed in dark blue, and the man at her side was robed in somber black.

The man slumped forward and appeared to be dozing, but the woman, scarcely more than a girl, sat erect, her eyes turning from one sloping, tree-girt bank to the other. Although she appeared engrossed in the scenery, she actually didn't see it. Her mind was swirling as quickly as the water cut by the bow of the canoe. Two inner voices were speaking to her, one kindly and comforting, the other rather cynical. Think, the tiny kind voice was saying, calm yourself, repeat your name. Who are you? Rowan, she cried silently, Rowan Malone. Really, the other voice jeered, are you sure of that Malone? It's mine, she replied; it was my father's. You're frightened, the voice jeered, but the other voice gained strength. Father Martin is beside you. What have you to fear? This wilderness, the cruel voice chuckled, and the men in this canoe. Oh, you've seen them looking at you, Rowan, especially the one they call Osa. *Osa*, your precious Father Martin told you, is a Spanish word meaning bear, and Osa is a bear of a man, isn't he? A bear of a man, hungry for a woman. It's going to happen again, Rowan, what happened to you in Montreal, in the house of Mme. Guilbant. It will be worse this time—there's more of them.

Rowan jerked her head, trying to drown out the words of that haunting voice. As she did, Osa swung around from his place directly before her, and she saw tiny eyes peering from his beard-matted face. Her own eyes turned instantly for reassurance to Father Martin, but he slumped forward, his wide-brimmed hat shielding his face. She caught a glimpse of the features in the shadow of the hat, and her mouth tightened with anxiety. He was desperately ill; never should he have undertaken this long, arduous journey.

And it's your fault he's here, the cruel voice insisted. If it weren't for you he'd be in Montreal where Reverend Mother could care for him, see he was made well. He's dying, and this is your fault. And when he is gone, who is there to stand between you and the bear?

Her hand clenched the gunnel until her knuckles whitened. But the other voice, calm and soothing, overrode the cruel one. Take heart, Rowan, it soothed. The priest may not be that ill. And the next fort, they say it is near. These men, wild as they are, are devout men and will never lay hands on a girl under the protection of a priest.

But if the priest is gone, what will hold them back? the other voice cried.

She must have made some sound, because Father Martin stirred and lifted his head. "What is wrong, my child?"

She managed a smile. "Stiff, I suppose. How are you feeling, father?"

"Stiff too and very weary, but soon we can both rest for a bit. It must be nearly time for our paddlers' next pipe."

He proved to be right. Hardly had he spoken when the steersmen called from behind them. "Time, *mes garçons*, for the blessed pipe. To the left bank."

His choice looked like a good one. The left bank in this area sloped gently down to the river and was covered with low grass and shrubs. The shrubs already wore fall's rich coloring and flamed in shades of gold and red. Through the grass a stream leaped lightly over pebbles on its crooked way to join the river.

As the men expertly nudged the canoe against the bank, Osa sprang out and, standing knee-deep in water, scooped the frail form of the priest into his arms. While he carried his burden ashore, the steersman also leapt from the craft and stretched a hand to assist the girl. Instead of taking it, she climbed out by herself. She didn't like the man. He was the most important man in the crew, the leader of the voyageurs, and his job required the most skill; but Armand was Osa's brother and she was more nervous of him than she was of the bear. Osa's small eyes glared at her with an animal lust, but Armand regarded her with malice, with an emotion approaching cruelty.

As icy water closed around her high leather boots and soaked the hem of her skirt, she swore under her breath. Reverend Mother had attended to the details of her scanty wardrobe for the trip, and her dress was a compromise between one proper for modesty and something that would prove serviceable amid the rigors of the wild country. The material was heavy serge, the skirt not as full as usual and much shorter, reaching barely to the tops of her boots. But neither Reverend Mother nor Rowan had fully realized what clambering out of a rocking canoe would entail, what making frequent portages over rocky, uneven ground would mean to a woman in skirts of any kind.

As she climbed up the grassy bank and paused to wring out her sodden skirt, she heard Armand laughing and speaking in whispers to the other voyageurs. Then Osa called and Beau hurried past her with his arms full of blankets, and she forgot about herself and hurried to where the two men were stretching the priest out on the blankets. Anxiously, Rowan knelt by the old man's side.

"You must eat, father," Osa was saying roughly. "Not for three days have you taken a bite."

Father Martin's eyes were closed, and his voice was so low that Rowan had to strain to hear him. "I thank you, my son, but I cannot eat."

Rowan appealed to him. "Osa is right; you must keep up your strength."

His eyes flickered open, and he smiled up at her. Such an ordinary face, the girl thought. Even in his youth he could never have had any pretensions to good looks. An old, unmistakably Irish face with a pug nose, an overlarge mouth, a receding chin. Yet such a face of goodness and strength. And when he smiled! His smile radiated charm, sweetness, and a gentle sadness. "I would gladly eat if I could, my child," he assured her. "But my stomach . . . alas, it will not retain food."

Beau touched her arm. "There's a little tea left. I've been saving it for our good father. I'll brew a cup for him."

As Osa and Beau left her side, Rowan looked after them. Such a difference between them. Most of the voyageurs were squat men with heavy shoulders and deep chests, overlong arms and short, powerful legs. Beau and Osa were both tall, although Osa was a head taller than Beau. But Osa was almost as wide as he was tall—a hideous, shambling figure of a man—while Beau deserved his nickname. He was the youngest man in the canoe, slender as a willow, with soft dark eyes in a handsome, clean-shaven face. Beau, she thought, the only one she didn't fear.

Her eyes flickered over the rest of the voyageurs as they strolled about, chatting to each other, lighting up small, stubby pipes. When she had first met them at Grande Portage she had been unable to tell one from the other. Armand she soon grew to know. He was the one with whom Father Martin had bargained for passage on the trip west. Silently she had stood by the priest's side while he pleaded with the short, powerful steersman.

"No," Armand had said bluntly. "I'll not take a woman in my canoe. They are frail things at best and could never stand the hardships."

"But surely there are women in *le pays d'en haut?*" Father Martin argued.

"*Oui, mon père,*" Armand agreed. His cunning eyes slid over Rowan. "Many women, but natives of the land. A white lady can't stand what these women accept as everyday living."

Father Martin hesitated, and Rowan could read his mind. Her heritage had been carefully concealed from the paddlers on the first part of their trip in the huge express canoe that had brought them from Montreal. The mother superior's last gift had been a wide-brimmed hat with ties that knotted under the chin. "Always wear it," Mother Michael-John had urged the girl. "Don't let the sun touch your face and neck. These men of the west are basically good men and devout, but their conduct with women is scandalous. They've their own code, and if they believe your blood is all white they will be respectful."

Clearing his throat, the priest said firmly, "Miss Malone will be no hindrance to you. We are traveling west so I may give her safely into the hands of her mother's people."

A smile flickered at the corners of the other man's

bearded lips. "And who might those people be, *mon père?*"

"Her mother is Aluski, sister of the chief of the Chilcotins. Her father"—and there was chill warning in the old man's voice— "was Eamon Malone, who was one of my best friends."

Armand's eyes roved over Rowan again, and his smile widened. "A *bois brûlée*. Never have I seen a breed with skin so white."

"Many of your own men are *bois brûlés*."

"*Oui*, but none pretend to be otherwise."

"Will you take us?"

"I will take you."

"In that case you will remember this," the priest said firmly. "Miss Malone will be in my care, and all respect will be shown to her by both you and your men."

Armand had agreed, but since the trip had started his eyes often darted toward Rowan with malice and a slow, patient expectation.

And so the steersman she knew from the outset. Osa, Armand's dull bear of a brother, she knew almost as quickly, and Beau, with his gentle eyes and gentle manner, she came to like. The rest of them all looked alike to her, but by degrees she sorted them out. Watching them, she named them one by one. Four-Finger Jacques, and the reason for his nickname was apparent. The index fingers were missing from both his hands. Rowan had questioned Beau about how Jacques lost them, but Beau colored and averted his face. Armand had overheard, and he bayed with laughter. "From putting them where he shouldn't have, mam'selle," he said, and lifting his voice, he shouted at Jacques, "Is that not right, *mon ami?* In drink your wisdom was gone, and it was the wrong Indian maid you approached!"

Then there was Portelance, with a somber, copperskinned face. Portelance was an Iroquois, and he seldom spoke. Jourdin and Lapointe were standing together beside the canoe. A ragged scar etched a red path across Jourdin's brow, and Lapointe was giggling his high-pitched giggle, which sounded constantly and irritatingly. Louis Grand was the last one. Why he was called large Rowan didn't know, as he had the same short stature as the other voyageurs. His expression was dull and vacuous, but when Louis Grand lifted his voice in their paddling songs, it soared above all the others, a sweet true tenor rivaling in clarity birdsongs in the woods.

She roused from her thoughts. Beau was standing beside her extending a steaming mug of tea. Gratefully, she took it and woke the priest from his doze. "Sip some," she coaxed, and he did.

The men had extracted a parfleche from their supplies, and when Father Martin had drunk the tea she went over to take her share. She liked the pemmican wrapped in its thin sheet of rawhide no more than did the priest, and during the early part of their travels had had to force it down. Now she was able to eat the rank, pounded meat and dried berries in their coating of grease as avidly as the men did. Although its taste was noxious, it was nourishing and even a small amount sent new strength through her body. As she ate she continued to worry about Father Martin.

"Beau," she said, "we haven't had fresh meat for days, not since those ducks you shot. Father Martin was able to drink the broth, and it seemed to strengthen him. Do you think you could get something else, perhaps a rabbit or a squirrel?"

"I'll try," he told her. "But hunting takes time, and we must hasten to bring the good father to the fort. Who knows how much time is left for him?"

She silently agreed, and when they were loaded in the canoe and again floating down the waters of the Nechako, she thought of the priest's chances. The doubts of the voyageurs about her own ability to measure up to the hardships of the wild country hadn't been realized. Each day seemed to toughen and strengthen her. She was able to look after herself, help with the cooking when fresh meat was available, and even handle her own bundles on the portages. It was the priest who felt the long, grueling

72

miles. Throughout the earlier part of the trip through the plains, Father Martin had remained spry and active. Once in a long time they'd come to a fur trading post, generally one of the Nor'westers, or sometimes on the bank of a lake or stream they'd see an Indian village. In these shelters they'd rest for a few days and then travel on. When the flaming colors of fall waned into a bitter winter they stopped at a fort, and there they wintered. The voyageurs, she admitted, had their own code of honor, and never at any of the places they stopped did they betray her origins. She was accepted as a lady and treated as one and took her place with the factor and his clerks at the head of the communal tables instead of below the salt with the half-breeds and the Indian wives and children. Sometimes she felt her duplicity, and once she questioned Father Martin about her conduct.

"Is this not a lie I'm living?" she asked.

He looked gravely at her. "If you're asked a direct question about your blood, then indeed you must tell the truth. But no one has questioned you so far." He added, "Remember, if this was known the burden for your safety would weigh more heavily on me."

Not only the weight of Rowan's safety but also the hard journey had taken its toll, and Father Martin began to fail. Where had it started? Rowan wondered. At that moment the canoe struck turbulent water, and from its bow Jourdin shouted, "White water ahead!"

From the stern, Armand roared, "Prepare to make portage!"

Sighing, Rowan started to gather her small bundles and those of the priest together. Father Martin grunted and fell heavily against her shoulder. Putting an arm around him, she steadied him. "I'm such a burden," he whispered.

"A very precious burden," she told him.

The canoe grounded, and in minutes they were all out. Armand walked along the bank for a few yards surveying the surge of white-tipped water. "We'll make it a *demi-charge*," he shouted back to his men. "Beau and Lapointe

73

will be on the towropes, the rest will unload at least half the weight of the supplies."

The men lifted out some of the bales, and Beau and Lapointe seized the two ropes and started the chore of towing the canoe through the edges of the turbulent water. It was always dangerous work. The footing was bad, and the powerful surge of the river at times nearly swept the canoe from their grasps. Frequently on *demicharges* a man would lose his footing and fall into the water, but all of them could swim like seals, and a mate would be tossing him a line in seconds.

The rest of the voyageurs were fastening tumplines across their foreheads to help support the heavy burdens on their backs. Osa had the heaviest load, but when he had it adjusted he turned and swept the priest up in his arms as though the other man were a child. Slinging her bags across her shoulder, Rowan toiled up the slope after Osa's huge form. She wondered at the man's strength and his doglike devotion to Father Martin. The memory of that terrible night in the pass of the sentinel mountains when a band of Piegan Indians, guardians of the passes, had swept down on their camp returned to her. The voyageurs had blended their own shouts with the bloodthirsty shrieks of the savages and had grappled with the Indians, wielding their rifle butts and slashing with short axes and the knives all the voyageurs wore in their belts. Osa thrust the priest and the girl back against a tree trunk, planted himself in front of them, and defended them with mighty, swinging arms.

The Piegans were driven off, but four of the voyageurs were wounded. Three of them weren't hurt seriously, but Osa had the iron head of a spear broken off in his shoulder. Father Martin moved among them, his bag in his hand, caring for their wounds. When Osa's turn came, the priest shook his head at the depth of the spearhead and plunged a knife into the fire.

"Take a deep breath, my son," he told the big man gently. "I'll be as quick as I can."

Standing beside them, a pot of boiling water in her

hands, Rowan turned her head away as the hot knife cut into Osa's shoulder. He made no sound, but sweat poured down his face, and his teeth gnawed his lower lip bloody and raw. Afterward, when the shoulder was bandaged, Osa took the priest's hand and kissed it.

Rowan tripped and nearly fell. A hand caught her arm, and she looked up to see Portelance. The lips in his grim, coppery face moved. "Take care, mam'selle. To hurt an ankle would be unwise."

Armand passed them, his back bent nearly double under the weight of his pack. "Move it up," he grunted. "Would you take all day on this short portage?"

Ahead of her, Osa plunged down a rocky slope, as sure-footed as a mountain goat. Rowan, the breath sobbing in her throat and every muscle in her body aching, followed him. At the foot of the slope on a grassy sward, Beau and Lapointe were wrestling the canoe into view. Osa gently deposited the priest in the shade of a huge fir tree, and Rowan sank panting beside him. Father Martin tried to help her remove the bags from her back, but his hands fell limply to his lap, and he leaned against the rough bark of the tree and shut his eyes.

"I don't think I can go further, my child," he whispered.

She took one of his frail hands in both of her own. Should she appeal to Armand to camp here? she wondered. Would he listen to her if she did? She turned to find his location and saw he was standing on the shore, one hand shielding his eyes as he scanned the sky.

"The shadows are lengthening, and the sun going to her rest," he called. "This is as good a place as any. Prepare camp."

Thankfully, Rowan hauled herself up and started to do what she could to make the old man more comfortable. She cut fir boughs, covered them with a blanket, and then stretched Father Martin, wrapped in more blankets, on their springy, sweetly scented surface. She used two of her own blankets to cover the priest, as he felt the cold severely, and then she fetched water and bathed his face and hands. Afterward she followed the tiny stream that flowed down from the woods until she found a little glade, and there she washed her face, neck, arms, and legs as well as she could. When she returned to the shore, she found that a fire had been kindled and Beau was kneeling beside the priest, holding a mug to his lips.

"Tea," Beau told her, "and the last there is. Osa is trying to find small game or a fish for the father's supper."

Rowan glanced over her shoulder. The rest of the men were gathered around the fire unwrapping pemmican, and some of them were firing up their short pipes. She drew Beau a little distance away from the priest. "How soon before we reach your fort?" she whispered.

He lowered his own voice. "By nightfall tomorrow. But if you hope to persuade us to go with you, that we can't do. As Armand told Father Martin, he must secure further passage from there. We've our duties at the fort, and we must stay there."

"I'm only thinking of getting to the fort. Father Martin can travel no further, and perhaps we can winter there and go on in the spring."

His gentle eyes looked with concern from her worried face to the sleeping face of the priest. "Pray we get there safely, that the good priest lives to see our fort, mam'selle."

She could smell smoke from the campfire, the tang of burning tobacco, and the sharp, pleasant odor from the freshly cut fir boughs. She fancied she could smell something else too and knew it was her own fear. "If he dies before we reach it, what will happen to me?"

Averting his face, he made no answer. She touched his arm. "Beau, what is Osa really like? He's so kind to Father Martin. I can't believe he's a bad man."

"He isn't bad," the young man muttered. "He's merely dull, with strong appetites. It's only when the drink is in him that he becomes . . . mad. But even then his brother can control him. If Armand wishes to, that is."

Her fear became stronger. "Does he not always wish to?"

Coming gracefully to his feet, Beau moved away. Over his shoulder he threw a few words. "Not always. Armand is the one to truly fear."

Without bothering to go and get her share of the pemmican, Rowan wrapped herself in a blanket and curled up as close as she could to the priest. She was exhausted, but sleep evaded her. Her mind roved back and then flinched away in horror from that night in the dark garret of the Guilbant house in Montreal. The faces of René Guilbant and his two friends flickered darkly through her memory.

It can't happen again! she silently cried. This time I'll die first.

7

While the girl slept and dreamt uneasy dreams of death, the old priest lay with his face turned up to the night sky, thinking of death. Such a narrow sky, he mused, merely a patch of velvety blackness snared between towering mountain peaks and edged with far-flung tops of hemlock and fir and cedar. So much narrower than the sky that had stretched over the village of his birth, nestled among the folded downs of County Roscommon. Still, the Lord lightened that sky with the pale sickle of a waning moon and scattered across it the glittering lights of a few stars.

This was the first time in the long procession of nights and days of recent weeks that he had roused for long from the exhaustion that had plagued him, seizing him unawares and drifting him into comalike sleep. My death is near, Father Martin thought, and for me the weary travail of my long life makes it a welcome one. But what of this child at my side? What of this sorely abused girl so dear to me, who even now, in sleep, turns with confidence toward me? Then peace soothed his troubled thoughts. If the good God, in His wisdom and mercy, takes this life of mine, it is His will and I must not question it.

Yet she is my responsibility, and should I now raise my voice, waken the voyageurs, and from them wrench a promise for her safety? In the light of the waning moon his brow furrowed. No, he decided, the promise will be given because the men are devout, but will their promise be kept? These men are akin to the country they work in, simple children of nature with that sudden cruelty that nature herself can demonstrate. To ask the vow knowing it would be mortal sin if the vow is broken . . . no. The Lord will find His own way, in His own time. Trust in Him.

Those were the words he had used in conversation with Reverend Mother when he told her of his decision to take Rowan back to her mother. The sense of peace deepened within him as he pictured her study, that refuge behind the high walls of the Convent of the Sisters of Ste. Claire. Sunlight had filtered through the budding leaves of the willow outside the window, falling across her desk and with mellow light outlining her face under the starched coif. Father Martin sat across from her, remembering this girl when he had taken her to a county fair—young Bridget Delaney, with her face glowing and bright ribbons threaded through her hair. Momentarily he had toyed with the thought of what their lives might have been if both of them hadn't been drawn to service for their God. Then he brushed his thoughts away. Young Bridget was long gone, and facing him was Reverend Mother Michael-John, her face as furrowed and careworn as his own. Both so old, he thought, so old.

She puts his thoughts into words. "You are too old," she told him with that bluntness she often used when they spoke in private. "I feel as deeply as you do for Rowan—after all, I raised her—but this trip is insanity."

"It's her wish, and this I owe her."

"Then send her with a younger man, one who can stand the perils ahead."

"Have you one in mind?" When she didn't answer, the priest continued. "I can think of no one. The men traveling to the west I've examined one by one, but either they would be unable to protect her from the voyageurs or they would be tempted by her beauty themselves. Would you have her endure again what brought her back to this convent, to you?"

The mother superior bent her head, and the priest followed her thoughts with no difficulty. The picture of Rowan as she had been the night he found her collapsed

79

against his door, a cloak drawn over the torn remnants of her nightgown, her face bruised, and her eyes mad with horror, flashed across his own mind. "Mme. and M. Guilbant are trying to atone for their son's sins," he told his companion. "They've offered funds to take the child home."

"Well they should! Have those rogues been given punishment?"

"They are at penitence. René Guilbant and his two friends excused themselves by swearing they were deep in drink and knew not what they did. I chided them severely and told them they wouldn't do in their cups what they wouldn't have done sober. Then they confessed they had discovered that Rowan has Indian blood and felt Indians were fair game for their advances. René and the other two have been chastised severely."

Fury flashed across her features. "That cannot return to an innocent girl what has been wrenched from her. To think I found the place in that household for the child myself, believing that Mme. Guilbant and her husband were devout and would give the little one a good home."

"Don't blame yourself. The blame for this I must share with her father. Eamon Malone and I should never have taken the child from her mother, never should have brought her east."

Reverend Mother brushed a hand across her brow. "How well I remember the little one when you first put her in my arms. And I am guilty of cherishing her too much. All of us—Sister Gabriel, Sister Paul, and Sister Peter—love her. Such a beautiful child, with those eyes and that long black hair. And then when she was barely sixteen to have to turn her out of this sanctuary."

He reached for his pipe, waited for the woman's nod of assent, and began to stuff tobacco into it. Smoke wreathed his head before he said slowly, "There again you attempt to take guilt that is not your own. Eamon was dead, and there were no further funds for his daughter's keep. I know you would gladly have kept Rowan on, but we suffer, as always, from lack of funds. It was necessary for her to earn her own keep, and for several years Mme. Guilbant kept her safe."

"That father of hers!" she burst out with renewed anger. "A gombeen on the face of the fair earth was Eamon Malone. I don't care if you called him friend. Draining the wares of his alehouse as though he hoped to drink them dry and putting not even pence aside for his own daughter!"

"Bridget, Bridget. Still the fiery temper of that colleen at the county fair."

At the sound of the name that no one but Father Martin had called her for fifty years, she smiled. "You said I was the fairest colleen there, Martin."

"Ah, so you were. With ribbons binding your hair and a smile on your face that rivaled the sun itself as it shone on the loch. But Eamon you never knew. He wasn't always a sodden wreck of a man in a dockside alehouse. Once he stood tall and fair, his red hair glinting in the western sun, a respected warrior among warriors renowned for courage."

Serene once more, Reverend Mother folded her hands before her and regarded the priest with interest. "You never have told about your meeting with him and why you feel so indebted to him."

"Then I shall tell you now. Perhaps it will temper your opinion of him." Puffing gray smoke, he stretched his legs comfortably before him. "It was like this. Years ago, when I was younger and more active, I made my way west, called by the need of lonely men in lonely places for what a priest alone could bring them—"

"Reckless with yourself even then, Martin."

"I was taken prisoner by Chilcotins and brought to their camp as a slave. There I found Eamon Malone, with bronzed skin and breechclout, already wed to the sister of the chief, and with a baby daughter by her. He told me his tale, which I shall recount briefly, a long tragic story of shipwreck and rescue by the Haidas of the coast. Because of his flaming hair they valued him, but they made him a slave. At a potlatch the chief of the Haidas gave

81

Eamon as a gift to the chief to the Chilcotins." His brow wrinkled in memory, and then he smiled, that smile of rare charm. "The twin sister of the chief, a comely maid called Aluski, looked with favor on young Eamon, and as she was a woman of influence she persuaded her brother to free Eamon from bondage and make him a brave. The ban against slaves is such that never may they marry the free members of the tribe. Eventually, after Eamon proved his courage in war and became a mighty warrior, the marriage was arranged."

"And when you arrived?" she asked.

"Eamon interceded for me, and so did their shaman, a wise old man who took a fancy to me. I too was freed, and it was then that Eamon told me of his plan for leaving the Chilcotins and bringing Rowan east."

"Did you try to dissuade him?"

"To some extent. I warned him what might happen to a child of mixed blood in the tight little society of Upper and Lower Canada. I also counseled that in Aluski he had a fine woman and might never again find her like. But Eamon was restless, always seeking that which never existed, and he determined to leave."

The woman's hands moved restlessly. "Why did the tribe let you go? How could they allow you to take the child?"

"Aluski," he said simply. "She loved enough to make the supreme sacrifice. If Eamon wanted to leave her, then she let him go freely. If Rowan had been a boy even Aluski would never have consented. But girls are valued less highly, and so we went."

For moments both were silent. Finally Reverend Mother stirred. "And now the girl would return, and she has no idea of her mother's people or even the land where she was born."

"That is true."

"She also wished to take vows," the woman said, and there was harshness in her voice. "She wished to join us as a novice, you wouldn't allow her to."

"Bridget, your affection is clouding your judgment.

82

You wish her safe, our Rowan óg, but it's not true vocation that spurs her request. It's only fear. She seeks a hiding place, a place to bury herself from a world that has bruised and maimed her. Would you be party to helping a girl take the veil who later may either regret her vow or, even worse, break it?"

She murmured, "You do well to chide me. When will you leave?"

He rose to his feet, and behind the desk she also rose. "As soon as the arrangements can be made. Perhaps in the west Rowan will find more mercy with her savage relatives than ever she has found in our civilization."

"The trip will kill you!"

Drawing himself to his full height, he looked sternly down at her. "If it does, then it will be the will of the God we both serve. Would you question His wisdom?"

"It is only that for so long we have found our paths together. I'm selfish, Martin. I grow old and would not lose the comfort of you."

His expression softened. "We'll both find comfort where we should." He stretched out a hand, and she took it in both of hers. For an instant he saw Bridget Delaney again and found himself saying tenderly, *"Slán leat mó ghrá gheal."*

Her eyes widened with shock, and then she smiled with a sad, secret understanding. "Perhaps now we may both say it." And she whispered the same words in English. "Good-bye, my own true love."

Then Bridget óg was gone, and as Father Martin closed the door, Reverend Mother's withered hands were reaching for her rosary.

Moonlight and starlight shone kindly upon Father Martin as the smile of memory made his wide mouth momentarily beautiful. A breeze from the river stirred the hair at his temples, and sudden pain flashed through his chest and down one arm. He accepted it, willing himself to make no sound, and by degrees it lessened until he was able to breathe again. Taking shallow breaths, he knew his time was near.

Time now, he told himself, to make his last contrition. His task was done, and he must leave the world and all its joys and woes behind him. One final prayer for Rowan, and his lips moved as he prayed for her safety. Then he folded his hands upon his breast and aloud, his voice sonorously drifting over the sleeping forms of the girl and the voyageurs, sent his final pleas toward the patch of sky flung over all of them.

His voice spoke on in Latin, deep and musical, the words of the ancient ritual warming and comforting him. But hardly had he spoken the last word when pain was on him again, this time in waves so terrible that he could no longer withstand the agony and sounds were wrenched from his lips.

Riding on that wave of suffering, his spirit faltered and then found the merciful curtain between the living and the dead. With gratitude he felt release and floated free beyond pain, beyond humanity, upwards toward the waning moon and the silver stars of the Master he had so long served.

8

Huddling on a rock, her face buried in her hands, Rowan was oblivious to everything and everyone around her. She didn't feel the warmth of the noon sun on her head and shoulders, the soft breeze from the river, and she didn't hear the voices of the men near the river or the rush as it ran rapidly between its banks.

Miles behind them, at the camp where they'd spent the night, was a fresh mound of earth and an upright wooden cross. In the pale light of dawn they had buried Father Martin. Lapointe and Jourdin dug the grave, Osa fashioned the wooden cross, and Beau, with painstaking care, carved a few words. *Father Martin Petrie*, his knife slashed out of the rough bark, along with the date of his death—*September 14, 1816*. Rowan had prepared the priest's body, closing his eyes, bathing his face, straightening his shabby cassock, and finally covering his face with a fold of the blanket they wrapped him in. When they lowered his body gently into the gouged-out hole, the voyageurs turned expectantly to Rowan. Numb with grief, she prayed, hardly knowing what she was saying. Tears were running down Beau's face, and Osa's huge body was shaking with childlike weeping.

Then they had silently loaded the canoe and as they drifted down the surface of the Nechako, Armand's voice called from behind the girl huddled alone in the middle of the craft. "Jacques, break out a keg of high wine. We could all do with a drink."

85

"Not me," Jacques called back. "Our factor would have my head."

Armand grunted. "Did they cut off your guts with your fingers? Lapointe, you can reach it. Have it out. The factor will never notice one keg."

"He'll notice," Jacques objected. "He checks too carefully for my liking."

"I'll take all responsibility," Armand said impatiently.

Lapointe called eagerly, "I'll get it. My throat has a dryness."

"Give it first to Osa," Armand ordered. "Perhaps then, brother, you'll stop your mewling for the dead priest."

Osa spoke thickly. "The father was a good man."

"The father is dead, brother. We've buried him and honored him, but we still live. Come, *mes hommes*, open the keg and pass it around."

The keg was passed first to Osa, who drank deeply, and then the length of the canoe. An arm thrust it past the girl, and Armand caught it and tilted it up. Wiping his sleeve across wet lips, he laughed and said, "That is better. Now, Louis Grand, strike up a song with your nightingale voice and let us be happy."

Throwing back his head, Louis Grand started to sing a hymn, but Armand shouted, "Enough! We're done with prayer. Give us a rollicking tune, something to lighten the stroke of our paddles. Sing to us about your girl."

Obediently, Louis Grand started the song. *"J'ai une fille graisse et jolie."* The other men's deeper voices joined his sweet, clear tenor.

Dimly, Rowan was aware of the smell of wine, the movement of the canoe, the words of the song. "Oh, I have a girl fat and fine," the men sang, "her arms grasp me, our legs entwine." The paddles picked up speed and flashed through the water, dripping fine sprays of silver drops as they lifted and fell. Rowan resented their merriment, resented the coarse words of the song. She almost resented the sun warming her. It should be raining, she thought, raining gray tears of grief for Father Martin. Who mourns for him but me? Then her thoughts shifted.

Many will mourn him. Reverend Mother will mourn him, and the Sisters of Ste. Claire, for all loved him well. The poor oppressed people in the slums of Montreal will sorely miss their Father Martin, who walked among them with compassion for their troubles, their misery, their sins. And I'm the one who brought him to this wild country and to this end. For weeks all I've thought of is my own fear, my own need of him. I never really considered *him*. I have sinned, thinking only of myself and bringing him to this death.

Then Armand called again, "The sun rides high in the sky. Let us stop for the blessed pipe and break fast. Osa, didn't you bag game in the night?"

"Two rabbits and a squirrel, *mon frère*. For the father I bagged them, but he didn't live to eat them."

"They won't go to waste. We'll light a fire and have them into a pot, and then we'll feast and drink more high wine."

Beau called back to the steersman. "I thought you wished to make the fort before nightfall?"

"That was for Father Martin's sake, and he no longer cares. A few hours longer, another night in the open, what does it matter?"

His voice had thickened, and Rowan realized he was becoming drunk. As the voyageurs unloaded at a rocky spit of land and kindled a fire, she could see many of them were feeling the strong wine. Osa's face was flushed, and he stared after her with gleaming eyes as she walked up the fall of stones and pebbles to perch herself on a large rock near the growth of trees that swooped backward and upward into the tangled fastness of a fir forest.

Jourdin cut up the rabbits and squirrel and flung the pieces into a pot of boiling water. Soon a delicious smell floated up the bank, and the men stood around the fire, savoring the odor of cooking meat, tilting up the keg of wine, and packing pipes with tobacco.

"Come closer," Armand called up to her. "Have some food and a drink of wine."

"I don't want anything," she called back.

"Too good to eat with us common men, isn't she?" Armand laughed coarsely. "And what is she but a squaw, the spawn of some white man and an Indian slut."

His words and the tone of his voice cut through the mist of grief that enclosed her, and she was suddenly alert. Why had he ordered the wine broken out? she wondered. Why a stop at this desolate point where there wasn't even a blade of grass? And with a sickening certainty she knew what moved in the depths of Armand's cunning mind.

Lapointe gave his senseless giggle. "Fair game for us. Indian maids are our right. We've taken them even when we've had to fight for them."

Beau said sternly, "She is under the protection of our church. Would you endanger your immortal souls?"

"Bah!" Armand spat on the ground. "She was the priest's ward, but as I've told you, he's dead. Dead men have no wishes. And did he ever ask one of you to swear an oath for this squaw? Speak up, did any of you swear?"

"That is true." Jourdin fingered the livid scar on his brow. "He asked none of us to vow."

Beau took a step toward Armand. "You play with words and lead these men astray. We all know what the good father's wishes were."

"Were!" Armand howled, throwing his arms wide. "As I've said, it's over. Who is with me?"

"Not I," Beau said, and went to stand a few steps apart from the knot of men.

Armand threw him a venomous glance. "The pretty boy saves himself for the girl who waits for him in Quebec. The rest of you—are you men or not? Portelance?"

The Iroquois's bronze face was impassive as he stepped to Beau's side.

"So," Armand grated, "another lily-livered one. Four-Finger Jacques, what do you say?"

Jacques held up both hands and showed them the stumps of his amputated fingers. "Before this I'd have joined you, but I've learned caution. I don't think this is a wise thing to do. The factor at our fort—"

"Silence!" Armand cut him off. "The factor isn't here, and I don't think he would trouble himself about a squaw. But you get over with Beau and Portelance. Jourdin?"

The man rubbed his scarred brow. "I'd like to but . . . a burial this morning and now . . . no." He took his place beside Jacques.

Wheeling, Armand surveyed his brother. Osa had drained the keg and was turning it idly in his huge hands. "Have I need to question your courage, brother?"

"I don't care about the rest," Osa said in his deep, rumbling voice. "On the dock at Grande Portage where first I saw this girl I knew she must be mine."

"Good man. But we'll give the other two their chances. What of you, songbird? Will you join us?"

Louis Grand lifted his vacuous face. "I've been thinking on it. One minute I think yes, then I think no. There's the church to consider, and the factor. On the other hand there's the enjoyment and sport—"

"You'll keep thinking on it forever, songbird," Armand said disgustedly. "Some time next year you might decide. Stand with the rest. This leaves one. Lapointe?"

"I've courage, Armand. I'd have a piece of it. I'm with you and Osa."

"So, we have three from eight. You five may squat beside the fire and eat squirrel and rabbit. We'll dine from sweeter flesh. And so that you may tell the factor you were restrained, I'll leave Lapointe to guard you. Get your rifle, Lapointe."

The man's wail was as high-pitched as his giggle. "You jest!"

"Get your rifle and force them to stay by the fire. When Osa and I are sated, *mon pauvre fou*, you may have your turn."

Springing to his feet, Osa flung the keg against the rocks with such force that it splintered. "Enough talk!" He lunged up the slope.

But Rowan no longer sat on the rock. When she'd realized what Armand was working the men up for, her fear came flooding back. When she'd seen Beau standing helplessly, she knew she could expect no protection from him. She'd slipped off the rock and inched up the slope to the first trees. Now she was running desperately through the forest, leaping along, her skirts caught up past her knees.

Behind her she could hear Armand shouting, "*Sacré chien mort!* The rabbit, she is gone! But the hound is hot on her trail. Run her to ground, Osa!"

The ground sloped steadily up, and for a time she ran blindly, looking over her shoulder, careening into trunks of trees. Then she forced herself to steady and started to pick her way, running as fast as she could, but watching for fallen logs, dodging leaning trees. If she was to escape she must use all her wits. Then her heart almost failed her. There was no escape. She ran from one danger into others. The great bears she'd been told about—the ones with the grizzled hides who could run faster than deer—inhabited the forest. Wolves were there, and maybe poisonous snakes.

Her foot touched a hard surface, and she looked down. The bed of a dried-up creek wound up the hill. The pebbles might slow her, but there were no obstacles. She decided to take it and turned up the steeper slope. She put on a burst of speed. Far down the hill she could hear something crashing through the underbrush. Was it Osa or one of the dreadful bears? Then her heel caught between rocks and jammed. She fell forward and landed heavily. The scaring fire of jagged stones lanced across her cheek, and her hands were scraped raw. Worse than that, when she hauled herself up she found she'd injured her ankle. For a few paces she limped along, and then, hearing the crashing behind her and men's shouts, she tried frantically to go faster.

No longer did she look for escape. She was looking for one of the terrible bears, for a swipe from a monstrous paw. She was looking for a wolf to tear out her throat. A waterfall, she sobbed, let me find some precipice to cast myself from. Any death at the hands of the wild would be more merciful than the fate that was following her in the guise of men.

Send me death, she prayed. Dear God, send me death!

9

On the side of the mountain high above the rocky spit but shielded from sight of it by a tall, dark stand of fir, a horse and rider appeared around a jagged rock cliff. The horse was small and stocky with short, powerful legs, and his piebald coat, white and black and tan, was already shaggy and uneven with the beginnings of a heavy winter growth of hair. Ahead of them a dog trotted, again heavily furred, a big black animal with the head of a wolf. The man astride the horse looked not unlike a voyageur. He was clad in buckskin fringed along the arms of the jacket, a bright scarf was at his throat, his feet were shod in heavy boots, but he didn't wear the red worsted cap trimmed with a turkey feather that all voyageurs wore. A wide-brimmed hat shaded a tanned face, and under it long blond hair fell to his shoulders.

As they reached a patch of sunlight glinting through the fir boughs, the rider reined his horse to a halt and sat in the saddle, enjoying the warmth of that sun. A fine day for a ride, Laurie Woodbyne was thinking, and a good day to get away from the confines of Fort Purline. Strange how the stockade that at times was a shield and a comfort at other times could prove so restricting. Part of the problem was the factor of the trading post. General Ezra Purline was a strange man, a man of conflicting faces. In some moods he was a martinet, violent and occasionally sadistic, in others he was an uncertain man, deferring to the men under him, unsure what decision to make. If he had stayed one or the other, he could have been tolerated, but one never knew which factor one would face.

That morning had been a good example of the factor uncertain of himself and everyone around him. Purline had called both Laurie and the third in command, a taciturn Scot named George Durran, to his office, which opened off the post store. As always, Purline was carefully dressed, his dark suit brushed, his linen immaculate. As they entered the office he rose courteously from behind his desk, his shoulders held militarily erect. Purline was tall, taller by half a head then Durran, and on eye level with Laurie. He had a spare, powerful build, and his black hair was clipped short. On the crown of his head he had a circular bald spot, but the factor wasn't vain about this and made no effort to brush hair over the spot to cover it.

"Be seated, gentlemen," he told them, and Durran and Laurie exchanged glances. They now knew which factor they faced. The martinet would have required them to stand—at attention if he could have managed it.

Sitting down, both younger men regarded Purline. All the man's features were oversized—his nose, his cheekbones, his jaw. Large ears stood out like bats' wings from his head, and his mouth was wide and thin. He should have been ugly, and would have been if he hadn't had deep-set, strangely beautiful eyes. Those amazing eyes now turned from one of his juniors to the other.

"The canoe of Armand," he said abruptly. "It's long overdue."

Durran nodded his red head. "Should have been here a couple of weeks ago."

"He started from Grande Portage about the same time as the flotillas did," Laurie agreed.

Purline was toying with small objects on his desk. He picked up a quill, moved it closer to the inkpot, shuffled some papers, and waited.

Durran crossed his legs, his eyes on Purline's hands. "Carvet told me that Armand took on two passengers at the Portage. An elderly man and a woman."

93

"Against all orders," Purline said with some heat. "He should have stayed with the flotilla, but what does he do but try to pick up some money on the side. That man is exasperating."

"You've often told us that Armand and his crew are the best men we have," Laurie pointed out.

Purline nodded. "Which is the only reason the impertinent fellow hasn't been sent packing before this. Do you think something has happened to them?"

Durran frowned, and one hand moved to stroke his short red beard, "Could be, general, specially with them carrying passengers. Carvet said the woman was young and pretty."

All three men mulled this over. Armand's and his brother's reputations with women they knew only too well.

"Was she white?" General Purline asked.

"Carvet said white as driven snow. And the old man with her was a priest."

Purline gave a sigh of relief. "Then we have no need to worry. Even Armand and Osa wouldn't try anything under those circumstances." His brow furrowed. "Those Nor'westers downriver, do you think they might have ambushed our men?"

This time Laurie answered. "Not with a woman in the canoe. They'd be more likely to help them than hinder."

"Why would a white woman be coming to this land?" Purline asked.

Neither Durran nor Laurie could even hazard a guess. Moving impatiently, Laurie asked, "What do you want us to do?"

"I don't know, Mr. Woodbyne. Both you and Mr. Durran are needed here. The canoes must be unloaded, the manifests checked. There're the men on wood details to supervise, and those dratted hunters are overdue again. So much to do and so few hands to do it with."

"Maybe we could ride downriver and check," Durran suggested. "The hunters are camped in that direction, and we could find out what's holding them up while we keep an eye out for Armand and his crew."

"I'm aware of what's holding them up, Mr. Durran. Whiskey! They begged for another keg, and I was fool enough to give it to them," Purline snapped. His manner suddenly changed, and he got to his feet, his body held rigidly. "You will remain here, Mr. Durran. Mr. Woodbyne, you'll leave immediately. Check the riverbanks for signs. See to the hunters. Take several days if necessary, but don't come back without news."

"Yes, sir." Laurie got to his feet. This was the general's other face—the martinet. He nearly snapped a salute and stopped just in time.

Outside the office, Laurie growled, "Damn pompous ass!"

Durran tugged at his beard. "He's neither pompous nor an ass. Most of the time he's the ablest factor I've ever served under. But once in a while . . ."

"Once in a while, what?"

"He fears."

"Fears what?"

Durran didn't answer. His short, sturdy legs were bearing him rapidly away, toward the gates of the fort and the river beyond.

On the mountainside high above the Nechako, Laurie grinned at the memory and patted his horse's shaggy mane. A good pony. He'd bought Moska from an Indian for a rifle, and he'd never regretted it. Moska certainly didn't have the size or the lines of the horses he'd ridden in England, but he had unbelievable stamina, and his unshod hooves could pick their way up a wall if they had to. Laurie's dog was waiting, his red tongue lolling from his mouth, giving him the appearance of grinning rakishly. Another good animal, and one who also lacked beauty. He'd taken Charlie forcefully from another Indian who had intended the ungainly pup for the stewpot. Laurie sometimes regretted calling the dog Charlie. It was an insult to a fine animal. Charlie was part wolf, and what the rest was was anyone's guess—maybe hound. He had the heart of a lion, the strength of several dogs, and he was ferocious. Laurie was the only one at the fort who could handle him, and even the voyageurs were afraid of the big dog. In the woods he was a comfort, for his senses were keen and he scented danger long before a man could.

As Laurie looked affectionately at his dog he saw the hackles lifting along the animal's spine. "What's up?" he muttered, and his hand groped for the rifle strapped to his saddle.

Laurie listened but could hear nothing. His eyes raked the surrounding forest. Was it one of the grizzly bears that wandered down in the fall and winter months? He looked back at the dog. Charlie was standing stiffly, his lips pulled back from white fangs. Sliding the rifle out, Laurie put it across his lap and urged the horse on with his knees. Something down the mountainside, he decided, and whistled softly to the dog.

Charlie moved out in front, and Moska trotted slowly along behind. They came out onto a shelf of rock, and from the edge of it Laurie could see the gleam of the river. Shading his eyes, he peered down at a spit of tumbled rock that jutted into the foaming water. He could only see the far end of it, but what he saw made him straighten in the saddle—a thin bluish spiral of smoke and a long birch canoe drawn up on the rocks. On the bow of the canoe was a circular design of red and black. Armand! So, he had found the errant voyageurs. He could guess what they were up to. Probably they'd broken out some liquor and were having themselves a time. Charlie gave a throaty growl, and Laurie's eyes flew to him. Then the man heard what the dog had heard long before. Something was crashing up the slope. He heard a muffled shout and then a high, shrill shriek. By God! That sounded like a woman!

"Find them!" he called to the dog.

Charlie lunged forward, and Laurie urged Moska at top speed. The bed of a dry creek angled down, and Laurie tried to head the horse into it, but Moska didn't care for the sliding pebbles and picked his way along the ridged grass border, his heavy hind legs braced, his front feet sliding.

Charlie had stopped and was waiting for them. With no hesitation the dog turned to the right and vanished through the firs. Cocking his gun, Laurie rode after him. Then came out into a small, grass-covered glade edged with the flaming, pointed leaves of the sumac bush.

In the middle of the glade two figures struggled. Osa, his eyes glaring madly, was grappling with a tall, slender girl. She wore a heavy blue outfit, and the skirt was ripped up one side, exposing flashes of long white legs. Black hair tumbled around her shoulders, and as Osa swung her around, Laurie glimpsed a white face with blood trickling down one cheek.

"Get him!" Laurie shouted to the dog.

In three bounds the huge animal was on the man, his fangs buried deep in Osa's arm. With an oath, Osa threw the girl from him. She flew across the clearing and crumpled across a log. One of the big man's hands fumbled at his belt for the short axe pushed through it.

He's going to kill Charlie, Laurie thought; he's going to axe my dog. Raising the rifle, he sighted along the barrel. Then another voyageur raced into the clearing, and Laurie recognized the short, powerful form of Armand.

"Stop him!" Laurie called. His rifle barrel moved to Armand's chest. "If you don't, I'll give it to you."

Armand wasted no time arguing. Laurie was the best shot at the fort. "Call off your dog," he panted.

Laurie called, and Charlie reluctantly released the voyageur and backed away, his hindquarters touching the ground, his front legs stiff and ready to propel him forward again. Osa had worked the axe free and was moving toward the dog, his own lips pulled back in a snarl. Before he reached Charlie, his brother was beside him, his hand forcing the axe down. "Osa," Armand ordered. "Drop it. Remember what papa told you. Always do what Armand says. Armand says to drop it. Get back to the canoe, my brother."

Osa faltered and his arm dropped. He shook his shaggy

97

head as though he were waking from a dream. Then, without a glance at either Laurie or the girl, he turned and shambled away through the trees.

Lowering the rifle, Laurie looked at the girl. She was propping herself against the log, one hand supporting the other wrist. His eyes moved back to Armand. "You've gone too far this time," he told the voyageur grimly. "Where's the priest? Have you hurt him?"

Armand drew himself up. "Hurt a priest? Never! We cared for the good father and did all we could for him, but he sickened and last night he died. This morning we buried him."

"And this afternoon you attacked his companion. When word of this gets back to the fort you'll be an outlaw, you and the rest of your crew. There won't be a place in this country for men who try to ravish a lady."

A sly grin crept across the other man's bearded face. "The lady is a *bois brûlée*."

"You lie!"

"Ask her."

Shoving his rifle back into place, Laurie dismounted. "Shut up and get back to the fort, you whoreson! I don't care what she is. She was helpless and you—"

"My brother," Armand interrupted, his voice silky. "I was only following Osa, trying to stop this outrage. Ask the rest of the men."

"The rest of the men will lie as you're doing. They're your crew, and I know how your code works. But you're not fooling me. Osa does nothing without your permission. You could have stopped him. Now, get out of here!"

This time Armand didn't argue. Turning, he followed his brother down the slope. Laurie strode toward the girl, pausing to pat Charlie's head. When he reached her side, she cowered away, her eyes wild. He spoke to her gently. "It's all right. You're safe now." He knelt beside her. "How badly are you hurt?" When he stretched out his hand, she whimpered and tried to crawl away from him. "Those damn animals," he grunted. "But they're gone.

98

I'm going to take you to the fort. Please trust me; I mean you no harm."

She was beyond reason or trust. As his hand neared her arm she bared her teeth, much as the dog had moments before. Pulling back his arm, he looked helplessly down at the pathetic, sprawled figure. The girl was mad with fright. If he tried to examine her injuries or lift her to his horse, she'd struggle and might do more damage to the wrist she was cradling in her sound hand. As he stared down at her, he thought, What's wrong with you, man? God's teeth, you pride yourself on the ease with which you handle savage dogs, wild horses, and small children. Use your head.

Backing away from the girl, he sank to the ground, both his hands in his lap where she could see them. Then he started to talk to her in a slow, even voice. He told her about his dog, pointed out Charlie's wide red grin, and he described how he had first seen the horse, Moska, and wanted him. As Laurie talked, the girl seemed to become calmer. She turned her head and looked at the dog. Much to Laurie's surprise, because Charlie never showed friendliness to anyone but his master, the dog came closer, sniffed at the girl's hand, and then lay down, his powerful muzzle against her knee.

"See," Laurie told her, "Charlie likes you. He wants to be friends." In the same tone he said, "My name's Laurie Woodbyne. What's yours?"

She whispered, "Rowan, Rowan Malone." Her chin lifted, and she added defiantly, "My mother is a Chilcotin, sister of their chief."

"Then you're a princess, and princesses should never be afraid of someone who wants to help them." He waited for a minute, and when she remained silent, he asked, "Can I look at your arm?"

Without a word she held it out to him, and he moved closer on his knees and took it into his hands. The hand fell limply from the wrist. "It's broken, Miss Malone. I'll have to put a rough splint on it to get you back to the fort. There's a man there, a canny Scot named George

99

Durran, who will set it. He doesn't hold a physician's degree, but he should." Laurie rose and cut a couple of lengths of small branch. Taking the scarf from his neck, he fashioned a sling. She bent her head while he knotted the scarf around her neck. Encouraged by her cooperation, he lifted her chin and ran a finger along the gash on her cheek. "Shallow," he muttered, "and it's stopped bleeding. Did Osa do all this?"

At the bear's name, she tensed. "My arm was bent under me when he threw me across this log. But I cut my face and hurt my ankle when I fell running from him."

"Your ankle?" He was about to lift her skirt when he stopped himself. Slow, Laurie told himself, slow. "Can I remove your boot?" he asked.

At her nod, he pulled the dark blue skirt back away from her legs. As he did, Charlie lifted his head from the girl's knee and growled deep in his throat. "God's teeth," Laurie said. "Are you growling at *me*, old boy? I told you he'd taken a fancy to you, Miss Malone. It's all right, Charlie. I'm not going to hurt her."

As he unfastened the boot, Rowan stretched out her sound hand and stroked the dog's head. It took a while to work the boot loose, and when it was off Laurie caught his breath. The foot and ankle were badly swollen, the flesh already darkening into an ugly purple. He shook his head. "I don't know. It may be broken or only badly wrenched, but the sooner I put you in George's hands, the better."

He glanced up and saw tears of pain running down her face, but she hadn't made a sound. "What are you doing here?" he asked abruptly. "This is no country for a woman."

"I was born here."

"Do you know anything about it?"

She shook her head. "My father and Father Martin took me east when I was a baby. I have no memories." Then she said violently, "It can't be worse than where I came from." The tears started to flow faster. "He's dead.

Father Martin is dead. He'd still be alive if I hadn't forced him to come—"

"Hush." Laurie patted her head as though she were a child. "I'll get water for you." He fumbled through his pockets looking for a handkerchief and found none. To think, he told himself, that the fop Laurie Woodbyne hasn't even a handkerchief. None of his friends in London would believe that. He'd already used his scarf as a sling, but after a moment he pulled out his shirt and, taking his knife, cut off a sizable chunk. With a courtly bow, he presented it to the girl. "For you. Dry your tears."

She stared up at him standing tall over her, the sun glinting from his pale hair, his shirttail dangling over buckskin pants, and she smiled. He caught his breath. What a beauty she was. Jet-black hair flowed from a center parting framing an oval face. Her brow was high and rounded, her nose slightly large and aquiline, her cheekbones high and sharply delineated. She had a mobile mouth with a tiny black mole near the corner of her lips. Her features, taken separately, hardly added up to beauty, but in that creamy white face they were exactly right. Her best features were her eyes—never had Laurie seen eyes like Rowan Malone's. They were a shade of blue he couldn't put a name to, darker than sapphires, and fringed with short, stubby, black lashes. Their setting made her entire face exotic. Over the high cheekbones her eyes slanted up at the outside corners as though she had Asiatic blood, as though she was related to the beautiful, ivory-skinned maids whom Marco Polo had met in ancient Cathay. Yet, Laurie brooded, perhaps Rowan Malone had every right to look like an Oriental princess. She had a strange mixture of blood, and it showed in her face. The few Chilcotins he had seen were quite Chinese in appearance, although they were much shorter and stockier than this slender girl. And this was the girl he was going to carry back to a fort filled with rough, women-hungry men.

As though she could read his mind, the smooth skin
101

wrinkled between those exotic eyes. "Are there women at Fort Purline?" she asked.

"Many. Outside the fort are lodges, permanent ones for the workers, and others set up when the natives come to trade. There are women there."

"Inside the fort?"

"Three. Two adult and a babe. The factor's wife, Nell, her baby daughter, and Nell's faithful Martha MacLeod. Martha, like Durran, is a Scot, and you'll like her." He whistled for his horse, and Moska trotted over. "Now for that water I promised you, and then we'll get you up on this beast's back."

He opened his leather water case, and she drank thirstily. Then, handling her as carefully as possible, he lifted her into the saddle. "Do you think you can hang on?" he asked. "It will be easier for you, and I'll lead Moska."

"I'll try," she said, and her voice was faint with pain. Moska took a few steps, and the girl moaned and fell forward across his neck. The horse stopped immediately.

"We'll have to do it this way," Laurie told her. Swinging up behind her, he put both arms around her and steadied her with his body. "Lean back against me."

Trustingly, she did, her slim neck falling against his shoulder, her head pillowed close to his face. As he felt her slender length against him, he could feel heat in his groin. Damnation! This was torture. How long was it since he'd had a woman? The last time he recalled when there was genuine enjoyment had been with Adèle Charloux in the soft, perfumed bed in her house in Montreal. Hatch's chief agent, M. Charloux, had taken good care of Laurie when he was there. His wife, tiny and mature and hot-blooded, during her husband's absences had taken even better care of the tall, good-looking Englishman. Now, with the memory of the Frenchwoman, he felt himself becoming hard. Damnation! This was all a girl who had nearly been raped needed.

With an effort he wrenched his mind away from both Adèle Charloux and the warmth of the girl in his arms. He wondered what the reception for Rowan Malone

102

would be at the fort. General Purline seemed to hate three things with implacable fervor—half-breeds, women, and Catholics—and this girl was all three. If Armand got to Ezra Purline first, the gates would be locked against this battered girl. He could almost hear the factor. "Take her to the lodges," Purline would say. "That is where a *bois brûlée* belongs."

Arguing that his own voyageurs had gotten her into this condition wouldn't change Purline's mind. He valued Armand highly, although occasionally the steersman drove the factor wild with rage. Armand, Osa, and the rest of the crew were the most daring, resourceful men at Fort Purline. They were the ones who made sorties against their archenemies from the Nor'westers' post at Fort George; they were the men who disciplined the natives if General Purline thought it necessary.

Laurie's mouth tightened. Shortly after he'd arrived at the post, he'd witnessed the general's peculiar brand of justice. A group of Salish Indians had run up a large amount of credit with the factor, promising to repay with the next season's catch of furs. Instead, they bypassed Fort Purline and took their furs to a rival trader. Armand and his crew had been sent to punish the Salish. Patiently the voyageurs followed the canoes of the Indians until they made camp and became sodden with raw whiskey. Then the voyageurs descended on them. They beat the men, broke their new rifles, took their store of ammunition, and holed the canoes. Before they left, the voyageurs ruined the food supplies and burned the trade goods. Two of the Salish women and three of their children had died of hunger before Purline would consent to deal with them. When they stood before him he told them grimly, "I'll give you food and guns, but find furs and bring them to pay your debt. Never cheat me again!"

Sickened, Laurie watched the miserable natives leave. Purline turned a triumphant face to his new aide. "Take a lesson, Mr. Woodbyne. You're new here and were sent to learn. That's the way you handle these thieving savages."

"I don't think I could do it," Laurie had muttered.

"Then you'll never be factor," he had been told.

Whistling to the dog, Laurie turned Moska toward the fort. No, Armand wouldn't suffer for what he'd tried to do. But damned if he'd take this gentle girl to the lodges outside the fort. I'll break the bloody gates down first, Laurie promised himself grimly.

Charlie moved out in front, and Moska plodded steadily along behind. Then the dog, the horse, and the man and woman on the horse's back disappeared into the fir forest in the direction of Fort Purline.

10

Rowan came floating to the surface of consciousness. Warily, like an injured creature of the wild, she willed her eyes to remain closed, her body to stay motionless. She was conscious of warmth, under her and over her, and of a dull ache down one arm and in her ankle. Cautiously her sound hand crept along the surface she rested on. It had to be a bed, the first one she'd been in for months. It yielded under her weight and was covered with something smooth and crisp, something that smelled fresh and clean. Sheets! She was in a bed with sheets. So accustomed was she to the hard ground, with only a blanket or at times a pile of fir boughs under her, that she felt a sense of wonder. Where could she be, and where were Father Martin, the canoe, and the voyageurs? Then memory came flooding back, and with it, her searching hand tensed beneath the sheet and her eyelids fluttered.

"She's coming round, Mr. Durran. Step back a few paces. Mr. Woodbyne said the lass is filled with fear of men."

It was a woman who spoke, and then came the deeper tone of a man's voice. "Aye, and no wonder for that."

Both voices held the soft burr of Scotland, but the woman's accent was thicker. The man's voice, though deep, was crisp and clear. Slowly, Rowan opened her eyes and looked up. Silhouetted against the rough beams of the low ceiling was the round, florid face of a middle-aged woman. Her eyes were sharp and gray, and her hair, plainly dressed, was a ginger color. Her mouth moved, and she said to Rowan, "Stay quiet now, lass, and don't waste strength with words. Ye're safe, and your hurts have been tended to. Ye're in Mr. Woodbyne's bed in the man's cabin. He be staying with Mr. Durran for a spell."

Rowan's eyes searched past the woman's face to the light flickering against the dark beams. "I can't remember coming here," she whispered. "I remember being on a horse, and then all went dark."

The ginger head nodded. "From weariness and pain ye lost all consciousness, and it was as well. Now, I'm Martha MacLeod, and I'll be at your side until ye're better. Here is Mr. Durran, who tended ye well."

Another head moved in beside the woman's. Rowan saw a craggy face surmounted by thick red hair. He wore no moustache, but from his chin jutted a short beard, a shade lighter than his hair.

"Are you the doctor?" Rowan asked.

"Nay, that title I can't claim, but I am the closest to one they have in this fort. My old granny, who some called a witch woman, taught me healing when I was but a lad."

Her eyes widened. "Are you a witch?"

He chuckled. "At times I wish I were, Miss Malone. But I have no gift for magic." He sobered and told her gravely, "Your ankle isn't broken, but it's badly sprained and must have rest. Only a small bone was broken in your wrist, and it was a clean break. The cut on your cheek is merely a scratch and will leave no scar. Now you must rest, for rest is the best healer of all. I've prepared a drink laced with laudanum that will send you back to sleep. Let your dreams be peaceful, for you are with friends."

She was about to thank him when she heard a harsh creak and her breath quickened. A soothing hand touched her brow. "Be easy," Martha MacLeod murmured. " 'Tis but the door opening. General Purline is here, and with him Mr. Woodbyne."

Martha's head and the man's were withdrawn, and she saw Laurie bending over her, firelight glinting in his blond

106

hair, his dark, long-lashed eyes looking down at her. She worked her sound hand free of the covers, and he took it in both his own. "Better?" he asked.

"Much. But I don't know how to try and thank you."

"Don't try. Here is the factor of our post, General Purline, who has come to see you."

Another head moved in beside Laurie's, and she tensed. Her fear of the blond man was gone, and she had trusted the two Scots immediately, but now she felt unease again. Because of the angle he was standing at, she couldn't see the factor's face. All she could discern was a huge, dark head with flaring ears.

When he spoke his voice was pleasant. "I'm grieved, Miss Malone, that this unfortunate incident happened with the men from this fort and in one of the company's canoes. You may rest assured I'll mete out punishment to them. Now, how do you fare?"

She murmured an answer, and he continued. "Mr. Woodbyne tells me that your traveling companion died on the trip. Have you any complaints about my men on that score?"

"No. They were kind to Father Martin and did all they could to prolong his life."

"I am relieved to hear that. Now, this is probably not my affair, but it would seem you are in my custody, and I feel I should know. Why is a lady like yourself in this desolate country, and what was your destination?"

Rowan wondered what to tell this man. She hoped one of the other three would intercede and spare her from answering. They were all silent. Even Laurie moved away, and she was left facing the monstrous, faceless head. Then her mouth firmed. Armand would tell him soon enough. Better total honesty.

"I was raised in the Convent of the Sister of the Ste. Claire, sir, and Father Martin undertook to return me to my mother's people." She took a deep breath. "My mother is Aluski, twin sister of the chief of the Chilcotin Nation."

For moments he said nothing, but she sensed that eyes

107

in the darkened face were scanning her own face, the tilted eyes, the high cheekbones. Then he straightened, and his voice seemed to come from a distance, cold and remote. "In that event, rely upon me. I'll speed you along your way with the utmost dispatch." The voice rose an octave. "Mr. Woodbyne, you will attend me in my office."

"I'll be along directly, sir."

"Now, Mr. Woodbyne. Right now."

The door creaked dismally, and Rowan knew they were gone. Then she felt a hand touching her brow again. A cup was pressed to her lips. "Drink, Miss Malone," a voice said, and both the voice and the gentle hand were those of the man called Durran.

In his office, General Purline stirred up the fire and put another log on it. Then he sank into the chair behind the cluttered desk and regarded the man standing before him. Quite a different man, Purline thought, from the one who'd arrived here. Apparently young Woodbyne had conducted himself well on the trip west and had won the respect of the voyageurs, but he'd still been somewhat soft, a bit of a dandy, on his arrival. Now the young man was hard and tough, his face, arms, and hands tanned, new wrinkles around his eyes, and a firmer set to his mouth. Even in the rough frontier clothes he wore, Woodbyne still had an elusive quality of elegance. Another quality he retained was an indefinable but infuriating streak of mockery. Because of Woodbyne's close relationship to Charles Hatch, Purline had forced himself to go slowly. How much had Hatch told this young man? Purline wondered. No matter, I'll break him down, I'll assuredly break this cocky young bastard.

"Well?" Purline finally asked.

"Well what?"

"I forbore questioning Armand and his crew members because it didn't occur to me that the man second in command to myself would be capable of such a disgusting ploy." When Laurie merely arched his arching brows even higher, Purline continued. "I now quite understand why the men felt they could perform that deed. You've been here long enough to know how unruly the voyageurs can be. I know how to handle them, but one thing I never interfere with is their treatment of native women. A factor must realize what kind of rein to use with these wild men and when to apply it."

"Are you saying that I should have stood by while they raped the girl, sir?"

"Of course not. Stop twisting my words. What I meant is that you were right to intercede on her behalf but dead wrong to think you could smuggle a half-breed into my fort in the guise of a white lady."

Although Laurie knew what the answer to his next question would be, he asked it anyway. "Where would you have had me take her?"

"To the lodges, of course. Some of the old women could have nursed her. And that's where she's going tomorrow. You'll take a litter and a couple of men to help you and get her out of this fort."

"Do you think that wise, sir?"

"What are you getting at, Mr. Woodbyne?"

"Miss Malone told you she was raised by nuns in a convent—"

"Papist mumbo jumbo! As a good Anglican, surely that cuts no ice with you."

"Perhaps I'm not as good an Anglican as you, sir, but this is hardly a Christian act you're thinking of. Regardless of her church, this girl has been gently reared. She *is* a lady. She traveled west under the care of her church, and I can assure you she knows less about the natives of this country than we do."

Purline's straight shoulders shrugged, but a glimmer of doubt crossed his large features. "Sit down, Mr. Woodbyne," he said slowly, "and tell me your thoughts."

Slightly encouraged, Laurie took a chair. For the moment the martinet was waning, and the uncertain factor appearing. He pressed his advantage. "If word of this gets out, and it will because our men talk, all the west will know the treatment this girl received from your hired men and from you."

"But she's a *bois brûlée*."

"Granted, but she may possibly have powerful friends in Montreal in the fur trade. And what of my father-in-law? Mr. Hatch, as you know, has a daughter—my wife. How will he react to news that his factor threw a wounded girl from his fort into the hands of savages?"

Purline rubbed his large nose and thought. Then he said hesitantly, "But she can't possibly stay. There's no place for her. She's in your cabin now, but you won't be able to remain in Mr. Durran's quarters indefinitely."

"Perhaps she could be of service to Martha and Mrs. Purline."

"And live in my house with my wife and daughter? No! You go too far, Mr. Woodbyne." Purline jerked to his feet, and more slowly Laurie rose. "For the present she may remain in your cabin, and I'll allow Martha to nurse her. When she is well I'll decide what to do. Good night."

Laurie took his leave. He knew he hadn't won, but at least he had a reprieve. For an instant he regretted not listening when Charlie Hatch was about to tell him about Purline's past. If he had, he might have learned something of value, something that might have helped the injured girl in his own bed. Then he crossed the width of the store to George Durran's rooms off the storehouse and wearily went to bed.

General Purline's office was actually a portion of his own cabin. A door connected it with the store, and another door opened onto the kitchen of the big cabin where he, his wife, his infant daughter, and Martha MacLeod lived.

As Laurie Woodbyne closed the door to the store area, Martha removed her ear from the door in the kitchen. She moved softly back to the woman who was standing before the hearth and put out a finger to touch the cheek of the baby the other woman was holding.

110

"Could you hear?" Nell Purline asked.

"Enough to tell that Mr. Woodbyne convinced him to leave the girl where she is until she heals."

"Thank God! I thought he'd have her dragged out tonight and taken down to those filthy hovels."

"Not all of them are filthy, Nell. Some are spotless. But give me the babe and sit ye down. Ye're that pale."

Handing Martha the baby, the younger woman sank on a stool before the fire. Nell's frail figure was draped in a shapeless gingham gown, and her bun of dark chestnut hair looked too heavy for her fragile neck. "Shouldn't you be getting back to her?" she asked.

"In a few minutes. She's sound asleep. I'll bide a while with ye and the babe." Martha rocked the child and smiled fondly down at her. "My fine wee lass. Have ye a smile for old Martha, little Dorrie?"

The child gurgled, and both women laughed with pleasure and bent over her. Round eyes stared up at them, and a fat fist waved from the tangle of blankets. For a time they played with the baby, and then Martha handed her back to her mother and stood up. Smoothing down her apron, she took a shawl from a peg. "Think ye'll be able to get on without me for a few days?" she asked.

Nell looked up from the child. "Little Moccasins will help out. Tell me, Martha, what's this girl like?"

"A bonny lass, pretty and soft-spoken and polite."

"I feel so sorry for her. Perhaps tomorrow I could come and see her."

"Best not to." Martha jerked her head toward the office door. "He'd be wild."

Nell sighed. "Yes, Martha, he'd never allow it. Go along and take good care of the poor girl."

"I'll stop in tomorrow and ginger Little Moccasins up if she needs it. Mind ye keep her moving."

"Don't worry. Dorrie and I will be fine. Good night, Martha."

After Martha had left, Nell sat on by the fire, her child in her lap, her face brooding. She spoke under her breath to the man in the next room. I followed you from India to England and then to this terrible land. Not for love, Ezra—that is long gone. She cried aloud, "Dear God, when will it end? When will this horrible bond that rivets us together be splintered?"

The office door opened, and General Purline stepped into the kitchen. Without even a glance in his direction, Nell gathered up her baby and fled toward the room where she slept.

11

Rowan stood at the small window to the left of the door, peering through the cloudy pane at the segment she could see of Fort Purline. She rested most of her weight on her right leg. After two weeks she was still favoring the left ankle, which was slow to heal. For a week she'd been confined to bed, and Martha MacLeod was with her most of the time. For the last week she'd managed to get out of bed, dress herself, and hobble around the cabin leaning on a rough cane. Martha slept nights in the cabin, but during the day she came only to prepare meals for the girl and to keep her company. At the moment, the older woman bent over the hearth, briskly stirring a steaming kettle of succotash. The combination of Indian corn, beans, and wild onion sent a savory smell through the room.

"What do ye think of the place?" Martha asked.

"It looks much like the forts we stopped at on our trip."

It did. Rowan could see the cabins, the store, smoke-houses, icehouse, blacksmith's shop, all built of logs, like the cabin she was in, their crevices packed with moss and clay. The buildings formed a hollow square and were protected by a strong log palisade. She couldn't see the far end of the palisade that faced the river, but she knew that the gates would be there, surmounted by a platform for the lookouts. Earlier that morning the square had been the scene of hectic activity. Indians, bearing loads of corn, logs, and bales from the latest brigade of canoes, had

113

scurried from one building to the next. A group of voyageurs had lounged in front of the store, smoking their pipes and idly watching the burdened natives. But now it was time for the noon meal, and the square was deserted.

"Drat!" Martha exclaimed.

Rowan turned. "What's wrong?"

Picking up a wooden pail, Martha said, "My own fault. I meant to fetch water when I came and forgot. Nell Purline sent a package of tea for ye, and a hot cup will do ye good. I'll go down and get some."

For a moment Rowan was tempted to let the other woman go. She was terrified of leaving the cabin, of having to see Osa and Armand's sneering face. Then she lifted her chin. She had to leave the cabin sometime. She took the pail from Martha. "Tell me where to go and I'll get it."

"Ye're not strong enough yet. Ye're still limping, and your arm—"

"I'll go slowly, and I've two arms."

"The voyageurs—"

"I'll have to face them sometime."

Martha looked doubtful, but after a moment she said slowly, "Aye, lass, ye're right. And Mr. Durran is at the river overseeing the unloading. Even those voyageurs don't go against The Durran. Here is where ye go."

Rowan listened, nodded, and opened the door. As she stepped out onto the hard packed surface of the square, she took a deep breath and walked slowly toward the gate. Charlie, his tongue lolling out, came bounding up and licked her hand. She patted his head, and he trotted along at her side. She was glad of the big dog's company. When she reached the gateway she could see a number of men gathered near the brigade of canoes, munching their lunches. George Durran was with them, and when he saw Rowan he lifted an arm in greeting. She waved back and turned away from the river. Now she could see the fort's setting. Its location was beautiful. A deep valley ran out from between two mountains, and the land sloped gently down toward the Nechako. Willow and ash lined the riverbanks, and the grass underfoot was studded with tiny wildflowers and shrubs. To the left of the stockade and shielded by thick growths of sumac, vine maple, and willow, was the stream that Martha had called a creek. It was much larger than a creek; actually it was a narrow, rather placid river. As she reached the bank she saw the little island the other woman had told her about. It was only about a hundred yards long and was a tangle of bushes and maple and poplar. Colors flamed there in rich fall array—the scarlet of sumac, the red and gold of maple, and the fine clear yellow of poplar. Although it was tiny, the voyageurs had given the island a name. They called it Ile Ste. Anne, for their patron saint.

She knelt in the soft grass and filled the bucket. Then she made her way back to the fort, walking more quickly and surely. As she reached the door of Laurie's cabin she breathed a sigh of relief and told herself, That wasn't too bad—I was all but invisible.

Rowan couldn't have been more mistaken. Many eyes had watched her—the voyageurs' as they hunched on the riverbank, the Indians' as they bent over fires before their lodges, and those of the man who pressed his face close to the window of his office and felt fury mount in his breast. Purline's hostile eyes followed the girl's slender figure until she vanished through the gateway, and then he flung open the door leading to the store and shouted at the clerk behind the wide counter.

"Mr. Holden, do you know where Mr. Woodbyne is?"

The clerk stammered, "I . . . I think he's at the smokehouse, sir."

"Well, don't stand there, man. Find him and tell him to get in here immediately."

The clerk departed at a run, and in minutes Laurie was in the office. Which general this time? Laurie wondered, and found out at once. He wasn't invited to sit.

"The guest in your cabin is now well enough to haul water," Purline told him frigidly. "You may not have noticed it, but she just set out for the creek. No doubt flaunt-

115

ing herself in front of the men and inflaming their passions."

"Carrying a pail of water is hardly inflaming to the passions, sir."

"Then you didn't see her. The way she was walking . . . an open invitation. We must decide what is to be done with her."

"You intend to send her to the lodges?"

"No. I want her off this post entirely." Purline rubbed his nose and then said evenly, "Be seated, Mr. Woodbyne. Two heads may be better than one. I've given much thought to this problem, and I feel I've reached a solution. She said she was trying to return to her mother's people. Well, we shall see she sets out for the Chilcotins at once."

"It's nearly the first of October, sir. The waterways will be freezing in a few weeks, and winter will be setting in. Where is the Chilcotin Nation located?"

Purline waved his hand in a vague circle. "North and west of us. I've no idea how far. As for winter setting in, she'll find Indian settlements along the way, and in one of them she can winter."

Laurie felt his temper rising and with an effort forced control on himself. Reason with this whoreson, he told himself; don't lose control. "She'll have to have an escort. Which of us will you send? Mr. Durran will no doubt volunteer, or I'd—"

"Don't be ridiculous! I can't spare a man."

"Who will paddle the canoe?"

A crafty look stole across the oversized features. "The luggage of both the girl and the priest was brought to me. As the priest was dead, I undertook to go through his effects. He had a quantity of cash with him, doubtless to arrange transportation for the next part of their trip. With it we'll hire a number of Indian paddlers to take the girl back to her own people."

"Which Indians?"

"Some of the men working around the fort would be glad to earn the money. Then there are the men who drift

116

in and out of the lodges. I was thinking of the Liar and the Dog's Head. Perhaps the Young Toad and the Big Rat."

Purline had used the nicknames of the Indian workers, the men who drew water, hewed wood, and transported ice and fish. Anger flooded through Laurie again, and once more he held it in check. "These men are heavy drinkers. They'll take the money, purchase liquor, and may desert the girl in the wilds. They may also ravish her as the voyageurs attempted to do."

"It won't be my responsibility once they are clear of the fort. Out of sight, out of mind." Swiveling around, he peered out of the window. "There she is now, coming back from the creek. Take a look."

Circling the chair, Laurie leaned forward. He could see Rowan with his black dog trotting along at her side. She was carrying a brimming pail of water, and she walked with a slight limp. Her hair was braided high on top of her shapely head, and she wore a white shirtwaist and a long dark skirt. Despite the limp, she walked with her body held proudly. A gust of wind caught her clothes and drove them back against her body. For an instant the lines of that body were clearly revealed, and he caught his breath. Small but perfect breasts were outlined, and the curves of full hips and long slender legs.

"See?" Purline hissed in his ear. "A woman the devil has spawned loose in my fort, and ready to unleash havoc."

Glancing at the factor, Laurie saw that though the man's voice held only disapproval, his face reflected lust. Purline lusts for her himself, Laurie thought. He left the window and retreated to his chair. When Purline swung around, his face was under control again.

"I'm a humane man, Mr. Woodbyne, and I don't relish the course of action I must take. You spent last winter here yourself, and you must know what I face. This fort is my responsibility, and so is the welfare of all the people it shelters. I know the temper of the men I employ. The voyageurs are difficult enough to control at the best of

117

times, but in the winter when they're idle they resort to drinking, gambling, and carousing with the women from the lodges. If we have this girl here, living alone and without a protector, they'll consider her open game. They'll fight each other for possession of her, and who is there to defend her? There are only a handful of men we may rely on—myself, you, Mr. Durran, Mr. Holden, and Mr. van Zzll. If we intervene they could turn on us. Do you understand my position?"

Reluctantly, Laurie nodded. The factor had stated the truth. Rowan would be like an open flame in a room filled with gunpowder. His arched brows drew together in thought. To send her west with a crew of drunken Indians was unthinkable, but where was a solution? Then one came to him, and he straightened.

"There is one alternative, sir. The voyageurs—even men like Osa and Armand—live by a strict code and don't dare break it. If they ever did they'd be outcasts from their own society. Under no circumstances will they ever touch another man's woman. Do you understand me?"

"I begin to." Purline's wide mouth hardened into a thin line. "And I don't like what I'm thinking. Do you mean to take this girl yourself?"

Thrusting both hands into the pockets of his buckskin jacket, Laurie could feel dampness trickling on his palms. He kept his voice steady. "I mean to give the appearance of taking the girl under my protection. If Miss Malone agrees, I'll move back into my cabin and stay there throughout the winter months. The voyageurs will believe there is only one possible reason for that."

"And I would agree. I doubt, Mr. Woodbyne, that a young, virile man like yourself could live a platonic life in a one-room cabin with a woman like that."

Laurie's temper flared, and this time he couldn't control it. "What evolves between Miss Malone and me would be our affair!"

"There you are wrong. Mr. Hatch has asked me for full reports on you, and in all honesty I'll have to tell him that the husband of his daughter has taken a half-breed woman."

Laurie was on his feet. "Mr. Hatch and I have a private agreement. The details he requested are solely concerned with my work. Do you fault that?"

"My reports thus far have been favorable. You do your work well, although you're somewhat soft with the natives. But control your temper. I'm going to speak to you as I would to my own son." Purline stretched out a placating hand. "I beg you not to take this step."

"To protect a helpless girl I'll take any step necessary. You may give Charlie Hatch full details."

Purline lurched to his feet, and dark color swept across his face. Raising a clenched fist, he shouted, "I know this type of woman only too well! Women are pure evil. In my lifetime I've known only two good women—my sainted mother and my sister. Women are described in the Good Book—the scarlet whore who sits astride the seven great hills. They leech men's strength, tempt them with their flesh, destroy their honor and their lives, and drag them down to the depths of hell! If you would save yourself, keep away from temptation. Return in time to your lady wife in England unblemished and still pure."

Laurie nearly laughed aloud. Purline should know his lady wife, the fair Esmie. But he didn't laugh. The other man's face was contorted with emotion; he looked crazed. Laurie wondered why Purline hadn't included his own wife in the short list of good women. If ever there was a saint it had to be Nell Purline. How she stood this man, Laurie had no idea.

He asked flatly, "Do you forbid me to do this, sir?"

Purline's arm dropped, and he braced himself against the edge of the desk as though suddenly exhausted. "No," he said in a hoarse whisper. "Do as you wish. Seek your damnation in your own way."

As Laurie stepped into the store and closed the door behind him, he thought, That man's completely mad when it comes to women. He bumped into the clerk, who was lurking near the door, one long hand clutching a bolt of red-and-blue calico. Through the shining circles of his pince-nez, Robert Holden's protuberant eyes were gleaming.

"Hear enough?" Laurie asked.

One of the pale, bulging eyes closed in a conspiratorial wink. "Most of it. Must admit, old chap, through the latter part of your debate I could have stood behind the counter and heard every word. Lucky the place is deserted. The old man was in rare form, baying like a bull moose in the mating season."

Laurie smiled at the other young man with that blend of amusement and exasperation that Bobby always managed to inspire. Taking the clerk's arm, he led him back to the counter. "Better get to work. If the general sticks his head out of that door, he's going to trample you like a bull moose."

Bobby went back to work piling heavy bolts of cotton on shelves behind the counter, and Laurie leaned against it, drawing deep breaths. The store had its own distinct smells, ones which he rather enjoyed. Bales of unpacked bundles were piled against the walls, the tables used for display were heaped with more, and the whole place, always cluttered, that day looked as though no order could ever be brought to it. But Bobby and the other clerk, Dutchy van Zzll, hadn't been idle. Tins of pins, needles, thread, and wool were piled on one table. Kegs of rum, high wine, and brandy were neatly arranged on their ledges, and tall bottles brimming with brightly colored beads sat ready for display. Laurie took another deep breath. The rancid odor of tanned and untanned hides still predominated, and that smoky hint of furs piled there during the winter months, but there were other smells— kerosene, spices, the sugary odor of the stock of hard candy, tobacco, and the sharpness from the liquor kegs.

"Where's Dutchy?" he asked the clerk.

"Back in the storeroom trying to bring order out of chaos. Since the brigades started to come in, this place has been bedlam."

"Always is at this season. Tell me, Bobby, did you really hear it all?"

Putting down a bolt of cotton, the clerk leaned nonchalantly against his side of the counter. "Every word. Admired the neat way you drove the old man into a corner. Tell you what—if you change your mind about your noble sacrifice and remain pure, I'd be willing to sacrifice myself. In the name of chivalry, of course, plus the fact that I got my first look at the bone of contention today. Zounds, but that's a woman!"

Laurie felt himself grinning again. There was no way to resent Bobby, no matter what he said. He decided, as he had many times before, that Bobby's family must have been delighted to see the last of the boy when he'd left England to make his fortune in the colonies. The boy was obviously well bred and probably came from a substantial background, but he had a weakness that actually was more an obsession. Bobby seemed to think of nothing, talk of nothing, and probably dream of nothing, but women. Despite his gangling body, his receding chin, his soft, baby-fine hair, Bobby was a red-blooded he-man. His prowess with the fair sex was amazing even to the voyageurs. Most of the boy's salary went in the effort to sate his craving. He spent freely on ornaments for the native girls, on money to pay off their husbands, fathers, or brothers. His trips to the lodges were more frequent than any other man's at the fort, and whenever a new batch of natives come to trade, Bobby was on the spot, looking over their women with covetous eyes.

Bobby was the joke of the whole post, the butt of every type of off-color remark, and yet even the roughest man there liked him. He provided amusement in dull lives, a constant source of ribald gossip. Some of his exploits in the pursuit of his obsession were fantastic. Bobby's name was frequently coupled with that of Little Moccasins, one of the native women who lived permanently at the lodges and did menial work around the post. Bobby had conceived a violent but unrequited passion for the woman and never gave up his efforts to seduce her. The amusing part of it was that Little Moccasins hated men with an emotion as obsessive as Bobby's love of women. She was a veritable Amazon, standing well over six feet in the huge, gaily decorated moccasins that had given her the nickname. She was handsome, with a strong vital body, smooth bronze skin, and long braids of black hair. Little Moccasins was always clean and wore fine-quality buckskin trimmed with flashes of vermilion and ornamented with beads. Copper bracelets jangled at her wrists, and around her strong column of a throat clustered strands of fancy shells.

Little Moccasins lived alone in a small, tidy lodge and spurned with vigor any effort of men to share her sleeping mat. All the men had wisely learned to leave Little Moccasins alone—she was stronger than most of them—but Bobby apparently couldn't stop his mad pursuit.

A month before, Bobby had crept into her lodge while she was still working at the fort, optimistically stripped off his clothes, and slid into the pile of furs where she made her bed. Some of the voyageurs who had been at the lodges witnessed the dénouement.

Later, Jourdin, between gales of laughter, had tried in broken English to tell Laurie of the scene. *"Sacrebleu!"* Jourdin sputtered. "Never in my life have I seen such a sight. Little Moccasins she go into her lodge, and soon out come bolting the good Bo-bee! He is naked as when his sainted mother bore him, and there is blood trickling down his side where the knife of the big woman has nicked him. Bo-bee go bounding along with his private parts still up and looking at the sky, and can that *garçon* run! His glasses are flying back behind his skinny shoulders on that black ribbon he wears, and he bounds along like a scared rabbit with timber wolf behind him. On his heels come Little Moccasins, and she giving war whoops that chill the blood, and in her hand she is got knife three feet long. 'I cut off your dirty pecker!' she is shouting, and I think she would have. But Chenette and Louis Grand and me, we pile on her and hold her down till Bo-bee gets to his cabin. Three of us strong man can hardly hold her." Clutching at his belly, Jourdin roared with laughter. "Such a man that Bo-bee. Such a stallion of a *garçon!*"

"Why are you grinning like a cat full of cream?" Bobby demanded, and wrenched Laurie from his thoughts.

"Just thinking."

Bobby gave his evil wink again. "Practically read your mind, old chap. Had your fingers crossed when you were swearing about your honorable intentions. Can hardly wait to mount the wench, can you?"

"Keep your mouth off her!" Laurie said coldly, and his amusement was gone.

"Oh, it's like that, is it? All right, Laurie, calm down. No offense intended."

"Are you going to spread this tale around the post?"

Holding up a thin white hand, Bobby said solemnly, "Word of honor. A murmur shan't pass my lips. The voyageurs will have to reach their own conclusions."

"Which is the way I plan it. That's the only protection the poor girl will have." Laurie's voice was milder. Bobby might be a womanizer, but he was a man of his word.

"You were speaking of work a short time back, old chap. The old man's not going to be happy with you if he finds you idling away your time."

"Right, best to get back."

"What are you doing?"

"I was at the smokehouse this morning helping Tapinawa and the Liar get venison on the racks. This afternoon I have to take out a wood detail. I'll be glad when this season is over. Too much work and not enough hands. By the way, when George comes in, tell him not to bother cooking supper. I've purloined some smoked buffalo tongue from the voyageurs and, believe it or not, a tin of English pudding."

"Hmm," Bobby said, licking his lips. "Snaggle any tea or coffee?"

Genuine tea and coffee were rare luxuries. Mainly they used substitutes for both. The leaves used for tea, particularly the white azaleas crushed for tea, were palatable, but the parched corn coffee was terrible.

123

Laurie closed his own eye in a wink. "A little of both. Stop around tonight and have a cup of real coffee."

"I'd like nothing better, but George was in a while ago, and his face was black as a Salish squaw's bottom. Have a feeling he'll be doing his promenade on the platform tonight." Gingerly, Bobby touched one of his earlobes. "That ruddy set of pipes! No matter how I bury my head I can't drown them out. Thank the merciful Lord he doesn't get fey often."

"Had he been drinking?"

"Not so I could tell."

"Then your ears may be safe. George has to be deep in his cups before he makes his promenade."

Bobby laughed. "True. But if he does, I'll wager it's the Macdonald tartan he'll be wearing."

"If he had a black expression, I'm not taking that bet. The Durran plaid he saves for his happy promenades."

Both men's chuckles were indulgent. Most of the men in the isolated forts developed peculiarities, and Durran was no exception. Sane and reliable as he was most of the time, he too had his mad point. Occasionally, and for no reason they could discover, Durran would dress himself in Highland garb—a kilt, a worn velvet coat, and a ruffled shirt—and through the night hours he would stride back and forth on the lookout platform high above the fort. His head would be thrown back, the magnificent mane of red hair and flaming beard outlined against the mountains, and from his bagpipe would come strange, unearthly wails. The Indians always gathered outside the stockade and gazed openmouthed at the man who strode like a Highland chieftain across the palisade. When his mood was good, Durran would don his father's plaid; when it was dark and gloomy it would be the Macdonald tartan that swung smartly around his knees.

"Fey," Bobby muttered, "and such a fine figure of a man George is. The girls would go wild for a man like that, and yet he never seems to look at them."

"And you never stop looking, young Robert. Don't you ever think of anything else?"

124

"What else is there to think of?" Bobby asked earnestly. Still smiling, Laurie swung on his heel and left the store.

When he returned at nightfall, weary and dirty and oozing sweat, Laurie found that Bobby was no longer in the store. A single oil lamp threw flickering light across the crowded room, and in one corner, perched on a bench and dozing, was Dutchy's small, misshapen form. Laurie didn't disturb the clerk. He moved quietly past the bench and headed down the short hall that led to the storerooms. Partway down, he swung open the door to the room that George Durran used as combination kitchen, living room, and bedroom. A rough arch led from it into the tiny cubicle that Laurie had been sleeping in. Both rooms were spotlessly clean, but they were bare. Aside from two hide-covered chairs before the crude hearth, a wooden chest and a bed in one corner, and a table and two chairs near the door, the room was in its original state. It was a place of rough log walls and a splintered planked floor. Over the chest Durran's bagpipe and his fife hung. In the chest underneath were his clothes and blankets.

On one of the hide chairs Durran was sprawled, gazing morosely into the tiny fire he'd kindled. On the flat stones at his feet sat a bottle and a mug, but Laurie couldn't smell the brandy that Durran drank in his moods.

"Greetings," Laurie called gaily. "I come bearing gifts." He thumped a bundle on the table. "Tonight we dine in style, but first I'd better clean up." Holding his sleeve to his nose, he inhaled. "Whew! I smell stronger than that ruddy smokehouse does."

Durran made no reply, and as Laurie peeled off his clothes and washed, the Scot didn't even glance up. Laurie found a clean shirt and pulled on a pair of pants. Opening the bundle, he began to spread out his treasures. "Smoked buffalo tongue from the plains, a good pudding, and, look at this, George—coffee and tea. Get that long face off you, man, and make the coffee."

With a grunt, Durran pulled himself to his feet and

reached for the battered pot. While he ground the beans and heated water he stayed silent, but when they sat facing each other at the table he finally spoke. "I saw her today."

"Miss Malone?"

"Who else? Bobby told me our lord and master summoned you to the office while the lass was fetching water. Is she to be thrown from his sacred fort, then?"

Putting down the knife, Laurie shoveled thick slices of tongue onto tin plates and pushed corn bread closer to Durran's elbow. "So that's what you've been brooding about. Cheer up, George. Miss Malone is to remain here until spring."

Dropping his own knife, Durran stared at the other man. "How did you manage?"

Smearing grease on a chunk of bread, Laurie said slowly, "I'm going to move back to my cabin. That is, if she agrees."

Durran lunged to his feet. "You're forcing yourself on her!"

"Sit down and let me explain."

Sinking back on his stool, Durran listened to Laurie's plan. When Laurie had finished, the Scot sat quietly for a time. When he spoke, he said almost exactly what Purline had earlier. "And how long will that last? She's a pretty slip of a girl, and you're a man."

Laurie was about to blurt out a hot answer, but he forced himself to speak evenly. "And not made of iron. But I promise you, George, it will only happen if she wills it to. I'm not a skunk who would force her."

George sighed. "You're not, and I apologize. You've done better for her with Purline than I could have. This is fine food. Let's enjoy it."

When they'd finished, they took their places facing each other on the chairs near the warmth of the fire. Durran crossed his heavy legs and pushed the bottle closer. "You'll be asking the lass tonight. Would you like a wee sip?"

"I'm tempted, but I don't think I should smell of liquor."

Tipping up the bottle, Durran poured a mug nearly to its brim. He took a long swallow, and Laurie noticed that his face was calm and placid again. "She'll say yes," Durran told him.

"You think so?"

"Aye. And in time you'll enter her bed and she'll be your wife, and a good one. Better than you deserve."

Laurie's eyes widened, and he took a look at the bottle. Could Durran be drunk? No, he wasn't yet, but he'd emptied his mug and was reaching for the bottle. At this rate he soon would be. "What makes you say that?" Laurie asked.

"I know." Wiping his lips, Durran looked solemnly across the hearth at the other man. "My old granny— Granny Macdonald, bless her memory—told me when I was only a lad."

"Your old granny told you about *me?*"

"Nay, not you. She had the second sight. She was born with a caul and knew things others didn't. That girl with strange eyes the color of Loch Katrine in the evening hours will be yours. For a time."

He *is* drunk, Laurie decided. He took his coat from a peg. He said good night to Durran but received no reply. When the door shut behind him, Durran reached for the woodbox, tossed a couple of chunks of wood onto the fire, and refilled his mug. While the fresh logs caught fire and flamed up brightly enough to wash the rough walls in a shifting tapestry of scarlet and yellow, the Scot slowly sipped his brandy. In the flames he fancied he could see the land of his birth, and nostalgia gripped him for heaths covered with gorse and sweetly scented heathers, for rounded hills and the tree-girt height of Ben Venue.

Over the memory pictures in the flames another memory took shadowy shapes and became larger until it masked the waters of the loch. It was a wizened face framed by a black bonnet, ribbons knotted under a sharp chin that curved up toward the hooked nose. Small eyes stared steadily into his. It was a face so old that no guess could be made about the woman's age. "Granny," Durran muttered, and the soft burr deepened. "My dear old Granny Macdonald. Did ye tell me true, granny, when ye parted the veil twixt past the future and gave me what comfort ye could?"

Logs crashed sideways and the face vanished, but Durran slowly nodded his head, and a pleased smile creased his face. "Ye told true, granny. A fine woman ye were despite the ignorant who would dub ye witch. A hard woman, as hard as the crags of Ben Venue, but with a good heart and the art of healing in your twisted hands. Ye raised me from a babe and when ye had to go, gave me all ye had—hope. I've waited the long years through, and the lass has come. But, first she must be another man's, and 'tis well the man is Laurie Woodbyne."

Springing to his feet, he threw open the top of the wooden chest and drew out a kilt, a shabby velvet coat, and a neatly darned ruffled shirt. Spreading them on the bed, he smiled and lifted down the bagpipe.

He stroked its length. "Ye shall wail this night for the lass with eyes the shade of Loch Katrine when twilight steals across that blessed land."

Soon he was dressed and striding across the darkened store, the bagpipe clasped tenderly to his chest. In his corner, Dutchy van Zzll opened bleary eyes, saw the Highland warrior, and muttered a weary curse.

12

Lights were gleaming from cabin windows all around the square, and pale strands of smoke drifted from chimneys toward the night sky. When Laurie reached the doorstep of his own cabin, the two tiny windows were spilling yellow light softly out across the hard packed earth.

He tapped on the door, and when it opened, Charlie stood between him and Rowan Malone. He sniffed at Laurie's hand, and the hackles along his back relaxed. Rubbing the big dog's head, Laurie smiled at the girl. "You've stolen my dog."

"Do come in," she said, and closed the door behind him. "I'm afraid Charlie does spend a lot of time with me, Mr. Woodbyne, but I've never encouraged him."

"Charlie has a mind of his own. If he's chosen you, you'll have no say in the matter, and he makes a fine guard dog."

"Please take a seat by the fire; the nights are becoming colder." She touched her lips and colored faintly. "I feel so foolish trying to make you welcome in your own home."

"It's your home now," he said gallantly, and chose one of the chairs near the blazing hearth. He sensed some difference in the cabin since he'd last seen it, but he couldn't put a finger on any changes. The rudely fashioned bed still sat in its corner, the pots and pans and dishes were piled neatly on the usual shelf. In another corner was the desk George Durran had built for him. It was the only fine piece he had. Durran was more skilled at carpentry than the man who did carpenter's work around the post. On its polished top were his small personal possessions. Silver gleamed from the edges of the three pictures and the old decanter, his brush and comb sat side by side, and in the middle were a quill pen and an inkstand. No, the cabin was the same as it had always been. The feeling of change must be coming from the girl sitting near him, her hair braided high on her head, a cameo brooch clasping the high-frilled neck of her shirtwaist. Perhaps it was the perfume that surrounded her, the scent he had inhaled when he'd held her in his arms on the way to the fort. It wasn't the smell of cologne from a bottle, but rather the fine odor of growing things, of fir forests and new grass. She seemed nervous and was pleating the silk of her skirt with one hand.

"It was good of you to come and see me, Mr. Woodbyne. I haven't met many people. There's only been Martha MacLeod, and Mr. Durran looked in occasionally to examine my wrist and ankle. . . ." Her voice trailed off, and then she said slowly, "This isn't a social visit, is it?"

She's damnably quick, Laurie thought, and was about to give her a reassuring answer when he changed his mind. She had a right to know the truth. "No, it isn't. I hardly know how to begin, Miss Malone."

"Perhaps I can help you. This concerns General Purline, doesn't it?"

"How do you know?"

"I'm only guessing. Although Martha never really says anything, I sense he doesn't like me, doesn't want me here. I could tell when he came to see me. His wife has never visited me, but she's sent me small gifts, and Martha says Mrs. Purline is kind. So it must be her husband. Does he want me to leave?"

"Yes," Laurie said bluntly. "But you must understand his position. This post is full of lonely men, men who are idle during the long winter and could raise mischief."

She was just as blunt. "You mean like the voyageurs did. Yes, I can see that. When does he want me to go?"

Laurie shifted in his chair. He admired her control. No

longer did she appear nervous. Her hands were folded in her black silk lap, and her face was composed. Before he could speak she continued in an even voice. "Father Martin had funds in his keeping for the remainder of our trip. I could hire a canoe and some men and continue until I find my mother's people."

"You've no idea what you're saying. The only paddlers you could get are Indians—"

"I am one myself."

"Allow me to explain. Some of the natives, the ones who live around the forts, have become corrupted—"

"Not of their own will!"

Color had crept up her neck and mantled her high cheekbones. The tilted eyes were bright with anger. He didn't attempt to placate her. "We've no time to argue moral values, Miss Malone. Be good enough to hear me out. Perhaps we have been corruptors, but many of the natives have become addicted to spirits and because of this would be untrustworthy for a woman traveling alone. They might desert you and leave you in the wilds. They might take the same course of action that Armand and Osa did. Now do you begin to understand?"

"I understand completely, but it would appear I've no choice in the matter. If I'm unwelcome, I must go."

Proud, Laurie thought—a proud woman. Under the pride he sensed terror, but she was trying to hide that terror from him. He admired her. As he spoke he gave her a reassuring smile. "All I've tried to explain is that a trip, at this time of year and with these men, is impossible. In the spring other plans can be made. We may be able to persuade some reliable men traveling into that part of the country to take you with them, to protect you until you reach the Chilcotins."

"General Purline will never allow me to remain until spring."

"You misjudge him," Laurie told her. Under his breath he told himself, You're a liar, man. Her assessment of the factor was quite correct. Some of Martha's feeling about the factor—and Laurie knew how Martha felt—must

131

have been transmitted to this girl. He continued, trying to sound confident. "The general and I spoke of this today, and we think we may have found a solution."

"And what is it?"

"Miss Malone, this must be your own decision. The only protection that can be given to you on this post is the appearance of being in a man's care, having a man living with you in this cabin. The voyageurs would accept this and wouldn't trouble you further."

The warm color seeped from her features, leaving them the color of ashes. Her hands gripped each other until the knuckles whitened. "What man?" she whispered.

"I'm making the offer." He watched her terror, and rage welled up within his breast. "All men aren't villains. And I'm not suggesting what you think. I mean to make up another bed, and all I'll do is stay under the same roof. In no manner will I give you cause for alarm. If you wish, I'll swear on a Bible!"

"Forgive me. It's only that men . . . they have been terrible to me. With the exception of Father Martin, I've never met a man I felt trust in."

"Then you haven't met many men. Most of them are worthy of trust. Will you trust me?"

She smiled suddenly, a smile that lightened her face and exposed its true beauty. "I'll trust you, and I thank you. You're kind. How will I be able to repay you?"

He got to his feet. "The payment I expect will be hard, tedious work. You'll have to look after this cabin and cook the meals. It may sound simple, but woman's work in this country is never light."

"I know litlte about it, but I'm strong, and Martha will show me how it's done." Her eyelids drooped, and she bent her slender neck. "Will you stay here tonight?"

"No. It will take a couple of days to make preparations. Another bed will have to be built and moved in. Perhaps you and Martha could make up curtains to shield both beds, with washing arrangements behind the curtains. It will be less awkward that way." He grinned.

"You may have made a bad bargain. I've a large appetite." He held out his hand. "It is a bargain?"

She laughed. "It is."

Trustingly she put her hand in his, and as his fingers closed tightly around it he glanced down and saw her breasts swelling against the shirtwaist, her narrow waist and rounded hips clothed in black silk. He made a hasty departure.

Outside the cabin he shivered and pulled up his coat collar. A cold wind was blowing from the northwest. What kind of bargain have I made? he wondered. Can I keep my part of it? For a moment he understood Bobby Holden's mad infatuation with the unattainable Little Moccasins.

A wild blast of sound came from the rampart, and he looked up and saw against the waxing moon a figure striding lithely along the lookout platform. As the strains of "Bonnie Dundee" burst over the post, Laurie threw his head back and laughed. He'd been right earlier, and there'd be little sleep for anyone that night. The Durran was in his fey mood and was as drunk as a lord. As Laurie drew closer he could discern the tartan Durran was wearing. The kilt swinging around George's sturdy knees looked like the Durran plaid. He should have taken Bobby's bet.

Then Laurie stopped smiling, and his arched brows drew together. What inspired joy in George Durran this night? Shrugging, Laurie headed toward the store.

Until the stars faded and blinked out in the gray light of dawn, the pipe howled. Down near the lodges the Indians watched the Highland warrior and listened, entranced with the strange music that outmatched in savagery their own. In one of the lodges Bobby raised his head, listened for a few moments, and then groaned and bent to his companion's plump breasts again. The voyageurs rolled restlessly on their narrow beds and cursed the Scot, but none of them dared challenge him. In Durran's moods he

133

was capable of tearing them to pieces. In his tiny cabin, Dutchy van Zzll turned his humped shoulder upwards and buried his head in a pillow.

General Purline lay stiffly on the bed in his cubicle. The shrill strains of the bagpipe had wrenched him from uneasy sleep, and as he listened to the savage sound, a savage desire stirred within him. He got out of bed and knelt on the cold floor, praying furiously. Although his words were addressed to his God, his thoughts veered to Rowan Malone and her breasts and hips, her long slim legs and ripe mouth.

Suddenly he pulled himself up, fumbled for a candle, and struck fire to it. Holding it aloft, he made his way to the curtained alcove where his wife and daughter slept. As he ripped back the curtain, the wavering candlelight spilled over the cradle and bed. Paying no attention to the sleeping baby, he strode to the bed, gazed down at his wife's white face and wide, frightened eyes. Without a word, he flung back the covers and threw himself across her frail body.

In the next cubicle, Martha MacLeod sat up in bed, pushed back one thin ginger braid, and cupped her hand to her ear. She heard muffled sounds and then a woman's moan.

"The beast," she muttered. "The foul inhuman beast!"

Folding her hands across her breast, she prayed to her own stern God. "Strike him down, Lord. Strike the beast down!"

13

Autumn lingered longer than usual in the valley snugly tucked between two mountains where Fort Purline nestled. October was a month of warm days and frosty nights. The leaves of maple, poplar, and sumac blazed in the valley, and along fir-covered mountain slopes patches of yellow and red flamed among the dark greens. All the people at the post worked long hours in the race against the winter that sent its warnings with turning leaves and frosted earth.

For Rowan it was a month of hard, unrelenting toil, tempered with a sense of peace and a strong feeling of accomplishment. Martha MacLeod, when she went about her own work, took the younger woman with her, and whether they were outside or in, she proved a fast, expert teacher. Rowan soon discovered that under the woman's plump layers were solid muscle and iron endurance. From the morning Rowan told Martha that Laurie would soon join her in the cabin, Martha was a support. She was the one who brought the gay cottons they stitched for curtains, directed the placement of the bed the carpenter carried in, and helped set up washstands within the curtained alcoves.

Martha's expression didn't betray her thoughts, but as they busied themselves sewing the blue, yellow, and white cotton, Rowan said, "Laurie is such a kind man."

"Aye," Martha muttered. "When it costs him little." After a time she said, "But Mr. Durran is the steady one."

135

Momentarily, Rowan wondered if the older woman was trying to warn her. Then, in the pressure of work, she forgot Martha's words.

Taking the girl with her, Martha went out of the fort to show her how to arrange nets for fish, gather wild rice that some called wild oats, harvest berries, and search for nuts. As she worked, she talked.

"It isn't only a matter of cleaning house and cooking meals in this land," she told the girl. "A woman must be able to provide some of the food. Unless, of course, ye are willing to eat salted and smoked meats and fish for months. The voyageurs do, and relish it, but fresh foods and some vegetables are needed. There are times when supplies run low and hunger stalks the land. And here is food in plenty for the gathering. I'll show ye camas roots, which are nourishing. Ye must be careful digging them. The ones with white flowers are deadly poison, the blue ones are wholesome."

Pausing in her work, Rowan stared. "How do you know so much?"

"Necessity, lass, and watching the squaws."

"Do you do all the food gathering for your household?"

"Aye. Nell is weak and sick some of the time. Even in the cabin she must have help, and Little Moccasins comes in to care for her and the babe." She turned and looked at the girl, who was standing knee-deep in the water of the creek. Rowan was wearing her leather boots, now cracked and worn, and the ragged blue outfit she'd traveled in. "We must do something about working clothes for ye. Those are only hampering ye."

Rowan looked ruefully down. "I know, but except for a few skirts and shirtwaists this is all I have."

"Come," Martha ordered.

They went to the lodges, and Rowan was fitted with tough buckskin skirts that stopped well short of her ankles. She purchased high buckskin moccasins that laced up her legs. From calico she made mannish shirts. After a time she found that the braids she pinned on her head were working loose and falling around her shoulders.

From then on she allowed the plaits to swing free, and to keep them clear of her face she knotted a leather, beaded band across her high brow. The autumn sun tanned her face, her neck, and her arms a clear amber. Although she didn't know it, she now looked like an exotic Oriental princess. All Rowan knew was that her strength was increasing day by day, and she gloried in the life and the free, supple feeling of her body. She spared little time from her work and paid no attention to the men at the post.

Once Laurie was in the cabin his prediction came true. No longer did the voyageurs stare at her with lustful eyes. Many of the men—but never Osa or Armand—would assist her with her burdens as she returned to the fort. The two clerks, Bobby and Dutchy, treated her with respect when she visited the store. She didn't see the factor often, and when she met him he merely jerked his big head in a nod and passed coldly by. Rowan was curious about his wife, Nell, who never seemed to leave the big cabin. The baby girl she saw frequently when Little Moccasins took the child for an airing. She carried the baby on a papoose board strapped across her broad shoulders, and once Martha stopped her and cooed over the baby.

"Isn't she a lovely one?" Martha proudly asked Rowan. "My wee Dorrie."

Dorrie was indeed a lovely baby, with a round face, dimpled cheeks, and wide gray-blue eyes. Her hair was fine and fair and curled around her face.

"How old is she?" Rowan asked.

"Nearly eight months, and she's a big girl for her age."

Rowan didn't ask Martha any questions about the child's mother, but her curiosity about Nell Purline was growing. Then one day as she went for water she saw Nell. The factor's wife was crossing the square toward her own cabin. When she noticed Rowan she averted her head and speeded her steps. Deeply hurt, Rowan went on her way. I've done nothing to the woman, she thought, and she didn't even nod at me.

The following day Rowan was spreading berries to dry

on the racks she had erected on the bank of the creek. She heard no sound, but she sensed she was no longer alone, that eyes were fixed on her back. She turned and saw a woman standing a few paces away from her. The woman held out a small hand. "I'm Nell Purline, and I'm sorry I haven't been able to welcome you sooner. Martha has told me much about you, and I'm so glad you are healed of your injuries and back to full health."

Rowan clasped the hand, and then she drew her own back and laughed. "I'm sorry, Mrs. Purline. I've got berry juice all over me."

Smiling, Nell bent and wiped her hand off on the grass. "It's sticky work. But please call me Nell; I always think of you as Rowan."

"It was kind of you to send me gifts. The tea was wonderful, and those cakes were delicious."

"I'm glad you enjoyed them. If you like, I'll send the recipe with Martha."

Nell continued to discuss food and recipes, but Rowan paid more attention to the older woman's appearance than she did to her words. Nell was short and fine-boned, and her dress looked three sizes too large for her. Around her shoulders she wore a heavy shawl, and she had a habit of hugging it around her. Above it her face was white and pinched. Her smile was lovely, and her eyes were like her daughter's, wide and gray-blue. As they chatted, another sound broke across their voices, that of a man's shout from the direction of the river.

Breaking off in mid sentence, Nell tugged her shawl around her and lowered her voice. "I must go back now, but I did so want to meet you."

"Will we meet again?"

Nell patted the girl's arm. "I'll seek you out, but not in the fort. Good-bye, Rowan."

As she watched the woman hurrying away, Rowan wondered about the factor's wife. Wasted and worn as Nell now was, she still retained a look of faded beauty. At another time, Rowan decided, Nell Purline had been much different. What had crushed her? The answer came immediately. Her husband, of course. His face flashed across Rowan's mind—that austere, suffering face of a monk with the monkish tonsured skull. Turning back to the racks, she laid out a fresh covering of leaves and began to spread the berries out. At least she had met Nell, and she found she liked her. She liked Nell very much.

In that autumn, life seemed good to Rowan, and she seldom thought of the man who shared her cabin. Laurie worked from dawn to dusk, coming into the cabin only to eat and sleep. Many nights he went out to work after supper and didn't return until she was tucked into her bed and sound asleep. Rowan was fulfilling her part of the bargain, and with that she was content. She had no idea she was slowly driving her protector wild.

It was well into November before Laurie broke. The night was a wild one. All that day a gale had been blowing, and in its icy blast was a threat of snow. When Laurie came home he was glad to sit beside the roaring fire and eat the supper the girl had prepared. With a satisfied sigh, he pushed away his plate and lifted the steaming mug. "Smells like the genuine article."

"It is." Putting down a pot, she sat down opposite him. "Nell sent a package of tea to me when I first got here, and I've been hoarding it. How did you like your supper?"

"Wonderful." He rubbed his stomach. "The venison steaks were delicious, and that bread! Never have I had its equal."

"The credit goes to Martha. She taught me all I know, including how to handle a bake oven." She pushed back a braid and asked, "Who cooked your meals before?"

"Usually I handled them myself. I tried a couple of women from the lodges but gave up when one tried to tempt me with boiled dog."

"Ssh!" She pointed at the dog sprawling on the hearthrug. "Charlie wouldn't care for that remark."

"He nearly ended up in a stewpot himself. Dog is considered a delicacy, but I haven't tried it myself."

The girl was moving around briskly, clearing the table

and setting a pot of water over the flames. Morosely, he regarded her. She wore a buckskin skirt but had removed the high moccasins, and he caught glimpses of trim legs and ankles. As she bent over the hearth, the collar of her shirt gaped and he saw the curve of one white breast. God's teeth, he grated under his breath, she doesn't even consider me a man. All I am is a fixture, good old Laurie who is treated as though he's another woman. Has the girl no sense? She must think she's back in that convent.

His thoughts went back through the preceding weeks. If he thought he'd suffered agonies with Esmie's locked door, he hadn't the faintest idea of what pure agony was. At least in the house in Mayfair he hadn't been forced to sleep, eat, and dress in a small room with a desirable woman he couldn't lay a finger on. He'd worked harder than any man in the fort since he'd returned to his cabin, putting in hours the others would never consider. Frequently, after his work was finished, he went down to the river and in the dark stripped off his clothes and plunged into the icy water. Work and cold water, he kept assuring himself, that's all that's needed to keep the promise so rashly given. Getting up, he picked up his coat. "I'm going out for a while."

She looked up from the dishpan. "It's a bad night, Laurie. Do you think we'll have snow?"

"We'll have snow," he muttered, and lunged for the door.

In the square he stopped and took a deep breath. A close shave that time—she'd nearly gotten something besides snow. Swearing under his breath, he wondered what to do, where to go. He thought of George Durran's snug room and then shook his head. Durran seemed to be avoiding him. The only time that Laurie had dropped in to see his friend, Durran had been glum and quiet. When Laurie rose to leave, the other man looked up and said brusquely, "I've a hunch the lass's dislike of men isn't just because of the voyageurs. There's something else there, something deep buried."

Laurie looked down at him. "What are you trying to say?"

"Go slow, man, go slow." Without another word, Durran had turned away and hunched over the fire.

No, Laurie thought, there's no haven with Durran. Fastening up his coat, he headed toward the gates. As he reached them, the threat earlier that day was fulfilled and snowflakes swirled through the air. He turned his coat collar up and plodded through the gateway toward the river. One thing was certain. He didn't dare swim that night. If he tried, he'd have lung congestion.

Through the curtain of snow he peered down at the dark water. He couldn't go on this way any longer. No matter how tired he was, no matter how much cold water and work, every night was the same hell. He'd stretch out on that damn narrow bed behind those damn curtains and try to sleep, but all he'd hear was the sound of her soft breathing, the rustle of her mattress as she turned in her sleep. He'd picture her body, long and slender and soft, and often he'd groan aloud in frustration. Some nights he'd find himself halfway across the cabin heading for her bed before sense returned.

Wind buffeted him, and he cursed under his breath. When he finally slept these nights, his dreams only increased his agony. He dreamt of Lila's warm arms, of Adèle Charloux's small body pillowed on its feather bed, even of Esmie and her violent lovemaking. And he wakened from those dreams in a narrow bed, his covers twisted and soaked with sweat. He was afraid of himself, afraid he'd break and rape her as Osa had tried to do.

Rowan, Laurie thought, what are you doing to me? And what is to become of you? Think, man, think. Useless to blame the girl—she trusted him completely. But he couldn't remain in that cabin with her. He no longer worried about her being expelled from the fort, for even Purline wouldn't dare try to throw her out with the snows of winter swirling through the air. The men would never stand for that. But the men—as soon as Laurie was out of the cabin the girl would be open game again. He pictured

141

her with the door broken down, with only Charlie to defend her, and he winced. He'd go to her defense, and then there would be bloodshed. Then Laurie thought of Durran. The man had never shown any interest in women; he truly seemed a man of iron. Perhaps he could persuade Durran to take her in. No! Jealousy raked at Laurie with painful talons. He couldn't bear to think of another man with her, another man watching the flash of long legs, the curves of delicious breasts. Admit it, he said to himself, you can't let her go. There's only one course left. You promised not to force her and you can't. But you can persuade her.

Turning, he strode away from the river. It was snowing harder, but he no longer felt the cold. "I'll make her mine. Other men have taken native women," he said aloud. "No matter how, by fair means or foul, I'll do it. I'll promise anything, but I'm going to have her."

When he neared his cabin he saw that the door was open and in the rectangle of light Rowan was standing. Her face was turned up, and snowflakes caught in her gleaming hair. When she caught sight of him, she called, "Isn't it lovely? It looks like fairyland." Running to meet him, she caught at his arm. "Look, the cabins are dusted with white. Snow is so kind to ugliness, isn't it?"

He looked only at her, at the flush of color on her cheeks, the brightness of the amazing eyes. "By spring you'll have had your fill of snow." He hurried her toward the cabin. "Let's get out of this. You're chilled, and I want to talk to you."

She went directly to the hearth and spread out her hands. "Brr! It was cold, but it felt wonderful." She swung around. "What is on your mind?"

He shook off his boots and hung up his coat. Then he pointed at a chair. "Sit down." Slumping in the one opposite, he wondered how to begin. "Rowan," he said abruptly, "I must warn you. You're in danger."

She glanced at the door, and he shook his head. "Not from outside this cabin. The danger is here, in this room with you." He leaned forward. "Don't you know anything about men?"

She spoke crisply. "More than you would believe."

"In that case you must understand why I can't go on any longer this way. I gave my word and it must be kept. I desire you so strongly I no longer can trust myself."

"I'll not hold you. I don't think that General Purline could force me to leave until spring. Not now that winter has set in."

"Right. But if I leave you'll still have the voyageurs to reckon with."

Her face was closed and cold. "I know, but I'm not the same person they terrorized on the trip. I've changed. I'm strong and I've Charlie. If necessary, I'll get a rifle."

She has changed, he thought; she's toughened and hardened. Aloud he said, "Then there would be bloodshed. There're more of them than the rest of us. They probably would win."

Her shoulders slumped. "What am I to do? I can't leave."

"There's only one way out. Rowan, would you . . . do you think you could be my wife?"

Springing to her feet, she walked around, lifting an object and putting it down. She paused beside the desk and picked up a picture in a narrow silver frame. It was an etching of a gracious house set against a mass of trees. She didn't recognize the trees. "You're already married, Laurie."

"Did someone tell you that?"

"No. But this picture, this is your home, isn't it? What trees are these?"

"Limes. Yes, that's where I was born. It's called Woodbyne Hall."

She picked up another picture. "This oil painting. At first I thought it was you, but the man is older."

He humored her. "My father."

Putting it down, she pointed at the third picture, a watercolor. Judith Hatch had painted it and given it to

143

Laurie before he left London. "To remember," she had told him kindly.

"This baby, with his fair curls and brown eyes and crooked finger—I thought again it was you. But it isn't. It's your son, isn't it?"

"His name is Chris."

"I don't feel you're a widower."

"I'm not, but I might as well be. I'll never live with my wife again. She's the reason I left England and came to this place."

"You're still married."

"I am, and I can't marry you legally."

Turning away from the desk, she walked over and stood beside him, looking down into the flames. "I can't marry you anyway. You're not of my church. But to live unwed with you would be even more sinful."

"We're not in civilization," he said impatiently. "We can't worry about these things. We're struggling to survive, and even churches will understand that."

"I'm not worried about a legal marriage," she murmured.

He sat forward and said eagerly, "If you'd like, we could have a native ceremony. Many men do, and we could go down to the lodges and—"

"No, these ceremonies mean nothing." Sitting down again, she kept her back straight, not touching the chair. "I saw the results of native ceremonies on my way west. I saw the men who had taken native wives and had children by them. I saw wives and children sitting at the table below salt while their husbands sat with the factors and clerks. I saw the women and children trying to eke out livings when they were abandoned and the men went back to their own countries. No, I don't wish that."

She has a mind, Lauric thought, a mind and a good discerning eye. Take it slowly; remember, promise anything. "Do you think I'd be like that?"

"I don't know. I know little about you."

"You know this much. I made a promise, and when I

144

no longer felt I could keep it, I told you. I made no attempt to take you against your will."

"Yes, I know that." She bent her long, slender neck, and twin braids swept forward against amber cheeks. "You're trying to help me, and that I know too."

She looks more and more like a native, he thought, but what a beautiful native. Desire for her flooded through him afresh. Any means, fair or foul, he reminded himself as he strode to the desk and pulled open a drawer. From it he took a delicate linen handkerchief, and for an instant he fancied that the yellowed cloth still retained a hint of lavender. It didn't. Any scent used on it had long before dissipated. Unwrapping it, he held up a heavy gold band. "This was my mother's wedding ring. I didn't put it on my wife's hand." And the reason, he said silently, was that my father wouldn't allow it. How would Sir Christopher feel about this? Laurie wondered, and shied away from the answer. "If you agree, Rowan, I'll place it on your finger and with it make you my wife."

She gazed at the ring and then at his face. "Would you swear vows on your mother's ring?"

"What vows?" he asked cautiously.

"That this marriage would be a true one and that you would treat me as a wife?"

"Yes."

"Would you swear never to leave me, to let only death part us?"

He almost blurted out yes. Then he paused. She was driving too hard a bargain. I can only go so far, Laurie thought. In silence he took his chair opposite her and looked down at the ring. Charlie growled in his sleep, and his tail thumped the floor. Other than that, the only sound was the wood crackling on the hearth.

"Well?" she prompted.

"I'll swear to care for you and cherish you and any children we may have. I'll swear to provide for you and for them. I'll swear while we're together to cleave to you only."

"But you won't swear you'll never leave me?"

"No."

"I'll have to. My vow must be that I can only be released by death—either yours or mine."

His head jerked up. "Then you'll marry me?"

"Yes."

He reached for her hand, but she pulled away.

"Wait. You've been honest with me. I must now tell you something that may change your mind."

"I won't change my mind."

"Don't speak in haste. First let me tell you this. You think I fear men because of my experience with Armand and Osa. That isn't true. I'm here because of men, three men, and they were drunk—"

"Rowan—"

"Please. You've had your say. Let me have mine. This is painful to recount. When my father died and I left the convent, Reverend Mother found a place for me with a French family. The woman was a fine person, and so was her husband. She gave me light work to do—sewing, writing letters for her, reading to her. I was only sixteen when I went to Mme. Guilbant, and for three years I had a good life. Then her son returned from France. His name was René, and he was different from his parents. Somehow he found out about my background, that I was half Indian, and when his parents were out he brought two friends and they came to my room and they—" Her composure broke, and she buried her face in her hands.

"Don't go on," he urged.

"I must. They were drunk, all of them. They did things to me . . . they forced me to do things. I almost went mad. When they finally left me I crawled to Father Martin, and he took me back to the convent."

With deep compassion, Laurie gazed at her. What a swine I am, he told himself—not much better than those three drunken brutes. George Durran had been right when he sensed that evil had touched this girl. He attempted to reassure her. "If you think this makes a difference to me, you're wrong. I still want you for my wife."

146

"Men!" Jumping to her feet, she glared down at him. "Do you think I told you this to beg your forgiveness? You've taken women where you want them, and I'm not asking that you're pure. I feel no guilt. Father Martin assured me no sin is attached to me. The sin belongs to the men who took me against my will!"

"Then why did you tell me?"

Sinking to the rug, she patted the dog's head. Charlie opened his eyes, and his long tongue licked out at her hand. Her voice was muffled. "In the time we've lived in this cabin you haven't touched me once, not a fold of my skirt or my hand. If you had, I'd have run from the door screaming. And I like you, Laurie. But because of the treatment I received, I don't think I could ever be a wife to any man. Once his hands were on me I'd be back in that garret with those men, and I'd scream and fight. I might kill. Now do you understand?"

All thoughts of himself and his own needs vanished in the girl's anguish. Leaning forward, Laurie gently tilted up her chin until their eyes met. "I understand, and now I'll make you understand. The union between a man and woman is nothing like the rape that was done to you. It's a beautiful act, filled with tenderness and leading to bliss. If you take me as husband I'll make another vow. I vow I'll teach you the meaning of that beauty. I'll make you a woman, and a whole one."

The strange blue eyes fixed on his face. "Do you think you could?"

"I vow I will."

She held out her hand. "Let us swear."

In that rude cabin, with only a dog as witness, the two swore. Laurie swore to remain with her as long as he could, but Rowan swore her marriage was to the death—of one or the other. As Laurie slipped the ring on her finger, he gently kissed her hand. Then he lifted her and carried her to the bed.

"You're my wife," he told her tenderly, "and I'll keep my vow. Soon you'll be a whole woman."

14

The first snow of the season was followed by violent storms until the days of lingering autumn warmth were only a memory in the valley of the Nechako. White banks drifted against the stockade and the log buildings of the fort, icicles hung from low eaves, and ice started to skim the river and creek.

The last promise that Laurie had made to Rowan seemed to be an impossible one to fulfill. Night after night he tried to keep his word, tried to break down her resistance to his maleness, and night after night she whimpered in fright and cringed away from his advances. No matter how tender his hands were, how gentle his voice, he met with no success. He knew that the girl was striving to banish from memory her abuse in the garret of the Guilbant house, but after a time he began to think that she'd been correct—she could never be any man's wife.

Finally he admitted defeat, retired to his own cubicle, and left her alone. In the confines of the snowbound cabin the tension between them was unbearable, and they both showed signs of strain. They tried to meet only at mealtimes, and their determined efforts to converse generally ended in an uneasy silence.

In late November Laurie was relieved when Purline, infuriated with the small amount of game sent in by the hunters, sent Laurie and Lapointe to check on them. The two men rode small, sturdy horses who were forced to wade knee-deep through drifts, and it was a hard trek for both the men and the animals. They were gone for four days. The night they returned, Laurie lingered in the stable. Moska had gone lame, and he was concerned about the horse. Under the smoky lamp, Laurie and the Indian stableman, Gerika, examined the animal's right foreleg.

The ancient stableman straightened, one hand easing the small of his back. "Moska lucky fellow. Pull muscle." Holding up a hand, he spread gnarled fingers. "This many days Moska be well again."

"You really think so?"

"Gerika knows horses. He be well."

Laurie breathed a sigh of relief, patted the shaggy neck of the horse, and picked up his rifle and his bulging pack. Opening the pack, he tore off a piece of tobacco and handed it to the old man. Grunting his thanks, Gerika crushed the tobacco in his palm, sprinkled it with lime, and popped the mixture in his mouth. He gave Laurie his toothless grin. "Good!"

Laurie shouldered his pack and plodded wearily across the square. God's teeth, but he was exhausted, and yet not so exhausted that he welcomed the sight of his snug cabin, yellow lights in its windows, smoke curling over the roof. Hell was waiting in that cabin, and although a couple of weeks ago he wouldn't have believed it, he had no desire to see Rowan's softly curved figure. Stamping snow off his boots, he swung open the heavy door and stepped into the warmth of firelight and lamplight. There was no sign of Rowan, and the curtains were drawn around her bedstead. On a tripod over a low fire a pot was suspended, and a delicious odor filled the cabin. On the table were a bowl, a mug, a jar of goose grease, and a fresh loaf of bread.

Putting his pack down, Laurie hung his coat from a peg and dished up the stew. It was as delicious as it smelled—rabbit meat, venison, duck, in a gravy filled with rice and onion. He ate two heaping bowls and wiped the bowl out with chunks of bread. Rowan might be no earthly use in bed, but she could certainly cook.

After he'd eaten, weariness came down in crushing

149

waves, and without a glance toward her corner he went to his own and pulled back the curtains. On the washstand was a clean towel, a dish of soft soap, and a steaming pitcher of water. She must have heard he was back, Laurie thought, and hurried around heating the stew and water for him. Poor girl, it was hell for her too. He stripped off his clothes, washed hurriedly, and got into bed. Scarcely had he lowered his head when sleep grasped at him, and as he sank gratefully into its depths, he thought, Damn, I forgot to pull those ruddy curtains.

Later he came awake wondering why he was pressed against the log wall. Then he felt silky warmth against his side. His hand moved and touched smooth skin. "Rowan," he whispered.

Her voice drifted through the darkness. "Talk to me. Tell me about England."

Without moving, he started to talk. He told her about his home in Essex, his boyhood, his school years. He told her about his father, his love for Sir Christopher, and about his brother, who was so different from himself. He told her about London, about the palace where the Hanoverian king George II held court. He described the tall townhouses of the wealthy and the crowded slums of the poor. He described fog blanketing the Thames and drifting up into the streets and alleys of the city. As he started to describe the English spring, with budding trees and soft gentle breezes, his hand stole out and caressed her thigh. She didn't move away, and his hand wandered further, stroking her hip, caressing her breasts.

No longer did he hear his own words; he didn't know or care if he was making sense. She moved closer, and he could feel her breath against his throat, her hot quivering body pressed against his own. Suddenly she pushed herself up on an elbow and bent over him. Thick scented hair tumbled over his face and throat, and then her lips pressed against his. His arms went around her.

Gently and slowly he made love to her. When the light of dawn pushed tiny, pallid fingers through the windows, he finally made good his promise. The girl in his arms had discovered womanhood, had experienced and enjoyed its mysteries.

Against his lips she whispered, "You have made me whole."

While the north wind hammered the fort and snow swirled around the cabin, they slept entwined in the warmth of each other's arms.

That night was a turning point both in Rowan's and in Laurie's life. Never had either of them known the joy that filled the rough little cabin with splendor. Laurie had snowshoes fashioned for the girl and brought her home a warm coat and hood of rabbit skins. As often as they could they left the stockade and wandered over the countryside. They crossed the frozen creek, and on the Ile Ste. Anne they discovered a secret place. It was a cave in the middle of the island, hidden behind a screen of tumbled boulders, with its entrance shielded by overhanging hemlock boughs. When they crept in the low entrance, they found that the floor was deep with river sand. Using their coats as blankets, they made love in the dry, snug, dark retreat. Afterward they kindled fires on the shore of the island and heated the pots of food they brought with them. As the short day waned they would trudge back to the fort, hand in hand, laughing like children.

Evenings held their own special magic. After supper they would sprawl in comfort on a bearskin before the fire, and then their voices would be low and at times serious. Laurie found he was making lines of poetry with no idea of meter or rhyme, and he would whisper them to Rowan. One night as they lay in each other's arms, gazing at pictures in the flames, he said softly in her ear, "Oh, my Rowan, tree of delight, with crowns of blossoms sweet and white—" With an embarrassed laugh, he broke off. "Never make much of a poet, I'm afraid."

Her arms tightened around him. "No need to, Laurie. Poets make words, you make love."

The love they made couldn't be hidden; it showed in

their every move, in their every expression. It shone forth from their faces and blazed from their eyes. And other eyes watched them. Not all were kind.

General Purline would glance from his office window, see them hand in hand, hear the echo of their laughter, and his hands would tighten into fists. "I'll crush them!" he'd rage. "They bring sin to this fort with their unholy lust."

His wife would see them from her kitchen window, and once she turned to Martha and said softly, "How happy I am for them." She added, as though speaking to herself, "Once I too knew how they feel."

Glancing at the younger woman's white face and frail figure, Martha only said, "Aye." But she was thinking of another fort, one ablaze with a southern sun, the parade ground brown and sere and dusty. Aye, she thought, her mouth tightening, and it brought you here to suffer.

Most of the voyageurs ran true to form. They'd nudge each other and make bawdy comments, but it was good-natured talk, and if Durran was near they'd say nothing. For Durran watched too, and although he said nothing to the voyageurs, if they spoke of Rowan he turned such a look upon them that fear coursed through their veins.

Armand was far from good-natured about Rowan and Laurie's happiness. One day as he saw them going toward the gates, he poked his brother in the ribs and growled, "There she is, the squaw who spurned us. Wallowing in it, isn't she?"

Osa looked down, his bearded face blank. "Who do you speak of, brother?"

Glaring at him, Armand spat, "You remember nothing, do you? If I asked what happened yesterday, you couldn't tell me."

"I remember papa. Papa said, 'Son, always obey Armand. Armand's smart. He'll look after you.'"

"Better remember that, dullard. Armand looks after you."

Armand had no affection for his brother; indeed, he couldn't recall anyone he had ever cared for. Number one, he'd tell himself—that's who to care about. But Osa was useful, and to control the big shambling brute was to control a deadly weapon.

Osa adored his brother, and now he tried to please him. His low brow furrowed with thought. "I remember a priest, a good man. He fixed my shoulder."

His brother raised shaggy brows. "*Bien, mon pauvre fou!* So, you remember Father Martin. Then you must remember the girl who just passed with her lover."

"Rowan!" Osa blurted. "The father was trying to keep her pure." His brow furrowed with the effort of remembering. "We didn't touch her."

"We almost had her, and then that damned English pig rode out of the forest and took her from us. For himself, he took her!"

Osa rubbed his forearm. "A dog bit me."

"*Fermez la grande bouche!* If you don't, I swear I'll bite you myself."

"What have I done, brother?"

"Talking to you is like baying at the moon." Armand strode away, and one hand fingered the knife in his belt. "One of these days I'll touch you, squaw, and you'll never forget that touch. Your face will never be pretty again."

All the people at Fort Purline watched the lovers. Bobby Holden looked after them and thought wistfully of Little Moccasin's tall, full figure. So preoccupied was the young man that for a time he didn't notice the odd reaction of his fellow clerk. Few people ever paid much attention to Pieter van Zzll, whom they all called Dutchy. To most of them Dutchy was all but invisible. He was a short man of indefinite age with a twisted body and stooped shoulders, one of which carried a small hump. His face was long and narrow, and faded brown hair fell lankly across his brow. When he smiled, which was seldom, the smile changed his face. Rowan had noticed the man because his smile reminded her of Father Martin. There was charm in that smile, a radiance, and more than a trace of sorrow. Dutchy lived alone in a tiny cabin in the southwest corner of the square. He took care of himself, cooked his meals, washed his clothes, and tidied his cabin. Never, in the years he'd been at the post, had Dutchy gone to the lodges. Because of this the voyageurs sneered, "Capon." Bobby, who was a kind man, was worried about his friend's celibacy. Sometimes while they worked together he would gently lecture the older man. "Dutchy," Bobby would tell him, "you need a woman." Dutchy would shrug misshapen shoulders. "What woman would want *me*?"

As the little man watched Rowan and Laurie, his thoughts strayed to his sterile life, his lonely cabin, and he grew restless. One afternoon as Bobby and Dutchy worked at bundling furs into bales, Dutchy spoke hesitantly to the young man. "You have wide experience with women, Bobby."

Behind the glittering pince-nez, Bobby's eyes glowed with fervor. "Wide indeed, old chap. It's my vocation in life, hunting the little darlings down."

Dutchy strapped up a bale of furs and patted the soft mass. "Would you help me?"

"Do what?"

"Find a woman."

Bobby dropped a bale, and it split open. Furs cascaded to the floor, but he paid no attention. "What kind of woman?" he asked cautiously.

"One to keep my house, cook my meals. A housekeeper."

"Something more than that, I'll wager."

Hot color flooded the smaller man's face. "Perhaps."

Slapping the counter, Bobby beamed. "Of course I'll help you. We'll have a look tomorrow. Bunch of fresh ones in, came in with a group of Salish with these furs. Have an eye on one little darling myself."

"We have to work tomorrow."

"We've both worked like dogs for months. Have a word with the old man myself. Get the afternoon off. George is a good chap, and he'll take over here."

Dutchy raised imploring eyes. "I'm not . . . not so sure. Maybe we'd better forget it."

"Rot, old chap. Strike while the iron is hot." Bobby peered at the other man's flushed face. "Don't worry," he said gently. "We'll just stroll past the lodges and I'll point them out to you. No one need know why you're there."

The next afternoon they were at the lodges. From a pale winter sky the sun glinted on the lodge area. The settlement was to the right of the gates between the stockade and the river. The dwellings were an odd mixture. A wide, rough trail led between two rows of permanent lodges, log and pole huts, some very large, with gabled ends. Past the permanent lodges hide tents had been hastily erected by the Indians who had just arrived. Near these were the round mounds of underground houses that burrowed deep into the earth. The only evidences of these winter houses were holes in the mounds of snow with the ends of wooden ladders protruding and long streamers of smoke from cooking fires curling up.

The area was a beehive of activity. Children and scrawny dogs raced around. Women bundled in fur and rawhide were tacking hides on stretchers, others were grinding corn on flat stones, still others were checking haunches of frozen venison and strings of wild fowl. The men were not as active. Inside the doors of lodges, Dutchy could see groups of braves gambling with cherry pits and splinters of wood. A few men lounged around outside smoking pipes and watching the women as they worked. Dutchy looked up at his tall companion, and Bobby gave him a reassuring smile.

"Nothing to it, old chap. Look them over, pick one you fancy, and leave the rest to me. Must be careful. If they figure you're an amateur they'll take half a year's pay." Lifting a long hand, he waved casually to a group of men hailing him. "Pass them by. New ones are down at the end. They've some fine-looking females."

Dutchy stopped. "I don't think I can do it, Bobby."

Bobby took the other man's arm. "Courage, old chap. Smile, look confident. Let me do the talking."

Dutchy smiled, and Bobby shook his head. "You're

just baring your teeth. If you can't manage a genuine smile, look sober and thoughtful."

Pulling his brows together in a ferocious frown, Dutchy tried to match his short steps to his companion's long, free strides. Bobby's hand tightened on his arm. "There's the tent I was thinking of. Take a look. Old fellow's got a batch of wives, some of them young and attractive, and a couple of daughters. Nubile little darlings. See anything you like?"

Dutchy stared at the women working around the tent. One of the older ones looked up, caught his eyes, and smiled at him. All her front teeth were missing. He turned his back. "It's not right! Looking at them as though they're not even human. What are we doing to these people?"

"This is no time to argue about exploitation."

"That's exactly what it is. Exploitation! We're taking their women, their country—"

"Calm down, Dutchy. We're businessmen, here for the business of gathering furs so idle, perfumed women in London and Paris can drape themselves in luxury, so overfed men who never step out of offices may become rich. We don't want their wild, forsaken country."

"Behind us will come people who will. Settlers will take this country and make it theirs. What is to happen to the natives who rightfully inhabit it?"

Bobby shrugged. "What always happens. But then, civilization progresses no matter what little people like us think. It's happened time and time again. What of merry old England? Ever thought how many races wrenched it from one another? And what have these noble savages done in the centuries this land has been theirs?" Bobby swung his arm in a wide circle.

Looking up at the snow-crowned peaks, Dutchy muttered, "It's still not right. This is their land."

"Bloody hell! Do you want a woman to warm your bed or not?"

Across Dutchy's mind flashed the image of Rowan and Laurie—their happiness, his own miserable existence. He took a deep breath. "I'm an exploiter too. I'll say no more."

With a wide smile, Bobby led him down the trail. "That's the spirit. Now, I'm going to be generous. I'll show you the little darling I've been thinking about for myself. Never let it be said a Holden is selfish. There she is, by that tent. The one stringing dried fish. Her name's Lorenawa, and she's a little beauty. Shuswap tribe, and she's a long way from home. Look at those sloe eyes and those haunches. Handfuls of beautiful ass! Like her?"

But Dutchy wasn't paying any attention to the Shuswap maid. He was watching the last lodge in the row. A woman had just pushed aside the skin flap and was walking toward them. She was short and heavy and bore a load of rush mats in her arms.

"Who is she?"

Bobby followed the other man's eyes. "Marinska. But forget about her. She's too long in the tooth, must be in her mid-twenties. Even the Indians don't bother with Marinska."

"Why not?"

"She's taboo. Lives in that lodge alone. Her husband brought her here, and she was the oldest of his wives. When they left he deserted her, drove her out of his lodge."

"How does she manage?"

"Does menial work around the fort. Looks after the voyageurs' digs. Weaves those mats and trades them for meat and fish."

The woman called Marinska had stopped, and she appeared to be bargaining with another woman. The other woman nodded, took a knife, and sliced off a chunk of frozen meat. As Marinska walked back toward them, she glanced at Dutchy. She didn't smile, but her long dark eyes met his. He whispered to Bobby, "Why did her husband abandon her?"

"She was barren."

"Did his younger wives have children?"

"How would I know? Look, old chap, I'm trying to

157

oblige, but I'm slowly freezing. Take another look at the luscious Lorenawa."

"No." Dutchy started toward the lodge Marinska was entering. "I'm going to talk to her."

"Wait." In long strides, Bobby overtook the other man. "If you have a yen for her, let me do the bargaining."

Dutchy raised his eyes. "She's an outcast too. No bargaining will be done. Thank you, Bobby, but now I'll carry on myself."

Bobby had been politely dismissed, and he stared after Dutchy's hunched back. "Poor ruddy devil," he muttered. "Well, might's well have a go at the lovely Lorenawa."

As the lanky Englishman approached, Lorenawa lowered her sloe eyes and studiously continued working.

"Now for some exploitation," he said in English. Without comprehension she bobbed her head, and he continued in the mixture of Indian dialects used in trading. "How would you like some pretty beads for that lovely neck of yours?"

She smiled shyly and continued to work. "Green and blue and amber," he said, and held up three fingers. "This many strands."

She glanced up, and the sloe-eyes widened. She wasn't looking at Bobby, she was staring over his shoulder. Turning around, he looked directly into a broad chest draped in a fur cloak. His eyes traveled up, and he saw the biggest, most ferocious-looking native he'd ever laid eyes on. Bobby couldn't back away; he was too close to the girl. "Just passing the time of day," he babbled in English, his eyes riveted to the shining hatchet the man clasped in one enormous fist. "Talking to your daughter."

"Squaw."

"Oh, your wife? Yes, indeed. Just passing the time of day talking to your—"

"How much?"

Bobby gasped with relief. A trader, but you could never tell. Some braves might slice an intruder's head off. "A dram of high wine."

"Not enough." Leaning past Bobby, the Indian pinched at the girl's bottom. "Fed well. Plenty fat. Good squaw."

Bobby was trying to breathe shallowly. A rancid odor came from both the girl and the man. Fish oil, he decided, the cherished fish oil used for a body rub. Never mind, old Tupa could take care of that.

"Two drams," he bid.

"And knife," the brave rumbled.

"All right. Two drams of high wine and a knife. No more!"

"Done. When?"

"Tonight."

"Throw in lodge. I sleep there." The brave motioned with the hatchet to a snowbank.

Breathing in the various pungent odors wafting from the lodge, Bobby shook his head. "I'll send for her."

The other man jerked his head and stepped aside. Bobby hurried down the trail. Now to find old Tupa. He didn't have to look far. She appeared at his elbow, her wrinkled face creased with a toothless, knowing grin. "When?" she asked.

He grinned down at her. "Always on the jolly old spot, Tupa. Tonight. This one is very ripe, so do a thorough job. Get that oil out of her hair, too."

"Tupa do good job. Always do good job."

He patted her shoulder affectionately. "And for your trouble you shall have three yards of blue cotton."

She squinted up at him. "Four. Flannel. Red."

"Your price has gone up."

She turned away. "Get some other. No good, the others. Tupa good."

"You win. Four yards of red flannel."

Over a skinny shoulder, she grinned at him. If Dutchy wants to take a lesson in pure exploitation, he should have seen that, Bobby thought ruefully. Where has the little chap gotten to? Then he pushed up the pince-nez on his nose and felt his mouth fall open. "My sainted aunt," he gasped.

Trudging toward him was Dutchy, his arms piled high

with bundles. A few paces behind him Marinska walked, her eyes on the man's twisted back. As Bobby watched, Dutchy paused and waited for her. Then, side by side, they walked toward the fort. As Dutchy passed his friend he smiled, that smile of rare charm. Openmouthed, Bobby stared after them. Then his mouth snapped closed. He caught sight of Little Moccasins' tall form, and he hastened toward her.

"How would you like some nice beads?" he called.

She snarled, baring large white teeth, and pulled her knife out. "Keep away, cur. I slice your neck!"

He stopped and shouted, "This is a ruddy strange love affair, little darling."

Another strange love affair was that of Dutchy van Zzll and the woman Marinska. She cared for his home and for him, and when she went to the lodges to barter for goods she walked proudly. Toward spring her posture was even prouder. Under her cotton dress her belly bulged, and she arched her back, pushing her swollen belly even further out. Often her man would walk by her side. As he gazed at his wife, heavy with his child, the sadness was missing from his sweet smile.

15

The Yuletide brought nostalgia to both Laurie and Rowan. Memories of other Christmas seasons filled Laurie's mind, the happy ones in his childhood with his father at Woodbyne Hall, the day he had married Esmie, and the Christmas morning when his son had been born. Rowan recalled other Yules too, those in the convent with the good Sisters of Ste. Claire. In earlier years her father, sober and neatly dressed, would come to see her on Christmas Eve to bring her small gifts. In his way, before drink had completely besotted him, he had loved his daughter, and she had returned that love.

When Rowan heard about the traditional party that the factor hosted on Christmas day, she was delighted. Martha told her that one of the storerooms was to be cleared, the walls decorated with fir boughs, and long makeshift tables erected to accommodate the guests.

"Will I be invited?" she asked the older woman.

"Everyone is invited, lass. The voyageurs, the Indians who work around the post, the clerks. We'll all be there."

Rowan immediately began to sort through the few clothes she had brought from Montreal to find something fit for the party. Smiling at the girl's enthusiasm, Martha trudged through the deep snow toward the Purline cabin. As she passed the store she heard a tap on a windowpane and looked up at Purline's office window. The factor held up a sheaf of papers and beckoned to her. When she entered the office he was sitting at his desk, a smile on his face, the papers spread in front of him. He appeared to be in good spirits.

Transferring the smile from the papers to Martha Mac-Leod, he told her, "I've finished the lists. Now, I want no effort spared to make this banquet a fine one. Hire as many of the native women as you require to help you. Have Gerika and Tapinawa cut boughs for the walls. I've already set the carpenter to work on the tables."

"What food do you want served, sir?"

He selected a list and peered at it. "For the clerks and the other whites, I think we'll have some of that buffalo tongue I had the voyageurs bring. Strange, the manifest called for eight, and I only counted seven. Oh well, they probably stole the other one. Some tongue and tinned ham. The hunters have brought moose and some partridge. These may be served for all. Make up a good pudding and have Nell bake lots of those little cakes. I'll provide China tea and Madeira wine for the clerks; the others will be served rum and high wine."

"Tea for the Indians and the voyageurs?"

"Tea muskey, Martha. There's little enough of the China tea. Mustn't be wasteful."

"Candy?"

He beamed. "Certainly. I'll have Mr. Holden supply you with a jar of peppermint sticks. The Indians love them."

Now she was smiling broadly. "It sounds like a fine party this year."

"It will be. Here is a list of the seating arrangements. Mind you follow it exactly."

Taking the sheet from his hand, she examined it. Her smile faded. "Are you sure about this one?"

He followed her pointing finger. "Absolutely."

"But she's—"

"Follow it exactly, Martha." He stood up. "That will be all."

Shaking her head, she left to start her work.

On Christmas morning Laurie and Rowan put aside their memories and prepared for the party. One corner of the cabin was piled with presents. Rowan was looking at hers with a childlike delight. She fondled the cloak of white fox skins that Laurie had given her, the fine new snowshoes expertly fashioned by George Durran. Picking up a little blue vase filled with dried wildflowers and fern, she smiled. Dutchy had tapped on the door, thrust it into her hands, and bashfully backed away.

She whirled around. "They're all so kind to me, Laurie."

He smiled at her. "Seems to me you were pretty kind yourself, knitting and baking gifts for everyone."

"And the party! I'm going to wear my silk shirt and the shirtwaist that Sister Gabriel made for me. It's covered with lace and—"

"Rowan."

His face was suddenly serious, and she gazed up at him. "What?"

"This party—" Breaking off, he looked down at her happy face.

"What about the party?"

"I was just going to remind you to wear your new cloak."

"How could I forget it?"

Picking up the cloak, she hugged the soft white mass to her breast. When they left the cabin she was wearing it, and the white fur collar framed her face. Her glossy hair was pulled back and fastened in a loose bun at the nape of her neck, her ears were hung with tiny cameo earbobs, and a matching brooch clasped the lace neck of the shirtwaist that Sister Gabriel had spent long hours sewing. On one wrist was a wide bracelet set with small blue stones that her father had given her, and the gold was echoed in the wedding band on her marriage finger.

When they entered the storeroom, they found they were the last arrivals. Three long tables, heaped with food and drink, ran the length of the big room, and all the people of the fort were there. The nearest table had been spread with a white cloth, and it glistened an array of china and silver. General Purline stood behind a chair, and Nell Purline was seated in the one next to it. Martha was there, and Bobby Holden, George Durran, and Dutchy van Zzll were also waiting. At the next table the voyageurs sat in two long lines. In front of them were heavy china plates and pewter mugs. The third one, crowded against the far wall, was bare, and tin plates and mugs were spread on the planks. The Indian workers crowded around this one, their eyes fastened on the tall candy jar and a keg of high wine in its center.

"Ah, Mr. Woodbyne, we've been waiting for you," Purline called. "Over here, beside Mr. Holden."

Laurie hesitated, and then slowly made his way to the table. Rowan stood where she was, huddled in her new cloak, feeling every eye fixed on her. "Where—" she started to ask, and then broke off.

Purline was watching her, smiling broadly. He pointed to the table against the wall. "Right over there, next to Marinska." He turned away, pulled out his chair, and called jovially, "Everyone be seated!"

Rowan sought her husband's eyes, but Laurie averted his head and stared at his plate. Both Holden and van Zzll studiously avoided looking at her, but Durran's hand closed into a fist on the white tablecloth. She stood alone by the door. Then she forced herself to move. She lifted her chin, loosened her cloak, and making her way through the close-packed tables, took her place beside Dutchy's wife. Marinska glanced sideways at the younger woman, and Rowan, holding her head high, said clearly, "Thank you for the lovely vase, Marinska. I shall always treasure it."

"The bottle my Pieter had, but I fill it with dried flowers." She added shyly, "I like the mitts you make me."

Squeezed tightly between Marinska and the stableman, Gerika, Rowan tried to eat. She waved away the tea muskey but allowed her mug to be filled with high wine. Why not? she thought defiantly. The food stuck in her throat, and she washed it down with gulps of the strong wine.

164

She wondered miserably why someone hadn't told her, why Laurie or Martha hadn't warned her. Involuntarily her eyes wandered to the factor's table. She couldn't see Laurie's face, but General Purline was staring at her, a tiny, satisfied smile hovering at the corners of his wide mouth. Before she turned her head, she saw Nell at his side, her neck, its heavy bun of hair seeming to weight it, bent over her plate.

She felt weak and nauseated. The fumes of wine filled her nostrils, and she smelled the mingled odors of moose meat, roast partridge, and rancid fish oil from the bodies and hair of the people surrounding her. Gerika was pressed against her side. He smelled strongly of the stable where he lived and worked. Despite his lack of teeth he was tearing at a huge hunk of moose meat, and grease was trickling down his chin. Bile rose in her throat, and she jumped to her feet, her cloak falling unheeded to the floor. I've got to get out of here, she thought. I'm going to be sick.

As she ran blindly across the floor, silence fell over the tables. Not even a spoon clinked or a hand moved. In that silence she reached the door and stumbled down the hall toward the store. Durran jumped to his feet. He divided a glare between the factor and Laurie Woodbyne. Purline smiled guilelessly up at the Scot, but Laurie met Durran's grim eyes and slowly got to his feet. Striding over to the Indians' table, he gathered up her fur and walked toward the door. Then Nell Purline's voice stopped him. Color was flaming across her cheeks, and she held out two small parcels wrapped in red paper. "Mr. Woodbyne, would you kindly give these to your wife with my compliments?"

Without a word, he took them and then followed Rowan. He found her in front of the store, bent double, retching. He put out a hand, but she slapped it away and ran across the square to the cabin. When Laurie entered the room he found her kneeling on the bearskin, her arms around Charlie, weeping into the dog's neck. Laurie knelt beside them, and Charlie raised his head, pulled back his lips, and growled.

"I don't blame you, old fellow," he told the dog, and put an arm around the girl's shaking shoulders. Charlie snapped at his hand. Hastily, Laurie pulled his arm away. "God's teeth! He'd actually bite me."

Jumping up, Rowan stood over him. Her cheeks were wet, but her eyes were blazing with rage and hurt. "Why didn't you tell me?"

"I was going to . . . this morning. I almost told you, but you were so happy. I just couldn't."

"You let me walk into it. Into that . . ."

Pulling himself to his feet, he took her hands and held them tightly. "Don't, Rowan, please. That's the way it is. You must have seen it at other forts on your way here. Marinska had to sit there too."

"He was enjoying it! That devil of a Purline. Enjoying humiliating me."

Laurie remembered the gifts Nell had thrust into his hands. "Nell sent you presents, darling, look."

She knocked them out of his hands. "Don't treat me like a child! I don't want any present. She didn't look at me, not once. Neither did you. You just sat down like a tame dog when Purline ordered you to. What kind of man are you?"

"Not much of one," he muttered. "I've never pretended to be much of a man. But that devil is my factor. My future is in his hands. He sends reports. I have to obey him."

"George Durran wouldn't. He'd have knocked Purline down!"

"Yes, he would have, and he'd never have gotten another position with a fur company. I'm sorry, Rowan. I promise you'll never have to go through anything like that again."

Now her face was cold and remote. She spoke without heat. "No, I'll never go through that again. I'll never go to another factor's party. I might as well accept the fact that I'm Indian and you're English. English and white and with a legal wife and son. And Nell couldn't help either. He rules her." Stooping, she picked up the parcels. She

166

opened the larger one and found two linen handkerchiefs edged with lace and embroidered with her initial. She read the words on the slip of paper pinned to them. "From Martha, with love." She tore the paper from the other. Inside was a tiny box, and nestled in it was a fine gold chain. "I'm so sorry, dear," Nell had written. "I can't give you this myself. Please try to understand."

Rowan lifted her eyes, now cold and dry, and gazed at Laurie. "I've a present for you."

"You've already given me two. That nice shirt you made and the scarf."

"In a way this is a present you gave to me. I'm with child."

"Are you certain? So soon?"

A wan smile touched her lips. "I'm certain. As for soon—it does happen. Are you displeased?"

"No, only surprised. I'm fond of children."

"I know." She glanced at the blond baby in the silver frame. "But this baby will be a breed."

Sinking on a chair, he pulled her onto his lap. "Don't use that word."

"A breed." She gazed into the fire. "Another little one to sit below the salt and eat from a tin plate."

His arms tightened around her slim body. "Our child, Rowan. We'll make our own world. You and me and our baby. We'll make a happy, secure world where we can't be touched."

"I'm no longer a dreamer, Laurie. There are other worlds that will always touch ours. And where they touch, they'll tarnish—as something was tarnished today. We've lost something, Laurie, and we'll never get it back."

"I promise you, darling, I promise we'll be as happy as we've been for this last month. Always, darling, forever."

"Nothing lasts forever," she told him sadly.

Both of them looked into the flames as though they were seeking a world that had never existed.

16

The end of the festive season arrived with the voyageurs' celebration of New Year's Day. Although the French-Canadians enjoyed the factor's party on Christmas Day, their own boisterous party was on *le jour de l'an*. Early that morning, attired in their best garb, all the crews of the canoes arrived at the store. Behind the counter, waiting in a solemn row, were the factor, Laurie, Durran, and the two clerks. Kegs of rum and high wine and tall pewter mugs stood ready.

Behind the kegs the factor stood, and the men filed by him, leaning forward to peck a New Year's kiss and receive a brimming mug of liquor. Then the voyageurs shook hands with Laurie, Durran, and the clerks, who each handed out small gifts of tobacco and sweets. Laurie shook Beau's hand, gave the young man a length of tobacco, and smothered a grin. From the corners of their eyes both Laurie and Bobby Holden were watching the factor, enjoying the sight of the rough voyageurs kissing his gaunt cheek. Purline hated this yearly ritual, but it was necessary, and he gritted his teeth and played out his role. Finally it was over, and as the last man left the store, Purline breathed a sigh of relief.

"Children," he grated, turning toward his office. "Grown men acting like infants."

"They won't act like children this afternoon," Durran said. "And by nightfall this place is going to be a prelude to hell."

Laurie, who had witnessed the last celebration of *le jour*

de l'an, nodded in agreement. By midmorning the voyageurs were well on the way. Through the daylight hours they feasted and played games of seven-up, poker, and euchre in their rough quarters. Kegs of wine were broached, and with it they washed down massive portions of salted venison, roasted beaver tail, and smoked salmon. They bet heavily on the games, and some of them began to turn ugly. As dusk settled over the stockade, the squaws they'd bargained for began to arrive. Beau started to tune up his cherished fiddle, and Lacroix took his battered guitar off the wall. The men raised their lusty voices in their paddling songs, and Louis Grand's marvelous tenor soared over all the rest.

"Behind our house we have a pond," they sang,

"En roulant ma boule!"

"Where three tame ducks swim round and round,

"Roulez, roulez, ma boule roulante."

Slumping on a bench in the store and gazing out into the dark square, Durran patiently waited. When he heard the burst of music and singing, he turned his head and nodded at Bobby, who was lounging behind the counter, the lights from the flickering fire striking splinters of light from his pince-nez. Bobby smiled. "Time?"

"Not quite, but they'll soon be dancing." Durran pulled himself to his feet. "If that leaping and cavorting can be called dancing. That's generally when the trouble starts. I'd better prepare."

"Better stick in lots of bandages, old chap."

Thumping his medicine bag on the counter, Durran rummaged through it. "Laudanum, camphorated spirits, flour for poultices." He closed the mouth of it and tied it with a rawhide strip. "Should give them all a dose of ipecacuam. That might take the edge off their high spirits."

Bobby's smile widened into a laugh. "They'll need the purge tomorrow."

In the quarters they were now dancing. Voyageurs leapt high into the air, clasping native women in their long arms. Beau and Lacroix sawed at their instruments, and the dance became even wilder. Armand singled out one of the women, hauled her into a corner, and threw her down. Tearing her buckskin skirt up, he fell over her body. The dancers paid no attention to the coupled figures. In the middle of the floor Chenette and Jourdin started to quarrel over the sloe-eyed Lorenawa. The little Shuswap was the prettiest girl there. With an oath, Chenette pulled his knife and went for the other man.

With a shrill giggle, Lapointe dropped his own woman. "Fight!"

The music trailed off, and Beau and Lacroix put down their instruments to join their comrades who were circling around the two fighters. The two crews cheered their own man on.

"Get him, *mon ami!*" Chenette's crew members bellowed.

"Cut him, Jourdin!" shouted the men from Armand's canoe.

The spectators jostled closer, and Louis Grand, shoved roughly by Lacroix, aimed a blow at the other man. Soon the crews from the two canoes were battling all over the big room. In the midst of the uproar Chenette and Jourdin fought on. Blood was running down Chenette's left cheek, and one of Jourdin's arms hung limply. In a corner most of the girls huddled around the heaving figures of Armand and his partner and watched wide-eyed.

From the direction of the door came a shouted Gaelic curse, and a gun blast roared over the heads of the struggling men. "Enough!" Durran shouted. He stood with his thick legs straddled, the leather bag dangling from one of his hands, the other grasping a smoking pistol.

As though by magic the men froze, the shouts died away, and they looked sheepishly at the enraged Scot.

"Let's have a look at the damage," Durran grunted. With one foot he kicked at Armand's form. "You hurt?" Then he saw the squaw's round face peering past the voyageur's shoulder, and he laughed. "Line up. First you, Chenette, then Jourdin. Never learn to keep knives out of it, will you?" He fingered Chenette's cheek. "Deep, lad— you'll carry a scar."

Durran sewed up Chenette's face and then the gash on Jourdin's arm. The two wounded men bore each other no ill will. After they were bandaged they collapsed on the floor, arms embracing, swearing oaths of undying friendship. Many of the voyageurs were only bruised and scraped, but Louis Grand of the silver voice had a broken arm. Under his matted hair, Osa had a lump on his skull the size of an orange. Gingerly, Durran poked at the swelling. "Might have cracked your skull, Osa. How do you feel?"

Osa's bearded lips spread in a wide smile. "Fine, M. Durran, Osa feel fine. Osa want drink."

"No more of that, lad."

Snarling, Armand kicked an empty keg. "It's gone anyway. Dirty pigs drank the last drop."

"Good!" Durran's eyes roamed around the room and settled on Beau, who was sitting forlornly on the floor, blood trickling down his brow, the shattered remains of his fiddle tenderly cradled on his lap. Durran tilted the boy's head back. "A few scratches on your scalp, but nothing serious. What happened to your fiddle?"

"Some *diable*, he hit me with her. I find which one, I kill him!"

"Sorry, lad. I can't mend fiddles, only men." Durran swung around to the cluster of native women. "Off you go, lassies. The party's all over."

A groan of protest greeted his words, but Armand was the only one to argue. "We hired them for the night. You're too highhanded. This is our affair!"

Durran wheeled and faced the other man, his hair flaming in the lamplight, his arms akimbo. He asked softly, "You have a yen to pick a fight with me?"

Armand looked around for support, but even his brother wouldn't look at him. He muttered and moved away.

Louis Grand, one arm cradled in a sling, tugged at the Scot's sleeve. "Can't we even have Lorenawa, M. Durran?"

Durran eyed the girl and told him good-naturedly, "I've

171

a hunch Lorenawa is the one who started this whole thing—not that you wouldn't have found some other excuse anyway." Tying up his bag, he lifted it. "Best get some rest, lads. I'll be by in the morning and give you all a big dose of ipecacuam." A chorus of groans erupted, and Durran paused at the door and grinned. "You've your traditions, and this is one of mine. See you at dawn."

Durran stood in the square for a moment. Snow, driven by a strong wind, swirled around him. He lifted his head and sniffed. Blizzard, he thought. The bad weather is about to begin. He started toward the steps of the store. As he passed Laurie's cabin, he glanced at the dark windows, pulled up his coat collar, and hurried on.

For days after the Christmas party Rowan didn't leave the cabin. She showed no further hurt or anger; in fact her expression was quiet and thoughtful. She cleaned the cabin, cooked excellent meals, and came obediently to Laurie's arms each night. But this passive creature was no longer the woman of gaiety and happiness whom he had enjoyed. Laurie shrugged and disregarded the change in his young wife's behavior. Women's moods, he thought—no doubt her pregnancy. In time she'll be back to normal.

Toward the middle of January, Laurie's prediction seemed to be accurate. The blizzards temporarily abated, and a pale sun beamed down on the fort. With the sunshine the cloud over Rowan also seemed to lift, and she was gay again, although her gaiety now had a hard, brittle edge. She persuaded Laurie that she should learn to handle a rifle, and he agreed it sounded like a good idea. Donning furs and snowshoes, they went out to the hills behind the fort. Laurie taught her how to load the gun, how to sight and fire it, and then he set up a target. He was amazed at her ability. After a few lessons she could load expertly, and her eye was good, her aim true.

"You're going to be as good a shot as I am," he told her proudly.

172

She smiled and kissed him, but she seemed somewhat abstracted. One day while Laurie was directing the long *traîneaux* of ice and wood the Indian workers were bringing into the fort, Rowan donned her rabbit-skin hood and coat and started down toward the lodges. She paused to watch the long sleighs with upturned ends, drawn by horses and dog teams, pass through the gateway. Laurie was riding on one, and he lifted a hand in salute. She waved back and then made her way through the snowdrifts down to the lodges. After a couple of hours of bartering she went home carrying a number of buckskin shirts, fringed and beaded, and a pair of leather leggings. From then on, even in the evening hours when she'd once worn skirts and shirtwaists, Rowan wore full native attire.

Old Tapinawa in his youth had been a mighty hunter. She bribed him to show her how to set up traplines for small game. The old man showed her how it was done, and he was as surprised as her husband had been at her speed and dexterity. From then on she was missing from the fort through most of the daylight hours, baiting the traps and retrieving the catch. Her skin, which had bleached through the winter months to its original white smoothness, became windburned and roughened.

Blizzards began again to swirl relentlessly through the valley, and they claimed three victims. A young squaw with a week-old papoose strapped to her back became lost in one storm, and the mother and child froze to death only yards from their own lodge. An elderly woman who was gathering firewood was caught in another storm, but her body wasn't found until the following spring.

Rowan would patiently wait until a storm abated, and then she would set forth, her rifle slung across her back and Charlie at her heels, to check her traps. Many of the men watched her leave the fort with worried eyes, and finally one of them spoke to Laurie.

He remonstrated with her. "The baby, Rowan—this isn't only dangerous for you but for the child."

She dropped a kiss on his brow. "Indians bear children

173

easily and become hardened to work. Don't worry, Laurie, I'm very careful."

She became overconfident. Toward the end of February she misjudged the weather and was almost a mile from the fort when the storm broke. She hung the two rabbits she'd trapped over her back with her rifle and with a mittened hand caught at the long hair on Charlie's back. "Take us home, boy," she told the dog. With unerring instinct he led her back to the fort.

As she staggered toward the gates, she thought she saw something dark wavering against the curtain of snow. Brushing snow from her face, she made out a man's figure. At first she thought it was Laurie, but as the man waded through the drifts toward her she recognized George Durran's powerful shoulders and jutting beard.

Catching her arm, he jerked her through the gateway. "You're plain daft. And I'm going daft worrying about you."

Her stiff lips tried to smile. "I bagged two rabbits."

"And for them you nearly paid with your life."

"I have to get home, George."

"You're coming with me. Time someone knocked some sense into you."

Outside the store he knelt and stripped off her snowshoes. Then he pulled her up the steps. Dutchy was baling furs, and he stopped to watch Durran lift the rifle and the small bloody carcasses from the girl's numb shoulders. Charlie followed as Durran, without a word to the clerk, led the way down the hall and flung open the door to his rooms. Rowan had never been in his quarters before, but all she saw was the fire blazing on the hearth. She headed directly toward it.

Stopping her, Durran pointed at one of the stools a good distance from the fireplace. "Sit there. Heat brings on chilblains. Let me check you over."

Meekly she did as he said. He knelt again, loosened the snow-packed leggings, and stripped both them and her high moccasins off her feet. Picking up a handful of snow that had fallen from their clothes, he rubbed her feet.

"You're lucky. Your feet aren't frozen. How are your hands? Wiggle your fingers." She wiggled her fingers, and he reached over and patted the dog, who had collapsed at her feet. "Good boy. You're the only reason this daft creature isn't frozen in some snowdrift."

She slumped on the stool while Durran put water on to boil. After a time he put a hot mug in her hands. She wrinkled her nose as the strong fumes drifted up.

"Hot toddy," he told her. "Rum and water. Get it down." Sinking onto the stool across the table from her, he asked bluntly, "Are you trying to kill yourself?"

"Usually I can judge the weather, but this storm came up so fast—"

"I asked you a question."

The hot rum was sending warmth through her body. Sitting up straighter, she met Durran's eyes. "No, I'm not trying to kill myself. I'm doing my work. Learning what is necessary for me to know."

"I've watched you, Rowan, and I know exactly what you're doing. Ever since that party you've been turning yourself into a native."

She shrugged, and her expression was hard. "That's what I am. Not allowed to sit or eat with the new masters of the land. So . . . I'm a squaw. And I'm learning how to be one."

"Then you're a failure. No squaw would go out to a trapline in this weather. This winter there's plenty of meat."

"Salted in kegs and reeking of brine. Smoked and hung until there's no flavor left."

"Still nourishing and capable of sustaining life. No, fresh meat is only an excuse. You're punishing your man and yourself and—" His eyes flicked over her buckskin shirt. "And the child you're carrying."

"How do you know about the child?" she whispered.

"I'm a spectator. I know many things. I know that Rowan is a fool."

Her eyes blazed. "If you're so wise, tell me what to do.

175

I'm neither white nor Indian. I've no place in either world. What do you suggest, spectator?"

"That you be yourself."

"Just what is that?"

"Someone wonderful, with a rich heritage from two ancient cultures. You're some of both. You don't have to be one or the other. Be Rowan and be proud. Teach your children pride because they'll inherit another heritage."

"Another heritage?"

"This land."

Her lips twisted. "A land being raped for profit, and when the profit is gone the white men will vanish. They'll hurry back to their own countries with their wealth."

"Not all of them." Turning sideways on his stool, he gazed across the room into the flames that leaped on the hearth. "Some of us will remain. True, the furs are being exhausted, but behind the fur traders will come settlers. Wagons will roll west, and this land will become a place of homesteads, in time of villages and towns."

Her eyes traced the lines of his profile—the sweep of bright hair, the bulging brow, and the high, arched nose. "What do you see for this land?"

"In time it will be one country," he said slowly, his brow furrowing. "It will be tamed, but its beauty, its mountain peaks and verdant valleys, will still delight the eye, win the heart. Men and women will die for this land, and they'll make it one—our Canada."

Like a small child she asked, "Will it be a great nation?"

"I don't know. It will be a blending pot of many different nationalities. In this fort we have a cross section. And these blood strains may wrench the young country into pieces."

"I don't understand."

He waved toward the bookshelves in the corner. "Neither do I, but I read and study and try to understand. I know this much. The Irish hate the English. The Scots despise both. The French-Canadians can't forget or accept their defeat on the Plains of Abraham, and hunger for *la belle France*. If we can't let go of the countries from whence we came, if we can't give total loyalty to this new land, then Canada is doomed."

"And the Indians?"

He sighed heavily. "In time they'll sit in judgment on all of us and probably find us guilty. And they may be right. But the old countries across the sea grow tired and full of people who would find a new home. This land is large and empty and must shelter all of us, including the native peoples." He swung around to face her. "This is only a guess, and the future is uncertain. We'll quite possibly live to see little of it, but teach your children so they may teach theirs. Teach them to have pride in all their bloodlines but to temper that pride with love of country."

The hardness and anger were gone from her features. There was wistfulness in the lines of her face, touching her mouth. She stared at the rows of books. "May I borrow some books?"

"Any time you wish."

Pulling on her boots, she laced up her leggings and walked toward the door. Charlie grunted and got up to follow her. She turned, her hand resting lightly on the dog's big head. "Thank you, George. I'll try to learn."

"Be at peace, lass."

As she walked home she felt at peace. When Laurie came in for supper he found rabbit meat bubbling in the stewpot, the black dog curled up on the hearthrug, and Rowan waiting. She wore a long, ruffled gingham gown, and her hair was piled high on her head.

His face glowing with pleasure, he took her in his arms. "I like that dress. I wish you'd wear it more often."

"I will. From now on my buckskins will only be worn for outside work." She buried her face against his shoulder, and her voice was muffled. "No longer will I punish you or myself for something neither of us can change."

He hugged her to him. Under her breath she added, What is going to be must be, but for now we'll have peace.

17

Toward the end of March the wind shifted, and there was a different feeling in the air. Snow didn't drift down as often, the sun peeked through gray cloud layers occasionally, and the winter-weary people of Fort Purline smiled at each other and nodded wisely.

One afternoon, as Rowan trudged across crusted snow to the lodges, she met Marinska, her arms piled high with bundles, coming from the settlement. Rowan stopped to speak to the other woman. A type of rapport had grown up between them; both were pregnant, and that was a common bond, but there was another one which neither woman ever put into words.

"Hello, Marinska, how are you?" Rowan asked.

"Good, Marinska good." She shifted her burden. "Getting hides and wood to make papoose board. When your baby come?"

"I'm not certain, but I think around the middle of September. What about yours?"

"Many moons." Setting down the bundles, she held up one hand and spread the fingers wide. "I think this many. *Neesitui.*"

Rowan had no need to count the fingers. She'd spent her idle hours at the lodges learning various Indian languages, and she had become quite fluent in many of them. Laurie didn't object. In fact he was glad to see her learn, as he'd never made the effort himself. Most of the natives he dealt with could speak broken English, and now when he had difficulty his wife could translate. "Five months,"

Rowan said. "We come due about the same time, Marinska."

Pulling aside her hide coat, Marinska rubbed her swollen belly. "Marinska too big for one. Maybe more." She peered at the girl's full fur wrap. "You big too?"

Rowan smiled. "Not very. I think I'll be having only one. I was wondering—Martha MacLeod is coming over to help me sew baby clothes. Would you like to join us?"

The woman's broad face beamed. "Marinska like that. You tell me when." She added proudly, "Pieter, he bring much cloth for baby. I sew with you."

So a little sewing circle was arranged. One afternoon a week, Martha and Marinska would arrive at Rowan's cabin, and they would sew, chat, and sip tea muskey. Once Rowan was surprised when Nell Purline came with Martha. She brought a batch of clean, neatly mended baby clothes. "These were Dorrie's," Nell told Rowan. "I thought they might come in handy."

Rowan was delighted, not so much with the gift as with Nell's presence that afternoon. The four women laughed and talked; Nell's pinched face eased, and she smiled frequently. Later, Rowan questioned Martha.

"I thought her husband had forbidden her to come to my cabin," she told the older woman.

"General Purline was away that day, lass, visiting the *bourgeois* at the Nor'westers' fort."

"But aren't the two companies deadly enemies?"

"That they are, but the two factors occasionally extend invitations to dine to each other. No matter what the quarrel is, they'll come to each other's aid in time of famine or sickness." Martha smiled at the girl's puzzled expression. "We are only two tiny groups in this—" She flung out her arm as though to encompass the wilderness surrounding them.

By April the shift in the wind was more pronounced, and it blew almost steadily from the south. The sky cleared and the sun beamed down. Snow started to melt into puddles, the jagged teeth of icicles began to drip steadily, and one night there was a grinding roar from the direction of the river. Wrenched from sleep by the noise, Rowan shook her husband's shoulder. "Listen," she told him.

Pushing himself up on his elbow, he listened. "Breakup time. Have a look in the morning. Winter is over, and spring comes fast in this country."

The next day she went down to the riverbank and saw that *breakup* was an apt term. The solid sheet of ice had splintered, and ice floes were bobbing downstream. Between the blocks, water danced and bubbled madly. Soon the bales of winter furs were packed into canoes, and flotillas left the fort and turned eastward. The snow melted rapidly, and streams flowed down into the valley, down into the creek and river, rushing in a swollen torrent to the sea. The trees budded and broke into full foliage, and the sky deepened its blue-gray into a darker hue.

With full spring, work at the fort picked up tempo. Most of the voyageurs had left with the flotillas, but the men left behind labored through the waning spring and the hot, dry summer that followed. Hordes of blackflies plagued the horses, dogs, and humans, and at times smudge fires blanketed the fort to keep away both the flies and the relentless clouds of mosquitoes.

Rowan continued to thrive on the life. She worked with Martha digging roots, setting out nets and drying the fish she caught, hauling water from the creek, searching the woods for berries. Most of the time she wore buckskins, and her face and arms tanned, but she kept her promise to Laurie. In the evenings when he came home she was always trimly dressed in the thin cotton dresses she stitched herself. Laurie was driving himself as hard as the men, but he worried about Rowan. One August evening as they sat on the doorstep of their cabin trying to escape the heat, he mentioned his concern to her.

Glancing at her stomach, now prominent under the crisp white-and-red gingham, he lectured her. "You mustn't work so hard. It can't be good for you."

"What about you? You're skin and bones from the work you're doing."

"I'm not about to bear a child." He slapped at a mosquito on his bare forearm.

Turning her head, she smiled at him. "You should see Marinska. She's huge and still is working harder than most of the men."

"Marinska has never known anything but hard work." He scratched his arm. "In England as soon as a woman is with child, she does little work—"

"She sits on a silk cushion and has servants wait on her." Her smile broadened. "You're thinking of wealthy women who can afford to be pampered. What about the poor women in the slums?"

"I know nothing about them," he confessed.

She stared up at the sunset, a sky magnificent with shades of gold and crimson and violet. "Women aren't made of silk and glass, Laurie. Actually, they're strong. In some ways they're stronger than men. This country isn't for the weak—they die quickly. Only the strong can survive."

"You've been reading more of George's books," he accused.

"I have. But I didn't get that information from a book."

As he mentioned Durran's name, Laurie felt a small twinge of jealousy. It wasn't only the man's books he resented, it was the number of times he'd seen his wife and the Scot in conversation at the store or in the square. What do they find to talk about? he wondered.

The thought of George Durran drove the rest of the conversation from his mind. But later he remembered some of Rowan's words. The weak die quickly, she had said. Anxiety gnawed at him. How strong was Rowan? Was it only willpower and pride that drove her on? What if she'd weakened herself by working so hard? What if he lost her?

"God's teeth!" he muttered. Without consulting his wife, he brought Little Moccasins to do the work. Rowan protested, but to no avail. This time Laurie was firm.

On the second day of September, Marinska went into

181

labor, and with Martha MacLeod as midwife, she brought forth twins. "See," Rowan triumphantly told her husband, "she had no trouble at all. Martha said it was an easy birth, and Marinska's older than me, and it was her first birth."

"It's not the same."

"A baby is a baby. Come and see them."

They went to Dutchy's cabin and brought with them gifts of tiny nightgowns that Rowan had made. Dutchy welcomed them exuberantly. A much different man, Laurie mused, from the one he had been before Marinska. Dutchy's face had filled out, and his expression was cheerful. Often as he worked in the store he would hum or sing a song.

"Welcome," Dutchy cried. "A drink of wine you must take. A toast to my son and daughter!"

Pressing wine upon them, he led them to the big bed behind crisp curtains where his wife waited. Marinska was propped up on pillows, and in the crook of each arm she cradled a baby.

"My son," Dutchy said, pointing at one child. "My daughter. We've called the boy Pieter and the girl for her mother. She is Mary. Healthy babes both, with straight limbs and strong backs."

"They're beautiful," Rowan told the parents. "Aren't they beautiful, Laurie?"

"Lovely," he agreed, but revulsion stabbed at his breast. He gazed down at them. Both babies had dusky skins, coarse black hair, and black eyes. Silently he asked himself, Will my child look like these? Will I have a black-eyed child with black hair, a son with a crooked little finger on a dark-skinned hand? The Woodbyne finger. God's teeth, he gasped silently, let it be a girl child!

Immediately he felt ashamed of himself and made a great fuss over the children while Dutchy beamed proudly and Marinska looked contented. But now his concern about the appearance of his own expected child banished the anxiety about Rowan's health from his mind. By mid-September he found he was becoming short-tempered, easily irritated. Will it never be over? he wondered. Will this suspense never be done with?

Early on the evening of the fifteenth of September, 1817, Rowan went into labor. Laurie sent Little Moccasins on a dead run for Martha, and then he rushed around the cabin pouring water into pots, building up the fire. When Little Moccasins brought Martha they found him bending over the bed, his face beaded with sweat, staring down at his wife.

Martha gave a hearty laugh. "It's the lass giving birth, not ye. Get ye gone to Mr. Durran. He's waiting to console ye till your babe is born."

"You'll need me here," Laurie babbled.

"Come now, Mr. Woodbyne. There's Little Moccasins and me, and Nell Purline will be with us soon. Would ye get in the way and hinder us?"

"Nell?" He drew Martha away from the bed. "Her husband will never let her come."

"This time he won't stop her," she said grimly. "Now, must I push ye from your own house?"

Taking another look at Rowan's face, he left. In the square he looked up at a full moon breasting a black velvet sky. Boy or girl, he prayed, let Rowan be all right. And let Nell come. His brow wrinkled. But she won't. I'll wager that old devil stops her.

The bet he made with himself was lost. At that moment Nell was preparing to leave her cabin. She was packing a basket in the kitchen, and as she reached for her shawl the door to the office opened and her husband entered. He glanced around the kitchen. "Is my supper not prepared?" he asked.

"Marinska will be here directly to make it. Dutchy is looking after their babies, and Marinska will look after Dorrie until I return."

"Where do you think you're going?"

She pulled her shawl around her thin shoulders. "Rowan has gone into labor."

"Do you think I'll allow my wife to pull from that wanton's body the seed of her profane lust?"

183

She stepped away from him. "I'm going to her."

His lips thinned. "Send Martha to her."

"Martha has already gone. But Rowan is young and very much alone. This is her first birth."

"I forbid it!"

"This time I'll not obey!"

He raised a clenched fist. "For all the years of our union I've tried to drive the devil from you, woman, to make you pure as my mother is pure. But you are still evil, still the Eve who for lust tempted Adam and drove him into exile."

"Evil or not, I'm still a *woman*, and another woman needs me." Picking up the basket, she started toward the door.

He was there before her, barring the way. "I can stop you."

"Out of the way! To stop me you'd have to kill me quickly. You wouldn't want that, would you? You prefer slow deaths."

At the contempt in her voice, his beautiful eyes dropped and he moved aside. She opened the door and stepped out. She didn't close it behind her. Kicking it shut, he raised his fist. "Kill you I will! In my own time, in my own way. Going to that heated slut. Helping her bear a sinful bastard by Woodbyne. In my own time—you, and her, and maybe Woodbyne too."

In Durran's room, Laurie was pacing the floor. The Scot, sitting comfortably in one of the hide chairs, watched the other man. "Sit down," Durran drawled. "You're acting as though you're the one having birth pangs."

Laurie glared down at him. "It's easy enough for you to talk. Anyway, why aren't you over there helping out?"

"Martha is there, and she's a good midwife. The women at the lodges always call for her if there's a difficult birthing. There's Little Moccasins too, and many a babe she's delivered. Strange—that lass hates men but loves children. An odd woman, Little Moccasins."

"Nell Purline is supposed to come too."

"I know."

"How?"

"She told me."

Laurie's eyes narrowed. "All the women confide in you, don't they?"

"Some."

"Even Rowan. I've seen you with your heads together."

Pulling himself from his chair, Durran reached for a bottle and a couple of mugs. "We speak of books and ideas. Is that wrong? Come have a nip of brandy, lad, and sit you down."

"I'm sorry, George." Sitting down, Laurie accepted a mug. "It's just that I've been going through hell. Rowan's worked so hard, maybe she's strained herself. Maybe . . ."

Without pouring brandy for himself, Durran set the bottle down on the floor at his feet. He leaned back and regarded Laurie's fine face, the dark arched brows drawn in a frown. "Rowan will be fine, and so will the babe."

"You're very cool," Laurie said, and immediately knew he'd heard those words before. Ah yes, the exact words that Charlie Hatch had muttered while they'd waited for Esmie to give birth.

It appeared that Durran could read his mind. "Laurie," he said slowly, "you have a son. Did you fret as much that time?"

"It was different that time. Esmie had swarms of nurses and the best doctor in London."

"And you didn't care as much for her as you do for Rowan?"

"I didn't care for her at all." In a burst of honesty, he confessed, "I only took her for her father's wealth, and even then I made a bad bargain." Draining his mug, he held it out to Durran.

The Scot shook his head. "Careful, take the drink slowly. By the time Martha arrives to tell you that you have a son—"

185

"Son?"

"Aye, a son. Rowan will bear you two sons."

Laurie squinted at the other man. "Have you been nipping at the brandy?"

"Nay, not a drop have I had. I seldom touch it."

Laurie felt his head nodding in agreement. Except when one of the Scot's rare fey moods was upon him, he'd never seen Durran take a drink. "*Two* sons? Your granny told you?"

Durran nodded his red head. Laurie thought, We're all mad. These lonely posts drive men mad. Dutchy is obsessed with his native wife and dark-skinned children, Bobby with his craving for sex, Ezra with his hatred of evil women and his ravings from the Bible, and now George Durran and his ruddy old granny. And I'm mad myself. I have to be. Here I am working myself into a frenzy about a native girl I took to satisfy my physical needs, a girl I don't even want children by.

The next minute he was on his feet, pacing the room. You need Rowan, he admitted, you need her body and her company. Without her you *would* go mad.

For two hours he paced while Durran silently watched him. Once Laurie swung around and said, "Let's have a drink. Why don't you join me?"

"We both need sober heads. Would you stagger in there drunk? As for me, if called I must go."

"Than you do believe there's trouble. Go check, George; have a look."

"Don't fash yourself. Martha's sensible. If there's cause, she'll call."

At last the ordeal was over. The door swung open, and Martha's ruddy face and wide smile sent relief through Laurie. "How is she?" he cried.

"She's fine and so is your babe. Go meet your son."

Laurie's eyes flew to Durran, and the Scot was smiling too. "My compliments to your granny, George, but no doubt it was a lucky guess. After all, there's only two choices." Squeezing Martha's thick arm, Laurie headed down the hall at a run.

186

She grinned at Durran. "The first one's hardest on fathers. I'll give them a few minutes, and then I'll get back. I sent Little Moccasins to her lodge and Nell home. The lass was exhausted."

He scanned her face. "Will she be all right . . . Nell, I mean?"

"He won't hit her; that's not his way. And it can't be harder on her than it ever has been."

"She should have left him years ago. She should never have come here with him. The man is unstable."

Martha gave him a bleak look. "Aye, that he is. Many's the time I've argued with Nell—in England and in India before that—but leave him she won't. He has her half convinced that she is evil, that she's the sole cause of his disgrace. So . . . she's bound to him and I'm bound to her."

"You're spending your life trying to shield her, Martha."

"Waiting, always waiting for that union to be dissolved. I can't leave Nell, and I can't abandon little Dorrie." She gave him a shrewd look. "But ye know about waiting. Perhaps both our destinies are to wait." She became brisk. "I must be getting back now. Rowan didn't have a long birthing, but the lass is weary and must have her rest. Good night, Mr. Durran."

The door closed softly behind her, and he sat on by the cold ashes of the hearth. He wondered whether to build a fire and decided against it. He was too tired; soon he would seek his bed. He thought of Martha's words—both of them waiting. Aye, he said to himself, many years I've been waiting. Since the night his grandmother had died, he'd waited.

Granny Macdonald hadn't been his grandmother; actually she was his great-grandmother. He thought of her as immortal and never had been able to picture her death. When the women caring for her called him into that humble cottage under the shadow of Ben Venue, he stood

187

above her bed, looking down at her face. In the candle-light he fancied he looked not upon a face, but upon a skull. Only her eyes showed life, and they were still bright and black and shrewd. Sending the women from the room, he knelt on the cold flagstones, his hands gathering hers into their hard young warmth. Her fingers pressed his, and he was surprised at the strength that still lingered in the twisted, dry bones of those withered hands.

At fifteen George Durran had the frame of a man, heavy-boned and wide, but the large bones carried little flesh. From the time he could remember, they'd never had enough food. Gruel and oatmeal mush was their staple diet, sometimes supplemented with an egg, and occasionally, on grand occasions, a chunk of stringy mutton. He was thin but strong and had often begged his granny to allow him to take a job as shepherd boy. She always refused. "Take your schooling, laddie," she'd tell him. "Or as good as ye can get in the village. Learn to read and write and do sums. I'll make our living."

Somehow the old woman had made it. Although the simple people of the district called her witch, they did so with respect and awe and admiration. Granny Macdonald was called in to nurse them in times of sickness, to birth babies, and to doctor sheep and cattle. She mixed medicines for them and read their futures. They were poor people, wrenching a miserable living from stony soil and barren hills, but they repaid as well as they could with copper coins, bags of oatmeal, a few eggs, and pieces of meat. Some nights other women would slip up the hill and into granny's cottage. These women were well dressed and came from towns and cities to see Granny Macdonald. When they appeared, the old woman would banish young George to the loft, and there he'd have to stay until they left.

Holding his grandmother's work-twisted hands, George felt tears brimming from his eyes, trickling down his thin cheeks. Her bright eyes flickered over his wet face. "Nay, George, ye be a man now. Tears aren't for men."

"You're all I have. There's no one else."

"There are cousins, but they be in other parts and know ye not. Aye, ye're alone. Your father, your mother . . . all the bairns dead, and I couldna save them. Only the youngest, my wee Georgie, could I save. But my life is spent. I sicken and would be free of suffering."

He buried his face in the quilts. "What will I do?"

Her hand feebly patted his head. "I'll tell ye. But don't speak, for time is short. Under this mattress ye'll find a little bag stuffed with silver—"

"Silver!" His head jerked up.

"Hush, do ye ken? Silver I have saved against this day. Ladies brought the coins, fine ladies in coaches with matched horses and clothes of silk. By night they came seeking potions to make men love them, and sometimes potions to rid themselves of the unwanted products of that love. Some came to have fortunes cast, but all paid in silver. The coins I hoarded and didna spend them on cream and meat and warm clothes."

"What will I do?" he repeated.

"Ye'll take the silver and go to Glasgow. There ye'll buy for five pounds an apprenticeship in the fur company. They look for strong young men to send to the colonies upon their business. There be enough to take ye to the city and to pay the price to these men."

The boy stared into her bright eyes. "I will be a fur trader in that far land across the sea?"

"Aye." Dry lids dropped over her eyes. "It's all I can do for ye."

"Granny," he whispered, and his voice was hesitant, "you've never foretold my future, and yet for others you did it freely."

"The others were not my kin. It's a dangerous thing to do, laddie, to part the veil and look through. The visions do not lie, but they can deceive if not read correctly. I couldna bear to do it lest I break my heart if I saw ill for ye."

The boy leaned forward eagerly. "Will you do it now, to give me what comfort you may?"

Her eyes opened. Then her head jerked. "If it be your

189

wish. Take my hand and sit quietly. Say nothing till I speak to ye."

Sitting as though he'd been turned to stone, he waited, clasping her hand. Her face was turned up to the ceiling, and a glaze seemed to dull her eyes. She was as still as the boy was, and her face looked even more like a skull. She's dead, he thought; her life has seeped away and she is gone. But he was bound by her command and didn't move. He was oppressed by the cold stale air of the room, the smell of sickness, the hunger pangs gnawing at his stomach. He was miserable and alone. Then a cracked voice came from her lips. It didn't sound like her voice.

"I see a land of wild beauty and of snow and ice and hardships. I see you prospering. You will rise in rank, and you will hoard your wages. I see you among log buildings with mountains rearing around you. There are people with dark skins and strange clothing. I see a woman, and she will bring you wealth." Her eyes blinked and turned toward the boy, and they were the eyes he knew. "Your lips are quivering with questions. Ask them, Georgie." And it was the voice he knew.

He pictured food that wealth could bring—rare roast beef, smoking puddings, strong ale—and his mouth watered. "Wealth?"

She smiled. "All wealth is not gold. That ye will learn."

"This woman will be mine?"

"I don't know."

His brows knitted, and he rubbed at his unruly mane of hair. "How will I know her?"

"She has hair black as midnight and skin like skimmed milk. Her eyes are blue, as blue as the loch when twilight shines across its waters. Her eyes will be strange, like no eyes ye've ever seen."

"Can you tell me more?"

"Ye'll love her, Georgie, but she'll belong to another man—for a time. Two sons she'll bear him, two tall lads."

"How will she bring me wealth?"

"I canna say. There will be two paths. If one is taken, she'll be yours. The other . . . never will ye claim her."

Her voice became strangely urgent. "Ye must never interfere. Ye must wait and let fate decide." Pain flashed across her features. "I must tell ye all. I saw terrible things. I saw a night of fire and murder and blood dripping. I couldna see past that." Her eyes closed. "There is no more."

The boy waited, but his grandmother didn't speak again. Toward dawn, while he still clasped her hand, he felt the last vestige of warmth seep from that hand, and he knew she was gone. Kneeling by the bed, he prayed for her and for himself. Then he kissed her cold brow.

In his room in that fort his grandmother had seen years before, an older George Durran remembered other forts. There had been one on the shore of James Bay and two on the wide, grassy sweeps of the prairie land. Then there had been Fort Purline.

Through earlier years, driven by the hungers of a strong young body, he'd taken women when he was forced to, as Bobby Holden did now. But always he'd waited for the woman his grandmother had seen. At Fort Purline she finally had come. Durran had recognized Rowan Malone immediately. When those oddly set eyes had opened, they'd looked past him to the face of the young man with thick silver-gilt hair. Woodbyne, shallow and selfish and self-seeking, had claimed her.

Pulling himself stiffly to his feet, Durran stared at the bagpipe hanging over the chest. Tonight? he wondered. Then he thought, no. Rowan had come, she'd mated with Woodbyne. Now she'd borne him a son. Another son would have to be born. He stretched his cramped limbs and went to bed.

He would continue to wait.

Laurie, after leaving Durran's quarters, raced across the square to his own cabin. As the door creaked open he could see Rowan, curled in a clean fresh bed, cradling a blanket-wrapped bundle in her arms. Looking up, she smiled radiantly at him. Her long hair flowed across the pillow, and her face was wan, with violet smudges shadowing her eyes. Never had she looked more beautiful to him. He bent over her and tenderly touched his lips to her brow.

She pulled back a corner of the blanket. "Your son, Laurie."

The baby was red and wrinkled, and little fists waved over the blanket. The tiny skull was thickly covered with black hair. Laurie bent closer. "His eyes look blue, Rowan."

"Dark blue. But Martha says they will darken. They'll probably be like yours—brown."

Or black, he said under his breath. Rowan took a little fist and gently spread the curling fingers out. "His left hand. The little finger is crooked like yours. Do you have a name for him?" Mutely, Laurie shook his head, and she continued. "Would you like to give him a family name? Perhaps Laurence, or your brother's?"

"No. I don't believe in sons having their father's given names. Too confusing. And I don't want my son called Ashbury." He asked quickly, "Why don't we name him after your father?"

"Eamon Seamus?"

"It has a good ring. We could call him Seamus."

"Seamus," she repeated, and nuzzled the black hair with her lips. "Are you pleased with him?"

"Delighted," he said heartily. "He's a sturdy little fellow."

To his relief the door creaked open and Martha entered the cabin. She beamed at them. "Ye've a bonny lad there, Mr. Woodbyne. He's a long one. Grow into a tall man."

"Yes, I think he will," Laurie said. "We're naming him Seamus."

The older woman nodded. "I'll stay the night, and perhaps tomorrow night too. Little Moccasins will be in to help during the daytime. Ye'd better bed with Mr. Durran a couple of nights."

Kissing Rowan again, Laurie poked a long finger gently at the baby and said good night. Rowan was exhausted, but sleep for a time evaded her. She heard Martha banking the fire and then the creak of the other bedstead as the older woman lowered her bulk onto the thin mattress. The cabin grew darker with only glimmers of light from the fire. Cradling her child, Rowan looked down into his face. Seamus, she thought, and you'll have dusky skin to go with your black hair and dark eyes. I love you, Seamus, but will your father? If your hair was fair and your eyes pale blue, would he have given you his name? And what is your name? Eamon Seamus . . . what? Malone is not really mine; I too have no name. Woodbyne is for neither of us, and yet you bear the Woodbyne finger.

Her eyelids drooped. I know so little, she thought wearily, so little. All I know is that I'm in love with the man I took from necessity. Not just his fine body, the beauty of his face, his lovemaking. I love Laurie. As for Laurie, not once in all these months has he said that he loves me. But now I have Seamus, and if necessary I'll love him enough for two.

From the direction of the other bed a prolonged snore rasped. Rowan smiled. She was still smiling when she fell asleep.

18

In 1822 violence was tracing bloody fingers across Europe. Civil war erupted in northern Spain, and royalist and liberal forces clashed. Chios's entire population of over thirty thousand Greeks were massacred by their Turkish enemies. While soldiers fought and died, French novelist Charles Nodier engaged in a different type of struggle and wrote his greatest work, *Trilby*. Across the English Channel Nash started construction on All Souls Church, and in the same year the Royal Academy of Music was founded. In Hetton, County Durham, the first British locomotive used for haulage chugged out of the station. That year the world received an immortal gift—Schubert's *Unfinished* Symphony.

The outside world and its events had no impact on the little settlement of Fort Purline, far west of the Shining Mountains. Life continued in its ordered fashion, the seasons changing and bringing with them their own quota of work and hardship. News filtered through to the fort once a year, brought by canoe and dogsled express from Montreal. By the time the rawhide pouches arrived—and they frequently had to be thawed before their contents could be extracted—the news was sometimes years old. Even so, copies of the London *Times* and the Montreal *Gazette* were eagerly read and reread, letters were worn to ribbons by handling, and there were barely enough Bibles, prayer books, and books of homilies to go around.

Rowan had learned to dread the annual arrival of the mail pouches. With the mail Laurie would go dark and sullen and sometimes would brood for days. He received no personal letters from Charlie Hatch. Any message intended for him was relayed through the factor and consisted of business details. Ashbury wrote duty letters that were like the man himself—stiff, dull, and mainly concerned with renovations on the house in Essex and the estate he was gradually enlarging. The letters from Judith Hatch were the ones that sent Laurie into the depths of depression, and yet her letters were the brightest, the cheeriest, the most informative. She gave him tidings of his friends and relatives, of events in London, and detailed accounts of his son's day-to-day life. Often she would slip in small pen-and-ink sketches of Chris. Laurie was able to keep pace with his son's growth from babe to toddler and then to young boy. For hours Laurie would sit at his desk, chin in hand, a sketch of his son propped up before him, his eyes hungrily scanning Judith's letters.

Rowan watched her husband with compassion and never intruded upon him during those dark days. Mixed with the compassion was another emotion, and this one she fought. As the years passed she found resentment growing for the little English boy so many thousands of miles away. She wasn't jealous of Laurie's love for his son, but for his second child, for Seamus, he had never shown any love at all. He wasn't hard on the boy, but he treated Seamus with an impersonal, detached kindness that he might have shown to any child at the fort. Seamus was devoted to his father, and from the time he could crawl he begged for attention. The child would pull himself up against his father's knees, his large black eyes fixed on Laurie's face, and would hold up chubby arms. Laurie always set the boy on his knee, but he never fondled him, never talked to him or even kissed his cheek.

The contrast between Dutchy van Zzll and his pride and love for his children and her own husband's indifference irked and then pained Rowan. Marinska and Dutchy had four children. The year following the birth of the twins, Pieter and Mary, Marinska presented her husband with a son whom Dutchy named for George Durran. Rowan was the godmother of their youngest child, her own namesake, an infant called Rowan Two.

195

The march of years at Fort Purline brought with it its share of comedy and tragedy. Bobby Holden continued his mad pursuit of Little Moccasins and twice was knifed by the enraged woman, once lightly but the second time seriously. George Durran examined the deep wound in Bobby's narrow chest and shook his head glumly. "Bad! I can't tell whether she hit your lung or not, Bobby. Won't you give up this mad chase?"

A grin creased the boy's pain-wracked face. "I'll live. Holdens are hard to kill. As soon as I'm fit again I'll woo the girl. Have to—she's my one failure. And somewhere under that cold exterior I know she has a yen for me. Stitch me up, that's a good chap."

Bobby was right. He was tough, and eventually he was able to resume his wooing of Little Moccasins. Strangely enough, although she continued to spurn him, never again did she use her knife on him.

Shortly after Bobby was laid low from love, tragedy struck the fort. Lacroix, traveling alone through the forest to check on the hunters, was attacked by a starving cougar. Lacroix fought the animal and managed to drive his knife through its throat, but in the struggle he was badly mauled. Somehow he dragged himself back to the fort, where Durran used all his healing skill on the wounded voyageur. Despite the precautions Durran took, the man's legs became infected, gangrene set in, and both legs had to be amputated at the knee. In the light of smoky oil lamps Lacroix was stretched on a table, filled with rum and high wine, and while four of his friends held him down, Durran sawed off the limbs. Knowing the future that faced a legless voyageur, Durran found himself hoping the man would die. But Lacroix, like Bobby Holden, proved tough and survived.

In the spring, plans were made to send Lacroix back to Montreal. The night before the brigade of canoes was due to leave, Lacroix appealed to his comrades. "Would you have me returned to Montreal to beg and starve upon the streets, *mes amis?*" he asked them. "Do you want me to crawl on stumps where once I had strong legs? Go down to the lodges, find an old squaw, and get from her what is necessary. Be men and let me die like one."

The voyageurs, their faces grim, turned away from Lacroix's bed. They drew lots, and Chenette and Portelance went to the lodges. In the morning Lacroix wasn't carried down to the canoes and sent east. He had died during the night. When Durran examined him, he looked long into the man's peaceful face before he pulled a blanket over it. He guessed what had been done, but all he said was, "His heart gave out. No doubt from the strain put upon it from the amputation." All the voyageurs crossed themselves, and no further questions were asked.

In the winter of 1819–20, famine stalked the fort. Game had been scarce that year, and the amount of fowl and venison brought in to be smoked and dried wasn't enough to last through the long winter months. Holes were cut into the thick ice that sheathed the Nechako and the creek, and the voyageurs and many of the Indian workers huddled over them for hours at a time, waiting for a tug on their lines. Many people went out of the fort to risk their lives setting up traplines in the forest. Rowan, warmly bundled in furs and accompanied by Charlie and either Beau or Portelance, set up her own trapline. She proved to be more skillful or luckier than many of the others and was able to bring back a fair amount of small game. She was heavy with child again, and this time her health suffered. Her body grew gaunt, and her face thinned until the bones were sharp and prominent and her eyes looked huge.

Laurie was occupied with his work and didn't appear to worry about her. If he did, he perhaps overestimated her strength and endurance. Durran worried, but this time he made no effort to stop her. Beau and Portelance were responsible men, and they would see she came safely back. Anyway, facing starvation as they all did allowed no reasonable basis for argument. There was no sense in Durran urging her to send Laurie, as he knew nothing about trapping. So the Scot waited and worried.

Toward the end of February the hunters tracked a herd of deer, driven down from the high country by wolves, and closed in on it. They returned to the fort with long *traîneaux* piled high with bloody carcasses. Jubilation broke out upon their arrival. Haunches of fresh venison sputtered and roasted on spits, savory smells of rich stew filled all the cabins, and the people of the fort feasted and gorged themselves to satiety. Durran took a heart and a liver to Rowan.

"These are the most nourishing of all the meat on a deer," he told her. "Mind you eat them yourself. Laurie and Seamus will do well enough with the other meat."

Seamus was tugging at the man's pants. At not quite three he was a sturdy boy, tall for his age and darkly handsome. Durran swung the child up. The boy's arms crept around the man's thick neck, and he laughed up into the Scot's bearded face. "A wee man you are, young Seamus," Durran said. The boy laughed with delight in the male strength of the arms holding him, in the deep voice.

Watching them, Rowan felt a pang. Seamus was gradually transferring his love for his father to Durran. She told Durran abruptly, "I'll eat the heart and liver myself."

Swinging the boy around wildly, Durran put him down. "Mind you do. We must look after Seamus's little brother."

"It's to be a boy, then?"

"Aye, a boy."

They both smiled, and the boy crowed with laughter. With the plentiful supply of meat the specter of death receded, and as time passed, Rowan's face filled out a trifle. On March 24, 1820, she went into labor an hour before dawn. This time the birth was a difficult one, and both Nell and Martha were deeply worried. Again Laurie waited in Durran's rooms, but this time it was the Scot who paced and Laurie who sat before the fire. Laurie watched the other man striding up and down the narrow confines of the room, pulling at his beard, and stopping occasionally to spill more brandy into his mug.

"What makes you so restless?" he finally asked Durran.

"The winter was hard on the lass."

Laurie stretched long legs toward the warmth of the fire. "It was hard on all of us, but Rowan is sturdy. She hasn't been sick a day in years."

Durran whirled on him. "Have you no eyes, man? Can't you see how thin she is, how the bones in her skull stick from her wee face?"

A burning log fell sideways and rolled onto the stones at Laurie's feet. Gingerly he took the poker and shoved it back. "You forget she had no trouble with Seamus, and the first birth is the hardest."

Durran snarled a curse and resumed his pacing. "With Seamus she was well fed and rested."

Laurie shrugged. The Scot, he thought, was getting to be like an old woman. But Rowan . . . was Durran too interested in her? He shrugged again. Nothing to worry about there. Rowan was devoted to him.

The hours dragged past, and Durran made no effort to prepare a meal. Toward the supper hour, Laurie rose and made tea and rough sandwiches of corn bread and cold venison. He offered some to Durran, but he shook his red head and continued pacing and drinking. It was close to eight when the door opened and Martha appeared. She leaned against the doorjamb, and her face was drawn and gray.

In two strides, Durran was at her side. "How is she?"

"She's safe, but it was a bad birth."

"The child?"

She looked past him to Laurie. "Ye have another son, Mr. Woodbyne."

As Laurie went past them, he grinned and clapped the Scot on his heavy shoulder. "I told you not to worry! And your old granny's right again."

Durran glared after him. "Daft!"

Martha nudged the door shut. "Aye, he thinks she's made of iron. He'll never know what the lass went through. For a while I thought we'd lose them both."

His expression softened as he looked down at her. "Worn out you are, and what a fine midwife you make.

You must have a drop with me; it will give you strength."

"Many a drop ye've had this day, Mr. Durran, but aye, I'll take a drop with ye."

Pouring generous amounts into two mugs, he handed her one and lifted the other. *"Slainte mhath!"*

"Down the hatch," she echoed, and drained her mug.

"Will you take another, Martha?"

"Nay, I must be getting back." Pausing at the door, she watched him lift down his bagpipe. "Ye'll promenade this night?"

"I'll stride the ramparts and make such music as will melt your heart."

"Ye'll keep Rowan awake with the swirls of your pipe."

Laughing, he pulled from the chest the tartan of the Durrans. "I'll make music to lull the lass into happy dreams."

She didn't argue. No one could sway The Durran in this mood.

When she got to Laurie's cabin she found him beside the bed, worriedly looking down at Rowan's face. "She's asleep," he whispered.

"I gave her laudanum to make her sleep."

"Her face—George was right. She looks like death."

"Death is behind her. We fought him off. In time she'll be healthy and strong. Have ye looked at your new son?"

When he shook his head she led him to the cradle and pulled back the blanket. "Rowan has called him Martin Petrie, for the priest who brought her west."

"Martin," he murmured, and bent over the cradle, his fascinated eyes devouring his son's face.

This boy was smaller than Seamus had been at birth. His face wasn't red but that shade of pink and white that rare babies have soon after birth. A tuft of hair glimmered silver-gilt on his small head, and his closed eyes were set like his mother's.

Spreading a fist, Laurie tenderly caressed the crooked little finger. "Martin," he repeated. "What color are his eyes?"

"Pale blue like a winter sky, and I think they'll not darken much." She gave him a gentle push. "Get ye back to Mr. Durran's quarters. Ye'll have a longer stay this time. I'll bide with Rowan until she gains strength."

Pressing her hand, he headed toward the door. As he passed the desk his eyes wandered to the baby in the silver frame. Except for the setting of the eyes, Martin at birth was a twin to his half-brother.

When Laurie opened the door he heard the first blast of pipes and groaned. Durran was pacing the lookout platform, his head thrown back, his beard jutting, and the kilt swinging around his knees. All through the hours of darkness the pipes bombarded the fort with wild swirls. Most of the people in the cabins cursed and sighed through a sleepless night. Rowan slept soundly, and towards dawn, as the chords of "Here's a Health to All Good Lassies" boomed over the roof, she smiled in her drugged sleep.

Two more years slipped by, marked by the growth of the children at the fort. Dorrie Purline was now seven, and she'd fulfilled the promise of beauty of her infancy. In summer she wore dainty muslin frocks sewn by her mother and Martha. Above the frilled collars her round face was dimpled and pretty; her hair had darkened to a honey color, and it hung to her shoulders in glossy ringlets. Her behavior was not as pretty as her face. Dorrie was high-spirited and willful, and she had an imperious manner that was far from pleasant. She was the undisputed leader of the other children, and she ruled Marinska's four and Rowan's two with an iron hand. Although her appearance was so feminine and her wide gray-blue eyes so innocent, she led them from one escapade to another. The youngest child, Martin, at only two managed to tag along after the older children, and he seemed to have an early flair not only for getting into mischief but for wheedling his way out of punishment.

Martin never received much disciplining from his father, as Laurie doted on the little blond boy. All the affection and attention he'd withheld from his older son he lavished on the younger. Martin accepted it complacently. At times Rowan wondered about the boy. She sensed that under Martin's beauty and charm there was scant feeling for Laurie, his older brother, or herself. She ceased to worry about Laurie's indifference to Seamus. For one thing, she admitted that if Martin was her husband's favorite, she had one too—Seamus. The love lavished on Martin by his father didn't seem to bother Seamus. He adored his younger brother, and he'd found his own male ideal in George Durran. It was a common sight to see Seamus at Durran's side, the boy's short legs pumping to keep up with the Scot's long strides.

Durran was fond of the boy and tried to keep an eye on him. One morning he saw a group of children gathered in front of the store. They'd formed a circle around Seamus, and, as usual, Dorrie was formulating their plan. Noticing Seamus's grave face, Durran stopped to listen.

"If you don't do it," Dorrie was saying, "we'll not play with you ever again. You're a coward, Seamus!"

Durran put a heavy hand on her shoulder. "Do what, young lady?"

Wide, innocent eyes were raised to him. "Nothing, Mr. Durran."

Durran swung around to young Pieter van Zzll. "Well, Pieter?"

The boy blurted, "Dorrie wants Seamus to let us tie him to a tree. Pretend he's a bad man and we're good Indians. Pretend we're going to burn him at the stake."

Durran's hand tightened on the girl's shoulder. "And you're capable of lighting that fire up, aren't you? You young devils run along, and if you get into any mischief you'll have me to reckon with. Mind you older ones keep an eye on Martin and Rowan Two."

The children, with Dorrie in the lead, ran toward the gates. Durran spotted Little Moccasins coming out of the voyageurs' quarters and beckoned her over.

"What you want?" she grunted in that surly voice she reserved for the despised males.

"You busy now?"

"Got work done."

He smiled up at the statuesque beauty. "Be a good girl and keep an eye on that pack of young ones. Dorrie's just bursting with ideas today."

"Dorrie bad girl. She need hiding. I watch." Little Moccasins scowled darkly and strode after the children.

Martha MacLeod appeared at Durran's shoulder. On one arm dangled a woven basket full of roots. Sweat beaded her face. "What was that all about?"

"Your wee Dorrie again. You look hot."

With her sleeve she mopped at her brow. "I am. For May it's overly warm, and digging is hot work. What's Dorrie up to now?"

"Trying to taunt Seamus into letting himself be tied up and burned."

"Dorrie is only playing. She wouldn't really do it."

"Like to lay a wager on that, Martha? You and Nell spoil that child; you're going to ruin her. Little Moccasins is right. Someone should paddle her bottom once in a while."

Martha sighed. "I suppose we do spoil the wee lass, but she's an only child and so much like her mother was at that age. I haven't the heart to hit the little one."

Vainly, Durran tried to picture Nell Purline, who became more like a wraith all the time, as a pretty, high-spirited child. "Doesn't Dorrie's father take a hand with her?"

"Not yet, but he will when she's older—when he sees signs of a woman's evil in her. But, thank God, not yet."

A sharp tap sounded on the window behind them, and both Martha and Durran jumped and spun around. Purline was pushing the pane up. "Come in, Mr. Durran," he snapped. "I have Mr. Woodbyne here, and I want to talk to both of you." Withdrawing his head, he slammed the window down.

Durran grinned at Martha. "The martinet today, judging from his tone."

When he swung open the door of the office, he decided he could have been wrong about the martinet. Laurie was seated in front of the desk, and behind it Purline sat, his usually erect shoulders sagging as though they bore a heavy weight. Taking his place beside Laurie, Durran waited.

Purline looked from one of the younger men to the other. "Well, have either of you gentlemen anything to report?"

Durran and Laurie exchanged puzzled glances, and then both shook their heads.

"I see," the factor drawled. "It would appear that I can't rely on my two assistants but must keep track of everything myself."

"Is something amiss, sir?" Laurie ventured.

"Yes, Mr. Woodbyne, something is amiss. Haven't either of you gentlemen noticed that for the last month no furs have come in? Have you noticed that except for the Indian workers, the lodges are deserted?"

Tugging at his beard, Durran said slowly, "Aye, I've noticed, but the furs from the winter's catch are already on their way east, and a good lot we had too. Few furs come to us in April or May."

"True, Mr. Durran. But in all your years in the trade, have you ever seen a month without even a rabbit pelt?"

"It does seem queer."

"It's more than queer—it's impossible. Well, Mr. Woodbyne, have you anything to say?"

Laurie shook his blond head. "I've no idea, sir."

" 'I've no idea, sir,' " Purline mimicked, his voice becoming savage. "*I* have an idea. The furs aren't getting through because someone is stopping the Indians before they reach here."

Durran leaned forward. "The Nor'westers? But they've been mighty well behaved since the two companies combined."

"It takes more than an amalgamation of the Hudson's

Bay and the Nor'westers to slow those scoundrels down for long. A Nor'wester is still a Nor'wester!"

Laurie moved restlessly. "But how are they doing it? Do you know?"

"Yes, Mr. Woodbyne. While you and Mr. Durran have been paying more attention to your private lives than to business, I've made it *my* business to find out. Those Nor'westers are sending *coureurs de bois* to intercept our Indians, and they're catching them before they get in here to trade."

"Are you certain, sir?" Laurie asked.

"I sent out some of the hunters to check the woods, and they've found proof that these woods runners are moving out in all directions, stopping the Indians on their way to Fort Purline, and bribing them with liquor for the braves, trinkets for their women, and sweets for the children. The *coureurs de bois* tell the natives that they'll get higher prices for their furs from the Nor'westers and also get better treatment. That is why our trade goods sit upon the shelves and no furs are in the storeroom. That is why our clerks lounge idly around."

With a certain admiration, Laurie regarded the other man. General Purline certainly was an able factor. "Surely, sir, with the little business we've lost thus far there's no reason for real alarm?"

Purline's big hand rubbed irritably over his bald spot. "I see I shall have to spell it out for you. Certainly we've lost little thus far—but what if it continues? When next spring arrives, what am I to tell Mr. Hatch and the other stockholders in London when we have few furs to ship? They're men of business, and this to them will be failure. They might replace us—you and Mr. Durran and myself—and send in men they consider abler. Worse than that, they might decide to shut down the post." His fist crashed down on the desk so hard that both younger men jumped. "I'll not allow that to happen. I was here when the first log was hewn for this fort, when the first rocks were rolled into position. This fort bears my name. It's my life's work! Now do you understand?"

Both men nodded, and Durran asked, "Have you a plan to stop this?"

"Yes, I've made a plan. I'm familiar with military strategy, and we'll proceed against them in a military manner. The Nor'westers have declared war, and war we will give them."

"What is your plan, sir?" Laurie asked.

"We'll take every able-bodied man in this fort and send out small parties to hunt these woods runners down. The hunters tell me they operate singly or in pairs. When they're found, our men will teach them such a lesson that never again will the *bourgeois* at the Nor'westers be able to force any of his men to intercept our Indians."

Durran was frowning. "You're not thinking of killing the *coureurs de bois?*"

"Of course not. I'm a Christian, Mr. Durran, and I do not murder. But I do want these runners beaten within an inch of their lives. I want them stripped of clothes and canoes and weapons. I want them crawling back to their cursed fort like worms. I want the fear of the Almighty God and General Purline put into them!"

Laurie shot a look at Durran's frowning face. "Will you lead our men, sir?"

"I'd like nothing better, but my place is here, at this fort. You and Mr. Durran will be in charge. Now, we'll decide on the men you'll take."

Durran was shaking his fiery head. "The fort is undermanned now. The brigades have left, and there are few men to handle the work."

"If this continues, there'll be no work for any of us. I'll give you all the hunters. Most of them are strong young men and handle themselves well in fighting. They're also excellent trackers. The cooper, the smith, and the carpenter will go with you. Again, they're strong and young. I'll send Tapinawa, who is old but still hale and was a mighty hunter in his day. Even the stableman, Gerika, will be pressed into—"

"He has a bad back," Laurie interrupted. "He would only delay us."

Rubbing his long upper lip, Purline considered. "True, Gerika is a bad choice. He'll remain at the fort. But you'll take all the voyageurs, and they are each worth five ordinary men. Mr. Durran, you're shaking your head as though you disagree."

"There's only one crew of voyageurs here—Armand's. If you take all of them this fort will be undefended."

Purline laughed. "What do you expect—an Indian uprising? You know as well as I that the palisade was built mainly to keep the wild animals and thieving Indians out."

"There are women and children here, general, and this is wild country," Durran said stubbornly. "I don't think we should take every man from this fort."

"Every man won't be taken. I'll be here, and so will Mr. Holden." Purline's mouth twisted with distaste. "Mr. Holden is much more zealous in his pursuit of women than he'd be in the woods fighting *coureurs de bois*. Mr. van Zzll will also remain. He'd be no asset, and besides, for the past few days he's been ill with intermittent fever. Surely that should reassure you that the women and children will be in safe hands."

"It doesn't reassure me," Laurie said abruptly. "I've a wife and two small sons, and I'm not reassured to think of four men here, one of whom is sick and another so old he can scarcely look after the stable. If you insist on this course of action I'll not go."

Purline's face flushed hotly, and his hands closed into fists. He seemed about to leap from his chair. "If I put it as an order, Mr. Woodbyne, would you disobey?"

Laurie was silent, but Durran said grimly, "We're not soldiers, we're traders. If called upon we'll risk our own lives, but we won't risk women or children. I side with Laurie. Some men must remain or I'll not budge an inch."

Both Durran and Laurie expected an outburst from the gaunt man facing them, but Purline merely rubbed at his lips, and his expression became cold and composed. "Perhaps I have been unreasonable. You may be right. I do have women of my own to consider. Yes, I was hasty. What men do you suggest we leave behind?"

"We can split up the voyageurs," Laurie said eagerly. "Take four with us and leave four."

"Very well. You and Mr. Durran will take Armand, his brother, Lapointe—"

"No," Durran said.

"Explain your objection, Mr. Durran."

"Armand is a rogue, and Osa follows his brother's lead. Lapointe is harmless enough by himself, but he tends to follow both Osa and Armand. You said you wished to stop short of actual murder. In the heat of fighting I doubt whether either Laurie or I could handle these men. They're too violent. I suggest they be left at the fort."

Raising shaggy brows, Purline looked at Laurie. "Well, Mr. Woodbyne?"

"Armand," Laurie muttered. "He *is* a rogue. I wonder if he should be left here."

Durran shot him an understanding look. "General Purline will be here, and Bobby and Dutchy. I was also going to suggest we leave Portelance. Of all the voyageurs he's the most reliable and has a level head."

"Very well," Laurie said. "I agree."

"Then we reach agreement, gentlemen. I'll send with you Jourdin, Louis Grand, Four-Finger Jacques and young Beau. The other four will remain to man the fort. Are there any questions?" As he spoke, Purline got to his feet.

The other men rose, and Durran asked, "When will we leave?"

"The day after tomorrow, before dawn. It will take a couple of days to ready provisions and summon all the hunters. I'll split your force into several groups and appoint leaders. You'll fan out in all directions. Remember, gentlemen, I want punishment meted out! I want the *coureurs de bois* to feel the heavy hand of General Purline! You are dismissed!"

Laurie stopped himself just in time. He'd been tempted to snap a salute and about-face, but there was nothing to

208

gain except further enraging their factor. In the store, Bobby Holden greeted Durran and Laurie with a grin and a sly wink.

"Heard it all, old chaps," he whispered. "You warriors are being sent out to do or die. Makes me rather glad not to be considered a warrior. A sensible Holden has no avid desire to return upon his shield." The boy's grin widened. "Notice the fire-eating old soldier stops short of actually fighting himself."

"Just as well," Durran muttered morosely. "The general would probably order the *coureurs de bois* lined up in front of a firing squad, and then there *would* be war. As for you, young Robert, best get to work."

"What work? As the old man told you, I'm idling in my time. It has some advantages. More strength left for my little darlings. Though I must admit there aren't any choice ones at the lodges. Place is ruddy well deserted."

Laurie grinned at the boy. "Why not have a go at Little Moccasins? Saw her honing up her knife this morning." His grin faded, and he said seriously, "Bobby, keep an eye on Armand, will you?"

"An eye is about all I can keep. If I ever laid a hand on the ugly blighter he'd rip it off." Bobby patted Laurie's shoulder. "But I'll watch him closely. Don't worry. And both of you take care. I've gotten rather used to your ugly faces."

On the square in front of the stable, Laurie plucked at Durran's sleeve. "Do you ever get the feeling that the factor is completely mad?"

"No, Ezra Purline is not mad—except in one area. Haven't all of us our mad points, Laurie? And the general, believe me, has some reason for his madness."

"I know nothing about the man's past. Once I had a chance to hear it. Like a fool, I refused."

"You won't hear it from me." Suddenly, Durran smiled and clapped the other man on the back. "Come on, Laurie, let's get ready to go to war!"

19

Fort Purline readied for war, and two days after the general's conference his forces prepared to leave the stockade. He had Durran draw the men up in two ranks in front of the store, and in the cold hour before dawn Purline strode down the steps to speak to them. Torches flared in the square, lighting up the men's buckskin clothing, glancing off the gay cock feathers in the voyageurs' red caps, and glinting from rifle barrels and short axes. The Indian hunters, the voyageurs, and George Durran and Laurie listened with grave, attentive faces as Purline spoke. He began by outlining what the *coureurs de bois* were doing to their trading business and the jeopardy their actions had placed the fort and its employees in. As Purline spoke he became more and more heated, and he ended by shouting, "Strike them down, men! Bring to these scoundrels the fear of God and Fort Purline!"

His excited listeners, with the exception of the Scot and Laurie, roared their approval and waved their rifles over their heads. Encouraged by this display, the general leaped up the steps to the store and stood silhouetted against the light behind him. Raising a clenched fist, he roared, "Strike them down!"

Frenzied shouts greeted this, and Purline waved and then disappeared. The men were milling around, talking excitedly, until Durran snapped, "Gather round." When they had formed a circle around him, he looked from face to face and spoke in a low, firm voice. "Listen to me, men. I think the general has given you the wrong idea.

There's to be no unnecessary bloodshed. We're not going out to kill those woods runners, only to scare them into stopping."

"The factor said to strike them down," Four-Finger Jacques protested.

"He didn't mean it that way."

Jourdin rubbed his scarred brow. "What if we have to kill to protect ourselves?"

Durran's eyes rested bleakly on the man. "That won't be necessary. They travel by ones or twos and will be outnumbered. If any of you lose your heads and kill one of those men, you'll have me to deal with. Understand?"

Heads jerked, and then in small groups the men slipped out of the fort. In all there were seven groups. Four of them were led by the voyageurs, Durran and Laurie led two others, and the last one was under the leadership of old Tapinawa. As the last man slipped through the gateway, Armand and Portelance pushed the gates closed and lifted the heavy bar into place.

"That Durran," Armand grumbled, spitting on the ground. "He always thinks he's boss. I hope one of the *coureurs de bois* crushes his thick head in. Durran I don't like."

Portelance asked over his shoulder, "Anyone you do like?"

"Certainly not you. But you like that white squaw, don't you? Always helping her with her nets and traps and carrying bundles like a tame dog."

The Iroquois's bronze face remained impassive. "Rowan is a fine woman. You're just mad because you weren't sent to hunt *coureurs de bois*."

"Left like a bunch of women with the women!" Armand headed toward their quarters. "I'm going back to bed. I suppose Osa and that fool Lapointe are still snoring their heads off."

When they entered the big untidy room, they found that Lapointe and Osa were still sound asleep. Kicking his boots off, Armand flung himself down on his bunk and pulled a fur robe over him. He tried to go back to sleep,

211

but it evaded him. All he could think of was the insult he'd suffered and the rest of his men moving through the woods on men's work. As the first pale gleams of dawn outlined the small windows and fell across the rough floor, he gave up, pushed back the robe, and swung his feet to the floor. With disgust he looked at his sleeping comrades. Lapointe gave a shrill whistling snore, and Armand aimed a kick at him. Opening bleary eyes, Lapointe blinked at his steersman.

"You want something, *mon ami?*" he asked.

"I want you to stop that racket before I stuff a boot in your mouth. I can't hear myself think."

Pushing himself up on an elbow, Lapointe asked, "What are you thinking?"

A sly smile hovered around the other man's mouth. "Seeing we aren't good enough to go with the rest, I'm thinking we'll have ourselves some fun." Picking up one of his boots, he threw it at his brother. It hit Osa's head, and he jerked upright. When he saw his brother grinning at him, Osa's bearded face split in a wide smile. "On your feet, brother," Armand cried. "Break out a keg of wine and let us drink."

Osa yawned and stretched his huge frame. "There's no wine, Armand. We drank all last night in farewell toasts to our friends."

"There's wine. Over there under that pile of furs. I stole three kegs from the storeroom yesterday. Two of rum and one of high wine."

"The factor," Lapointe said, and gave his high giggle.

"The factor is busy playing general, and Dutchy is sick in his cabin. Holden will be busy sniffing around Little Moccasins." Armand's grin widened. "Out of that bunk, Osa, and get your brother a drink."

While Osa went to do his bidding, Armand turned to Lapointe. "What do you say to a game of seven-up?"

The other man spread his hands, "That I would like, Armand, but no money do I have. My last was spent on a woman from the lodges. But I have a good knife with a keen blade. That I would wager."

"Your knife you can keep." Sinking back against the robe, Armand put both hands behind his head.

Osa, who was pouring the wine, looked up with sudden interest. "A woman I could use. I can't remember when I had my last."

"You can't remember your last anything, my good fool," his brother snorted. "As for women, the only women at the lodges are old crones belonging to the hunters. Most of them are toothless and built like a piece of rawhide."

Passing brimming mugs to Armand and Lapointe, Osa drained his own in one swallow. He poured another, and his small eyes flared redly. "A woman I need! I am about to split my pants with the need."

"Shut your mouth!" his brother bellowed. "We all need women, and there are none."

His shout wakened Portelance, and he sat up in bed and shook his head. Then he saw the mugs in the other men's hands. "Where did the drink come from?"

Lapointe giggled. "The good Armand, he stole it."

Portelance pointed at Osa. "Where's he going?"

Sitting up, Armand stared at his brother. Osa had pulled on his boots and coat, slung his rifle over his back, and was pouring wine into a large leather flask. "Where *are* you going?" he demanded.

"To get a woman, brother."

"I told you there are none at the lodges. Where will you look?"

Osa jerked his shaggy head. "In the forest. I will hunt one down like a deer. I need a woman." Holding the keg up in enormous hands, he gulped wine from it.

Lapointe was giggling, and Armand laughed. "Look at the stupid bear. Going to the woods for a woman! He can't remember what he did yesterday, but he'll find a woman where we can't."

"I remember," Osa protested. "Papa said, 'Osa, always obey Armand.' "

His brother bellowed with laughter. "That's what papa
213

said, and Armand orders you to go into the woods and don't come back without a woman."

"I bring woman," Osa promised, and strode from the quarters.

Portelance asked quietly, "Why did you do that, Armand? You know Mr. Durran said we were all to stay here."

"Durran, Durran! Can't you get it through your thick head that he's gone and we're here." Turning his head, Armand called, "Lapointe, what are you staring at?"

Lapointe, his mug clutched in his hand, was at a window. "Rowan and Martha MacLeod are going by. They're out early."

Pulling himself up, the steersman sauntered over. "So they are. And the white squaw has her two brats with her, and Martha has Dorrie Purline. Where do they go?"

It was Portelance who answered the question. "They've dug little garden plots in that low stretch below the burial ground. They go to seed their plots."

"I'd like to seed that white squaw's plot," Armand muttered.

Portelance looked pointedly at Lapointe, and with a nervous giggle Lapointe said, "Remember, *mon ami*, the code. Rowan belongs to another man."

"It's my brother who forgets, not me," Armand reassured him. But his eyes, as they followed Rowan's slim figure, were hot with a mixture of lust and hate.

The noon sun blazed on the small group having their lunch near the rectangles of turned earth. Martha's plump figure was perched on a big rock next to Rowan, and at their feet Seamus, Dorrie, and little Martin sat on the grass. Pouring cold tea muskey into a tin cup, Martha handed it to the younger woman. She rubbed at the small of her back. "Getting old," she told Rowan. "That bending gets to my back."

Rowan took a sip of tea. "You'll never get old, Martha."

Pushing aside her own cup, Dorrie hugged her rag doll to her and scowled. "Don't like that stuff, Martha. I want some berry juice with honey."

"I didn't bring any, lass." Leaning forward, Martha patted the child's curls. "Would ye like Martha to get a cold drink of water for ye?"

"Don't want water." Dorrie smiled and held up her doll. It had been skillfully made, and the tiny dress it wore was of the same gay print as Dorrie's dress. The eyes were blue buttons, and the hair loops of yellow yarn. "Jane wants a drink of berry juice too, Martha."

Attracted by the bright doll, Martin stretched a dimpled hand toward it. His brother batted the hand aside and said sternly, "Dolls are for girls. You play with the soldiers Mr. Durran made for you."

Martin started to cry, and Rowan took a hand. "That's enough," she said firmly. "All three of you play nicely or I'll call Little Moccasins and she'll take you back to the fort."

For an instant Dorrie's eyes blazed, and then she dimpled and smiled again. "Yes, Rowan," she said demurely, and took Martin's hand. "Come on, boys, we'll play fort. My doll, Jane, can be a beautiful lady, and your wooden soldiers can guard her."

"Mind you stay where we can see you," Rowan called after the children. She whistled to Charlie and pointed to the children. He loped after them.

"You're good with the dog and the bairns too," Martha told her. She stretched and then caught at her back again. "That was hard work. We've got the corn and pumpkin seeded, but there's still so much to do."

"It can wait." Rowan mopped at her hot face. "We got an early start, and I'm tired too. Let's find some shade and rest."

Pulling herself stiffly up, Martha pointed up the slope. "Nearest trees are up there in the burial ground. Let's walk up. We can watch the bairns better from there too."

Rowan picked up her rifle and slung it across her back. She'd learned never to go far from the fort without it.

There was always danger from wild animals. Cougars and an occasional wolf were at times driven by hunger from the mountains and prowled around the fort. She told her companion, "I've never been in the burial ground."

"It's peaceful." Martha toiled up the slope, and Rowan followed her. They found a huge cedar and sat down in the shade. The fallen needles exuded a faint perfume as they crushed them.

Rowan gazed around at the rude crosses. "I had no idea so many were buried here."

Martha pointed to a line of crosses. "That's where the Indian workers have been buried. That long line over there is where five voyageurs lie. Their canoe overturned in the rapids; all perished, but only five bodies were recovered." She moved her finger to the right. "Young Gerald Randolph, who came out here as a clerk and died from lung congestion his first winter. He was a nice lad. And that one closest, that's the Purlines' plot."

"Purline?" Pulling herself up, Rowan wandered among the crosses.

Martha followed her. "Two wee babes, both boys. One lived a week, the other only two days."

Looking down at the tiny, sunken rectangles, Rowan murmured, "I didn't know Nell had borne any child but Dorrie."

"Three she brought to term and lost those two. She's carried so many babies I've lost count. Nell's frail, and each miscarriage takes its toll on her strength." Martha added darkly, "In the end this may kill her."

Ezra and Nell Purline's private life had never crossed Rowan's mind before, but now she found herself wondering about it. She found it hard to picture the austere general as a passionate lover. She wandered on until she stood before the last cross. Words had been cut into it, but they were badly weathered and it took moments to read them. "Henry MacLeod," she read aloud. "Born 1749, died 1815." She paused. MacLeod . . . for the first time she realized that Martha had been married. She'd never heard the woman called anything but Martha and had thought she was a spinster.

"Aye." Martha rested a hand gently on the top of the cross. "My man, and a good one he was too. Henry was the general's orderly in India, and before that he was with the general's father. When he left Dardeshi he stuck with the general, and I stayed with Nell. After a time Henry told me, 'Martha, I be older than ye, but it would be fitting if we wed.' And so we did. He was a comfort and a good man, and I've missed him."

"India," Rowan murmured. "I've read in George's books about that country. What is it like?"

"Hot and dry in the summers and sodden wet in the rainy months. Full of hostile heathens and wild beasts, and a forsaken place at the best of times. With its own beauty, I guess, though it never claimed me."

Rowan swung around, her face bright and eager. "Tell me about India."

"To do that I'd have to tell ye about the general and Nell." Martha retraced her steps to the shade of the cedar tree.

Rowan followed her and sank cross-legged beside the older woman. Pushing back one long braid, she said earnestly, "I've never once asked you anything about Nell's past."

"Aye, I'll give ye that."

"I'm fond of Nell. She's been kind to me and the boys. I'd never hurt her or gossip about her."

Martha's sharp eyes settled on the girl's face. "Ye've been good to Nell since ye came here and have lightened her burdens a little. Your tongue isn't loose, and ye have no malice in ye." She sighed. "No one have I had to talk to since Henry, God rest his soul, died. Mr. Durran knows some of this, but he never speaks of it to me, nor do I to him. Aye, Rowan, I'll tell ye about India, and Nell and Ezra Purline. Perhaps it will ease my own burden a little."

Settling more comfortably, Rowan waited. Martha gazed down the hill at the children and the big dog play-

217

ing beside one of the garden plots. Slowly, and gravely, she parted to speak. "All my life I was with Nell's father's family. When her mother died in India, Colonel Burns sent Nell and me back to England, and I took Nell to stay with her cousins. One of them, Patience, was Nell's age, and the two girls were close as sisters. They were happy years, but as she got older Nell hungered to be with her father. She pestered and coaxed him in all her letters until he told us to come. Nell was seventeen when we went back to India."

"What part of India was he in?"

"Assam, in the Khasi Hills, with the garrison stationed at a little town known as Dardeshi. It was a fort, but nothing like the one we can see from here. The native town was all mud-daubed huts and brick, but the garrison was set higher on the hill, and there were barracks for the sepoys and cottages for the white officers. There were thick jungles where dangerous animals roamed—tigers and leopards and elephants—but much more dangerous were the hill tribes. They were a handsome people, but proud and cruel and violent, and they hated the British. Earlier they had fought many battles, but by the time Nell and I came to Dardeshi Colonel Burns had brought peace to the district."

Assam, Dardeshi. Rowan rolled the rich names through her mind as though she was speaking them. Little by little, as Martha spoke, the vista Rowan could see—the log palisade, the bend of the Nechako River, and the masses of dark fir, hemlock, and cedar—faded. Instead she looked toward an alien settlement high on a hill, its buildings strange and exotic under a southern sun.

218

20

Colonel Geoffrey Burns came to Dardeshi with mixed emotions. He was glad to be out of Bengal, to have a command of his own, but he was a professional soldier, and a good one, and he knew that his new post would prove a challenge for any soldier. His superior officer, Brigadier General Lamont, had left no doubt in Burns's mind on this point.

In his office in the white rococo building in Calcutta, the general leaned back in his chair and said, "Jeff." With that one word Burns knew that the formalities were over.

"Yes, John?" he replied.

"I'm handing you a hot potato. Never get the idea that this posting is a favor. The Dardeshi area has been a boiling pot ever since the East India Company moved into Assam." Getting to his feet, he picked up a ruler and pointed at the map behind him. "The valley of the Brahmaputra River. Rich in tea and cotton and silk. Here are the Khasi Hills. The hill tribes are fierce and rebellious, and their leader is a wily old fox named Tantio Rao. He's a genius at military strategy and repeatedly has sent down his armies on the natives of the valley, hindering the shipment of goods. Here is the town of Dardeshi." The ruler thumped the map. "Notice where it's located—in the foothills of the Khasi Hills. This pass right behind it is called Hajarial, and this is where the hill tribes filter through to the Brahmaputra Valley. If the Pass of Hajarial can be controlled, the rebels can be controlled.

To date we haven't had a commander there who can control it."

Burns nodded his large, sandy head. "I see, John. A hot spot it is."

"We're giving you a strong garrison and the best officers I can round up. The rest is up to you. Good luck, Jeff."

Burns needed more than luck, and he knew it. When he got to Dardeshi he rode through the area with his senior officers, and he shook his head. Turning to Major Campbell, he put his thoughts into words. "The pass could be held, but casualties would be terribly heavy. What's this Tantio Rao like?"

"In his sixties and, according to all reports, so fat he has to be carried. But he has a good mine and is an educated man. He has two sons, and they've been educated too. Sounds as though both his boys are much like their father. But Tantio Rao and his sons are mild compared to his nephew. The prince Vitria is a devil, a pure devil."

Burns raised sandy brows. "But Tantio Rao runs the show?"

"He does, and with a heavy hand. Even Prince Vitria doesn't go against the old fox."

Burns rubbed his chin and appeared to be deep in thought. Major Campbell regarded his new commander with interest. Colonel Burns had been preceded by a fine reputation. He was short and rotund with thinning sandy hair and a big, bluff, good-natured face. His expression bordered on dullness, and Major Campbell wondered if the reports had been exaggerated, but he was a cautious man and he decided to wait and see how fast the new officer reacted. He didn't have long to wait.

"We know where Tantio Rao's headquarters are?" Burns asked abruptly.

"Certainly, sir. About ten miles through the pass, on the crest of the Khasis."

Swinging lightly back into the saddle, Burns turned his horse's head toward Dardeshi. "I'm going up to see him," he called over his shoulder.

220

Campbell spurred his horse and drew level with the other man. "You're going to what?"

"I'm going to see him. You say he's educated and intelligent. I'm going to parley."

"It's suicide, sir. That pass—the men will be cut down. Tantio Rao doesn't have a rabble of peasants; he has a small but disciplined army."

Burns smiled grimly. "Exactly, and we've little chance of halting it by force. We'll have to use words."

"Very well, sir. I'll give orders. We'll leave only enough men to guard the garrison."

Still smiling, Burns flicked at the dust on his tunic. "I'm taking one British officer, one native officer, and six sepoys. All will come on a volunteer basis, major."

"You won't get clear of the pass, sir."

"Ah, yes, we'll get to Tantio Rao's stronghold safely. You said the old man is a fox. Foxes are sly and cunning. He'll be curious to know what I want."

"Once there," Campbell said doggedly, "he'll have you. He can hold you for ransom, use you as a threat to the garrison, or even boil you in oil. You've no idea of the barbaric tortures these natives can—"

"Major Campbell! Must I remind you I've spent many years in India? My wife died and is buried in this country. My daughter Nell, who was born here, is now in England and bothering me continually to allow her to return. I know India."

"Yes, sir. Sorry, sir. I spoke without thought. I'll make arrangements." Campbell glanced at the man riding at his side. How could he ever have imagined this man was dull? "Colonel."

"Yes?"

"I'd like to go with you."

Burns turned in the saddle. "Thank you, major. I should be honored to have you along."

The short column rode out of Dardeshi the following morning. One sepoy rode ahead bearing the regimental colors, and behind him rode Colonel Burns and Major Campbell in the black-and-silver dress uniform of the

Twelfth Bengal Rifles. Then the native officer, Rissaldar-Major Dowlah, rode proudly with his five sepoys. No white flag was carried. Burns had vetoed the suggestion. "If they're going to attack, a white flag won't stop them. And I won't carry that color in our ranks."

As their horses clattered over the rocky defile winding through the pass, Campbell held his breath, waiting for the first shot. He looked straight ahead, as the other men did, but he knew that even if he scanned the overhanging cliffs, he would see nothing. But he felt them. He sensed eyes riveted on them, rifles aimed, and the skin between his shoulder blades tingled. Burns proved to have been right. They saw nothing until they approached the head-quarters of Tantio Rao. The stronghold, built of reddish rock, was perched high on a hill, and a narrow road, permitting only two men to ride abreast, wound steeply up to high gates arched in stone. As the column trotted toward the road, they saw three mounted men, richly dressed, riding down to meet them. Behind them they heard more horses clattering over the rocks, but not one head in the tiny British force turned.

Pulling their horses up, the three natives waited. Campbell whispered to the colonel, "The one on the right is Cherta, elder son of Tantio Rao. I don't recognize the one behind, but the one on Cherta's left is Prince Vitria."

Burns studied the two princes. Cherta was round-faced and rather pleasant-looking. The man in the rich purple robes trimmed lavishly with gold was tall and lean. He was handsome, as handsome as the devil Campbell had likened him to. Burns met his eyes, and a cold shiver ran down his spine. Whatever Tantio Rao proved to be, Burns was glad it wasn't Vitria he had to deal with.

Without a word the three men wheeled their mounts and trotted up the road. From behind his own men, Burns could hear the thud of many hooves, the jangle of weapons and trappings. They passed under the looming stone arch into a courtyard. In its center was a fountain that sent jets of water high into the air, and the sun shining through them formed a rainbow. A good omen? Burns wondered. Then his attention snapped back to their advance escort. The three men had dismounted and were waiting on the steps of the building. Burns snapped an order, Campbell echoed it, and the sepoys dismounted.

Cherta gazed down at them. Out of the saddle he proved to be short and plump. One hand rested on the jeweled dagger hilt at his waist. He pointed a finger at Burns and then at Campbell and spoke in English. "You and you, come. The rest stay here."

Burns looked up at him. "My men come with me."

Vitria whispered to his cousin, and Cherta nodded. "All come."

In close formation they followed the two princes, their standard-bearer marching ahead. The only sounds made as they walked down the long corridor were the creak of leather boots, the jingle of spurs, and the silken rustle of their flag. Double doors, richly inset with gold and jewels, silently opened, and they were in an audience chamber. A strip of multicolored carpet led to a dais where Tantio Rao reclined. He wore robes of apricot silk, and his head was bound with a gold turban. Silken cushions cradled a soft, gross body, fat past the point of obesity. Two veiled girls in transparent clothing bent over him, holding a goblet to his lips, placing sweetmeats in his mouth. When he saw the British officers, Tantio Rao lifted a regal hand and the girls moved softly past the couch and edged through the curtain of hanging silks. Absently, Burns noticed that the man's hand was tiny, beautifully formed, his fingers ringed with jewels.

The two princes bowed deeply to their ruler and stepped to one side of the dais. The British officers were allowed to approach to the foot of it. As he stopped, Burns noticed one of the silk curtains moving, and he smiled an inward, grim smile. He'd wondered why they hadn't been disarmed. None of them had rifles, but Rissaldar Dowlah, Campbell, and he all wore sidearms. Now he knew why. The place was probably bristling with hidden riflemen.

Burns inclined his head. "Excellence."

223

"Colonel Burns," Tantio Rao responded. His voice was thin and high-pitched like a young boy's, but his eyes, as tiny as raisins buried in a suet pudding, were as old as time.

The two men, one reclining comfortably, the other standing at attention, steadily regarded each other. At that moment there was no one else in the room for either of them, perhaps no one else in the world. Burns waited for Tantio Rao to speak. Finally he did.

"You interest me, colonel; never before have I had a British officer as guest."

"I don't come as guest, Excellence."

Tiny, unblinking eyes peered at Burns. "What do you come for?"

Burns didn't hesitate. "As you must know, for you know my name, I'm officer in command at the garrison at Dardeshi. I was sent from Calcutta to prevent further raidings into the valley of the Brahmaputra. I come to make peace."

"Then you waste your time. Peace we'll never have, not until the last of your race leaves this country. You are a brave man, colonel. I must tell you I admire courage, even foolhardy courage like yours. You and your men are now delivered into my hands, and I must decide what use to make of you."

"Kill them!" Prince Vitria sprang forward. "Let me do it. Slowly, by inches. Let me do it!"

The gold turban moved until the huge, moonlike face of Tantio Rao was turned on the prince. "Do I grow so senile that you must speak for me, nephew? You will now judge the wisest course for our people?"

Virtria's eyes fell, and he stepped back. The tiny eyes looked at Cherta. "And you, my son, do you offer advice?"

"Do you ask it, my father?"

"I ask."

"Hear this man out."

The gold turban dipped in a nod. "Wise advice. Take heed, Vitria. Cherta hates the British as much as you, but

224

he uses the caution a wise leader must exercise." The moon face swung back to Burns. "Speak."

"Granted you have me and this small group of men, but orders have been left in Dardeshi. No ransom, no threats concerning us, will change those orders. You may deliver our bodies in pieces, and my orders will be carried out."

"What orders, Colonel Burns?"

"The pass will be held. No longer will your men ride through the Pass of Hajarial to raid the valley."

"Your men will die, colonel."

"So will yours, Excellence."

"There are other ways into the valley besides the pass."

"Long and hard. And Dardeshi commands the valley. My regiments can move into it and cut off your forces."

"The garrison has recently been strengthened?"

"Do you need to ask?"

The moon face split into a smile. Tantio Rao's teeth were like his hands, tiny and exquisite. "No, I have a good spy system. Speak on."

"I offer tribute."

"Have you the authority?"

"I have. For every bale of cotton, for every container of tea, for every bolt of silk that leaves the valley, the East India Company will pay tribute. The more goods that move out unhindered, the more your tribute will be."

The man in the purple robe leaped again, this time straight at Burns. "Cut his tongue out. These men killed my father." Vitria whirled on his uncle. "Your brother they killed. Now they try to buy us!"

Tantio Rao touched the lowest of his many chins. As he did, pendulous breasts were briefly outlined under apricot silk. "Yes, my brother was killed by the British. But patience, my nephew, patience. Revenge in good time, and when the time is right." One tiny, exquisite finger jabbed at Vitria. "Leave us. This is no time for anger to drown sense." The high, boy's voice was unchanged, but Vitria swung on his heel, shot one look at Burns's impassive face, and stalked out of the chamber. Tantio Rao

225

turned to his son. "Cherta, does your mind speak for you, or your hate?"

"As you taught me, my father, my mind will speak."

"Let it."

The plump young man advanced a few steps and stood at Burns's elbow. He held up a hand. "On this hand we have useless slaughter of our people. Many British can we kill, but more would come behind them."

The gold turban dipped in agreement. "The garrison we can slaughter, the white women we can take and use as we wish."

Burns spoke roughly. "Lay a finger on an Englishwoman and this land will run with your blood."

Nodding, Cherta raised his other hand. "Tribute will add to our wealth, our arms. In time it will be different. Let us wait for that time."

Tantio Rao beamed at his son. "You have voiced my decision, my son." Raisin eyes shifted to Burns. "For this time there will not be peace, but a truce. The valley will remain untouched by us, the town of Dardeshi will slumber under the Hills of Khasi. We will take tribute, and no longer will we raid. Colonel Burns, I find I admire you. You are truly a sahib-*bahadur*, and I admire brave men. We can never be friends, but this I will warn you. I feel, and both my sons feel, as Prince Vitria does. We temper our emotions with reasoning, but if once, only once, we are cheated on tribute, we will make war."

"You'll not be cheated, Excellence."

The gold turban dipped. "You will be provided with an escort to the Pass of Hajarial. My son will take you. The truce begins from this moment."

Both Burns and Campbell bowed, and then they swung around and smartly marched from the chamber. Behind them their men strode. The courtyard was deserted, but near the fountain, with its arching rainbow, their horses were tethered. As they prepared to mount, Vitria appeared at Burns's side. In a low voice he grated, "You've not won, British swine! One day I'll settle with you and listen to the music of your screams. Dardeshi will run with blood, and it will be yours."

As they followed Cherta down the narrow winding road, Burns brooded about Vitria. The man was a fanatic, and there was no doubt that he was dangerous. As they turned their horses into the rocky defile of the pass, he shook off his gloom and turned to the major. Campbell smiled at him. "My compliments, sir. You've accomplished what no other commander at Dardeshi ever has."

"We'll wait and see on that, major. But if the old fox's word is kept, and I think it will be, I'm going to send for my daughter. I haven't seen Nell for over ten years, not since her mother's death."

"That will be a happy day for you both, colonel."

Burns nodded. A very happy day, he thought. But no man is infallible. Geoffrey Burns would live to curse the day that Martha brought his daughter to Dardeshi.

Nell Burns had a tremendous impact on the garrison at Dardeshi. The British women on the post were the wives of the older officers, and they were faded and weathered by their years in India. Their time was occupied with their children, their households, and the small social events they arranged to escape the bordeom. Nell, who had been only another pretty girl in England, suddenly found herself the beauty of the regiment, the only single girl on the post. The older women she quickly won over with a combination of deference and pretty manners, and by passing out with a lavish hand gifts of English soap and toilet water.

Most of the senior officers regarded their commanding officer's daughter indulgently, remarking to their wives that they hoped their own daughters would have Nell's nice manners and charm. Silently, they compared her to their own women and yearned over her young curves and fresh face.

Shortly after her arrival, Major Campbell remarked to Captain Brock, "Strange how white women go to one extreme or the other in this climate. Either they bloat completely out of shape or become as lean as dried meat."

Brock nodded glumly. His own wife had bloated and was an immense woman whose corset had to be laced, and her shoes put on for her, by servants. "Let's hope Miss Burns isn't here long enough to lose that freshness."

"Yes," Campbell agreed. "Let's hope this is a short visit."

Campbell wasn't considering the girl's possible loss of beauty in his desire for her to leave Dardeshi. He found he didn't care much for her. He admired her looks, but under the silken skin and innocent eyes he sensed an unruly spirit, one that could wreak havoc in the small community if it was unleashed. To himself he muttered, Let's hope Colonel Burns keeps a tight rein on her.

Colonel Burns didn't apply any rein to his daughter. From the moment he took her into his arms and felt the soft contours of her woman's body, from the moment he looked down at the face so like his wife's, he was lost. The girl's wide gray-blue eyes smiled up at him, her chestnut hair curled brightly around a dimpled face, and to him Nell could do no wrong.

The junior officers—three lieutenants and two cornets—took one look at the English girl and fell head over heels in love with her. They danced attendance on Nell, and it went to her head like wine. Shamelessly, she played one young man against another, nearly driving them all wild. She was drunk with power, infatuated with the country, considering it romantic and never seeing the perils it held. The mud and brick native town was exotic and wonderful to her. The garrison, with the white boxes of officers' bungalows under gold mohur trees, she thought enchanting. Nell reveled in the ease of the life, the number of whiteclad servants ready to cater to her every whim. Life smiled on her, and most of the people in the garrison smiled too. The only men who didn't admire her were Major Campbell and Rissaldar-Major Dowlah. The rissaldar was devoted to Colonel Burns, but the daughter of his commanding officer worried him. Finally Dowlah took his worries to Martha MacDowl. Dowlah liked Martha and valued her calm good sense. She heard him out, her brows knitted, and then she sought her young charge out.

Nell was in her bedroom, humid air filtering through the latticed windows. She was clad in a flimsy dressing gown gaping open over her corset cover and was sitting before her dressing table, brushing her long, bright hair. Martha glanced at the white riding habit draped across the bed, touched the high, polished boots, and sat down in a wicker chair. "Going riding again, Nell?"

"Uh-huh. With Lieutenant Hamilton."

Martha nodded. Rodney Hamilton was her favorite among the young officers. He reminded her of Geoffrey Burns in his youth. The boy had sandy coloring, a compact build, and a plain, freckled face, but he was calm, methodical, and already a fine soldier. If anyone could handle her spirited young charge, Martha thought, it would be Rodney.

She watched the girl's animated reflection in the mirror. "Been doing a lot of riding lately, Nell."

Nell shrugged a rounded shoulder. "I enjoy riding."

Martha wondered how to proceed. Much as she loved the girl, she knew Nell, knew her arrogance and temper. Martha was only fourteen years Nell's senior, and sometimes it wasn't easy to handle her. Finally she said, "That's what I want to talk about."

Putting down the brush, Nell swung around, her dimpled face framed in flowing waves of thick chestnut hair. "Why are you looking so sour?"

"Rissaldar Dowlah told me something I didn't like."

Nell pouted. "He's an old gossip."

"The rissaldar never gossips, lass. But other people may be beginning to gossip about ye."

"I've no idea what you're talking about." Raising white hands, Nell began to dress her hair high on her head.

"The rissaldar understands the protocol of garrison life. Ye don't."

"Rubbish. I was born here."

"And what do ye remember?"

Putting a finger to her full lips, the girl thought. "I remember my ayah, how soft and comfortable her lap was. I remember daddy and mother coming in to say good night to me. They were going to a party, and daddy wore dress uniform, and mother had on a green silk gown and a feather boa."

"I was talking about garrison life. It's a narrow life and a narrow circle of people. If a woman's reputation is tarnished she might as well leave India. She isn't invited to any of the social—"

"Martha!" Nell swung around again. "Will you get to the point? Lieutenant Hamilton will soon be here, and I'm not even half ready yet."

"The point? Aye, lass. Ye've been doing a lot of riding lately with the young officers—"

"With a sepoy as guard. You know daddy never allows me to leave the post without a guard."

The older woman's mouth set. "Ye've been bribing your escort to leave ye alone with your young men. Ye sit on banks of streams and let them hold your hand and whisper sweet nothings in your ear. This isn't done. Sooner or later the ladies will learn of your conduct and will start to whisper. They'll call ye loose and wild."

"The ladies like me, Martha."

"They do now. But if they decide your moral conduct is poor they'll turn on ye, and mark my word, so will their men. Ladies rule the social life in a garrison, and ye'll be an outcast."

Nell's eyes widened. "I didn't realize. It's all so harmless, Martha."

"It doesn't look harmless, lass." Martha put her hand on the girl's shoulder. "Be a good girl and keep your sepoy with ye when ye ride."

After this talk Nell's conduct became more circumspect, and Martha breathed a sigh of relief. She hadn't wanted to bother Geoffrey Burns about his daughter. He had enough on his mind as it was.

At the precise moment that Martha was lecturing his

daughter, Colonel Burns was in his office poring over the latest reports from Calcutta. He'd sent urgent messages to Brigadier General Lamont explaining his position. After the dry, factual report he'd added a personal letter. "What are you trying to do to me, John?" Burns had written. "I know the situation at Dardeshi appears to be stable. Tantio Rao has kept the truce, and the valley is at peace, but as I've warned you repeatedly, his nephew, Prince Vitria, is stirring the hill tribes into revolt. He's preaching discord and telling the tribesmen that his uncle is selling out to the British, intent on gaining the money from tribute for himself and his sons. If Vitria ever overthrows his uncle this place will explode. In the meantime, you are moving more of my sepoys out and even transferring my most experienced officers."

The papers that were ranged on his desk threw Burns into a state of mental turmoil. Picking up Lamont's answer to his letter, he reread part of it. "It's your own fault," was written in the general's neat script. "You've done too good a job, Jeff. I can appreciate your position, but try to appreciate mine. The goods are moving out of the valley of the Brahmaputra in larger amounts than they ever have, and Dardeshi is at peace. The troops and officers are more needed at frontier points where heavy fighting has erupted. I'll do my best for you, but I can't replace the troops and I'm afraid, as you'll note in your orders, that I must claim even more of your officers."

With a muttered curse, Burns crumpled the paper and then looked up. Major Campbell was standing in the doorway. "More trouble, sir?"

"Come in, major. Have a seat, and you'd better get yourself a drink. Here, have a look at this."

As his eyes scanned the lines, the major's eyes narrowed. "Ye gods! More troops being transferred out, and more of the officers too."

"They're stripping this garrison. The damn fools!" Burns ran a heavy hand over his thinning hair. "You'll notice that you're being recalled to Calcutta for assignment. I'll miss you, major."

231

"You'll still have Major Hewitt, sir, and he's a good man."

"And a sick one. Major Hewitt should be sent home. Malaria has undermined his health to such a degree that the man isn't fit for duty. Notice how many officers I'll have left."

"Hewitt, Captain Graves, Lieutenant Hamilton, and Cornet Peters. But I see they're sending you another lieutenant."

"Green as grass. Just arrived from England."

Campbell glanced down at the paper. "Ezra Purline. He's General Oswald Purline's son. He'll be a fine soldier."

"Still right out of military school and won't know a rissaldar from a jemadar."

Campbell chuckled. "He'll catch on. Bearing the Purline name, he can't help but be a good soldier."

"Any further word from the spies on Prince Vitria?"

"Still stirring up hell in the hills, sir. Agitating for all-out war. I'm surprised that Tantio Rao hasn't put a stop to him before this."

Burns frowned. "Don't think the hill tribes don't know our strength to a man. Their spy system is superior to our own. Have a hunch that many of our house servants give full reports."

"No doubt."

"Sometimes I wonder if I should ever have allowed Martha to bring Nell here."

Rising, Campbell drained his glass and set it down on the desk. "You must admit it's been a comfort having them with you, sir."

Burns's frown vanished, and he beamed. "That it is. Nell lights up the house. She's a good girl."

As Campbell left the office, his own brow crinkled into a frown. Astute a soldier as Burns was, he was completely blind when it came to women. He had no idea what the two women in his bungalow were actually like. The daughter Burns doted on, in Campbell's opinion, had the makings of a wild little wanton, and Campbell had the feeling that if the right man appeared that's exactly what Nell Burns would be. Martha MacDowl—Campbell's mouth relaxed—now, there was a fine woman, but his colonel didn't know what Campbell had observed. Martha was devoted to more than Burns's daughter—she was quietly but passionately in love with Geoffrey Burns.

The major shrugged. It was none of his business. Best to get to his own bungalow and let his wife know she'd have to start packing. Sad as he was to leave Dardeshi and Colonel Burns, he'd be relieved to get his family out. His sixth sense told him there was trouble brewing. However, Lieutenant Purline would be arriving shortly, and at least Burns would have another good officer to back him.

Two weeks after Campbell and the other reassigned officers had left, Ezra Purline arrived. By that time the garrison was much depleted, and Purline could have had his choice of several bungalows standing untenanted. He decided to move in with Rodney Hamilton, and for a time the two young men hit it off well.

Purline made almost the same impact on the ladies of the garrison as Nell had made on the men. All the officers' wives doted on him. His manners were exquisite, he endeared himself to them with his gallantries, and at every opportunity he read or recited poetry to them.

The men, with the exception of Hamilton, were far less enthralled. Colonel Burns detested the lanky young man at sight, the other officers were suspicious of a soldier who seemed more at home with a book of poems than a sword, and Rissaldar Dowlah watched Purline narrowly. "Mark my word, sahib," the native officer told Lieutenant Hamilton. "That's one's a bad one."

The two men were standing in a corner of the parade square watching Purline putting a squad of sepoys through drill. Purline cut quite a figure. His tall, thin figure seemed designed to carry his immaculate uniform, and his face, under the topi, was large-featured and stern.

He had a good head of thick black hair that waved back from a broad brow and deeply set, beautiful eyes.

Hamilton grinned at Dowlah. "Much as I respect your opinion, sirdar, I think this time you're in error. Purline is a good chap, and remember, his father was General Purline and his grandfather—"

"I know, sahib. I served with General Purline years ago, but this is no son of his."

Hamilton regarded the older man with interest. He did respect Dowlah's opinion. The rissaldar was an old trooper, and his dark face, above the grizzled beard, was wise and knowing. "What bothers you about Lieutenant Purline?"

"He's not a sahib-*bahadur*."

Throwing back his sandy head, Hamilton laughed. "The poor chap hasn't even had a taste of combat, and you decide he isn't a brave man. Come now, sirdar."

"Wait," the other man warned.

In a short time Hamilton no longer worried about Dowlah's words. He was too concerned about Nell Burns. Hamilton had never attempted to delude himself about his feelings for the girl. He loved her deeply, and he was the type of man who loved only once. For a while he'd believed she returned his affection, and he had hopes that she might marry him. When Purline arrived, all this changed. From the moment Nell and Purline met, a flame erupted that couldn't be concealed. They were drawn together as though both of them were powerless to prevent it. Nell no longer would ride with either Hamilton or Cornet Peters. She rode with Ezra Purline. Again she sternly refused to allow the sepoy detailed to her to accompany them. As soon as they were out of sight of Dardeshi, she sent her native escort away, and Nell and Purline rode the hills by themselves. They stopped in copses of trees that bordered little streams; they sat on grassy banks and talked. Purline held her hand and gazed into her eyes. He wooed her with gentle, poetic words, and soon the inevitable happened. Their first tentative, closed-mouth kisses became open-mouth, passionate embraces. Nell came

234

gasping into the young officer's arms, and his hands fumbled through her clothes and caressed her breasts. The day came when they could stand it no longer. They ripped off their clothes and lay naked in each other's arms. She gave herself to him freely, gladly, and thought she loved him and he loved her.

This time Martha was sick with anxiety. She tried to talk with Nell but met with complete failure. "I love him, Martha," the girl breathed. "In time we'll marry."

"Ye're the talk of this post! How many invitations have ye received from the ladies lately?"

"Bunch of dried-up old prunes. What do I care? I don't care about anything but Ezra. We love each other, and we'll be married."

"Ye don't love, ye wallow in lust. For that ye'll both pay. Anyway, he's not a man to marry the likes of ye. When his time comes to wed he'll pick the daughter of a general, not a lowly colonel's girl."

Nell's face flamed. "I *hate* you."

Gripping the girl's shoulders in powerful hands, Martha shook her. "It's gone past flirting, hasn't it?"

Nell wrenched herself away. "It's not your business. Stop meddling!"

"I'll tell your father."

Drawing herself up, Nell looked coldly at her companion. "Tell him."

Martha never had a chance to tell the colonel. The situation in the Khasi Hills had worsened and was out of control. Early one morning a runner came to the colonel's bungalow and handed the officer a bundle. The wrappings were of apricot silk, and Burns stared down at it. "Where was it left?"

"The gates, sahib-colonel," the sepoy panted. "In the night they brought it. Like shadows they move."

"Summon all the officers to my office," Burns snapped, and the man left at a run. Looking up, the colonel saw Martha and Nell in their bedroom doorways. "Get back to bed," he ordered.

All the officers were in his office when Burns got there.

Setting down the bundle, he gingerly opened it. The delicate apricot silk was stained with darker marks, and on the silk was a tiny exquisite hand. Jeweled rings flashed on the fingers. "Tantio Rao," Burns said heavily. "Prince Vitria has sent news of his uncle's downfall. I wonder how that devil ever got to the old fox."

"In his zenana," Major Hewitt said. "I received a report from Salika a few minutes ago."

Every head swung toward the major. He sprawled in a chair, mopping beads of sweat from his brow, and his skin was a leaden color. Sick again, Burns thought despairingly. "What happened?" the colonel asked aloud.

"Vitria bribed three of the women, promised them titles and wealth. When Tantio Rao and his sons went to their women's quarters—"

"His sons too?" Captain Graves asked.

"All three. Their wine was poisoned, and Tantio Rao and his sons died. Then Vitria cut off this hand himself and ordered that the three women poisoners be beheaded. That's the way that devil keeps his promises!" Breathing heavily, Hewitt leaned back.

Captain Graves rubbed his short fair hair. "Salika is a responsible spy."

"The best," Hewitt said. "Some of the women talked to him. Vitria also stripped off his uncle's gold turban. Said he was saving it for Colonel Burns."

Burns thumped his desk with a heavy fist. "There's one promise Prince Vitria made that he'll try to keep. He promised Dardeshi will run with blood."

"We've got to stop him," Lieutenant Purline muttered.

Lifting hostile eyes, Burns regarded Purline. "Do you have a suggestion, lieutenant?"

Purline rubbed at a jutting ear. "They'll come through the pass, sir."

"And the sun will rise in the east. Of course they'll come through the pass. Tell me, lieutenant, how long can we hold the pass with the number of troops we have?"

"I don't know, sir."

"Well, I do. Not long." Wrenching his gaze from Purline's reddening face, Burns swung around to the major. "Did you get messengers off?"

"As soon as Salika reported, colonel." Hewitt wiped at his brow. "But reinforcements will take awhile to get here."

"Thanks to those bloody fools in Calcutta! In the meantime we've women and children here." Burns's hands knotted into fists. "I don't have to explain what would happen if they fell into Vitria's hands."

Hamilton moved closer. His face was so pale that the freckles stood out in blotches. His voice was steady. "Buy time, sir?"

"Exactly. Gentlemen, we *must* buy time. No matter what the price. If those fiends come through the pass they'll wipe out the garrison. Now, how to do it."

"Lieutenant Purline's suggestion about the pass, sir," Captain Graves said.

Burns looked up at the younger man. "It will be guarded, of course, but we must engage Vitria's attention, keep him occupied for a time." He rubbed at his square chin. "There's only one thing he'd give time to now."

Major Hewitt went even grayer and gestured at the water jug. Cornet Peters poured a glassful and handed it to the major. "You have an idea?" Hewitt asked.

"There's only one way." Colonel Burns reached for his sword belt and buckled it on. "I'm going up to the stronghold and parley."

The officers stared at him. It was Cornet Peters, who was not only the junior officer but also the youngest man there, who spoke. "Sir, Prince Vitria will never parley. He's intent on war."

Burns picked up his topi. "I know, but he's a sadist. It will be his style to toy with me for a time, to pretend to listen to my arguments. That will buy time, precious time for us."

Pulling himself from his chair, Hewitt braced himself against the edge of the desk. "When he's through toying, he'll be ready to torture."

"Slowly," Burns said. "That's his style. More time."

Purline's face was drained of color, and sweat beaded his brow. "You won't have a chance," he whispered.

Savagely, the colonel swung on him. "We all know that, lieutenant. Do you realize what he'd do to our women and children? I asked you before, do you have a better suggestion? Either make it or be silent!"

As Purline backed away from Burns, Hewitt took a step forward. "How many men will you take with you, colonel?"

"None."

"You can't go alone, sir. I volunteer to accompany you."

As he looked at the major, Colonel Burns's expression softened. The man was swaying on his feet; he wouldn't even be able to get into a saddle. "You're needed here, major. You'll be in charge. But thanks."

Straightening his shoulders, Captain Graves said solemnly, "I'll go with you, sir. Two British officers will buy more time than one."

"You have a wife on the post, captain, and three small children."

"You have a daughter. I'm a soldier, sir."

Burns's wide face creased into a smile. "You are indeed. Get ready to ride. We leave in two hours." He beckoned to Lieutenant Hamilton, and the two men left the office. In the compound, Burns directed his steps toward his bungalow and said to the younger man, "I don't want Nell to know. I'll tell Martha, and she can break it to the girl after Captain Graves and I leave." Without changing his tone, he asked, "You love Nell, don't you, Rodney?"

"I do."

"I'd hoped . . . but never mind that now. I want a promise. If Prince Vitria's forces get through and attack the garrison before the relief column arrives, I want you to promise me that you'll do what is necessary about Martha and . . . and Nell."

"I don't think I could, sir."

Grasping Hamilton's arm, Burns swung him around.

238

He stared steadily into the other man's eyes. "You know what I mean. They can't fall into that devil's hands. Will you do it?"

The lieutenant took a deep breath. "If it's the last resort—yes."

"Good man." Burns squeezed the arm he held. "Major Hewitt will be officer commanding, but he's coming down with malaria again. So, to all intents and purposes, the post will be in your hands. As soon as Graves and I clear the pass, take half the men and stand guard at Hajarial. If the relief column doesn't get here soon you probably will have to take the rest of the men. That pass must be held whatever the price! Any questions?"

"Rissaldar-Major Dowlah will insist on accompanying you and Captain Graves, sir. Whom shall I give his command to?"

"He'll insist, but Dowlah won't be allowed to go. He's needed here." Burns's hand dropped away from the other man's arm. "Now I'd better get ready and speak with Martha."

He'd taken several steps before Hamilton's voice stopped him. As Burns turned, Hamilton said quietly, "We'll hold the pass, sir." The young man snapped a salute and walked away.

As Burns and Graves rode out of the settlement and turned their mounts toward the pass, Nell was preparing to leave the bungalow. While she adjusted her wide-brimmed hat and pinned it into place on her thick hair, she wondered why Martha was in her room with the door shut. Martha hadn't come out to say good-bye to daddy, and that wasn't like her. As Nell stepped out on the red-flagstones of the wide, colonnaded veranda, few sounds broke the silence. All she could hear was a native maid humming as she swept off the walk, and the gentle sighing of the breeze through the gold mohur tree over her head. Nell shrugged. She had her own problem, and worrying about silence where there generally wasn't any was none of her concern.

She walked slowly down the dusty road to the parade square. She must find Ezra and talk to him. She couldn't wait any longer. It was a blessing that her father had left on patrol, because she now had a chance. She saw Ezra heading across the compound, going toward her father's office. She speeded her steps and then noticed Laura Graves coming from the direction of the gates. Nell tried to arrange a smile on her face. None of the other women were friendly to her now, but she liked Laura. She was younger than the rest and was still rather pretty. Then Laura saw Nell. She stared straight into the other girl's eyes, lifted her chin, and passed without a word. Nell stared after her. Laura's eyes were red and swollen as though she'd been weeping. For a moment Nell watched her with puzzled eyes, and then she hurried after Ezra's tall form. All the women were cats; Laura was as bad as the rest.

"Ezra," she called. "Wait for me."

He turned and waited, but one polished boot was beating an impatient tattoo in the dust. The impatience was echoed in his voice as he said, "I haven't time now, Nell. Major Hewitt collapsed, and I've just seen him to his quarters. I have to take charge of the regiment."

She gazed up at him, her eyes devouring his face. "Where's Rodney Hamilton?"

"He's taken some of the men to stand guard at the pass."

"But why?"

Something flickered in the beautiful, deep-set eyes. "Martha will tell you all about it. I must go, Nell." He strode into her father's office and closed the door.

Nell flushed with anger. "Well!" she said. She was tempted to throw that door open. Ezra must listen. Whom else could she talk to? Martha? No, not about this. What had Ezra meant when he'd said Martha had something to tell her? Angrily, she swung around and retraced her

240

steps. The same maid who had been sweeping the walk was now dusting furniture in the small drawing room.

"Where's Miss MacDowl?" Nell asked the girl.

"In her room, miss-sahiba. She crying."

"Crying?"

Without knocking, Nell opened Martha's door. The older woman had collapsed in a heap on the bed. She lifted a swollen face. Perching on the edge of the bed, Nell put an arm around the other woman's shoulders. "What's wrong?" she whispered.

"Has he gone?"

"Daddy? Yes, the captain and he left about an hour ago. Martha, what's wrong? I saw Laura Graves, and she looked as though she'd been crying her eyes out, and now you. The whole post is so quiet, and Ezra looks so . . . so queer. Tell me."

Struggling to her feet, Martha dipped a towel in a ewer of water and bathed her eyes with it. "Your father asked me to wait until he was gone, lass. This morning . . . Tantio Rao and both his sons have been killed. Prince Vitria is leading the hill tribes now."

Without comprehension, Nell stared at Martha's swollen face. "I don't understand."

Rage blazed from Martha's eyes. "Nay, ye don't. Too busy dallying with your Ezra to understand anything. Well, I'll tell ye. The heathens will sweep across Dardeshi with that devil leading them if they aren't stopped."

"But we've troops here, Martha. Rodney is on guard at the pass now."

"If the relief column doesn't get here, how long can Hajarial be held?"

Slowly, Nell pulled herself to her feet. "Where did daddy go?"

"To the heathens' stronghold to buy time."

Now Nell understood. "Oh, God! I must get to Ezra!"

Martha was still flaming with rage. "What can that do for your father?"

"Not for daddy, Martha, for me."

The fresh color had drained from her face, and she

241

looked years older. Nell took two steps and crumpled to the floor. Dropping the towel, Martha ran to her. "Lalla!" she called.

The maid ran in and knelt by the girl sprawled on the floor. Martha was cradling Nell's head in her lap, smoothing back the thick hair from her high brow.

"Miss-sahiba *gora*," Lalla cried.

"Aye, she's pale."

"I get *pani*. She has *bahut* grief."

"Aye, fetch fresh water, Lalla." To herself, Martha muttered, "And she feels much grief, but there's more to it than that, I'll wager."

For three days after her father left Dardeshi, Nell moped around the bungalow. She lost weight, and her face was pale and drawn. Martha, eyeing that ashen face with dark-circled eyes, sighed but said nothing, nor did she ask any questions. The fourth day Nell dressed, arranged her hair becomingly, and pinched color into her cheeks. She walked to her father's office through the hushed compound. A sepoy was on guard at the door, and he reported that Lieutenant Purline had left orders that no one was to be admitted except on army duty. Nell tried again the following day and again was turned away. She went miserably back to the bungalow, which now was as hushed as the rest of the settlement.

Some of Martha's thoughts were with the girl, but mainly the older woman brooded with anguish about Colonel Burns. She'd loved Geoffrey since she could remember with a quiet desperation that accepted the fact that she could never be more to him than a servant. So she'd contented herself with serving, first his wife who had died so young, then his daughter. Yes, I love him, Martha admitted, and he's dying in those hills. She didn't think of the colonel as dead, only in agony, and when a week had passed, she was close to collapse.

Finally, the fate of Colonel Burns and Captain Graves was known, but the news was brought first to Purline, and it was hours before either the colonel's daughter or Martha was told.

Rissaldar Dowlah arrived early in the morning and woke Purline. Purline rubbed sleep from his eyes, took one look at the dark face with the grizzled beard, and blurted, "They've attacked, then."

"Not yet, sahib, but there is news. Lieutenant Hamilton says to come."

He would say no more, and the two men rode in silence to the entrance of the Hajarial. Over their heads, in niches among the rocky cliffs, sepoys perched. All of them were craning their necks, looking down at the pass. As their horses clattered into the narrow defile, Purline saw a group of soldiers gathered near the end of it. As they drew closer, he spotted a number of bodies scattered among the rocks. They were natives, clad only in loincloths and turbans, with curved knives at their waists. Tribesmen, he thought, and felt his breath catch in his throat. As the rissaldar and Purline dismounted, Hamilton turned an expressionless face in their direction.

"Over here," he called to Purline.

Purline moved to the other officer's side and looked down at two bundles on the stony ground. For a moment he only stared, and then he groaned aloud. The two things on the ground bore no resemblance to men, and it was only by the tattered remnants of their uniforms that he could tell one man from the other. From a gaping hole that once had been a mouth, a wisp of gold-colored cloth protruded.

"When?" Purline asked.

"A short time ago." Hamilton waved a hand at the tribesmen's bodies. "They tried to drop them and run, but we were ready. Only one got away."

A muffled sound came from one of the things at their feet, and Purline jumped. Bending over Burns, he tugged at the gold cloth. "He's alive! He's trying to speak."

Hamilton grabbed the other lieutenant's hand. "They're both alive. Their tongues have been hacked out."

Purline backed away. "Eyes burnt out, ears . . ." In

horror he looked down the blackened torsos until he saw what was below the waists. Bile rose in his throat, and he gagged. "The bloody bastards! How could they do that and keep them alive?"

"Skill," Hamilton said, flipping open his holster flap and pulling out his revolver.

Still backing away, Purline cried, "I'll get the surgeon. I'll go back and—"

"Don't be a fool!" Hamilton bent over, but Dowlah, who had been standing like a statue, caught at his arm. "This I will do, sahib."

"No, rissaldar, this I'll do."

The revolver roared twice, and Purline screamed and ran. He'd gone only a couple of yards when he tripped and fell head-long. Propping his head up, he spewed vomit.

Hamilton didn't turn, but Dowlah snapped at the nearest sepoy, "Take two men and get the lieutenant back to Dardeshi. He's suffering from a touch of the sun."

Waiting while the soldiers lifted Purline into the saddle and led the horse away, Hamilton stared down at the two bodies. Then he stuck his revolver back into the holster and muttered to Dowlah, "He's suffering from a touch of yellow. You were right about him."

Dowlah's turban dipped in a nod. He pointed at the bodies, and Hamilton rubbed his brow. "Not to the fort. The women . . ."

"I'll take care of it, lieutenant." Stooping, Dowlah gently pulled the cloth from Burns's mutilated mouth. Dark clots of blood fell from it. "Prince Vitria kept his promise."

Hamilton straightened his shoulders. His voice was icy. "Detail some men for burial and get the rest back into position. They'll come now."

"Not until nightfall. Then they'll come like ghosts."

"We'll be ready." Throwing back his head, Hamilton looked upwards toward the Khasi Hills. Raising a clenched fist, he shouted, "We're ready, you bastards! We're going to hold this pass!"

244

As the echoes reverberated through the cliffs, Dowlah raised his own head. He muttered, "Yes, we'll hold. But for how long?"

The rissaldar's prediction was accurate. At dusk they came, hordes of them, creeping down the defile. But the British force, enraged by the horrible deaths of their officers, fought like madmen. Dowlah and Hamilton and Cornet Peters were everywhere, rallying the sepoys and urging them on. Under the barrage the forward surge of tribesmen wavered and then broke. The natives who got through the Hajarial were ridden down and slaughtered by the sepoy cavalry.

Prince Vitria's army was turned back that night and the next, but casualties among the sepoys were high, and more men had to be brought out from the garrison. The third morning after the attack began, the rissaldar brought Hamilton back to Dardeshi. The lieutenant had been shot in the right leg, and his left arm dangled limply. He refused to go to the hospital but insisted on being carried to Major Hewitt's bungalow. There, in the bedroom where his senior officer was propped up against a stack of pillows, he gave his report. Hewitt, fighting his own sickness, sent for the surgeon and Lieutenant Purline. Both men entered at a run. The surgeon knelt beside Hamilton and started to slice his trouser leg off. Purline stood beside Hewitt's bed. The big shadowy room was cool, but sweat dripped down Purline's face, and his hair was damp with it. Standing behind Hamilton's chair, the rissaldar regarded Purline sardonically.

"Lieutenant Purline," Hewitt said weakly, "as you can see, Lieutenant Hamilton is badly wounded. You'll have to take over his command. Leave ten sepoys here and take the rest to the pass. You'll move out this evening—"

"But Cornet Peters," Purline broke in. "Surely he can handle it. You're not well, sir, and with Lieutenant Hamilton wounded someone must be in command here."

Hewitt's fever-bright eyes searched the other man's

face. Then his eyelids drooped and his eyes closed. "Cornet Peters was killed last night. As for command . . . there's none left. Most of the women are at the hospital nursing the wounded. We'll station some of the sepoys there. Martha MacDowl has taken charge of the nursing staff. You're the only able-bodied British officer we have. You and Rissaldar-Major Dowlah will leave with the troops—such as they are—at dusk. Do you understand?"

"Yes, sir." Purline snapped a salute.

"Dismissed," Hewitt whispered.

As the door closed, Hewitt opened his eyes and looked at Hamilton. The younger man was biting his lip with pain as the surgeon probed at his leg. "What do you think about Purline, Rodney?"

Mutely, Hamilton shook his sandy head. Hewitt's bright gaze sought Dowlah. "You may make the arrangements concerning the women and children, rissaldar."

"Yes, sahib. One man at Miss Burns's bungalow, four at the officers' mess hall where the children will be gathered, the rest at the hospital."

"They understand what is required of them?"

"They understand, sahib. When the signal is given they'll do it as quickly and as painlessly as possible."

Hamilton raised his head. Blood spots flecked his lower lip. "And you, sir?"

"Mrs. Hewitt is at the hospital with the women, Donnie and Mary are with the children in the mess. As for me—" Pulling one hand from under the sheet, Hewitt showed him what he held. Then he shoved the revolver out of sight.

Hamilton grunted, "Purline's all we have."

"Yes," Hewitt sighed. "He's all we have."

Dusk had settled over the compound when Rissaldar-Major Dowlah entered Hamilton's bungalow. The wounded man was in bed with his native servant at his bedside. Hamilton was dozing, but as Dowlah bent over him, he opened his eyes. "Something wrong, sirdar?"

246

Dowlah spoke rapidly for some minutes, and then Hamilton grunted and tossed the sheets back. He shifted around until he was able to rest his bandaged leg on the edge of the bed. "Help me dress, Nikai," he told his servant.

Nikai protested that the sahib wasn't able to leave his bed, but Dowlah shoved him aside and helped Hamilton himself. Buckling the pistol belt around the officer's waist, Dowlah pulled Hamilton erect and, with Nikai's help, got the lieutenant to the veranda. Two sepoys were waiting. One of them took Hamilton's sound arm from Nikai, and the other waited for orders.

"Three horses," Dowlah told the waiting sepoy. "Saddle them and have them at Colonel Burns's bungalow."

By the time Dowlah and the sepoy half-carried Hamilton down the road to the bungalow, he was sagging between them. Another sepoy stepped from the shadow of the trees and spoke in a low voice to the rissaldar. Dowlah nodded, and although the living room windows were dark, he thumped heavily on the door. After a few minutes, the waiting men could see a flickering light approaching the door, and then it creaked open. Nell Burns, her hair in pretty disarray about a flushed face, was holding an oil lamp high in one hand.

Her eyes traveled from the native soldiers to Hamilton, and she gasped. "Rodney, you're wounded!"

"Aren't you going to invite us in?" he asked.

She stood aside. "Of course, come in."

Dowlah and the sepoy lifted Hamilton into the small room, and the lieutenant's eyes went past the girl to the closed doors of the bedrooms. Pulling her dressing gown closer around her, the girl waited. Finally, Hamilton looked at her. "Is Purline here, Nell?"

"Really, Rodney, what a question." She gave a little laugh. "As you can see, you got me out of bed. I've not been feeling well since daddy—"

"Don't mention your father! I asked you a question."

She drew herself up. "How dare you! Of course Lieu-

247

tenant Purline isn't here." She flung out her hand. "Would you like to search my room, look into my bed?"

"Yes," Dowlah grunted, and took a long step toward one of the closed doors, but Hamilton stopped him. Searchingly, he looked down at the girl he loved, studying the pretty face framed in tumbling waves of bright hair. Then he raised his voice. "Lieutenant Purline has orders to take the detachment out to the pass. The men are waiting for him at the parade square."

"Do you want to search my room?" she repeated.

"No, Nell, I can't do that to you. If you do see Purline, tell him this. Tell him there're worse things than death. Tell him it isn't too late. He can still come. Tell him—" He broke off abruptly and said to Dowlah, "For God's sakes, get me out of here!"

"But sahib—"

"Get me out, sirdar. Get me on a horse."

As Hamilton stumbled between the two men toward the door, Nell stepped closer. Her face was white. "What are you going to do, Rodney?"

He looked down at her coldly. "What I have to do. I'll lead the men myself."

"But you won't have a chance. You're wounded and—"

"Get out of the way, Nell. That's the least you can do."

Hamilton didn't glance at her, but Dowlah looked directly at her, and she flinched from the contempt in his dark eyes. Outside a sepoy was waiting with three horses. They hoisted Hamilton into the saddle and carefully set the boot on his wounded leg into the stirrup. Straightening his shoulders, Hamilton gathered the reins in his sound hand.

Dowlah jerked his head at the two soldiers. "Take the lieutenant to the parade square. I'll be there directly." He turned back to the bungalow and called softly, "Rambir." The guard stepped out of the shadow of the gold mohur trees. In the dusk his red coat looked black, and the white crossbelts, cuffs, and collar were startling. "You may leave here," Dowlah told him. "Go down to the officers' mess and help Carawal with the children."

"But rissaldar-major, I was told to remain here in case the rebels break through and the miss-sahiba Burns—"

"You have your orders, Rambir."

"Yes, sirdar." Touching his turban, the man walked away.

Dowlah looked at the bungalow where Colonel Burns had lived, and something moved in the depths of his eyes. "In a way I hope they do come," he whispered. "I'd like Prince Vitria to attend to you two himself." He strode rapidly away to join Hamilton and the troops on the parade square.

From one of the darkened windows, Nell watched the guard and the rissaldar leave, and then she sank weakly into a rattan chair. Her knees felt like jelly, and sweat was trickling down between her breasts. Her hands clenched into fists, and the nails bit painfully into her palms. When Ezra had appeared that afternoon, she'd been so happy to see him. He looked dashing in his uniform, so strong, so manly. I've nothing to fear, she thought; now we can talk. Removing his topi, he glanced around the drawing room. "Where are Martha and your maids?" he asked.

"They're staying at the hospital, caring for the wounded. I'm alone, Ezra. Oh, I'm so relieved that you came!"

His arms closed around her and his mouth sought hers. They kissed passionately, and his hands worked at her clothes, stripping them off her body. He didn't appear to notice that the dress he was ripping off was black, her mourning for her father. Nell thought of it briefly but then decided, Daddy's dead, he can't help—only this man can. They made love on her bed, and Nell was astonished at the man's passion. Ezra seemed in a frenzy of desire. He's mine, she exulted, he loves me.

Later, as cool air filtered between the lattices and the room darkened, Purline whispered in her ear, "You must help me, Nell. You're the only one I can turn to."

"I'll do anything I can, darling. What do you want?"

"I've been ordered out with the remainder of the troops tonight. To take command at Hajarial—"

"What about Rodney and Cornet Peters?"

"Peters is dead and Hamilton is badly wounded." Pushing himself up on an elbow, Purline peered down at her shadowed face. "It's certain death up there, Nell. Do you want me to die?"

"No," she said firmly. "I can't let you die."

"Then help me. They'll come for me. Major Hewitt is too sick to get out of bed, but Hamilton and that damned native officer will come. You must tell them you haven't seen me—"

"But the sepoy on guard outside. Rambir saw you come in. They'll know I'm lying."

"I know," Purline said urgently. "But Hamilton's in love with you. He won't humiliate you in front of those native soldiers. They'll go away and I'll be safe."

"You've planned it all, haven't you?" she asked, and her voice was dull.

"Everything, darling. There's no reason for dying—and the way those devils torture! Hewitt and Hamilton are fools to think they can hold that pass. They should pull back into Dardeshi and defend it until the relief column gets here." Bending his head, he nuzzled hot lips against her throat. "Help me, Nell. Don't let me die."

She pulled herself away from him, away from his sweating skin, away from his clinging arms and moist mouth. She stood over him, naked, and looked down at the naked man sprawled on her bed. It was so dark she couldn't see his face, and for this she was glad. "If the relief column gets through . . . you know the penalty for this?"

"Court-martial."

"You fear to die. What about dying in front of a firing squad for cowardice, for desertion of duty?"

Sitting up, he said eagerly, "I figured that out too. There'll be a court-martial, but my family—because of the Purline name they'll go easy. They'll never put a Purline in front of a firing squad. Will you do it, Nell? Will you lie for me?"

Reaching for her dressing gown, she pulled it on. Then she struck a wax match and lit a lamp. In the yellow circle of light, Nell Burns and Ezra Purline stared at each other. Finally the silence was broken by a heavy thump on the front door of the bungalow. Picking up the lamp, she moved away from the bed. "I'll do it. I'll lie to Rodney. But it isn't for you, Ezra, it's for me." Softly, she closed the door behind her.

So she'd lied to Rodney and he'd known she was lying, and his eyes as he left had reflected only disgust. Now she sat in the dark drawing room, huddled in a chair, listening to the staccato clatter of gunfire at the pass. For a time the sounds almost died away, and she sat straighter, her hands clenched, wondering if the rebels were through the Hajarial. Then the firing of guns began again, and this time there seemed to be more of them, many more. Some instinct told her what had happened, and she whispered, "They're here. The relief column is here."

Nell Burns was right. Shortly before dawn the relief column arrived, and the tide of battle for the Pass of Hajarial turned. By the time the column got to the rocky defile, few of the men from Dardeshi still lived. Only a handful of sepoys fought on. Lieutenant Rodney Hamilton lay dead, and at his side, still breathing but critically wounded, was Rissaldar-Major Dowlah. Dowlah lived long enough to make a report to the major of the column, to tell him of the deaths of Colonel Burns and Captain Graves. Dowlah also told him in detail about Ezra Purline and Nell Burns. The description of the officers' torture sent the British soldiers howling through the pass as though they were demented. They slashed and killed until the rebel bodies were piled in heaps. Prince Vitria was cut down and his mangled body tossed on top of one of the piles of corpses as though it were a piece of rubbish. Then the major turned his attention to Dardeshi and to Lieutenant Purline.

Long before the major arrived at the bungalow to arrest her lover, Nell had her chance of talking to Purline and reaching an agreement with him. They faced each other across the width of her bedroom. Purline was neatly dressed in uniform, his sword at his side, and Nell had donned her black mourning gown.

"They'll soon be here for me," he told her.

"I did what you asked, Ezra. I saved your life."

He bowed, and there was mockery in the movement. "For that you'll always have my gratitude."

"I need more than gratitude. You must marry me as soon as possible."

He laughed. "Don't be ridiculous. I've enough problems without that one."

"I'm with child."

"That's your problem, Nell."

Sunlight was seeping through the lattices. Bending, she turned down the wick of the lamp. "I'm afraid it's your problem too, Ezra. It's your child."

He shrugged. "It could easily be Hamilton's. The way you threw yourself at me, like a bitch in heat—I've no proof it's mine."

"You know better than that!"

He picked up his topi. "I'm sorry, Nell, but that's the way it is."

"No," she said quietly. "You'll marry me. You're terrified of dying. If you don't marry me you'll be committing suicide. Do you realize what would happen to you if I talked? If I tell of tonight, of my father's death, of how you dishonored Colonel Burns's daughter?"

"Whom would you tell?"

"Daddy has many friends in India. You'd never leave this country alive."

Purline frowned. "It would seem you have me."

"It would seem I do."

"And I am forced to marry a loose little strumpet, a woman who unmanned me with her flesh, with her ungodly passion. Yes, Nell Burns, you're the one responsible. If it hadn't been for you I'd have been fighting at the Pass of Hajarial. You did this! And now to be saddled with you, to have to look at you every day, to have to remember the shame you brought me to—"

"You're blaming me because you're a coward!"

He struck her full in the face. "Never say that word again. We'll be married, and I promise you this. I'm going to make your life hell. I'll never let you go, and I'm going to punish you for bringing me to this. The bonds that bind us will be much stronger than love ever could be."

She faced him, her shoulders straight, her chin lifted. Nell was a soldier's daughter, and not yet had Ezra Purline begun to break her spirit. "Yes," she said coldly, "a strong bond will hold us together. It will be riveted of shame and disgrace"—she looked directly into his eyes—"and hatred!"

21

As Martha MacLeod's voice faltered and trailed off, Rowan slowly returned to the hill over Fort Purline. The sere browns and dusty greens of Dardeshi faded, and again it was Maytime above the Nechako River. Below the burial plot Seamus and Dorrie were still playing, but little Martin had curled up on the grass and appeared to be sleeping with his blond curls pillowed against the broad back of the dog.

Rowan's legs had gone to sleep, and she shifted until they were stretched out in front of her. She rubbed at a numb calf. "What happened then?" she asked Martha.

"Exactly what Ezra Purline had believed would happen," Martha told her wearily. "Major Hewitt and the officers with the relief column would gladly have hanged him on the spot, but they were cautious men. The name Purline had been mentioned in English history books, and the men of that family had played important parts in building the Empire. Ezra was sent under guard to Calcutta. There was a short hearing there, and then he boarded ship, still guarded, to be court-martialed in England."

"And Nell?"

"Nell and I followed Ezra to Calcutta. They were married, and the four of us—Henry MacLeod remained with Ezra because of his loyalty to Ezra's father, and I stayed with Nell—went back to England. On the voyage Nell lost her first baby."

"How long were you in England?"

"For five terrible years. The court-martial was held secretly, but word leaked out and Ezra's friends and relatives disowned him. Except for Patience Burns—Nell's cousin—all Nell's relatives turned their backs on her. Ezra found it impossible to get any work, so we lived in a cramped little flat in London. That's when Henry and I were wed. I never loved him, but I did become fond of him, and Henry proved a strong and comforting husband. I've missed him."

Rowan darted a look at the older woman's drawn face. "Did Purline have a private income?"

"He had nothing. But Nell had a small inheritance from Colonel Burns, and we eked out a life on that. Our life was grim. All we had was each other. Ezra clipped his wavy hair short and began to go bald. More and more he turned to the Bible, and more and more he turned against his wife. Nell had a strong spirit, but he wore at it day by day until she began to half-believe she was a wicked woman who had ruined his life and her own."

"Why did you leave London?"

Martha's sandy eyebrows drew together. "Ezra was devoted to his mother and his older sister, Margaret. They were both lovely women in a cold, fair way, and he worshiped them as emblems of goodness and purity. No matter how other people treated him—his uncles and brothers and cousins—he was always convinced that Margaret and his mother still loved and understood. Then one night Nell and Ezra went to a theater, to try and forget the life they lived in that flat. In the lobby they came face to face with his mother and sister. I think if the Purline women had looked at him with disgust or even hate he might have stood it, but Nell said they glanced at him as though he were a stranger, with no sign of emotion or recognition, and then passed by."

"It must have shattered him," Rowan said slowly.

"It did. For days he was like a dead man. Then he went to a man named Charlie Hatch who had a number of fur trading posts in the colonies. Ezra humbled himself to this man and begged for a chance to prove himself."

255

Martha's mouth hardened. "I almost felt sorry for Ezra at that time. Charlie Hatch I only saw once, but he reminded me of an English Prince Vitria—a cruel, cruel man. Hatch humiliated Ezra, toyed with him, dubbed him general, but finally agreed to send him to the colonies to learn the business. We were in Montreal for a time and then at three forts, each one further westward. Ezra threw himself into the work and proved to be a valuable asset for the Hatch Company. When this fort was planned, Ezra was put in charge of erecting it and running it. It's his life's work and the only thing he has pride in." Martha sighed heavily. "That's the whole story, Rowan."

The girl's eyes were fastened on the Purline plot and the two tiny graves. "Not quite, but . . . I don't know how to ask."

Martha followed her eyes and sighed again. Slowly, she pulled herself to her feet, knuckling the small of her back. "Aye, I know what ye're thinking."

Rowan stood up too and slung her rifle over her back. "If he hates his wife and thinks her evil—why those graves? Why Dorrie and all the babies she's lost?"

"In those short months at Dardeshi, Nell lost all passion, but Ezra Purline is a man who needs women. Much as he loathes his wife, at times his lust is too strong to keep him away from her. When that happens he takes her brutally, without tenderness or feeling. Each pregnancy weakens her further, and her husband is well aware of that. He wants Nell dead, lass; he wants to be rid of her." Martha started down the hill. "I can speak of this no more, Rowan."

Deep in thought, Rowan followed her. When they reached the garden spots, she bent and scooped her younger son up. He stirred in her arms, her eyelids fluttered, and then he was sound asleep again. She hugged his warm body close to her breast. The other two children were tired too. Seamus trudged along at her side, and Dorrie clung to Martha's skirt. The sun was low on the horizon, and the shadows were lengthening into twilight. Rowan realized they must have talked all afternoon. As they walked through the gateway, she saw Portelance high above it, standing on the lookout platform. Lamps were burning in the store, Purline's office, and the kitchen of his home. On the opposite side of the square, old Gerika squatted in front of the stable, his toothless gums moving as he chewed his cud of tobacco and lime ash. Near him Armand and Lapointe lounged. Lapointe, whittling at a piece of wood, gave the group of women and children a cheery greeting, but Armand looked only at Rowan, and his expression was ugly. There was no sign of Osa. The stench of rum surrounded the two voyageurs, and she merely nodded and walked on, but Martha stopped to chat with Lapointe.

Directing her steps across the square toward her cabin, Rowan glanced toward the yellow rectangle of Nell Purline's kitchen window. Behind the pane she caught a glimpse of Nell moving around the room. She saw the shawl pulled over the shapeless dress, the tight bun of hair at the nape of the long slender neck, and the delicate profile. She pictured the young Nell, the one whom Martha had described. Nell Burns, glowing and pretty, unruly and high-spirited, who had captured Rodney Hamilton's heart. Nell Burns, indulged by her father, courted by young officers, the beauty of the regiment. Tears blurred Rowan's vision. How much more merciful it would have been if Nell had perished at Dardeshi.

Blinking away tears, she paused on her doorstep, looking back across the silent square. Armand lounged against the log wall, and he was still staring at her. She hugged Martin to her breast and found herself wishing that Laurie and George Durran were not pursuing *coureurs de bois* through the forest; she wished they and all the other men were at the fort. The evening air was still warm, but she was shivering. Was this hushed, brooding stillness the way it had felt at Dardeshi, she wondered, waiting for the tribesmen of Prince Vitria to break through the sepoys at the Pass of Hajarial? A sense of foreboding gripped her. Inside the cabin she barely took time enough to put Martin on his cot and light a lamp before she barred the door.

That night Charlie slept beside her bed, and close beside the shaggy black dog she propped her rifle.

Rowan didn't sleep well that night. Several times she woke from bad dreams, the covers tangled and soaked with sweat. Twice she got up and checked on Seamus and Martin. Shortly before dawn she gave up and rose and dressed. She put wood on the banked fire and took down her tin of tea muskey. When she went to the lean-to for water she found the pail was empty. Leaving Charlie with the sleeping children, she picked up the bucket and her rifle and left the cabin. The first tentative hint of sunrise sent opalescent fingers of light streaming over the dark fir forest to the east. She saw a shadowy form on the platform above the gates and guessed it was Portelance. He turned, saw her, and called down, "Rouse Armand and Lapointe, Rowan. Osa is without the gates."

Obediently, she turned back to the voyageurs' quarters and pounded on the door. After a time, Lapointe stuck a sleepy face around it. She gave him Portelance's message, and he shouted back over his shoulder. Rowan waited while the two men trotted across the square to unbar the gates. As they pushed them open, she walked toward the front of the fort. Osa stumbled through the gateway, his silhouette strange and distorted. He carried something across his shoulders, and for a moment she thought he bore the carcass of some animal, perhaps a small deer. Then Rowan distinguished a dark fall of hair, a flash of white buckskin, slender legs, and small feet shod in moccasins. Dropping the bucket, she ran toward the gates.

Armand was crowing with delight. "He has done it, *mes amis!* This dull bear has found a woman where we couldn't. You've done well, brother."

"You ordered me to find a woman. Papa said, 'Always do what Armand says.'"

"Put her down," Lapointe said eagerly. "Let us have a look at your prize."

Heaving her off his shoulders, Osa dropped her to the

hard packed earth. He stood beside her, his thick legs straddled. "She's mine," he rumbled. "Through the woods I pursued this deer, and I caught her."

Armand called, "Get down here, Portelance. Have a look at the deer our bear has caught."

Portelance was already climbing down the ladder. He looked closely at the girl sprawled at Osa's feet. "I don't like it. She's only a child."

"You like nothing," Armand said. "And she is big enough. Lots there for all of us."

His small eyes glaring redly, Osa fingered the axe in his belt. "She's mine."

"Of course," his brother said soothingly, "you caught her. But after you, then I come, and perhaps Lapointe too. Portelance isn't interested."

As the men continued to argue, Rowan dropped to her knees beside the girl. She could smell rum fumes from the men, and she knew that all of them except Portelance were deep in drink. Osa looked and sounded at his most dangerous, and Rowan's whole impulse was to run back to her cabin, but she found she couldn't. The Indian girl's hands were bound with rawhide thongs, and so were her slim ankles. Brushing back the girl's long dark hair, Rowan saw her face. She was snarling like a terrified animal, her lips drawn back from her white teeth, and she was very young. She couldn't have been more than fourteen. Her skin was smooth and a soft bronze in color, and her eyes were as black as a night sky. The short buckskin dress was fringed and decorated with beads and streaks of vermilion, and around her throat dangled a shell necklace supporting one large pendant of polished jade.

Bending close to the girl, Rowan tried out some of the Indian dialects she'd learned. The girl appeared to become calmer, but she kept shaking her head. Finally Rowan found that the girl could understand some French and a little of the Coast Salish. Rapidly, Rowan asked questions and the terrified child answered. Then Osa intervened. Stooping, he lifted the girl as though she were a

259

doll. Rowan sprang to her feet and caught at the man's thick arm. It was Armand who struck her hand away.

"Clear off," he warned. "Keep out of our business."

"You can't do this," Rowan cried. "Make Osa set her free."

Armand shoved her against Portelance, and he steadied her. She gazed at his impassive bronze face. "Portelance, you must stop them! None of you understand. Her name is Atai and her brother is—"

"Clear off!" Armand raised a clenched fist.

Helplessly, Rowan watched Osa carrying the girl toward the voyageurs' quarters. Behind them, Armand and Lapointe strode. Lapointe gave his silly high-pitched giggle as Rowan turned to Portelance. Before she could speak, he spread out both hands. "It's not my affair, Rowan. I can do nothing. Armand and Osa, they would kill me."

As he climbed the ladder to the platform, Rowan heard another voice. General Purline was standing on the steps of the store. "What's going on here?" he demanded.

She ran toward him. "I must speak to you."

He made no effort to disguise his dislike. "I've nothing to say to you."

"This fort, you value it," she said rapidly. "You must listen."

One large, well-shaped hand rubbed his chin. Then he stood aside. "Come in."

Lamps were still burning in the store, and Bobby Holden, his hair uncombed, was leaning against the counter. Pushing the pince-nez higher on the bridge of his nose, the young man gazed curiously at the factor and then at Rowan.

"My office," Purline said, and led the way.

He sank into his chair but didn't invite the girl to sit. In silence he waited, and finally she said, "Osa has brought a girl from the woods—"

"An Indian?"

"Yes, but—"

"Then there is no need to say more. As I have made

abundantly clear, I don't interfere with the voyageurs and their native women."

Gazing down at him, at the clipped hair and the naked gleaming spot on the crown of his head, at the roughhewn features and jutting ears, Rowan felt disgust and rage welling up within her. She thought of Nell lying for this man while he cowered in her bed and of a wounded, gallant man who went out to die in Purline's stead. She understood why Purline seldom challenged Osa and Armand. He was a coward, and he feared them. She almost turned to leave, and then she remembered Atai and stood her ground.

"This is more than the welfare of an Indian maid," she said softly. "The safety of your fort is at stake. This isn't the wife or daughter of one of your tame Indians. This is Atai, sister of the chief of one of the Teton tribes."

"Teton?"

"Sioux. Atai is a Sioux."

He snorted. "Impossible. The Sioux are a people of the great plains far to the south and east of us. We've never had Sioux in this area."

"They're here now. Atai told me that her tribe, greatly lessened in numbers, were driven from their homes by the Chippewa. As you must know, the Chippewa have been armed by white traders with guns and ammunition—"

"Supposing she did tell you the truth? What has this fort to fear from the remnants of a tribe of Sioux?"

"They're proud and mighty warriors. The braves will track the girl here, and if you allow the voyageurs to abuse Atai, her brother will wreak terrible vengeance."

Propping his wide chin on one hand, he appeared deep in thought. For a time she had hopes, but these were dispelled when he said slowly, "I can't interfere with the voyageurs."

Rowan took a deep breath. "In the name of mercy you must! Atai is a child, no older than fourteen. You've a daughter, sir. What if Dorrie—"

"Don't bring my family into this sordid discussion." He got to his feet and towered over her. Looking down into

261

the tilted blue eyes, he said grimly, "Despite her age or tribe, she is only a squaw. You of all people should know how I feel about squaws."

She didn't flinch. Lifting her chin proudly, she stared back. "And about any woman, regardless of the color of her skin. I won't try to persuade you further, but this I can promise you. The Sioux will come, and with them will come this fort's doom—and I hope yours."

Swinging around, she walked out. Bobby Holden scuttled away from the door and moved back behind the counter. As Rowan stepped out of the store door, she heard the first piteous scream from the voyageurs' quarters. Her rifle clenched in her fist, the breath sobbing in her throat, she ran toward the sound. Armand and Lapointe moved away from the wall to meet her. They stood stolidly, their rifles leveled.

Her shoulders slumped. Slinging her own rifle over her back, she picked up the bucket. As she walked blindly in the direction of the gates, she could still hear the child's screams.

The sun was directly over the fort and Bobby Holden was missing his noonday meal, but he didn't mind. He was admiring Little Moccasins's tall figure and Amazonian good looks. While Laurie was away, she was helping Rowan, and she'd been sent to the store with a list of supplies. Although Little Moccasins still spurned Bobby's advances, her attitude toward him appeared to have become somewhat milder. Measuring out powder and shot, he said to the Indian woman, "Rowan appears to be stocking up for war."

"She damn good shot."

"I hear she is. I know little about such things. Must admit I'm better at making love than war. Which brings me to what I've been mulling over." He paused and then asked plaintively, "Do you suppose for a change we could speak in the trading dialect? I could make my thoughts much clearer to you."

She fingered a braid of coarse black hair. "Speak Onglis. My Onglis good."

"Well, if you insist, little darling. I've been thinking a great deal about you and me lately. I doubt very much if I shall ever leave this wilderness, and I'm deucedly attracted to you. I've a feeling that one of the chief reasons for my abysmal failure with you is that I've used the wrong approach in wooing—"

"Speak Onglis, cur!"

"As you wish. I was wondering if you'd care to marry me."

She laughed. "You want Little Moccasins to jump stick with you."

He gave her a weak grin. She'd used the derogatory term for a native marriage ceremony. "Something of that sort, I suppose."

Throwing back her head, she roared with laughter. "Jump stick with *you?* Not little Moccasins. Not by damn sight!"

He adjusted his gleaming pince-nez and wistfully regarded the smooth column of her throat. It wasn't far from that throat to the jut of her full breasts. He thought, By jove, absolutely smashing! Must weigh five pounds each if they weigh an ounce! Clearing his throat, he asked diffidently, "What must I do to win your favor?"

She sobered and examined the young man with calculating eyes. "Not jump stick. Marry. Like this." She placed one hand across her brow, shading her eyes, while the other hand made a circular movement around her throat. Moving back, Bobby gazed apprehensively at her knife sheath. Was she threatening to cut his throat? Then his face cleared. "Aha! A wide-brimmed hat and a collar. You mean you want a legal marriage with a minister." Taking the lid from a glass jar, he offered it to her. "Have a sweet, little darling. What turns your charming feminine mind toward a man of God?"

She selected a long red-and-white striped peppermint stick and sucked noisily on it. Around it, she mumbled, "No jump stick. You die—Little Moccasins gets nothing."

Rather miserably, her suitor regarded her. She had abandoned sucking the candy stick and was greedily biting it off in large chunks. He watched her large white teeth crunch down. Does she want to marry me only to kill me off for my estate? he wondered. Aloud he said gravely, "Don't get any ideas. I'm worth more alive. I'm afraid dear old dad cut me off without a sou. Little dustup about a chambermaid he fancied himself. And I haven't saved a shilling from my pay, so it will be to your advantage to keep me alive. That way I can work and make money for you."

She nodded. "You work, make money. Not go to lodges to waste on girls. You try and Little Moccasins gut you like deer."

Stepping around the counter, he gazed up at her. "Does this mean we're engaged?"

"We marry."

He slid a tentative hand up her arm. "In that case, seeing we're as good as married, how about a little kiss?"

She slapped his hand down, but the expression on her broad face was close to coquettish. "After man marry up, cur."

"One thing I think we should discuss. If we're to become man and wife, I would appreciate it if you could call me something besides cur. Call me Bobby." She tried to say the word and failed. "Very well," the young man conceded, "that seems a little difficult. We'll shorten it. Say Bob."

Her lips, sticky with peppermint but delectable, rounded. "Boob!"

"Like this." He mouthed, "Bob."

"Boob. My Onglis good. I call you Boob."

"I think I'd rather be called cur." Bobby slipped an arm around her waist, and this time she didn't repel him. We make progress, he told himself, and raised his other hand to squeeze her breast. "What a luscious creature you are. I think I won't have to go to the lodges again. You're enough woman for any man, little darling."

"Shut mouth, Boob."

He lifted his eyes. Her expression was abstracted. She drew away from him and in two strides was at the window. Over her shoulder she grunted, "Get gun!"

He stared at the broad expanse of her back. "I'm afraid I'm no fighter. I confess I don't know how to handle one of the infernal contraptions."

"For me, not you." Whirling, she pulled a rifle from a hook on the wall and expertly loaded it. "Take one and hold it, Boob."

Obediently, he lifted another rifle down. "You must have ears like a wolf. What is it?"

She kicked open the door and with her free hand practically lifted him to the top of the stairs. "Look."

His mouth sagged open. "My sainted aunt! I've never seen natives like those before. What tribes are they?"

"Sioux."

They marched across the dusty square. The man in the lead was young and handsome. His features and coloring reminded Bobby vividly of the young voyageur Beau. There was a difference. This man's face showed no hint of kindness or gentleness. He wore a breechcloth of white buckskin, and a short cape hung from his broad shoulders. It was ornamented with pieces of jade and trimmed with feathers. Dark hair fell to his shoulders, and around his brow was a beaded band with a single eagle feather thrust through it. Two other men followed a few paces behind the young man. They were both tall and strongly built. The one on the left was an older man. His cheeks were slashed with red lines that Bobby thought were paint. As they drew closer he could see that the red marks were partially healed knife cuts. The third man was the youngest. His face was round, and a bandage was wound around one arm.

"My sainted aunt," Bobby repeated admiringly. "They're certainly fine-looking chaps."

"Bad medicine," Little Moccasins muttered.

Tearing his eyes from the Sioux braves, Bobby looked around the square. Behind the Sioux was Portelance, his rifle held in steady hands. Old Gerika was coming out of

265

the stable. As usual his jaws were moving rhythmically, and he clutched an old-fashioned musket. Armand and Lapointe were leaning against the wall of their quarters with rifles cradled in their arms. In the doorway to Dutchy's cabin, Marinska stood. Her youngest child was clinging to her skirt, and her two little sons, Pieter and Georgie, were standing beside her. In one hand Marinska clutched an axe.

Then Bobby saw Rowan. She was walking toward the Sioux. Martin toddled along behind her, and his older brother was trotting to catch up. Reaching out a long arm, Little Moccasins pulled Martin up beside her and called to Seamus. The older boy turned his head and then obediently came to her. Martin was struggling to get loose from Little Moccasins's grasp, and Bobby leaned down and scooped up the child.

Rowan moved closer to the Sioux and stopped. The young man in the lead held up a hand, and the three braves halted. He said something to the girl, and she replied. Bobby whispered to Little Moccasins, "Can you understand?"

"Sioux brave say he's Takuimo, chief of his tribe. He say he wants talk to our chief."

Clutching the squirming child, Bobby looked nervously toward the factor's office window. "Where's the old man? He should be out here. Maybe I'd better get him."

"Stay, Boob. He come."

General Purline was walking from his cabin with a stately tread. He was impeccably dressed, his dark suit neatly brushed, his linen snowy, with a gray silk stock at his throat. On his head he wore a tall beaver hat, and he carried a gold-headed cane. The hat made him look even taller, but when he reached Rowan's side and stopped in front of the Sioux chief, Bobby saw that the three natives were much taller than Purline. With a sense of shock he realized they were all as tall as Osa.

In a clear, confident voice, Purline instructed Rowan. "Ask him who he is and his business."

"He told me his name is Takuimo and he's—"

266

"Do as I tell you."

Again she spoke to the young chief, and he answered in his cold, hard voice. With her eyes on the handsome young man's face, she translated, "His name is Takuimo and he's chief of a tribe of Sioux who have been driven north by the Chippewa Nation. They fought many battles, and many of their warriors are dead or wounded. Chief Takuimo is resting his people before going south again to join with other Sioux tribes. He is here because his young sister, Atai, is missing. The two men with him are his brother, Okima, and his sister's affianced, the warrior Skeska. Yesterday Atai went to gather roots in the forest and didn't return. They found traces of a struggle, they found her basket, and they found tracks. They say she was brought to this fort by a large, powerful white man against her will."

"By jove," Bobby whispered excitedly to Little Moccasins, "these are quite the trackers if they can deduce all that."

"Shut mouth," he was told.

Martin was whimpering against his chest, and Bobby realized he'd been crushing the boy against him. He loosened his grasp and soothed the boy. His other hand, holding the empty rifle, was damp with sweat. The conversation between the factor and Rowan that he'd eavesdropped on that morning ran through his mind. Anxiously he waited to hear Purline's answer.

Purline was taking his time. He'd locked his hands behind him under the tails of his coat, and he was rocking back and forth on his heels. He glanced sideways toward his cabin, and Bobby, catching a flicker of motion from the corner of his eyes, swung his head around. On the doorstep of the large cabin Nell Purline was standing, her shawl hugged tightly around her, little Dorrie clinging to her hand. Nell's face was ashen, and her eyes looked huge and frightened.

Purline said abruptly to Rowan, "Tell Chief Takuimo that he is mistaken. There is no Indian maid of that description in my fort."

"I won't lie."

"Then I'll tell him. He seems to understand some French." Raising his voice, Purline started to speak slowly and laboriously in French.

A bay of laughter broke across his words. Digging Lapointe in the ribs, Armand shouted across the square, "Are you afraid of these running dogs, *mon général?* A brave man who allows mangy savages to scare you!"

Purline whirled on him. "Be quiet, you drunken fool!"

Armand laughed again. "He can have the little deer. She's of no further use to us." Turning to the door, he called, "Come, my brother, bring your prize out. Her people have come to claim her."

His eyes glaring from his matted face, Osa staggered out of the doorway. In his massive arms the Indian girl dangled like a broken toy. "She screamed too loud and hurt my ears," he said. "I sought to quiet her and took her neck in my hands. Here." Lunging across the square, he tossed the girl at her brother's feet.

"My God," Bobby muttered, quickly turning Martin's face to his chest. He saw Little Moccasins put out a powerful hand and drag Seamus behind her.

Bobby was sickened. The girl lay in a tangled heap, the buckskin dress ripped half off her body, and the smooth curve of a bronze hip and the curve of a tiny breast showed. Her head was canted to one side, and her long hair fell across her face. "He's broken her neck," Bobby whimpered.

Little Moccasins raised her rifle. "Now all hell break loose, Boob."

General Purline was as ashen as his wife. Sweat beaded his brow and trickled down his nose. He stared down at the pathetic heap at his feet and then up at the young chief's face. Takuimo didn't show any emotion. His face looked as though it had been carved from amber. The carven lips moved, and he said a few words.

Rowan raised damp eyes from the girl's body and said huskily, "He says he must have the man who did this."

268

"Osa?" Purline turned and looked at Osa. As he did, Armand raised his rifle and aimed it at the factor's chest.

"Try it, *mon général*. Try and deliver my brother to this savage and you're dead."

For moments everyone in the square stood as motionless as the Sioux warriors. Lapointe's rifle pointed at Takuimo, Portelance had his weapon aimed at the backs of Okima and Skeska, and Armand's rifle pointed steadily at Purline.

Purline spoke; his voice was loud, but there was a quaver in it. "Tell the chief I'm sorely distressed by this tragedy but I can't deliver my man to him. Tell him that Osa is dull-witted and can't be held responsible for his actions."

Rowan translated, and the reply she received was only a few terse words. "Takuimo says he must have this man. If you give him Osa he'll leave in peace."

"No! Offer him gifts. Any of these dogs would sell their sisters for gifts. Tell him I'll give him rum, tobacco, cloth goods for his women. Tell him I'll give—"

Rowan turned her head away. "I won't offer him this insult."

"I command you to translate. Tell him the gifts I'll give him. Tell him I can supply his tribe with arms and ammunition to use in their war against the Chippewa."

"You can't command me! Tell him yourself."

Purline's mouth snapped open, but another voice cut across the square. It was Takuimo's, and he spoke in almost unaccented English. "The Indian maid with blue eyes has given you her answer. She will not offer me this insult. I'd advise you, chief of this fort, not to try and buy my sister's life with a handful of trade goods."

Purline's eyes widened. "You understood everything we said."

Narrow, dark eyes impassively regarded Purline's quivering face. "I was taught your language and also French by a missionary when I was younger than her." Without looking away from Purline, the chief pointed at

269

the girl's body. "I ask only one gift from you. This Osa who killed my sister must leave with us."

Glancing at Armand and his leveled rifle, Purline shook his big head. "I'll not give you my man."

Without turning his head, Takuimo spoke to the two men behind him. The one with red knife wounds on his cheeks took a step forward and spoke swiftly and forcibly. After a moment, Takuimo's head dipped in a nod. He bent over to lift his sister's body, and the other man spoke again. This time Takuimo shook his head and muttered something.

"What are they talking about?" Bobby asked Little Moccasins.

"Warrior with scars say he was to be Atai's husband. He carry her. Chief say no, Skeska, she my sister."

As the chief lifted the dead girl, her neck lolled over his arm. Skeska brushed the hair away from her face, and Bobby gasped. Her eyes were wide open, staring sightlessly up, and her mouth gaped as though she'd died screaming. Her thin throat was mottled with ugly bruises.

Takuimo raised his eyes from his sister's agonized face and spoke to Rowan. This time Bobby didn't need a translation because Rowan said in English, "Chilcotin. My mother is sister to the chief of the tribe."

Takuimo's hard eyes swept from the crown of Rowan's glossy head down to her moccasins. "You have other blood than Chilcotin," he told her. "And so do your man children." He jerked his head, and Bobby's arms closed convulsively around Martin's small body. Takuimo's head swung toward Dutchy van Zzll's cabin. "And there is a Salish woman and four mixed-blood children." The young chief looked at Nell Purline. "The chief of the fort's woman and girl child." His gaze returned to Rowan. "What does this Osa do, and what kind of name is that?"

Osa answered himself. "I'm a voyageur," he said proudly. "My name means bear. That is my brother Armand over there. He is smarter than me but not so strong."

Takuimo nodded gravely. "Yes, you are a bear and

strong." He took a step backward, and Bobby saw Portelance steady his rifle on the man's back. The chief looked down at his sister's face, then he looked at Osa, and last at the factor. "You, chief in your tall hat and with your men around you with firesticks, listen well to Takuimo. One day my people will learn wisdom. Instead of Chippewa fighting Sioux, we will band together and fight our last war, and it will be against you with your white skins who maim our bodies, break our spirits, grind our pride into our country's soil. We will teach you a terrible lesson!"

Purline said nothing, but Rowan, with sadness in her face and voice, said softly, "In the end you will be defeated."

"Perhaps. But we will be remembered!"

Takuimo grunted a couple of words to Okima and Skeska, and with them at his heels, he walked regally from the fort. The last thing Bobby saw was the girl's head bobbing loosely against her brother's arm, her black hair drifting back like a dark cloud of smoke. He didn't realize he'd been holding his breath until he felt a pain in his chest and expelled it.

"Whew!" he said. "I'm glad to see the last of those three. Must admit they took it well."

"Think so, Boob?" Little Moccasins stretched out her arms. "Give Martin here. I take boys to Rowan."

As Bobby handed her the child, Purline said cheerfully, "Faced them down, didn't we? Don't ever point a gun at me again, Armand. I'd no intention of handing your brother over to those savages. Just to be on the safe side we'll keep the gates barred, and there'll be two men manning the lookout tonight. We'll take it in shifts. Portelance and Lapointe will take the early watch, Armand, you and Osa, the second. Mr. Holden and Gerika will take the third." Teetering on his heels, he looked coldly down at Rowan. "As for you, you'll hear of this when Mr. Woodbyne returns. You disobeyed me, and you proved hysterical in your assessment of these savages. Your proud and warlike Sioux left with their tails between their legs."

She didn't look at him, but as she walked away she called over her shoulder, "They were armed with knives, and rifles were pointing at them. They'll be back."

"Hysterical women," Purline muttered. As he passed his cabin he snapped at his wife, "And you, standing there like a brazen hussy letting those men stare at you! Get into the cabin, Nell, and take my daughter with you."

Bobby hefted the empty rifle he still clutched in a sweaty hand. "General, I've never stood watch."

Purline slapped the young man's shoulder. "Never mind, Mr. Holden, it's merely a precaution. Gerika will be with you, and I'll come up myself for a time during your watch."

Paying no further attention to the men, Rowan walked swiftly over to Marinska's cabin. The door was ajar, and Marinska was bending over the bed in the alcove. Standing by her side, Rowan looked down at Dutchy's flushed face. "How is he?"

Marinska shook her head. "Not good. I give him medicine Mr. Durran left, but Pieter not good."

Taking the woman's arm, Rowan drew her away from the bed. The children were playing on the floor. Georgie and young Pieter were wrestling, and the older girl, Mary, was playing with a rag doll. The baby, Rowan Two, held a bright ball of wool in her chubby hands. Keeping her voice low, Rowan said, "The Sioux will be back. You know that, Marinska."

"They come back."

"Will you bring the children and come with me?"

The Indian woman looked tenderly at the small twisted form in the bed. "I stay with my man."

"Then let me take the children."

The older woman hesitated and then said firmly, "Children stay with father." She touched Rowan's hand. "You go. Go quick."

Rowan bent and kissed the broad cheek. "Good-bye, Marinska," she said.

Leaving the cabin, she trotted across the square to her own. The wind drifting down from the mountains brought a clean, fragrant scent that mingled with the woodsmoke from the chimneys of the cabins. She took a deep breath of that air and stepped into her own cabin. Little Moccasins had put out cold food for the children's lunch, and while they munched it she was packing a buckskin bag.

"Did you get the ammunition from Bobby?" Rowan asked.

Little Moccasins jerked her handsome head. "Over there. I pack food, water bottle, blankets."

"Make up another bottle of that berry juice and honey the children like."

"Already done, Rowan. My canoe on creek, hidden in willows. Paddles in it. I show you where." She lifted calm, dark eyes. "Marinska say no."

"Dutchy's too sick to take, and she won't leave him. I wanted the children, but she says they have to stay with their father."

"Dutchy give Marinska children." Little Moccasins's hand sketched a bulge in the air over her own flat belly. "Marinska and children stay with Dutchy."

Rowan was working with her rifle and a powder horn. "Where's Martha?"

"In bed. Walk like this." Bending her straight shoulders, the big woman hunched across the floor.

"Can she walk to the creek?"

"Have to. We help Martha."

Rowan looked up at the woman beside her. "You'll come, won't you?"

"Little Moccasins stay too, Rowan."

"Why? There's nothing to keep you here. I can see Marinska, but—"

"Stay with my man. Stay with Boob."

"Boob? Do you mean Bobby Holden?"

"Boob and I marry with—" Little Moccasins sketched a collar around her neck.

Rowan was staring at the other woman. "Marry? With a minister? I thought you hated Bobby."

"Little Moccasins always want Boob."

"Then why did you chase him away with a knife? You even cut him several times."

The wide brown face split into a smile, and she tapped her brow with a long finger. "Me plenty smart. Girls in lodges good for Boob one night, maybe two. He get girls easy. Boob never get Little Moccasins. Now, marry him and make good man of Boob."

Rowan was smiling. There was no doubt that Little Moccasins was plenty smart. She had what she wanted, a legal marriage with the young Englishman. Then her smile faded and she said urgently, "Chief Takiumo was making a head count. We must get the children out of here. Talk to Bobby. Persuade him to come with us. Both of you come. It's your only chance."

The other woman nodded agreement and then sighed heavily. "No use. Boob say safer in fort. Lots men with guns. Boob damn fool. Little Moccasins stay look after damn fool. Can't come. But I help you."

Putting down the rifle, Rowan studied her children. Martin was pushing bread crumbs around on the table, but Seamus was watching his mother with wide, grave eyes. Such a sturdy little boy, Rowan thought, such a calm, sensible child. Even at five he was highly sensitive as well. She had a hunch he knew only too well what was going on. Climbing down from the chair, he took one of her hands in both of his and squeezed tightly as though trying to comfort her.

She knelt beside him. "We're going on a picnic, Seamus. I have to go get Dorrie and her mother and Martha. You do what Little Moccasins says and tell your little brother what fun picnics are."

"I will, mommy. I'll tell Martin."

Rowan moved quickly out of the cabin and along the square. The gates had been closed and barred, and Portelance was still on lookout. She didn't approach Nell's kitchen door but circled the Purline cabin and went in the back way. Inside the lean-to she paused to listen for the sound of the factor's voice. The lean-to was a dim place, and in the corners cordwood was piled. Dried pumpkin strips hung from the rafters, and she could smell brine from the kegs of salted fish and game. Opening the door, she looked down the narrow hall. Four curtained cubicles lined the hall, and then she saw Nell in the doorway of the kitchen. She called, "Nell, are you alone?"

Nell stepped into the hall. "The general is in his office, Rowan. He didn't want lunch. Dorrie's here and Martha's in bed. That gardening work yesterday gave her a stiff back."

Parting the curtains of Martha's cubicle, Rowan beckoned to Nell. Martha was propped up on pillows and her face was drawn with pain, but when she saw Rowan she smiled. "Told ye I was getting old, lass. My back's played out."

"Can you walk?" Rowan asked.

"Aye, but bent over as though I'm ninety. Why?"

"I'm taking the boys and getting out of the fort. Little Moccasins is lending us her canoe. I want you two and Dorrie to come with us."

Martha looked bewildered. "Why?"

"The Sioux will be back. We must leave and as fast as we can."

"But Nell said there were only three and they left quietly."

"Don't you understand? The chief's sister was raped and brutally killed. These are proud warriors. They'll make a bloodbath of this fort."

"But three men—"

"Martha, those were only the leaders. The rest of the tribe's out there. He said many of the warriors were killed or wounded, but who knows how many are left? If they take this fort they'll want Osa and General Purline. But they want Nell and Dorrie too. As for the rest . . . they'll slaughter all of us."

Nell stepped closer. "Won't we have a better chance here? There're the voyageurs and Gerika and Bobby. Surely they can defend the fort."

"There aren't enough men to fight them off. They'll come over the wall and . . ." Her voice trailed off, and then she said firmly, "I'm not going to waste time arguing. Trust me. Get Dorrie. Dress in warm clothes. Tell the child we're going on a picnic. Now, Nell, now."

"Rowan's right," Nell told Martha. "I saw the chief's face, how he looked at Dorrie and me. I'll help you dress and then I'll get Dorrie ready." She turned to Rowan. "Shall I pack food?"

"No, Little Moccasins is packing food. We'll bring the boys and pick all of you up at the lean-to. Be quiet. Don't let the general know."

Nell was already pulling Martha's clothes on. She bent to lace the older woman's boots. "There'll only be Dorrie and Martha. I'm staying."

Martha caught at her hands. "No! You owe him nothing."

Nell smiled. "You're wrong, Martha. I owe Ezra a great deal. Oh, not what you're thinking. It's certainly not loyalty or affection keeping me here, but I must stay. We're bound together with something stronger than steel. I won't, I can't leave him."

Looking at Nell's dreadful smile, Martha's mouth set stubbornly. "Then leave me be. I'm staying too. Rowan can take wee Dorrie."

Hooking her hands under the older woman's armpits, Nell hauled her to her feet. "You've stayed too long now. You've wasted your life on me. I'm past needing you, Martha, but Dorrie will. You'll go, if I have to drag you down to the canoe."

Martha's eyes blazed, but at that moment the curtain snapped open and all three women jumped. Dorrie's blond head poked into the cubicle. She looked at her mother and then at Rowan. "What are you and Rowan doing, mummy? I thought Martha was sick."

Her mother bent over her. "Martha feels much better, dear. You and Martha are going on a picnic with Rowan. It's a secret, and you mustn't tell your father."

The child clapped her hands. "A picnic! Are Martin and Seamus going? Are Pieter and Mary and Georgie—"

"Martin and Seamus are going," Rowan told the girl.

"But Marinska's children are staying home. Their daddy's sick."

Blue-gray eyes so much like Nell's stared up from the child's round face. "I won't drink that awful tea! And I'm going to take my doll with me."

"Fine," Rowan said. "Take Jane. Little Moccasins is making up a bottle of berry juice. You like that." She looked intently at Nell. "Won't you change your mind?"

"No. I'll have Dorrie and Martha waiting in the lean-to. Do you know where you're going to . . . to have your picnic?"

"Yes, but I can't tell you."

"Why not?"

Rowan glanced down at the child's attentive face. "Because they could make you tell. They have ways. Little Moccasins and I will do our best to hide our tracks—"

"Tracks!" Dorrie cried. "Are we going to play Indian like those three men who were here today? The ones who picked up the sleeping lady?"

"Yes," Rowan said grimly. "We're going to play Indian."

Nell frowned. "They're expert trackers. Do you think you can fool them?"

"We can only try." Rowan kissed Nell's thin cheeks. "God be with you," she whispered.

As she ran back to her own cabin, she thought, God be with all of us.

By the time they got down to the canoe hidden in a clump of willow opposite Ile Ste. Anne, the sun was low on the horizon. Rowan, who had been taut with anxiety for hours, was dripping sweat. Of the group the only calm ones were the imperturbable Little Moccasins and Seamus, who never appeared ruffled.

Rowan and Little Moccasins had the two boys and the packs ready in a short time, but Martha and Dorrie had been delayed. When Rowan slipped into the lean-to expecting to find the woman and child waiting, she found that the general had changed his mind about having a meal and was sitting in the kitchen. She inched open the door leading to the hall and listened. She could hear his deep voice, the piping tones of Dorrie, and once in a while Nell's light voice. Rowan was rigid with fear that impetuous Dorrie would decide to tell her father about the picnic. She knew that Martha, waiting in her sleeping cubicle, and Nell, working in the kitchen, must be just as much on edge. Finally she heard a chair being scraped back, and then the sound of a door closing. The general had returned to his office. Hardly had the door closed when Martha and Dorrie were brought to the lean-to by a white-faced Nell. Martha stood with her head averted while Nell knelt beside the child. She hugged the little girl and kissed her tenderly. Dorrie, who was ablaze with excitement, seemed suddenly to sense her mother's tension. Putting up a hand, she stroked Nell's cheek.

"If you're going to be lonely, mummy, I'll stay with you."

"No, dear, you go along and have a good time with Martin and Seamus."

Dorrie pushed her rag doll into her mother's hands. "Take Jane. She'll keep you company till I come back."

Pushing the child gently toward Rowan, Nell got to her feet. She clasped the doll to her breast. "Go quickly," she said faintly.

They left as fast as they could and found Little Moccasins patiently waiting behind the lean-to. With her were the two boys and Charlie. Despite the fact that she'd slung the heavy bag of provisions and a roll of bedding over her back, she took Martha's arm and helped the suffering woman along. Martin was lagging behind, so Rowan picked him up and pushed Dorrie and Seamus along in front of her.

"We must all be quiet," she whispered. "Remember, we're Indians. Don't raise your voices, and do as you're told."

Nodding their heads, Dorrie and Seamus tiptoed along with exaggerated caution. Martha glanced back at Rowan.

"How do we get through the gates? Nell said the general ordered them barred."

"Portelance is on watch, and I hope to persuade him to let us out. Now, around behind the store. We'll keep behind the buildings until we near the gates."

The voyageur was standing with his back toward the fort, leaning on the palisade, gazing out over the river. So silent was the group of women and children that he didn't hear them until Rowan called softly up. Swinging around, he peered over the platform and then climbed agilely down the ladder.

He glanced at Martha, bent almost double with pain, to Little Moccasins and the heavy packs on her back. "General Purline gave orders," he told them. "Nobody comes in or goes out."

Little Moccasins grasped at her knife. "Open gates, cur, or I slice neck."

He turned an impassive brown face on her and shook his head. Rowan touched his arm. "Please, Portelance, let us go."

"Orders, Rowan, my orders are—"

"Look." She pointed at the children standing before her, at the boy she held in her arms. "Would you have their lives on your conscience? You should have too much there now. You made no effort to stop Osa and Armand, Portelance."

He looked down at the three small faces and then, without a word, lifted the heavy bar. Little Moccasins, as she passed him, rasped, "Keep eye out. I come back soon."

As they cleared the fort, Rowan urged, "Hurry, Martha, walk faster."

"I can't, Rowan. I'm trying, but I can't move any faster."

"Wait," Little Moccasins grunted.

Taking the bedroll, she slung it across the rifle over Rowan's back. Then she lifted Martha's short, stout body and draped her across her broad shoulder. With long strides, Little Moccasins led the way around the palisade toward the creek. With Dorrie's and Seamus's help, Rowan pulled the canoe clear of the willows and held it while Little Moccasins lifted Martha and lowered her into it. In moments they had the bundles in, the children lifted into the middle, and Rowan climbed into the stern and picked up a paddle. Then Charlie leaped in, spraying all of them with water. Little Moccasins steadied the canoe and then, with a tremendous heave, pushed it away from the bank. All the children waved to her, and she lifted one regal hand in farewell. As they drew away she started to cut a bough from a fir.

"What's Little Moccasins doing?" Dorrie asked.

Rowan was propelling the light craft along with powerful strokes of the paddle. "She's going to wipe out our tracks, Dorrie, and the place where the canoe was hidden."

"Like Indians do!" Dorrie exclaimed, and turned around to Martha. The woman was crouched in the bow of the canoe, her face turned back toward the fort, tears dripping down her cheeks. "Why are you crying, Martha?" When Martha made no reply, Dorrie cried, "Why is she crying, Rowan?"

Rowan blinked back the tears in her own eyes. "Martha's back hurts her, Dorrie."

Wide eyes searched Rowan's face, and then the child's mouth twisted and she started to cry. Little Martin, clinging to his older brother's hand, began to whimper.

"I want to go back," Dorrie howled. "This is no fun. I want my mummy!"

Rowan winced. Sounds travel clearly across water. Her eyes searched the banks. Dorrie's howls were piercing, and soon Martin would stop whimpering and start crying at the top of his lungs. "Quiet them!" she told Martha.

Seamus had already put his arm around his brother and was whispering in his ear. The younger boy subsided immediately. Martha spoke softly to the little girl, but Dorrie's mouth only opened wider. Leaning forward, Martha slapped the child across the face. It was the first time a hand had ever been laid on Dorrie in punishment, and the shock stopped her screams. Crawling along the bottom of the canoe, she buried her head in Martha's lap. Martha stroked the honey-colored ringlets. "There, there, wee Dorrie. Martha's sorry, but ye must be quiet."

"We're not playing, are we?" Dorrie moaned. "You're taking me away. I'll never see mummy again."

Martha's arms tightened around her. "Ye have Martha, Dorrie. Martha will always be with ye." Across the child's curls, she looked toward Rowan. "Where are we going?"

"I'm circling the island. We'll disembark on the other side."

"Why not this side?"

"That mudbank on this side will show tracks too clearly. The other side is mainly rock. But the current is swifter over there. Everyone sit still, and don't talk."

Martha was staring at the island. "Shouldn't we try to get further away from the fort?"

"We haven't time. Daylight is waning, and the children need shelter. The nights are cold. There's a cave on the island where they can sleep. It's the best we can do, Martha. Now, please don't talk. The paddling is difficult through this stretch."

The water on the far side of the island was rough and Rowan's arms were aching, but Little Moccasins's lessons in handling a canoe had been thorough, and eventually Rowan nudged it against the rocky shore. Tall trees hid them from the other bank of the creek.

Seamus crawled out after Rowan, and both of them stood in cold water while they helped the other three out. Dorrie and Martin were easy enough—Rowan swung them out onto the rocks—but Martha could scarcely move, and it took time and strength before she was standing on the shore. Seamus did his best to help, but Rowan was exhausted and had to sink to the bank to get her breath back.

"The rest of you go on up to the cave," she panted. "Seamus will show you where it is. I'll hide the canoe and bring up the packs. Keep your voices down. Dorrie, you help Martha. Let her lean on you."

They set off with Seamus, holding Martin's hand, in the lead. Martha, leaning on Dorrie, slowly followed. Charlie stayed with Rowan, sprawling beside her until she finally forced herself to her feet. She unpacked the canoe and hauled it up on the bank. Cutting boughs, she spread them over the canoe and stood back to look it over. It wasn't a very good job; keen eyes could spot it, but it was the best she could do. Shouldering the packs and her rifle, she trudged into the trees, following her companions. She found them sitting around the mouth of the cave. Martha had propped her back against a big boulder that still held the warmth of the sun. Dropping the packs, Rowan rubbed her own aching back. She shielded her eyes and scanned the sky. To the west a spectacular sunset threw streamers of gold and scarlet and purple across the sky.

"We'll have supper now," she told them. "Then I'm going to bed all of you down in the cave—"

"No!" Dorrie cried. "I'm not sleeping in a dark wet cave. I want to go home."

"It's not wet. It's dry, with clean sand on the bottom of it," Rowan said patiently. "It won't be dark. I brought a small lantern."

Dorrie flung her head back until her ringlets danced. "There're animals in caves. Big ones with long teeth. They'll eat us!"

Martin's blue eyes widened, and he threw back his head and wailed. Seamus immediately cuffed him, and Rowan took a step closer to the girl. "That's enough, Dorrie. One more outburst and I'm taking you across my knee. Understand?"

Dorrie glanced sideways at Martha for support, caught a glimpse of the woman's haggard, sad face, and changed her tactics. "I'll be a good girl, Rowan. What kind of food are we having?"

Opening the leather bag, Rowan spread food out. Soon the children were eating cold duck, cornmeal bread and jam, and small cakes. Rowan urged food on Martha, but she shook her ginger head. "If ye have tea, I'll have a sip, lass."

"We've something better than tea." Rowan pulled out the bottle of berry juice sweetened with honey. Carefully, she measured the liquid into four tin cups. She poured twice as much for Martha as she did for the children.

Dorrie pouted. "I want the big cup. Martha has more than us."

Rowan handed the cups around. "She's bigger than you."

Martha looked over the rim of her cup. "Aren't ye having any, Rowan?"

"No, I'll have water."

Looking from the tin cup to the children, Martha raised sandy brows in a silent question.

"It will be easier this way," Rowan told her.

It would be easier. She'd laced the drink with laudanum. There'd be no chance of any of them staying awake or crying out this night. She packed the remains of the food away and found the lantern. Crawling into the cave, she lit the lantern and arranged a snug nest of blankets. The children were yawning as they stretched out, and Martha's eyes were heavy. The Scotswoman was in the middle, with Dorrie cuddling up to her on one side and Martin's blond curls resting against her other arm. Seamus curled up beside his brother.

"Sleep well," Rowan told them. She kissed her sons, touched Martha's cheek, and patted Dorrie's head.

"Can't you sleep in here with us, mommy?" Seamus asked sleepily.

She kissed his firm cheek again. "I'll be near, Seamus."

She sat beside them until they were all breathing in heavy, regular breaths. When Martha started to snore, Rowan turned the lantern out and crawled out of the cave. She sat in front of it, a blanket over her shoulders, the rifle across her lap. Charlie pressed closely against her side, and she patted his head, glad of his company. The last brilliant colors of sunset were fading in the westward sky. A moon, close to full, was appearing over the dark mass of firs, but clouds surrounded it, and as she watched, they drifted across it, veiling its silvery

283

brightness. It would be a dark night and a cold one. The wind, whistling down from the mountains across the water, was chill. Hugging the blanket around her, she thought back over the day. Had she panicked? she wondered. Had she taken Martha and the children and run when it was foolish to do it? Would they have been safer in the fort?

In the silence of the little island with its tall trees, doubts gnawed at her. The silence was broken only by the lapping of the water against the shores, the rustle of wind in the trees over her head, and the faraway cry of some night bird in the forest. She remembered the expression in Takuimo's eyes, Skeska's scarred face as he'd brushed back the hair from the face of the girl he was to have married. Some instinct deep within her told her she wasn't wrong.

Her thoughts strayed to Laurie and George Durran and the rest of the men. Again she wished fervently they were back in the fort. If they'd been there that day this would never have happened. She knew George Durran would have taken the Sioux maid from the voyageurs and freed her. What would Laurie have done? She shook her head. She admitted that the man she loved, with whom she'd lived for six years, in most ways was still a stranger to her. In all those years he'd never said he loved her. He'd told her he loved her hair, her eyes, her body, but never had he said he loved *her*. Martin was so much like his father, and she sensed that Martin was incapable of deep feeling for anyone. But Seamus—in the darkness her lips curved in a smile—Seamus with his black eyes and coarse black hair, Seamus with the rosy color in his dusky face. Ah, yes, Seamus loved. She'd often imagined that he was like her mother, like her mother's people. Suddenly, she hungered for the mother she couldn't remember. Aluski, a woman who had loved enough to give up her man and her only child.

The night bird called from the forest again, and she was wrenched from her thoughts. Was it actually a bird? Her hands tightened on the cold metal of her rifle barrel.

She pictured dark figures slipping stealthily through dark trees, heading for the fort, and she shuddered. If the Sioux tracked them to this island, what could she and her dog actually do against them? They loved children. Would they kill the children? If they didn't, if they took the little ones with them, what would their fate be? She pictured Seamus and Martin and Dorrie as captives, and her mouth hardened. She'd never allow that to happen. One of her hands left the rifle and felt for the knife at her waist. If the Sioux came she could do only one thing—the same action that long before Colonel Burns had asked a young officer named Rodney Hamilton to do for his own women.

She was cold and cramped and terrified, but she sat on, gripping her weapons, straining her ears for sounds in the night. One part of her mind wandered to the people at the fort. They'd be starting supper by now, she thought, and in her mind she could see Nell moving around her kitchen, bending over the hearth.

It wasn't until she tasted salty moisture on her lips that Rowan realized she was crying.

22

At Fort Purline it was the supper hour. In the van Zzll cabin, Marinska sat beside her husband's bed trying to coax him to drink a little broth. On the lookout platform, exposed to the raw wind from the northeast, Lapointe had joined Portelance on watch. Little Moccasins was heating up a pot of succotash in Rowan's cabin. Neither Armand nor Osa had any interest in food. They were sharing a keg of rum that Armand had just stolen from the room behind the store. Osa seemed depressed, but Armand was in high spirits. As he drank, his thoughts dwelled more and more on Rowan.

"She's gone," Armand told his brother. "Sneaked out before sundown with Martha MacLeod and the three brats. That squaw thinks she's smart, but Armand's smarter."

"Armand's smart. Papa said that," Osa dully agreed.

"Papa was right, brother. I know where they went. That white squaw thinks no one knows about her spot on Ile St. Anne. How wrong she is."

Osa nodded but made no answer. He had no interest in Rowan.

In the flickering light of a single oil lamp, Bobby Holden still worked in the store. He was hanging lengths of tobacco from hooks on the wall. On the hearth of the crude fireplace, a small fire was kindled. It was smoking, and he coughed occasionally. The door of the factor's office opened, and Purline shoved his big head around the edge of the panel. "Still working, Mr. Holden? Might as

286

well call it a day and have your supper. I heard you coughing. You're not coming down with an illness like Mr. van Zzll, are you?"

"No, sir." Bobby coughed again and covered his mouth. "That fire. Smoking badly tonight."

"Hmm." Strolling over, Purline looked critically at the hearth. "Chimney's not drawing properly. Probably the direction of the wind. Let it die out. No one will be in here anyway."

The lanky young man rounded the corner of the counter. "Portelance was telling me that the lodges are now deserted. He said the women and children all went into the forest this afternoon. Said even old Tupa is gone."

"I'm certainly not responsible for the movements of the hunters' families."

"Don't you think it odd, sir?" Bobby asked bluntly. "Those Sioux here, and then the Indians run for cover. Frankly, I'm wondering if Rowan might have been right about them."

"Rubbish, Mr. Holden! I was a soldier for years, and I assure you those Sioux won't dare try anything. For one thing they've no idea how many armed men are inside this stockade. No, I know savages, and they'll keep clear of us."

"I'll keep that in mind when I'm up there in the dark with Gerika tonight," Bobby muttered morosely.

"You don't seem reassured." Laughing, the factor clapped a big hand on the younger man's shoulder. "Rely on my judgment. Don't worry any further, and you get along to your cabin now."

Bobby nodded and took his leave. Purline barred the door, raked some ashes over the smoldering fire, and then made his way through his office to the kitchen of his own cabin. The fire there was drawing perfectly, and Nell had his supper prepared. She dished up stew, put a loaf of fresh bread and a jar of goose grease on the table, and reached for the coffeepot. Sitting down, Purline glanced around the table. It was set for only one.

Picking up a spoon, he dug into the stew. "Aren't you eating, Nell?"

"I'm not hungry."

He accepted a cup of coffee and spooned some sugar into it. "I suppose Martha is still laid up. What about Dorrie? Did she eat earlier?"

Nell removed the stewpot from the tripod. "Neither Dorrie nor Martha is here."

His spoon dropped with a clatter. "What do you mean?"

"Rowan took her boys and Dorrie and Martha. They're all gone."

"They can't be! I left orders that under no circumstances were the gates to be opened."

Nell didn't look at him. "They're gone."

He slapped a hand on the table, and the coffee sloshed, amber liquid spilling down the side of the cup to form a small pool around it. "Of all the ridiculous situations. First that hysterical squaw and her dire warnings. Then young Holden scared out of his wits because a pack of squaws leaves the lodges. Now I find my servant and my own daughter have left the safety of this fort. Why didn't you stop them, Nell?"

"I was glad to see them go. I believe Rowan is right."

"You've always been a fool! The danger is outside the palisade, not in here." He added grimly, "If anything happens to Dorrie I'll hold you responsible."

Removing her apron, she hung it on a peg. "I'm responsible for everything, aren't I, Ezra?"

"Where are you going? Aren't you going to clean up the kitchen?"

"It will wait until morning." She turned toward her sleeping cubicle. "I'm not feeling well."

He eyed her with interest. "You never feel well anymore, do you? Go along to bed then, but one thing I assure you. When Woodbyne returns I'm going to tell him a few home truths about the squaw he's living with. I won't have her upsetting my fort. If he can't handle her, he can get rid of her. I don't want her here."

His wife was paying no attention to him. Stepping into the cubicle, she pulled the curtains closed. He glared at the green-and-white gingham for moments, and then his face cleared. No real harm done. Martha and Dorrie would probably have an uncomfortable night, but it served them right. As for the Indian woman, in time he'd deal with her. As he thought of Rowan he felt a stirring in his loins. An instrument of the devil, that woman. Look what she'd done to the voyageurs, look how she'd hypnotized young Woodbyne. And what about Laurence Woodbyne? Had that disgusting Charlie Hatch confided in his son-in-law? Did Woodbyne's mocking aura stem from the fact that he knew about India, about Dardeshi? But Dardeshi was behind him. The past was dead. He'd made a fresh start, and this fort was a success. If it weren't for Nell and her damnable eyes and white face, he could forget all of it. Nell wasn't well. Each day she seemed to get weaker, her face more wan. Soon—he took a deep breath—she might be dead, and he'd be free of her.

Getting up, he took a rag and wiped the pool of coffee off the table. Then poured a fresh cup. Time he was getting to bed himself. It had been a long day and an upsetting one, and he was tired. He decided he wouldn't undress. He'd promised that ass of a Holden he'd check in on the third watch, and he'd better do it. Holden certainly was a useless ass. Anyway, Ezra Purline decided, I'll be in a snug bed while that Indian slut and Martha are cowering under a tree somewhere. With the thought, he smiled. Serve them both right.

One by one the lamps went out in the cabins, and darkness settled over the buildings. At ten o'clock Portelance and Lapointe left the lookout platform and Osa and Armand took their places. By that time Armand was feeling the rum, but Osa was soddenly drunk. Settling down on the platform, he braced his giant shoulders against the logs of the palisade and sat with the keg of rum between his legs.

"Stupid nonsense," Armand grunted. He leaned back against the log wall with his back to the river. "Standing up here in the wind when we could be down in the quarters. Right, Osa?"

He received no answer. Leaning over, he jerked his brother's head up, scanned his face, and then let it drop. "Passed out, you big dull bear. Ah, well, you might as well sleep."

Drunkenly, he started to think of Rowan again. For years he'd lusted after her and hated her. This could be his chance. He could follow her to the Ile Ste. Anne. If he judged her correctly, she'd be on guard before the cave, that cave where the pig Woodbyne and the white squaw used to make love. Many a time he'd followed them and from outside the cave had heard their voices, their husky whispers, the rustle of their clothing as they'd stripped naked. He'd sweated, picturing the blond Englishman and the beautiful *bois brûlée* with their bodies entwined, their lips pressed hotly together. He probably could lure her away from the cave, but when the voyageurs heard what he'd done he'd be an outcast. The code would be broken, and even Osa would be forced to disown him.

Armand rubbed his chin. There was a way! It could be blamed on the Sioux. He'd entice the girl away from the cave, have his way with her, and then kill her. He'd mutilate her as a savage might, and that would be most enjoyable. He imagined his knife slashing at her white body and groaned with pleasure. Teach the squaw to spurn him. Yes, it could be done. He'd wait until the next watch. Neither old Gerika nor that stupid Holden would know he'd left the fort. He'd climb the palisade and then— He thought of the girl and his knife and started to smile.

He was still smiling when two dark forms came over the log wall behind him. He had no warning. The knife slipped into his back while he was thinking of his knife in Rowan's soft body. He lived for a few moments, long enough to hear the Sioux warriors working around his sleeping brother. He could feel blood seeping from his back, forming a warm pool under him, and he wondered if they were killing Osa. He died without knowing his brother's fate.

Four of the braves securely lashed the unconscious man with rawhide. Then they lowered him over the palisade. Other Sioux, waiting on the ladder, caught the huge body, groaned under its weight, and let it drop to the ground. Then a stream of brown bodies clad in breechcloths swarmed up the ladder and, from the platform, stared hungrily down into Fort Purline.

In his cabin, Bobby Holden moaned in his sleep and rolled over. Lifting his head, he stared around him. By Jove, but that had been a nightmare! Good to see his familiar room, the fire banked on the hearth, the remains of the pot of succotash Little Moccasins had brought on the table. Fumbling on the floor, he found his pince-nez and looped the cord around his neck. Swinging his bare legs out of bed, he stared around the room. The curtains were drawn over the window, but their edges were rimmed with light. Had he overslept and missed his watch? Was it morning?

He shivered and pulled the skirt of his flannel night-gown around his spindly shanks. Heaving himself reluctantly up, he padded across the cold floor and opened the door. His eyes widened, and he snapped his pince-nez up on his nose. The square looked as though he'd wakened and found himself in hell. The huge pile of cordwood that the general had ordered piled in the middle of the square had been kindled and blazed up in ragged flames. Red and gold sparks flew upwards, and those colors were echoed in the ocher-and-vermilion-painted faces of the savages around it. Firelight burnished their bronze bodies and glinted from their shoulder-length hair. They wore breechcloths and moccasins, and bows and arrows were slung across their naked shoulders; war clubs were either strung around their necks or grasped in their hands;

knives were at their waists, and most of them carried spears.

Standing motionless by the fire was the young chief. He no longer wore his short, ornamented cape. His handsome face was painted with red and yellow, and in one hand he held a short club studded with jade.

Bobby looked around wildly. Where were the general and the voyageurs with their guns? Then he saw some of the voyageurs. At the foot of the ladder to the lookout platform, Armand's body sprawled. Blood dyed the back of his buckskin coat, and the top of his head was missing. Near the door to the voyageurs' quarters, two more bodies were crumpled. They were horribly mutilated, but Bobby recognized the bright sashes. Lapointe's was green and red, and Portelance's blue and yellow. There was no sign of the factor.

Then he heard shots and a bellow he recognized, and his eyes were wrenched further down the square. In front of Rowan's cabin was a group of struggling figures. One of them was Little Moccasins. She was naked, and her coppery body thrashed about among four warriors. Her hair was loose and fell in a straight black mass to her waist. She held a rifle but had reversed it and was using it as a club.

With no hesitation, Bobby galloped to her aid. "I'm coming, little darling!" he shouted.

One of the warriors swung around, and his eyes widened. The lanky young man, clad in a billowing white gown, his pince-nez perched precariously on a long nose, made a ludicrous sight. Bobby had no weapon, but barehanded he descended on Little Moccasins's attackers. He pulled and hauled at their slick bodies until one brave turned and, almost negligently, thrust his spear into Bobby's narrow chest. His eyes bulged, red stains mantled the white of his nightgown, and he crumpled. Little Moccasins appeared to go insane. With inhuman strength she bludgeoned the warriors, driving them away from Bobby.

She stared down at him. "Boob. My poor damn fool!"

One of the battered Sioux raised his spear, sighted carefully, and drove it deep into her back. Still she stood, wavering, blood flowing redly down her flanks, staring down at Bobby. When her knees gave she fell close enough that one of his hands could reach hers. Bubbles of pink foam trickled from his mouth as he whispered, "Sorry, little darling . . . forgot rifle . . . not a fighter but a lover . . ."

Little Moccasins didn't hear him. She was dead. Bobby lived long enough to see her scalped. Then he was glad to die.

Across the square a group of Sioux was battering down the door of the van Zzll cabin. Skeska, his red wounds blending with the warpaint on his cheeks, was directing them. The chief, who had watched the deaths of the wild young Englishman and the gigantic Indian woman, strolled toward them.

"What is holding you up?" Takuimo called. "Can a simple slab of wood defeat the strength of many warriors?"

"It's barricaded," Skeska told him. "But soon it will be down."

Takuimo nodded. "This is the house of the Salish woman and her children." The door splintered from its hinges, and one of the braves wrenched it aside and leaned it against the log wall. Waving the men aside, Takuimo stepped to the gaping hole. A chest of drawers had been pushed against the door, and over it Takuimo peered into the cabin. "There is the Salish woman, her children, and her man. As I suspected, he is white."

Lamps burned beside the bedstead, and in front of them Marinska stood, her short legs straddled, a hatchet in one strong hand. At her side her son, young Pieter, stood in the same posture as his mother. His chubby hands grasped a chunk of firewood almost as large as he was. The three other children crouched on the bed, their black eyes gleaming with terror. Rowan Two clutched at her father's hand. Dutchy was delirious, and his head rolled from side to side. His eyes, in a flushed face, wandered without comprehension around the room.

At the chief's side, Skeska, wild with bloodlust, shrieked, "Stand aside, my chief, and let us finish them!"

Holding up a hand, Takuimo said quietly, "Wait." He looked the room over. His hard eyes wandered from Dutchy's humped form to the children and then settled on Marinska's broad face. "I'll be generous, Salish woman; take your young and leave. We'll satisfy ourselves with this white man."

Her head shook so violently that the long braids bounced. "To kill Pieter, you first kill my son and me!"

Shoving aside the chest of drawers, Skeska sprang into the room. He raised his war club and charged at Marinska. In one mighty leap his chief was upon him. Grasping the older man's arm, Takuimo wrenched and the club passed harmlessly over the woman's head. Skeska turned glaring eyes on his chief. "Let me finish them."

"It would seem you forget who is leader," Takuimo said evenly. "I told you to wait."

Skeska stood eye to eye with the young man, and then his eyes dropped and he stepped back. Takuimo gazed down at little Pieter. The child's chubby arms trembled from the weight of the piece of wood, but his eyes flamed defiance. "Put down your weapon, little warrior," Takuimo said. "What's your name?"

"Pieter van Zzll. I'm called for my father. My mother is Marinska."

"Marinska," Takuimo muttered. "You would fight like a she-wolf for this white man? You would see these children slaughtered rather than give him to us?"

"I would," she panted.

"Why?"

"Pieter took me when I was an outcast, when I was called barren. My life was no better than one of the village dog's. But he took me and gave me children. He gave all of us kindness. For him I would see my children dead. I would die myself."

"I admire courage and loyalty." Takuimo glanced at Skeska. "Take a lesson in loyalty, Skeska. You're a brave man and a mighty warrior, but if ever again you challenge

294

me we'll fight to the death." His eyes traveled back to Marinska. "We don't need your lives. Because of you, your man has his. Stay in this cabin. No harm will come to you." Turning on his heel, he strode out of the doorway and gestured to one of the braves. The shattered door was lifted and leaned back to cover the opening. Takuimo took a knife from its sheath and carved a mark on the wood. He shouted across the square. "Let no man go past this. If this cabin is touched, the man will deal with me."

More warriors were dragging old Gerika from the stable. "What of this old one?" one of the warriors called.

Takuimo glanced their way. "Kill him."

A war club rose, arched over Gerika's matted hair, and crushed his skull like an egg. Skeska moved up beside the chief. He spoke slowly and sullenly. "I shouldn't have disobeyed, but I keep seeing Atai's face, and my mind churns with grief. Only blood can heal my hurts."

"I see my sister's face too, my friend, but the Salish woman and her sick man had nothing to do with Atai's death. If you think me soft, watch well." Takuimo caught sight of his brother's tall form and rounded face. "Okima, gather the warriors. We are ready for the chief of these people. The man with his tall hat and his woman and girl child. Bring them out, but harm them not." He spoke in a lower tone to Skeska. "Have men erect a strong stake near the fire."

Both Okima and Skeska hurried to do his bidding. Takuimo took up a position near the fire. He watched his warriors break down the door of the Purline cabin. He watched other warriors driving a thick stake into the ground near him. Above the crimson and yellow paint on his cheeks, his dark eyes were calm and cold and hard.

Nell Purline was dragged from the cabin. She wore a long flowing nightgown, and her chestnut hair, glinting with red lights in the flames, tumbled to her shoulders. She sagged between two warriors, and if they hadn't been holding her she would have crumpled to the ground. Then more warriors came from the cabin. Among them was

Purline's tall figure. He was dressed as he had been earlier that day, but now his linen was crumpled, the silk stock was disarranged, and he didn't wear the beaver hat. He was offering no resistance to the men holding him. His skin was gray, and sweat trickled from the end of his fleshy nose. The last man to leave the cabin was Okima. He trotted over to his brother. He snorted disdain. "The proud chief we had to pull from his bed. But the girl child is not in there. They must have hidden her."

Skeska ran over to the two men. "All the buildings have been searched, and there's no one in hiding. The blue-eyed Chilcotin woman and her two children are missing too."

"So." Takuimo fingered the hilt of his knife. "She's a clever woman. Of all in this fort I read understanding of us only in her eyes. She's taken her children and the chief's daughter and run."

"We can bring them to earth," Okima said eagerly. "By the light of dawn we can pick up their tracks. A woman and three children can't go far."

Skeska nodded. "They can't hide from our eyes, Takuimo."

"That can wait," Takuimo said. "We have business now."

Flanked by his brother and Skeska, he took a few steps toward the captives. Purline suddenly wrenched his arms from the hands of the men holding him and ran to meet the Sioux. He fell to his knees on the hard packed earth of the square. "Mercy," he babbled. "Give me mercy. Do what you want with the rest, but spare me. I'll give you all the goods in the store. I'll give you anything—"

"Silence!" Takuimo said sternly. "Get this worm to his feet." He waited until Purline was roughly hauled upright, and then he looked contemptuously down at him. "The great chief of this strong fort has courage only when surrounded by his men and firesticks. I have already killed your men. If we wish your goods we'll take them, but we didn't come for trinkets and blankets and rum. We came for the man called bear, and him we have. We came for

296

you and your woman too. Shortly you will know how I feel, how Skeska feels. Tie this worm to a stake."

With folded arms, Skeska, Okima, and Takuimo waited while Purline was lashed to the stake with rawhide strips. Then Takuimo spoke to a warrior and pointed at Nell. The man grabbed the front of her nightgown, slashed it from neck to hemline, and wrenched the material from her body. She stood in pathetic nakedness, her thin milk-white body revealed to all their eyes. So thin was she that her breasts were only tiny, rose-tipped buds and her rib cage was etched starkly under them. Only her thick hair, falling in reddish waves, softened that wasted form. She lifted wide eyes to Takuimo's expressionless face. "Will you kill me now?" she asked softly.

"In time." He turned to her husband. "Your wife will die as Atai died—slowly. Many of your men raped my sister. Many of my men will rape your wife. When they are done, her neck will be twisted—slowly. This you will watch. If you close your eyes or look away you'll be prodded with a knife. After you've watched her die, your turn to die will come. Slowly."

Saliva was dripping down Purline's square chin. His eyes rolled wildly from Takuimo to his wife's pinched face. "Do what you want with her, mighty chief. She's a wanton, a slut! She's the scarlet whore who sits on the seven great hills! Make her suffer. Rape her. Kill her. But please spare me."

The men who had been holding Nell Purline had dropped her arms and were staring at her husband. As she walked toward the man lashed to the stake, one of the warriors sprang after her. Takuimo raised a hand, and the Sioux stopped. As though there were no one else in the fort, she walked up to Purline and stared up at his face.

Her voice was clear and calm. "The years roll away, Ezra, and again we have Dardeshi. You were a coward then and you're a coward now. There have been times since we married when I almost accepted your preachings, almost believed that it was I who caused your desertion." She drew herself up, her narrow shoulders as straight as once they'd been. "Rodney Hamilton died for you, Rissaldar Dowlah died for you, the sepoys died for you. As long as you live, you don't care who dies in your stead." She waved a hand. "Look over there. Portelance and Lapointe died because you're a coward. Little Moccasins and poor Bobby lie in pools of their own blood because of you." One slender hand pushed the heavy hair from her face. "Now I'll die. But no matter how painfully I die, these men are more merciful than you've ever been."

Turning her back to Purline, she went directly to Takuimo. Gray-blue and black eyes met, and between those two people of vastly different worlds for an instant was complete understanding. The woman said nothing, but the man bowed his head and murmured, "I'll give you the mercy he never has shown you."

Putting out a sinewy arm, he drew her face against his hard bare chest. His other arm rose, and firelight glinted on the knife blade. With precision he drove it between two of the bony ribs. His aim was strong and true. Nell Purline died instantly. For seconds they stood, his arms supporting the frail body, a study in copper and white. Then he lifted her as gently as he'd lifted his dead sister, and carried her to the stake. He laid her at her husband's feet, face up. He pointed at her torn nightgown. "Cover her. All but her face."

When it was done he stepped away from the man bound to the stake. Purline followed the chief's movements with terror. Skeska pointed at the factor. "Now we kill him."

Takuimo shook a regal head. "He desires life."

Okima stared at his older brother. "You're going to let that . . . that creature live? The mangiest dog in our village would fight for his mate!"

Turning to his warriors, Takuimo said sternly, "This night you've dipped your weapons in the blood of brave people. That big woman and that silly young man"—he pointed toward the bodies of Little Moccasins and Bobby—"died fighting. The voyageurs battled well. Don't soil your knives on this thing on the stake. Twice this night I've given mercy—to the Salish woman and to her." His finger pointed down at Nell Purline. "To the chief of this fort I'll not give it. Let him live and look upon and remember a wife who was a better man than he is."

Both Skeska and Okima nodded gravely, and the rest of the warriors raised their spears in agreement. Skeska said, "The blue-eyed Chilcotin—will we pursue her?"

Takuimo deliberated. "I would like to, if only to add her to my wives. Noble sons the Chilcotin would bear a man. But . . . no. This fort houses many more men than the ones we've slain. Against many men with firesticks our losses would be great. Our lives we need for our war with the Chippewa. We'll follow the men who carry the man called bear. We will punish him, and then we must leave this valley."

A warrior stepped forward, a young one with a wound in his shoulder. "Do we set flames to these buildings before we leave?"

Takuimo shook his head. "When they return, let the white men see our work. Let them look upon their chief and his wife. We're done here. Skeska and Okima will come with me. The rest of you go to our camp and prepare the children and women to move. If you're ready before we return, head south. We'll follow."

All the warriors waited respectfully until he moved away from the stack of burning wood. Skeska and Okima fell into step behind him, and the other men followed. Not one of their heads turned to look at the still figure lashed to the stake.

Time passed, the fire burnt down until only a few flickering tongues of flame lighted the square. The wind died, and a gentle rain started to drift down. Drops fell against Nell's face until it looked as though the dead woman wept. A cold gray dawn began to break above the mountains. It was only then, in that dawn's light, that a dark shadow that had stood motionless in the darker shadows of the van Zzll cabin moved.

Stalking across the square, Marinska stood stolidly in

front of the stake. Purline lifted his big head and looked at the woman with empty eyes. "Untie me," he whispered.

She stroked the knife stuck in her belt, and then her hand fell to her side. Leaning forward, she spat full in his face. Stooping, Marinska lifted Nell's body in her arms and stumbled into the Purline cabin.

Throwing back his head, Ezra Purline stared sightlessly up at the leaden sky. After a time the rain washed the spittle from his cheek.

23

It was well past dawn when the three Sioux leaders arrived at the glade in the forest far west of Fort Purline. None of them showed signs of fatigue. Tirelessly, they had trotted along through the balance of the night, moving among the tangled trees and underbrush with ease.

As they came into the clearing, they saw Osa with his back propped against a hemlock trunk, his four guards sprawled out on the grass a short distance from him. The warriors weren't sleeping. As Takuimo, his brother, and Skeska appeared, all the men sprang to their feet. The clearing they'd picked was a lovely spot. A tiny stream bubbled merrily through it, and along its banks clustered clumps of white azalea and blue camas flowers. The rain drifting down was light—more mist than rain—and refreshing.

One of the warriors came to meet the three leaders. He raised his spear in a gesture of respect.

Takuimo lifted a hand. "Hail, Zabacta. How did it go?"

"It was hard work, my chief; the big one is heavy as a buffalo. Finally we forced him to walk, and then we moved faster. Were any of our brothers slain?"

"No, Zabacta, none were slain. The voyageurs proved mighty fighters, but we caught them while they slept, and one was deep in spirits. Still they managed to wound three of our warriors. It was well there were no more of these men or we'd have lost many braves."

"And the chief? Did he fight well?"

Okima snorted, and Takuimo said, "Their chief hid in

his bed like a woman until he was dragged from it. He's no real man and should crawl on his belly like a snake. Enough of this night. Later you will hear it sung around our campfires. You will have your parts because you captured the bear." He glanced around. "Where is my sister?"

Zabacta led the way to the far side of the clearing, where a tanned deer hide covered a small mound. Stooping, Takuimo pulled back a corner of the hide, and they all gazed down at Atai. Hands had closed her eyes, her tangled hair had been combed and neatly braided, the torn buckskin dress had been drawn over her little body.

"She will soon rest at peace," Skeska said. "Soon her killer will be dead, and she may rest."

"Yes," Takuimo sighed. "We'll give her peace."

Swinging around, the chief led the way to where the voyageur sprawled. Osa's eyes were heavy and red-rimmed, but he was conscious. His arms and legs were lashed tightly with rawhide strips, and both his wrists and ankles were swollen and raw.

Zabacta pointed at the voyageur. "He fought his bonds for hours. It was well we tied him securely, for indeed he is a bear."

Reaching down, Skeska brutally wrenched Osa's beard until his massive face was lifted toward them. *"Eh sum okit,"* he ordered.

Osa stared without comprehension, and Takuimo said, "I don't think he understands any dialect." In French, he gave the same order. "Look at us."

"I'm looking," Osa protested. "But that man, he pull my beard."

"Bear," Takuimo said slowly, "do you know why we took you alive?"

Osa's shaggy head shook. "I was drunk. I don't remember. My brother, Armand, he stole rum and we drank."

Lifting his spear, Skeska drove the point of it against the huge man's throat. "You remember Atai!"

The voyageur didn't wince as the sharp spear drew

302

bright blood from his throat. His brow furrowed in thought. "Atai?"

Okima called to the warriors, "Bring my sister."

They stripped away the hide, and two of the men lifted the rough litter they'd carried the girl on. They trotted over and put it down on the grass. Pulling his spear away, Skeska forced Osa's head around until he had to look directly down at her. "Look, and tell me you don't remember!"

The wrinkles smoothed out of the voyageur's brow. "Ah, the deer. Yes, I remember her. She ran like a deer, but I caught her. Armand told me, 'Osa, I order you to bring back a woman.'" He looked proudly up at them. "And I did. I always obey Armand. Papa said, 'Osa, always obey Armand. He's smart.'"

Skeska looked puzzled. Taking his hands from Osa, he turned to Takuimo. "What's wrong with this man?"

Takuimo touched his brow. "He's simpleminded. I think we took the wrong man. It's his brother we should have here. We killed this Armand on the platform."

Throwing back his head, Skeska howled, "He was killed with one prick of a knife!"

Okima rested a hand on the man's powerful arm. "We have the bear. Whether he is simpleminded or not, his hands took Atai's life."

"Yes," Takuimo agreed. "The bear must pay."

Osa had been paying no attention to the Sioux. He was still staring at the girl's face. "I didn't mean to hurt her. She screamed and hurt my ears. I only took her neck in my hands and squeezed. It was the rum. Rum makes me do bad things. I do remember the girl. Armand's wrong, I can remember."

Takuimo looked searchingly at the voyageur, and then he turned his back. "Zabacta, take the men and dig a deep pit. I'll pace it off."

Skeska and Okima remained by Osa's side while the other men worked. They dug rapidly into the soft soil until they had a deep hole roughly eight feet by five. The bottom of it they lined with fir boughs, and then Skeska

303

lifted the girl's body and carefully lowered it to Zabacta. As Zabacta stretched her out on the fragrant boughs, Takuimo nodded to two of the men. They hoisted Osa and dragged his heavy body to the edge of the pit.

Osa looked down into the hole and then raised puzzled eyes. "What do you do?"

"You have injured us," Takuimo told him. "You dishonored my sister and then you killed her. Now, through eternity, you must lie at her side. She's dead, and her agony is past. The agony to come is for you."

Osa's brow furrowed again in his obvious effort to follow the other man's words. As Skeska watched, his straight dark brows drew together. "I take no pleasure in this," he muttered.

"No more do I, but it must be done." Takuimo's face was as cold and hard as the knife at his waist. "Listen, bear, try to understand. We're going to bury you alive—"

"Ah," Osa triumphantly said. "You are going to kill me."

"No," Takuimo explained patiently. "We'll only put you in beside my sister. You'll die in your own time. Skill is required to do this so death does not come quickly from falling earth. We have this skill. Boughs will be arranged so the soil does not fall and smother you. Hollow reeds will be placed so some air does get to you. You will die of hunger and thirst. Maybe you will die mad from terror." His hard eyes ranged over Osa. "You're a strong man, and you may live for days. Mercy I will not have! Do you understand now?"

Osa nodded his great head. "I understand. I took your sister from you. If you had hurt Armand, I would hurt you. It is fair."

"Lower him," Takuimo told Zabacta.

It took the strength of the four warriors to place Osa beside the girl's body. Then they arranged the reeds, and Okima handed down more boughs to them. They placed these with great care until only Osa's face was still exposed. Skeska turned his back, but both Takuimo and Okima stood looking down into the grave. Osa stared up

304

at them with steady eyes, but he said nothing. Abruptly, Takuimo ordered, "Cover his face."

More boughs slid into place, and the men started carefully to replace the soil. No sound came from the grave. Finally, it was done. Sod was laid gently over the raw soil, and Takuimo bent over the mound to check the reeds. He rose and nodded at the four braves. "Well done."

"How long do you think he'll last?" Okima asked.

"A long time. He'll not die easy," his brother told him.

"He'll die well," Skeska said.

"Of all the men I've known he is the bravest. His heart is as great as his body." Takuimo raised his spear. "The bear is brave!" he shouted.

Six spears flashed up. "Brave!" they echoed.

"Our people wait," Takuimo said. "We must leave this land."

Breaking into their tireless trot, they loped from the clearing into the forest. With unerring instinct they swung east and then southward and on noiseless feet left the valley of the Nechako.

24

A small flotilla of yellow canoes floated down the Nechako River, and the men in the canoes were exhausted but filled with a sense of satisfaction. In the lead canoe, George Durran wearily shifted his position and watched water falling in silver gouts from the flashing paddles. At his side Laurie slept heavily, his chin resting on his chest, his broad-brimmed hat shading his face.

Yes, Durran was thinking, the job was done, and General Purline should be pleased at their speed. They'd been lucky. Their scouts brought word that the *coureurs de bois* had gathered in one place to celebrate before making their way back to the Nor'westers' fort. All the men from Fort Purline had crept stealthily around their camp in the night hours and, before the woods runners were properly awake, had overwhelmed them. There had been a little resistance, and several men from both parties had been wounded, but no one was killed. The general's orders had been carried out. The woods runners were mauled, their clothes were stripped from their struggling bodies, their weapons were destroyed, and their food supply was ruined. Durran ordered that the canoes not be holed. "We'll go back by water," he told his men. "It'll be easier and faster than traveling through the forest."

They were drawing near to the fort now, and soon the men would be able to get a well-deserved rest. Durran hadn't been able to fall into slumber like Laurie, and he wondered what was bothering him. He found himself looking from one bank to the other, sweeping the forest with keen glances. There seemed no apparent reason for concern. It was a fine, clear day with the sun beaming down. From the canoe behind his, he could hear the voyageurs singing one of their rollicking songs as they bent over their paddles. Voyageurs? Could he be worried about Rowan at the fort with Armand and Osa? He shook his red head. Little Moccasins was staying with Rowan, and that woman was as good as two ordinary men. Besides there was Purline, Bobby Holden, and Portelance. No, Rowan would be safe.

From the bow of the canoe, Tapinawa called, "Mr. Durran, fort dead ahead."

The voyageurs gave a mighty shout, and Laurie stirred and raised his head. He pushed his hat back from his eyes. "Uh . . . what's going on?"

"We're home," Durran told him.

"God's teeth but I'm glad of that." Laurie stretched and yawned. "I smell like a piece of venison that's been out in the sun too long. Be good to get a warm bath and sleep in a decent bed."

Durran was staring at the fort. "Strange, the gates are standing wide open."

"In the daytime they generally are."

"I'd have thought while we were gone Purline would have kept them barred. And there's no sign of life around the lodges. At the first sight of a canoe the natives usually come tumbling out of them and gather at the landing." Durran peered at the stockade. "Can't see any sign of smoke, and it's noonday."

Laurie stretched lazily. "It's pretty warm. Maybe they're having a cold meal."

Reaching for his rifle, Durran called to Tapinawa, "Speed it up."

The paddles flashed, and in minutes the canoes were at the landing. Durran was the first man out. As the rest of the men disembarked he snapped, "There's something amiss. Proceed with caution and have your weapons ready."

Shooting a look at the Scot's grim face, Laurie reached

for his own rifle. They trotted up the bank toward the gateway. Durran led the way with Laurie at his heels, and the other men fanned warily out behind them. When they entered the fort the first thing they noticed was the huge mound of ashes in the center of the square.

Jourdin grabbed Durran's arms. "The doors. They been broken down! Look—van Zzll's, Rowan's, the Purline cabin!"

"My God!" Laurie pointed past the pile of ashes.

They broke into a run. On the stake, Purline sagged, his head drooping forward. Jourdin slashed at the rawhide thongs, and Durran lifted the factor's chin. He touched the base of the man's throat. "He's alive," he grunted.

The rawhide parted, and Purline slumped forward. Laurie and Beau caught him. Purline's eyes opened, and his cracked lips moved.

"What's he trying to say?" Laurie asked.

"Water," Durran ordered.

Tapinawa scurried to get it, and the other men gently stretched the factor out. Kneeling beside Purline, Durran tore off the silk stock and opened the filthy shirt. His hands moved over Purline's body, and then he looked up at Laurie. "Not a sign of a wound." Taking a dipper of water from Tapinawa, he held it to the factor's lips. "Slowly, general, slowly. There, that's enough for now."

Abruptly, Laurie swung around and looked at his cabin. The door hung from the hinges. "God!" he groaned. Leaving the group gathered around Purline, he ran toward his home. "Rowan!" he shouted.

Durran looked up at Jourdin. "Check around."

Louis Grand, followed by Four-Finger Jacques, came panting up. "We already have, M. Durran. There's blood. Bloodstains on the floor of our quarters, bloodstains on the lookout platform. But there's no one here!"

"Marinska here," a voice said from behind them.

Durran was on his feet in one bound. "What happened?" Grabbing her shoulders, he looked down at her broad, impassive face. "Where's Rowan?"

308

"Rowan's gone," Laurie shouted. "My boys! There's no one here."

Durran shook the woman savagely. "Where's Rowan?"

"Everyone dead," Marinska said dully. "Except him." She stabbed a finger at Purline's sprawled figure.

As Durran's nerveless fingers fell from her shoulders, Laurie ran up. "Make her talk," Laurie rasped. "What happened here, Marinska? Where're my wife and children?"

She raised long, dark eyes. "Look behind you."

Laurie whirled and then raced toward the gates. Rowan, with two of the hunters at her heels, was walking toward them. She carried her rifle in one hand, and she walked slowly, as though she'd aged. Her face was smudged with dirt, and her buckskin skirt was soiled. Laurie pulled her into his arms, and she buried her head on his shoulder.

"The boys?" Durran shouted.

"Safe," Rowan said faintly. "On the Ile Ste. Anne. With Martha and Dorrie."

Durran pointed down at Purline. "Jourdin, you and Louis Grand carry him in to his bed. Give him a little water, but not too much at one time. I'll be there shortly." He spun around. "Jacques, get those gates barred and get up on lookout. Beau, Tapinawa, take some of the hunters to the Ile Ste. Anne and bring back Martha and the children." He called to Laurie, "Bring Rowan to your cabin." Taking Marinska's arm, he said, "You come with me."

Scooping up his wife, Laurie carried her to the cabin. When he got there Marinska was huddled by the fireplace and Durran was standing over her. Durran pointed to a chair, and Laurie carefully lowered Rowan into it. "Get both of them brandy," Durran ordered.

While Laurie located the bottle and poured some in tin cups, Durran looked from one woman to the other but said nothing until the cups were empty. A little color seeped back into Rowan's face, and Marinska straightened her sagging shoulders.

"Where are Dutchy and your children?" Durran asked Marinska gently.

"Children safe. Cabin. Pieter dead."

"Was he killed?"

She shook her head. "Died from sickness. Two days ago."

Leaning forward, Rowan patted the other woman's head. "Leave her alone. I'll tell you." Slowly, her voice at times faltering, she told them about the Sioux girl and Osa. She recounted the arrival of the chief and her own flight to the island. "The day after . . . the massacre I left Martha and Charlie with the children and came back. Marinska and I buried them . . . Nell, Portelance, Armand, Lapointe. We found a cart and put them on it, and we pulled it up the burial ground. We buried Little Moccasins and Bobby in one grave. We buried the three voyageurs in one grave. Most of them had been scalped. Then Dutchy died of fever, and we buried him. . . ." She covered her face with her hands. "We buried all of them. There were vultures and it was hot and we had to bury them fast or—"

"Rowan!" Kneeling at her feet, Laurie gathered her into his arms. "My God, Durran, can't you see the shape they're in? Leave them alone!"

"I can't," Durran said grimly. "They bury the dead, and they leave that man lashed to the stake. Purline's had no food, no water. They pulled the dead past him and left him in torment."

Laurie stared up at the Scot. "Why didn't the Sioux kill him too?"

Durran shrugged. "Rowan, why didn't you cut Purline loose?"

She shook her head. "Can't tell . . . promised Martha. Sleep . . . I want to sleep."

"Put her to bed," Durran said. He turned to the Indian woman. "Well, Marinska?"

Pulling herself to her feet, she staggered toward the door. Over her shoulder, she grunted. "Marinska go to children now. Soon, take them away. Back to my tribe. Pieter dead."

Much later, after Rowan was sound asleep in her bed and the children and Martha had been brought back from the island, Laurie and Durran met in Purline's office. Laurie jerked his head toward the kitchen of the Purline cabin. "How is he?"

"In bad shape." In the lamplight Durran's face was drawn. "If we hadn't got back he'd have been dead in a couple of hours. But he'll make it. He's a strong man."

"Who's looking after him?"

"Right now, Jourdin is. Louis Grand can take over later tonight. In the morning the natives will probably be coming back to the lodges. Some of the hunters are out looking for their families now. I'll get one of the women, perhaps old Tupa, to nurse Purline."

Laurie rubbed his brow. "Thank God some of them survived. Osa and Armand—those ruddy fools. What about Osa? I'd forgotten all about him."

"Vanished. I imagine the Sioux have dealt with him by this time. But we'll send a couple of voyageurs and some hunters out to search tomorrow. Maybe they can pick up tracks."

Pouring more rum in both their glasses, Laurie took a long swallow of his. "If Rowan hadn't acted swiftly, the boys and her . . . and Dorrie and Martha—" He broke off. "Why isn't Martha nursing the general?"

Durran shook his red head, and lamplight glinted from it. "Refuses to go near him. She's taken Dorrie to Bobby Holden's cabin. Says they're going to stay there."

"Just what in hell did happen here, George?"

"Only three people know—Rowan and Martha and Marinska—and I've a feeling they'll never tell."

"What could Purline have done to deserve this? Maybe they blame him for the massacre."

Durran shrugged heavy shoulders. "He's not the only one to blame. Osa and Armand started the whole thing. Portelance didn't lift a hand to stop them. Purline—he's guilty too, but . . ." A tiny, sardonic smile lifted the corners of Durran's mouth. "Have you ever thought, laddie, it may be something Purline *didn't* do? Anyway, he'll live. In a week I've a feeling he'll be the same man he's always been."

As soon as Laurie returned to his cabin to care for his wife and sons, Durran opened the door to the store. Instead of turning down the hall to his rooms, he went outside and stood on the steps. Lamplight shone from windows around the square, from Purline's cabin, Rowan's, the voyageurs' quarters, and the cabin where Bobby Holden had lived. The windows of the van Zzll cabin were dark, and Durran's gaze lingered on them. Slowly, Durran's eyes ranged around the square, settling at last on the mound of gray ashes and the tall stake. Nell Purline dead and buried, and Ezra Purline still alive. Dardeshi again? he wondered, and nodded his head. Would Purline be able to live with this new memory? Durran's head nodded again. The man had managed to live for years with the Pass of Hajarial.

Lifting his head, he stared at the cold brilliance of the stars. "Ye were right," he said softly. "Ye told true, granny. A night of fire and murder and blood dripping. Ye saw true. Thank God ye never saw the man who lies yonder, for no real man is he, only a creature that walks like one. But Rowan and her boys are safe. How much longer, granny, how much longer?"

Ezra Purline, as George Durran had pointed out, was a strong, rugged man. Two of the women from the lodges cared for him. One was old Tupa, and the other a younger woman, a widow called Carafa. They tended him well, giving him the medicines that Durran prepared and brewing broths and tea for him. In ten days he was able to sit in a chair and within a fortnight returned to his office. The day he was able to get to his office and sit in the chair behind the large desk, he summoned Laurie and Durran.

Purline was neatly groomed, and although gaunt, he

looked fairly well. His manner was crisp and businesslike, although he jerked his head toward the two chairs facing him. When his two aides were seated he said, "Gentlemen, I require a report on the raid against the *coureurs de bois*."

Tersely, Durran gave him the details. When he'd finished, the factor nodded his big head. "Well done, gentlemen. That should prove a deterrent against further actions by the Nor'westers." Leaning back in his chair, he folded his hands. "I suppose you've both been filled in on some of the details that led to the tragedy that occurred here during your absence." He paused. Laurie nodded, and after a moment, Durran jerked his head. "I had an instant decision to make when the three Sioux leaders arrived. They demanded that I turn Osa over to them. Much as I was tempted to do it—because his actions with the Sioux girl put all of us in jeopardy—I realized how the voyageurs would accept it. As you know, if I'd given Osa to the Sioux for torture and death, this fort would have been shunned by voyageurs, and never again could we have persuaded any to work for us. So, as commanding officer, I made the decision."

Bending his head, he stared down at his folded hands. "In view of what happened that night, I almost wish I had given them Osa. Young Mr. Holden's death was a loss. Soon I'll have the painful duty of writing his family about his terrible fate. We also lost three voyageurs." He raised his deep-set eyes. "Has any trace been found of Osa, Mr. Durran?"

"None. The hunters tried to track the Sioux, but rain had washed out their tracks."

Purline sighed. "We may rest assured that Osa is dead. Those Sioux are incredibly savage and bloodthirsty. I begged them on my bended knees to kill me and spare my wife, but the chief . . . he laughed at me. They killed Mrs. Purline before my eyes. The chief said they would allow me to live so I could hang there helplessly and die slowly while I looked into her dead face."

He paused again as though waiting for a comment.

Durran said nothing, but Laurie murmured, "Mrs. Purline was a fine woman, sir; you've suffered a grievous loss."

"Yes, Mr. Woodbyne, I have, and I'm a shattered man. Later that night—or was it toward morning? I really can't remember. Anyway, Marinska appeared. At first I thought she was a ghost. I'd believed everyone in the fort was dead. I begged her to untie me, but the woman seemed quite mad. Later, Mr. Woodbyne, I opened my eyes and saw your woman. She was helping Marinska with the dead. I called to them repeatedly, but they must have been in shock. Neither of them came near me. When they left, I hung there dying of hunger and thirst in the glaring sun. That's all I can remember."

Laurie said quickly, "Terrible, sir."

Purline straightened and crashed a fist on his desk. "I want revenge, gentlemen! I want those savages pursued and wiped out! I want—"

"Too late," Durran interrupted.

"What do you mean, Mr. Durran?"

"I said it's too late. It was too late when we got back here. They move quickly, and they had three days' start on us. Even if there had been a chance of catching up with the Sioux, I wouldn't have dared. We didn't have enough men to challenge them."

"I suppose you were right. Anyway, I was ill, and the command was yours and Mr. Woodbyne's. Now, about the squaw in Mr. van Zzll's cabin. I understand that the poor chap died of his sickness. I want that woman off this post, and I want those children off too."

"They're gone," Durran said crisply. "Marinska and her children left about ten days ago."

"They'll be fine, sir," Laurie said. "She was going back to her tribe. For the children's sake they'll take her in. She might even marry."

"Thank you for your reassurance," Purline said acidly. "I'm not concerned with their welfare. That woman, mad or not, left me to die." The deep-set eyes glared at Laurie. Is he going to order me to send Rowan away? Laurie wondered. But Purline didn't say anything further

314

about his ordeal. Instead he asked, "Have you anything to report, Mr. Durran?"

"Aye. I've sent messages to the nearest of Mr. Hatch's forts—Fort Timberline—asking for aid. We're short of men here. We need another crew of voyageurs and a couple of clerks. I'm certain they'll send replacements."

"Well done. You've managed quite capably. Now, I understand that Martha and my daughter have been staying during my illness in Mr. Holden's cabin. Would you tell Martha she may now return?"

Durran got to his feet. "I'll send her to you. Is that everything?"

"That is all, gentlemen."

After the two men left his office, Purline sat deep in thought. Durran had seemed quite brusque. Was it possible he had any knowledge of what actually had happened that night? Purline shook his head. No possible way anyone could know. Marinska—she was an ignorant savage, and she'd always disliked him. The Sioux had shut her into her cabin, and she wouldn't have dared leave it until they'd left the fort. As for Woodbyne's woman—she'd left him tied there merely for spite. Well, she knew how he felt about her. He'd deal with her later. Purline smiled, and he was still smiling when the door to the store opened and he glanced up to see Martha standing in front of his desk. "Sit down, Martha," he said pleasantly.

"I'll stand."

"As you wish. I realize that both you and Dorrie have had quite an ordeal, but it's over now. I know the child is doubtless grieving for her mother, and the sooner she is back with me the better. I shall also be glad to have you handling the meals. Tupa and Carafa have done their best, but believe me, no one can cook like you."

"We're not coming back."

"What?" His head jerked up, and he looked directly at her. Her face was cold and set. "Explain yourself!"

"In the morning we're leaving. I've made arrangements

315

for paddlers to take Dorrie and me to Fort George. We'll get further transportation east from there."

"Martha," he said gently, "you're distraught. I greatly fear this horror has unhinged your mind. Pray be seated and compose yourself."

She laughed bitterly. "Unhinged my mind. Compose myself. Come, Ezra Purline, ye've known me long enough. We're leaving, and ye'll not say nay."

He was on his feet, staring at her. "I certainly can't prevent you from leaving. In fact, it's a good idea. I'm tired of you! But my daughter will not leave this fort."

She lowered her voice. "Shall I tell about Dardeshi, general? Shall I tell about ye cowering in a woman's bed rather than do your duty? Do ye want your men to know what happened here the night of the massacre? Shall I tell Mr. Woodbyne of ye begging on your knees for the Sioux to rape your wife and kill her, but to spare your miserable yellow skin?"

"How do you know?" he whispered.

"Marinska."

"She was shut in her cabin. She couldn't—"

"She climbed out the back window. She watched and listened. When Rowan came back here the next morning, Marinska told her everything. When they'd buried the dead, Rowan came and told me. Marinska refused to cut ye down or give ye even a sip of water, and Rowan was terribly upset." Martha laughed again. "I told Rowan to let ye be. To let ye die."

Collapsing in his chair, Purline covered his face with one big hand. "How many know?"

"Only the three of us."

"And Marinska's gone." He uncovered his face, and it was dreadful. "Nobody would believe that white squaw."

"Rowan's husband would, and so would The Durran. They'd both believe me. And The Durran knows all about the Pass of Hajarial."

"Nell told him!"

"Nay."

"You did!"

316

She shook her ginger head. "Our lips were sealed. Ye're Dorrie's father. The Durran heard about ye long ago. One of the officers of the relief column met him in Montreal. He told Mr. Durran all about Dardeshi."

Purline groaned. "He's known all these years."

"The Durran doesn't talk, and he doesn't sit in judgment."

Purline took a deep breath. "Very well, you've won. You're gaining your own way by blackmail. Where will you take Dorrie?"

"To Montreal. Then we'll take passage to England. Nell's cousin, Patience, will take the child in. Patience loved her mother, and she'll love Dorrie." Martha stared grimly down at him. "I know what ye're thinking, but don't try to regain custody of the bairn. Ye want Dorrie only to torture her, to make her suffer as ye made Nell suffer. Ye'll never have her. I'll tell Patience everything, and she'll never give the bairn to ye."

"Take her!" he shouted. "Take her, and both of you get out of my fort!"

"We're going." At the door she turned and said sternly, "Don't try to revenge yourself on Rowan. Your reputation is in her hands. If she tells the truth, there isn't a man in this land who will work for ye or with ye. Goodbye, *general*. I hope ye rot in hell!"

As she slammed the door, Tapinawa looked up from his post behind the counter. He called to Martha, but she paid no heed. Outside the store, on the steps, Rowan was sitting. Pulling herself up, she walked at Martha's side. She asked, "Did he agree?"

"He had little choice, lass."

Tears blurred Rowan's vision, and she groped for the older woman's hand. Martha took the girl's hand in her own strong, calloused one. "Don't cry, lass."

"It's the first time I have since . . . since it happened. I helped Marinska and didn't cry a tear. But, Martha, Nell!"

"She's gone, Rowan. She's at peace."

"But her death. What a horrible way to die."

317

"It was quick. Marinska said the Sioux chief showed Nell mercy, and I think he did."

Rowan rubbed her wet eyes. They'd reached the Holden cabin, and they stopped on the doorstep. "Will you stay at Patience's house with Dorrie?"

"Nay. Patience has her own little family. Three children. Dorrie will fit in well. And Patience, while she looks like Nell, is much different. She's stronger and steadier. She'll raise the bairn well. Dorrie will need a firm hand, for she is like her mother. As for Nell, I loved her, but I never deceived myself. She lived in hell, but she helped make it. I'll pray Dorrie will be different."

"What will you do?"

"I've some saved, and Henry, may he rest in peace, left me a little. Perhaps I'll take a little cottage by the sea and make a life for myself." Martha smiled warmly at the girl. "Maybe find a man to share it with. I'm not that old, ye know."

Rowan clung to the other woman's hand. "You'll never be old, Martha MacLeod." She felt her eyes brim with hot tears again. "You loved him, didn't you?"

"Geoffrey Burns? Aye, lass, that I did. But there's room for more than one love in a heart. Perhaps I'll find another."

"I'd like to come down and see you and Dorrie off in the morning."

"Nay, don't come, Rowan. It's easier this way. Just turn and walk away."

"I hate to say good-bye to you," the girl sobbed.

Martha squeezed her hand and then pushed her gently away. "Life is a series of good-byes," she said. Opening the door, she stepped into the cabin and softly closed it. Martha MacLeod never did say good-bye, and that was the last time Rowan ever saw her.

Tears streaming down her cheeks, Rowan stumbled across the square. Her tears blinded her, and she walked right into someone. It was a man. His arms went around her, and she sobbed on his shoulder. She thought it was

Laurie. When she brought herself under control she realized it wasn't her husband. It was George Durran. He didn't speak, nor did she, but all the way back to her cabin she saw the look of compassion on Durran's face.

25

For weeks after the massacre at Fort Purline, Rowan existed, whether awake or asleep, in a nightmare world. At nights she would awake screaming from terrible dreams to see Laurie's concerned face as he bent over her. Time after time in dreams she'd relive the hours when Marinska and she had worked against the heat and the circling carrion birds to give the dead decent burial. Again she would prop up Nell's naked body while Marinska struggled to clothe the poor corpse in a gingham dress. Against her hands she'd feel Dutchy's humped shoulder as she rolled him off the bed onto the cart. She'd see the mutilated bodies of Lapointe and Portelance, the color of their beloved sashes. She'd fight to untangle the stiffened forms of Bobby Holden and Little Moccasins.

Her waking hours were no easier. She was afraid to look from the window for fear she'd see the tall, lithe form of Little Moccasins, the top of her head a mass of dried blood and oozing gray matter, striding across the square. She was afraid to listen for fear she'd hear the echo of Lapointe's high giggle. She feared to go to the store lest she see the ghost of Bobby leaning against the counter, light glinting from the round lenses of his pince-nez.

As time passed, the memories of horror lessened. Without knowing, General Purline helped her. He took the reins in his capable hands and soon had his fort back to something near normal. Fort Timberline responded to the call for help with despatch. The factor sent not only a full crew of voyageurs but also four others to make up the complement of the crew of Armand's canoe. The steersman of the new crew was a middle-aged man known as Chichi. He was jovial and smiling, but he ruled his men well and wisely. Beau, to the other men's surprise and his own delight, was appointed steersman of his own canoe. He proved to be a wise choice. The handsome French-Canadian handled his own men as firmly as Chichi handled his.

In the latter part of August, two new clerks arrived. They were brothers, Mike and Tim O'Casey, and although they were Black Irish in looks, with swarthy skins, blunt features, and masses of tightly curling black hair, their temperaments were bright and carefree and jolly. Rowan found that with the O'Casey brothers behind the counter she could go into the store again. Against their laughter and jokes not even the ghost of Bobby Holden could prevail. A short time after their arrival the brothers made a trip to the lodges to select, from the new arrivals flooding in there, a couple of suitable girls. They chose twin sisters, plump, pretty girls, and after making a deal with their father, they brought their prizes triumphantly back to the fort. The factor had given the brothers Bobby Holden's cabin, and with their girls the brothers settled happily in. Neither of the Irish boys could pronounce the sisters' Indian names, so Mike, two years the elder and two inches taller than Tim, called his girl Biddy. Not to be outdone, Tim called his girl Middy.

. The voyageurs chuckled, nudged each other, and riotously questioned the brothers about just how they managed to distinguish between the girls, who were identical twins. Mike solemnly assured them that Biddy had a black mole in a strategic location, but when the girls were dressed it could be confusing.

Shortly after they'd taken their brides, the boys took Middy and Biddy to the lodges for a native wedding ceremony. Afterwards they threw a wild party at their cabin. They invited everyone from the lodges as well as from the fort, and soon the cabin was overflowing with guests and the party moved out into the square. Middy and Biddy passed through the crowd serving roasted fowl, barbecued fish, and boiled venison while Mike and Tim spiked huge mugs of coffee with Irish whiskey.

Rowan, Laurie, and George Durran stood watching the festivities with mugs of whiskey and coffee clasped in their hands. Both Laurie and Durran wore wide grins. Laurie leaned across his wife. "Want to make a bet on how soon the old man comes bolting out of his office to break up this sinful display?"

"You'd lose your money." George waved his mug. "Here he comes now."

Much to both men's astonishment, the general didn't come to stop the party. Not only was he tolerant and rather genial, but his arms were piled high with gifts. He brought candy for the children, tobacco for the men, and for the brides he had lengths of cotton, two round mirrors, and tortoiseshell combs. Purline even accepted a mug brimming with the potent brew and for a short time sipped it and beamed on all. When the musical part of the evening began he beat a hasty retreat to his cabin, and for once Rowan agreed with him. Even in her cabin with the doors and windows closed, the noise was unbelievable. Both the O'Casey brothers played fiddles, and Beau and Jourdin ran to get theirs. The Indian braves, not to be outdone, formed their own band of drums and finely wrought handclappers. Durran, after several mugs of Irish coffee, appeared resplendent in Highland dress to promenade on the lookout platform with his bagpipe wailing.

The musicians didn't bother trying for the same tune. The O'Caseys played an Irish jig, the voyageurs one of their paddling songs; the Indians beat out a tune that sounded like the prelude to another massacre. But The Durran, high above the square, managed to outdo all with a spirited rendition of "The Reel of Tulloch."

For a time both Laurie and Rowan laughed helplessly, and then she sobered. The O'Casey boys had brought more than cheer and laughter with them. They'd brought a piece of news that vitally concerned Rowan and her sons. While the wild music swirled through the square, she talked to Laurie. They argued for hours, finally reached a decision, and when it had quieted down a little, they went to bed. A reluctant promise had been forced from Rowan, and she lay for hours watching the shadowy ceiling, sick at heart.

The next morning she sought out George Durran. He was in his rooms, his eyes sunk in dark circles from his musical night, blundering around trying to wash his dishes. As she entered his room, he clutched at his brow. "Softly, lass, softly. No need to slam the door."

"I didn't slam it, and don't expect sympathy from me. You earned your head."

"From the look on your face you bring troubles, and it's a poor place to come. I can barely stagger, let alone think."

Sitting down at the cluttered table, she rested her own aching head in her hands. Durran wiped his hands on a rag and came to sit opposite her. "Out with it," he said.

Lifting her head, she spread both hands in a helpless gesture. "I always bring my problems to you. I shouldn't. It puts weight on you, and I've no right."

"You've every right. Tell me about it."

"If only Martha were still here. Until she left I didn't know how dependent I was on her. She was like a mother to me."

"Even if Martha MacLeod were your mother, there comes a time to walk alone."

"I know." Her tilted eyes searched his face. "But I'm a mother, and that's why I'm here. Ever since the massacre I can't stop thinking—"

"They're gone, lass. Let them rest."

"I've already accepted that. It's the boys. I keep thinking they might have been . . . they might be dead too. This is a hard land, George. Death comes so quickly. Martin and Seamus might drown, a wild animal could kill them, they could die of fever like Dutchy did." She took a deep breath. "I was raised a Catholic. I *am* a Catholic. What is your church?"

"My parents were Presbyterians, but as for me—I claim no church. I've a firm belief that, regardless of church, we all worship the same God."

"I agree with you, in principle. Can you understand a person who is raised in a church believing in the mores, the tenets, of that church?"

His red head nodded. "Aye, lass, that I understand."

Jumping to her feet, she paced the small room. "Laurie doesn't! He tells me it's superstitious nonsense. He tells me Martin and Seamus are his sons and he regards them as Anglicans. He tells me that if I go ahead with my plan General Purline can ruin his career. Laurie tells me—"

"I've heard enough of Laurie. What is your plan?"

As she paced, her buckskin skirt swirled around her ankles. She wore low moccasins, and Durran caught glimpses of her ankles, of her slender legs. With an effort he wrenched his eyes away from those shapely legs and fastened his gaze on her flushed face. Over the high cheekbones, her eyes blazed. "If the boys had died that night, George, my beliefs tell me that never would they be allowed to reach heaven. You see, my faith warns that if children die without baptism their little souls don't go to purgatory and thence to heaven. For eternity they must remain in limbo. I torture myself thinking of them there. George, this life for children is so uncertain."

"I know, Rowan. You asked Laurie for permission to have the boys baptized?"

"I did." Swinging around, she caught his hand. "Mike O'Casey tells me there is a young priest at Fort George. He is Father Laurent, and soon he'll be leaving the fort, traveling west. The priest intends to spend a few days here, and I thought I might persuade him to baptize the boys. Neither of them were born in wedlock, but he might take the circumstances into consideration." Her voice broke. "Laurie made me promise I wouldn't approach Father Laurent, wouldn't ask him. He said the factor would disapprove of this 'Papist nonsense.' "

"So he would. Purline is a strong Anglican and loathes those of the Catholic faith."

"What's wrong with Laurie now? He stood up for me when I first came here and risked the factor's disapproval to become my protector. What's happened to him, George?"

Miserably, Durran regarded her. How could he tell her the truth? Laurie was currying favor with Purline for only one reason. He wanted to get out of this fort, this country. Laurie wanted to go to Montreal. Purline was his ticket out. He couldn't risk incurring the factor's displeasure. Aloud he said, "You've it in your power to force General Purline to do as you wish, Rowan."

"How do you know?"

"I guessed. Martha MacLeod took Dorrie, and Purline let them go. She wouldn't leave you defenseless against him. You must have the same weapon."

"I have. Last night I thought of using it." Her chin lifted proudly. "Martha made me promise I wouldn't use it unless Purline directly threatened the boys or me. Martha was afraid he might revenge himself on us, and Purline hasn't even looked at us."

Durran moodily regarded the clutter on the table. He moved a tin plate, touched the saltcellar, and then folded his restless hands. "He's afraid. He's always afraid. Now he's afraid to meet my eyes for fear of what he might see in them. Have you noticed that where once he turned to me for everything, he now turns to Laurie?" She nodded, and he continued. "He knows Laurie is ignorant of his past, has no knowledge of the Pass of Hajarial or the night of fire and murder. Martha was forced to give my name to Purline, to tell him what I knew. Now Purline waits for a chance to send me away, to rid himself of me. But I do my work and will give him no excuse."

She gazed down at him. "You actually want to stay here, to work for a man like him?"

"I do, but enough of that. This promise you gave Laurie—how was it worded?"

She put a finger to her lips. "I promised that when Father Laurent arrives here I'll not approach him. I'll not ask his help."

"When he arrives at Fort Purline?"

"Yes."

He beamed. "Then your solution is clear."

"I don't understand."

"Think, lass. The priest must travel from Fort George."

"Of course he must, but how can that help?"

"You've come to the wrong man, Rowan. Go to a man who knows the route, who knows where the stops are made for meals, for the voyageurs' pipes."

"You mean—"

"I mean go to a man of your own faith."

Her smile was as wide and bright as his. "Why didn't I think of that?"

"Your heart was thinking for you, Rowan; let your mind think."

She rested a hand affectionately on his heavy shoulder. "I will. Thank you, George. I don't know what I'd do without you."

She left the room at a run, the buckskin skirt swirling up around her long legs. He sat where he was. He fancied that through the rough cloth of his shirt he could still feel the warmth of her hand. In his mind he pictured her graceful legs, her lovely face framed in black braids. Groaning, he put his head in his hands. Affection was all he could expect. Good old George . . . George who loved her with all his heart.

Rowan went directly to the voyageurs' quarters. Sitting in front of the building, their shoulders hunched against the sun-warmed logs, were Chichi and Louis Grand. When she asked for Beau, they told her he was inside. She hesitated, and Chichi assured her that Beau was alone. She found Beau seated on the edge of his bunk, carefully fashioning a small wooden box. Looking up from his work, he smiled at Rowan and held out the box. "Do you think she'll like it?"

Rowan didn't have to ask who "she" was. Beau talked

nonstop about his girl in Lower Canada. She admired the box, the cleverly carved flowers, and the raised heart. "Angeline will like it, Beau. Any woman would."

"I'll carve our initials right here." He pointed at the heart. "She's such a fine girl, my Angeline. So pretty and so wise. All my wages she saves, and in time we'll have enough to buy a farm near our village. Then we'll marry and have eight children—four strong boys to help me farm the land and four pretty girls to help their mother with the hens and cows." Eyes warm with his dreams looked at Rowan. "Angeline and I already have names for the little ones. The first girl will be Rowan."

Sitting on the bunk at his side, Rowan gave him back the box. "Will your children be baptized?"

"Of course."

"Mine aren't. Neither of the boys have been baptized."

"That's terrible. You must have it done." He sliced off a chip of wood and held up the box to inspect his work. Then he said cheerfully, "Mike O'Casey told me a priest will soon come to stay for a few days. You must have the father do this immediately."

"I can't. Laurie made me promise not to."

"General Purline?"

"Yes. Laurie's afraid for his career."

"The factor never interferes with us, with the voyageurs. The priest will come here to hear our confessions. You must bring the boys here—"

"I promised, Beau. I gave my word to Laurie that I wouldn't. But Father Laurent has to come here. Surely, if we could meet him downriver—"

"What is this you say? Are you asking me to . . . Rowan, I'm sorry. If the factor ever learned of this I'd be discharged. Never could I find another job in the west. All my years of work, all the time Angeline has waited for me— You can't ask this of me!"

His handsome face was distressed, and Rowan thought, No, I can't ask this. General Purline could destroy this man, and with him, his patient Angeline. Getting to her feet, she said wearily, "I'm sorry, Beau, I just didn't know who else to go to. You're right, I can't ask this."

"Wait a minute." He turned the box in his well-shaped hands. "Angeline is wiser than me. If she was here, what would she say?" His face cleared. "My Angeline would say, 'You must help this woman and her little boys. The children must be baptized.' Yes, Rowan, I'll help you. I must have another man, a man to assist me with the paddling." He grinned wryly. "Assist me with the good father."

She sat down again. "How will we do it?"

With the point of his knife he drew a jagged line on the wooden floor. "The voyageurs from the Nor'westers' fort always stop here for a meal and a pipe." The knife made a little X. "It's about ten miles downriver. We'll be there waiting for them—"

"Can we depend on these voyageurs' help?"

"Their help—yes. They are of our faith. Their silence—no. In drink they might talk, and we'd be exposed."

Her dark brows drew together. "Then how can we reach the priest?"

"The part of the trip before this stop is long and tiring. The priest will want to stretch his legs, to ease his stiffness. He will walk in the woods. We'll lie in wait and bring him to you and the boys."

She nodded. "What other man will you ask?"

"I was thinking perhaps Four-Finger Jacques or Louis Grand." He shook his head. "I'll speak to Jourdin."

"Jourdin! But he talks so much, and when he drinks he talks more."

"True, but on this point we can trust Jourdin. In his little village near Montreal he has a wife and ten children."

"*Ten.*"

Smiling, Beau made a motion outlining a big paunch over his trim waist. "Every time our Jourdin goes east with the canoes, his wife swells up like this. When he goes back the next time there is another babe in his woman's arms. This secret Jourdin will keep." He bent over his gouged-out map. "This is how we do it."

Their dark heads close together, the two conspirators made plans to kidnap a priest.

A few days later the canoe bearing the priest and his paddlers from Fort George stopped at the traditional place. After a spartan meal, Father Laurent took a stroll through the woods, enjoying the exercise and the solitude. He had no intention of straying far from the voyageurs. He could still hear their voices, could still smell the smoke from their fire, when a rough bag came down over his head and both his arms were grasped from behind. He'd had no warning, not even a crackle of a broken twig or the stirring of the heaps of dry autumn leaves. The bag smelled atrociously of smoked fish, and he fought to get his breath. He was a young man and a fairly strong one, and he put up a fierce fight, but he was no match for the arms gripping him. They dragged him along, deeper and deeper into the forest. He was numb with terror. His voyageurs had warned him about the wild animals, the huge bears and savage wolves that inhabited the forest. Then his sense of humor came to his aid. Wild animals would hardly bag his head, and assuredly those were human hands on his arms. Although he couldn't make out the words, a voice was muttering soothingly to him. When they came to a rough spot, he was lifted and carried over it. Eventually he was set on his feet, and he could feel the hard hands leave his arms. The bag was pulled from his head, and he could hear the soothing words clearly. "Please, good father, do not cry out. We've brought you on God's work and intend you no harm."

Gasping for breath, his hair standing on end, his face suffused with heat, Father Laurent turned wrathfully on his captors. He saw a tall, handsome young man and another, shorter and heavier and older, with a scar etched across his brow. Both men sheepishly lowered their eyes.

"What's the meaning of this outrage? Do you hope to hold me for ransom?"

"Don't blame Jourdin or Beau, Father Laurent," a woman's voice said. "They are only helping me."

The priest swung around. A woman was standing a few feet away, and for a moment he thought she was a native princess. She was tall and dressed in beaded, fringed buckskin. A band around her brow restrained two long, glossy black braids, and she was the most beautiful creature he'd ever seen. Beside her stood two small boys, the fair one only a toddler, the other boy taller and older. Although the younger boy showed no sign of Indian blood, the other did. *Bois brûlés,* the priest thought, and handsome ones at that. "Where do you come from?" he demanded.

"Fort Purline."

"What is so important that it's necessary to abduct me?"

One of her amber hands waved toward the children. As she moved, her sleeve fell back and he saw that the skin of her arm was as white as his own. "These children have never been baptized, father."

He ran a hand over his rumpled hair. "Couldn't you wait for this until we reached your fort? In a few hours we would have been there."

She shook her glossy head. "I've promised not to approach you at the fort. My only chance was to catch you before you arrived."

"Well, I'm most certainly caught." His tone was milder, and he looked around for his two captors. Both men were patrolling the edges of the forest. "To whom was this promise made?"

"To my husband."

"He is a . . ."

"Yes, he is white. He is Laurence Woodbyne, and he's second in command to the factor."

Father Laurent glanced at the blond boy again. Except for the setting of the little fellow's eyes, he would have thought him white. "Are you married?" he asked gently.

Her chin lifted proudly. "No. Laurie is not of our faith. He's an Anglican, and that's why I had to promise not to ask you. These two men who help me would lose their jobs if this is ever known."

"Then the children were born out of wedlock. Why did you accept this union, daughter?"

"I had no choice. I was alone, with no protector. The men of the west are basically decent men, but they're rough. I was in danger from them. Laurie's and my union has been a true one, and our marriage has been a real one."

The priest rubbed his chin. "I can't do this without consulting with others of my order."

She waved an expressive hand at the forest surrounding them. "Here there is only you."

"You have committed sin, my daughter."

The strange blue eyes met his squarely. "My children haven't."

"What is your name?"

"Rowan. My name is—" She hesitated and then said defiantly, "Rowan *Pas-de-Nom*. My boys are Martin *Pas-de-Nom* and Seamus *Pas-de-Nom*."

His heart went out to her. Rowan No-Name, daughter of some white man and an Indian woman. Her children, again nameless. A memory stirred, and he asked quickly, "Rowan! Were you once called Rowan Malone?"

"Yes," she said eagerly. "Did you know Father Martin Petrie?"

"I didn't have the honor, but I've heard much about him and about you. The mother superior of the Convent of the Sisters of Ste. Claire—"

"Mother Michael-John!"

"Exactly. Reverend Mother and I are firm friends. In fact, she asked me to look for you as I traveled west and to do what I could to be of assistance. Yes, Rowan, I'll baptize your sons." He fumbled at his shoulder. "I fear I have lost my bag."

From a distance, Beau had been watching them. Seeing the priest's gesture, he trotted over to them, taking from his own wide shoulder a black bag. "Here, father. When we banged your head I took this that it might not go astray."

The priest took it and smiled. "It would seem, Rowan, that you pick good accomplices," he said drily. "They forget nothing. You, young man, lift the older boy. His mother will hold the younger."

"We must hurry—" Beau started to say.

"We cannot rush the Lord's business, my son," he was told.

Despite his words, the young priest wasted no time. From his bag he drew a lace-trimmed linen stole and a tiny vial of holy water. While Beau and Rowan held the boys, Father Laurent performed the ceremony of baptism. Afterwards, perched on a rock, his head averted, Father Laurent heard Rowan's confession. Only then would he allow Jourdin and Beau to take him back toward his own camp. They were just in time. They heard the sounds of men's voices as the Nor'westers fanned out to search for the missing priest. Beau pointed Father Laurent in the right direction, and Jourdin and he slipped back to join Rowan and the boys.

The meeting in the woods was a closely guarded secret. No matter how drunk or talkative Jourdin became, this was one thing he never spoke of. When Father Laurent arrived at Fort Purline, the young priest never by word or look betrayed that he knew Rowan. He realized at once how General Purline felt about him, that only hospitality forced the factor to be pleasant. But Purline gave Father Laurent a bed in his own cabin and fed him lavishly.

On the night of his arrival, the priest took his place opposite his host in the kitchen. As Carafa shuffled around setting out their supper, Father Laurent gazed out of the window. Rowan was passing the cabin, a pail in one hand. "Who is that lovely girl?" he asked the factor.

Purline craned his neck. "A squaw, father. You've met Mr. Woodbyne. That's his woman." He turned deep-set eyes on his guest. "I've tried to prevent these unholy unions, but to no avail. You mustn't fault me. I do my best to fight against sin."

Father Laurent, although young, was a good judge of character. Although his face remained expressionless, his eyes were unfriendly as he regarded the oversized features of the other man. Turning his head, he tried for another glimpse of Rowan, but she was gone. Such a beautiful woman, he thought. Then, with deep compassion, he asked himself, And what is her fate to be? Most likely that of other native wives—a short time of happiness and then desertion. He felt his hands clench into fists, and he said slowly to his host, "Yes, General Purline, I believe you know a great deal about sin."

Purline studied him. Papist devil, he thought, always talking in riddles.

Rowan had seen the priest at the factor's window, and as she continued on her way she was smiling. She was not fond of deceit, but this time it had been necessary. She saw Martin and Seamus running toward her, and still smiling, she hastened her steps to meet them.

26

Five years passed like gray smoke wavering from the chimneys of Fort Purline. In the outer world, events both large and small took place. War raged in the Mediterranean. The ancient Acropolis at Athens was captured by Ibrahim, and at Salona the Greeks destroyed a Turkish fleet. Another Turkish fleet was destroyed at Navarino by a combined force of Greeks, French, and British. John Clare, the peasant poet, wrote *The Sheperd's Calendar,* and in London, Carlton House Terrace was designed by Nash. In the same city, James Simpson constructed sand filters for the purification of the water supply. Far across the ocean, on King George Sound, a settlement, later to be called Albany, was founded. In *le pays sauvage,* a trading post called Fort Langley was constructed near the mouth of the Fraser River.

Except for the new trading post, which was west and south of them, the inhabitants of the little world in Fort Purline paid scant attention to the events in the larger world. All that vitally concerned or interested them were the events that occurred in their fort. The years between 1822, always referred to as the Year of the Massacre, and 1827 were filled with smaller, less earth-shaking happenings.

In the spring of '23, Louis Grand lost forever his silver voice. He had his vocal cords pierced with a knife in a fight with another voyageur over the favors of a handsome Salish girl. Never again was he able to speak, let alone raise his gorgeous voice in song.

In the fall of the same year, Rowan lost her faithful Charlie. The big dog died, as he had lived, in his mistress's service. While helping their mother gather berries, Martin and Seamus wandered between a brown she-bear and her cub. As the huge bear came lumbering in for the attack, Charlie flung himself into the defense. He sprang at the bear's throat, sank sharp fangs into it, and dangled there until, with one swipe of an enormous paw, the bear flung him aside. The dog's gallant attack gave Rowan time to level her rifle, take careful aim, and fire. Her aim was true, and the bear fell a few feet short of the terrified children. Men on a wood detail were working close by, and they came running. Laurie paused only long enough to see that his sons were safe before running to his wife's side. Charlie was still alive, and Rowan cradled his big head in her lap. His tongue licked out as he feebly tried to reach her hand. Laurie took one look at the animal's slashed stomach and raised his rifle, but Rowan shook her head and reached for her own weapon. It was her finger that pulled the trigger and put the faithful animal out of torment. Later she buried his body near the mouth of the cave on the Ile Ste. Anne.

Laurie went to the lodges and found a pup who looked much like Charlie. Rowan accepted the dog, named him Nicko, and raised him. Nicko eventually attained Charlie's size and proved a strong protector, but Rowan couldn't love him as much as she had her first dog.

When the brigade of canoes left the fort for the east in April of 1824, Beau said his farewell to his friends. His Angeline had sent word to tell him to come home, that now they had enough savings to get married. Although he was eager to get to his waiting bride, Beau wept when he said good-bye. Rowan was saddened to see him leave, but she didn't shed a tear. Since Martha MacLeod had gone, Rowan seldom wept. She remembered the older woman's words. Life indeed was a series of good-byes.

Shortly after the brigade of canoes drew away down the Nechako, the population of the fort was increased by four. Middy and Biddy, only two days apart, gave birth to twins. Biddy gave Mike O'Casey identical daughters, and Middy presented Tim with twin sons. The O'Casey boys were ecstatic and celebrated their new status as fathers in their usual fashion. They threw an enormous party and, after passing out food and drink, began their musical efforts. As the three groups—Irish, French, and Indian—strove to outdo each other, George Durran made his way to his lonely post on the lookout platform. With stately grace he raised his bagpipe, and from it came a blast of sound that made the combined efforts of the musicians in the square below sound weak. Tim O'Casey, as drunk as Durran, stared at the figure promenading above him. Then, for the first and also last time, a man challenged Durran during his promenade. Inflamed by drink and pride that he'd fathered sons while his brother Mike had merely produced daughters, Tim swarmed up the ladder. It proved a mighty battle. Tim was younger than Durran by many years, and he was strong and agile, but The Durran was no man to challenge. With a wild cry he went into battle. In a whirl of arms and legs, they fought until Durran, with one powerful heave, grasped Tim O'Casey, whirled him high over his head, and tossed the Irish boy into the square. Then Durran picked up his pipes and calmly finished "The Flowers of Edinburgh."

When the tune was done, Durran climbed down the ladder and pushed his way through the crowd surrounding Tim's limp form. He found the young man sprawled senseless on the hard packed earth. Tim's fiddle had been shattered, and so had his right leg. Calling for his bag, Durran expertly set and splinted the broken limb. After he came to, Tim O'Casey shook hands with Durran.

"George," he told the Scot solemnly, "I've learned something today. Never try to move onto another man's piece of turf."

"Aye, laddie," Durran agreed. " 'Tis dangerous."

For Rowan those five years were a period of peace. Her relationship with Laurie had settled into a comfortable, warm, and rather secure marriage. The doubts and anxieties that once had plagued her had either vanished or abated. She loved Laurie, but now she understood him, and no longer did she wait for the moment when he would declare his love. She sensed he never would. Both Laurie and Rowan were involved with their home, their work, and their children.

Seamus, at ten, was a strapping boy, as tall as some of the voyageurs and with a powerful build. He's given up looking for attention from his father and now ignored Laurie as completely as Laurie ignored him. His days were spent with George Durran, learning carpentry and taking lessons in writing and reading. He helped his mother with the rougher work, and Rowan had taught the boy how to handle a rifle. Seamus rivaled both his parents in this skill.

Martin was seven, and he was tall for his age, but he had his father's slender build. As he grew older the boy more and more resembled the Woodbynes. His hair was silver-gilt, smooth and thick, his features were beautifully modeled, and he had his father's elusive quality of elegance. As well as Laurie's physical beauty, Martin had his father's charm, but with it went some qualities that Laurie didn't display. Martin was proud and arrogant, and both pride and arrogance were clearly shown on his frequent visits to the lodges, where he lorded it over the native children. Unlike his brother, Martin hated work. He preferred to follow his father as he went about his duties, and Laurie purchased a small pony for his younger son and taught him how to ride. Laurie's love for Martin was overt and showed in his every word and gesture.

The two brothers were no longer close. Their interests were as different as their appearance, and Laurie's obvious preference was bound to drive a wedge between them. Rowan realized this but was forced to accept it. In time, she'd think, in time this too will work out.

The only time a shadow fell across their cabin was when the annual mail arrived. Each year the same thing would happen. With the arrival of the books, packages, and letters, Laurie would retreat from his family. For days he'd be grim and unapproachable. Even Martin learned to steer clear of his father until the cloud lifted.

The mail in '27 was delayed, and many of the inhabitants of the fort chafed with irritation. For Rowan it was only a reprieve. In the middle of August, when the mail canoe finally came into view, she decided to take the boys and go into the forest to dig roots. She packed a lunch, slung on her rifle, and whistled for Nicko. Then, with Seamus, Martin, and the dog, she left the fort. She also left Laurie to his mail.

In the store the general, affable and in good spirits, passed out the contents of the pouch. He handed Durran his thin sheaf of letters and gave the O'Casey boys their large share before he turned to Laurie. "More mail than usual this time. Lots of news from home, Mr. Woodbyne."

Nodding, Laurie scooped up the thick pile and left without a word. Putting aside the voyageurs' portions for their steersmen to get, Purline took his own stack and retreated to his office.

He sorted his mail out. Letters from M. Charloux in Montreal, reports from other factors, a short duty letter from Nell's cousin in England that would only tell Purline of Dorrie's health, and a thick letter from London. Selecting the letter from London, Purline looked it over. It bore Charlie Hatch's ornate seal, but the crabbed handwriting was not as firm as usual. The man was getting older, Purline thought. Slitting it open, he read the contents. Then, more slowly, he reread it. A wide, delighted smile creased his big face. Finally! The day had finally arrived. All his years of work and dedication had come to flower. Jumping from his chair, he flung open the door to his kitchen and poured a generous amount of Madeira in a glass. Returning to his office, he sipped wine and reread a portion of the letter.

"I have good tidings for you," Hatch had written. "Due to some family problem, M. Charloux is forced to leave Montreal and my service to return to France." Here Purline sipped a little wine and grinned widely. He'd only met

338

M. Charloux's wife once, but he'd heard many stories about Adèle Charloux's romantic indiscretions. He could make a guess as to why her husband was intent on leaving Montreal. He read on. "I'm appointing you chief agent in M. Charloux's place. As you know, this is quite a promotion, but because of your devotion to your work I feel you've earned it. You'll be in charge of all my forts, will be called upon to make decisions concerning them, and will be accountable to no one but myself. As soon as possible I wish you to secure transportation and proceed with all despatch to Montreal. M. Charloux has agreed to delay his own departure until your arrival. As for the management of Fort Purline, I have two suggestions. I've written my son-in-law, and Laurence Woodbyne, if he decides to, will become factor. In the event that Mr. Woodbyne turns this post down, Mr. Durran will take over as factor. I sense you have no high regard for Mr. Durran, but his record proves that he is honest and reliable." With a perplexed expression, Purline read the last few sentences over. Why would Charlie Hatch be uncertain that Woodbyne would accept the position of factor? Purline's thin, wide mouth smiled again. There could be only one reason. Mr. Woodbyne must be going to be offered something much more attractive. In that event the man might be leaving his native family. It looked as though at last that white squaw would be getting her well-earned punishment.

Leaning back in the chair, Purline tossed off the rest of the wine. His eyes wandered past the open door to the kitchen. From where he sat he could see the faded white-and-green gingham that curtained off the area where Nell had once slept. Since her death he'd allowed no one to set foot in that alcove. Her bed was as it had been when the Sioux had pulled her from it. The small objects she'd treasured—her silver comb and brush, the bottles of scent and pieces of English soap—still were ranged neatly on her table. The last water she'd used to wash in had long since evaporated from the bowl, and dust had settled thickly on every surface in the tiny room.

Nell was long dead and buried, and he was free. Purline regarded his future with optimism. What a wonderful life lay ahead of him. With his savings and the large share he would receive in company profits, he'd be well on the way to wealth. As soon as he arrived in Montreal he would rent one of the gracious mansions standing in the shadow of Mount Royal. He'd engage a woman as housekeeper and employ a large staff of servants. Later . . . maybe he'd take another wife. Perhaps the daughter of a French fur baron. Frenchwomen were reputed to be fine, docile wives. He'd select a young one, a girl inclined to plumpness, with dark, flashing, Gallic eyes. His hand reached out and caressed the leather cover of his Bible. The Lord would not give a man such strong appetites of the flesh unless He expected that man to satisfy them. He was hungry for a woman. His abstinence had been long enough. Yes, he'd take a plump pretty girl, and he might even have children by her. A son . . . he'd like a son.

Pushing back in his chair, he folded his hands across his vest. Could he ever return to England? His mother, although very old, was still alive, and dear Margaret lived with her. Hunger to see the two women tore at him. If he returned covered with honors, perhaps with a knighthood in sight, his mother and sister might well welcome him. Yes, it was possible this could happen.

Although his mind was a continent and an ocean away, he still stared at the curtains that shielded his wife's alcove. Finally his eyes focused on it again. Lifting a big fist, he shook it gleefully toward the alcove. "I lived to defeat you, Nell Burns. You've plagued my dreams for years, but I've won. Now I'll regain the reputation and honor you stole from me!"

As the echo of his voice died away, a low laugh tinkled through the cabin, a cool, mocking laugh that brought him to the edge of his chair. Against the gingham curtains wavered a slight figure. He could see the outlines of a naked female figure, but through it he could still see the faded checks of the gingham.

"Nell!" he cried.

The form seemed to solidify, and now he could discern chestnut hair falling loosely to the apparition's waist. Wide gray-blue eyes stared steadily into his. The bloodless lips moved. "Yes, Ezra, Nell. You've seen me in dreams. Now you see me while you're awake. So, you make plans for a noble future. Do you think I'll leave you alone and let you enjoy that future? No, Ezra. You've forgotten something you said yourself. A strong bond rivets us, too strong for my death to break. In your lifetime I'll give you no peace, and I promise you this. When you die I'll be waiting. Judgment will be delivered against you for Dardeshi and the night of the massacre. We all wait for you—my father, Rodney, Dowlah. Portelance, Lapointe, Bobby Holden, and Little Moccasins will be there. All of us wait."

"Nell," he implored. "Give me peace."

The form was dissolving, but he heard the faint laugh again. "Peace you will never have, Ezra Purline."

"There are no ghosts!" He jumped to his feet. "You're only in my mind. You don't exist!"

As he stood there shaking, the door to the store flew open and Tim O'Casey stuck his Black Irish face around the panel. "Are you all right, sir? Did you call?"

Purline mopped at his dripping face. "No, Mr. O'Casey, I didn't call. I must have dozed off and had a bad dream. Back to work."

"Yes, sir," Tim said, and shut the door. Purline clung to the edge of his desk with both hands. He looked down at Hatch's letter, at the rest of his mail, at the empty glass with a few dregs of wine discoloring its bottom. Could someone have drugged it? He forced his eyes up, toward the kitchen door. Sunlight fell over the gingham curtains. One of them seemed to move. Frantic with fear, he wrenched open the door to the store. Behind the counter, Tim was unrolling a bolt of cotton for two Indian women.

"Mr. O'Casey, do you know where Mr. Durran is?"

Tim waved a freckled hand. "Just went past, sir. He's in his room."

He followed the factor's figure with speculative eyes.

The old man looked like death. What could be wrong with him? A few moments later, Durran asked himself the same question. Without knocking, Purline flung open the door and stumbled into Durran's room. Durran was stirring a pot of stew, but after a glimpse of the older man's face, he put down the spoon. "This is a surprise, general. I believe this is the first time you've visited me."

Purline didn't look at Durran. Crumpling in a chair by the hearth, he shielded his face with one hand. "Give me a minute. I've had a shock and must gather myself together."

Reaching down a bottle, Durran asked, "Would you like a sip of brandy?"

Purline shook his head. Returning to the hearth, Durran picked up the spoon and began briskly stirring the stew. Finally, Purline seemed to regain control. His hand fell away from his face, and a little color had crept back into his cheeks. "Forgive me for bursting in like this, Mr. Durran. I received a letter from Mr. Hatch that contained excellent news. I've been promoted and will be leaving shortly to take the position of chief agent in Montreal. M. Charloux is resigning."

"Congratulations."

"Yes, the tidings were extremely gratifying and fill me with joy."

Durran ironically scrutinized the other man. Purline's hands were still trembling, and if the tidings had filled Purline with joy, he'd hate to see the factor facing bad news. Durran spared a thought for Laurie. The position of chief agent was the one the man had coveted for years. How would Laurie react to the news that Purline had it? Aloud, Durran said, "I'd imagine that Laurie will be promoted to factor of this fort."

"He'll have that opportunity, but his father-in-law appears to have reservations about Mr. Woodbyne accepting the position. In that case, you'll be the new factor."

Durran murmured, "You overwhelm me, sir."

"I knew you'd be delighted. That's why I hurried directly to you. I know during the last few years my work has prevented me from seeing much of you, but now I've a suggestion to make."

"Which is?"

Purline gripped his hands together to try to disguise their trembling. "The duties of a factor are much more involved than your present ones. For one thing, there are reports to prepare, letters to write, books to keep. As these have never been your concern, I feel it only right for me to teach you them. For that reason I was wondering . . . would you object if I move into your quarters for the remainder of my tenure?"

Durran's eyes widened. "All I can offer you is that tiny room off this one. Hardly what you're used to, sir."

For the first time, Purline looked at the rooms. "Hmm . . . yes, your quarters are rather cramped." He brightened. "You must move into my cabin. There's lots of room. Carafa comes daily to tidy the place and cook my meals, but at night I'm alone, very much alone. Perhaps you could move in today, and tonight I could start teaching you your new duties."

"Has Laurie turned the position down, then?"

"Not as yet. I've had no time to consult him."

"In that case, general, you may be trying to teach the wrong man. Laurie is the one who'll probably have to learn."

Purline stroked his square chin. "That's possible. Mr. Durran, I think I'd like the brandy you so kindly offered." He waited, accepted the mug from Durran, and continued, "Somewhere—I can't remember from whom—I once heard that you come from a family of spiritualists."

Durran's red brows raised. "Spiritualists?"

"Something about a relative of yours. It might have been a grandparent who was mentioned."

Durran chuckled. "You must mean my granny Macdonald. Nay, she was no spiritualist, general. Granny was merely a wise old woman with healing hands, and a little talent for seeing into the future."

Clearing his throat, Purline muttered hoarsely, "I'd have sworn I heard she was a witch."

"Nay, she was no witch."

"She must have known about potions," Purline said eagerly. "And you must know something about them too. You must know how to ward off evil."

Tugging at his short beard, Durran stared at the other man. "Nay, of this I know nothing. All I know is how to heal a little and how to judge a man's character. My judgment tells me you've been frightened. What has frightened you?"

"Frightened!" Purline blustered. "I'm certainly not frightened. A trifle upset, perhaps, but certainly not—" Breaking off abruptly, he drained his mug. "Very well, Mr. Durran, I'm terrified. Let me explain. Martha told me you have heard about a place in India called Dardeshi. Is that correct?"

"It is, sir."

"Martha told me that your information came from an officer who once was sent in relief of that fort during a tribal uprising. Because of my family's prominence in military affairs and the envy and petty jealousy it engendered, I was subjected to a character maligning at that time that was unbelievable. No doubt the tale you heard was much distorted, but I'll not bother to go into the true facts now. Let me say this. Many people died at Dardeshi. For years I've dreamed of them. Then, right in this fort, another tragedy occurred and more people died. My wife was killed before my eyes. Since that night I've dreamed of those dead, too. But today"—he took a deep breath—"today, in broad daylight, with my mail in my hands, in my own office . . . I saw a manifestation of pure evil."

"What did you see?"

"My dead wife, Mr. Durran, exactly as she was the night those savages slaughtered her. She was standing in my kitchen, and I not only saw her, I heard her voice. She threatened me with terrible things. That's why I came to you. You must exorcise this dream who appears in my wife's guise. You must drive her from me!"

"Ah." Durran sank back in his own chair. "You come

344

looking for a witch. You want the black arts to drive this memory of your wife from your mind."

"It wasn't a memory. It wasn't in my mind. I tell you, man, she stood there. She laughed—I heard her voice!"

"Nay, general, she wasn't real. I knew Nell well, and never would her gentle, sweet soul do what you say. There are no ghosts, only people who can't live with that which lies heavily on their consciences."

"You really think so?"

"Aye. You say you've dreamed of the dead for years. Today you simply heard sounds, saw an image conjured up by your own mind, by your own memory."

Shifting in his chair, Purline rubbed distractedly at his brow. "Have you any suggestion, Mr. Durran?"

With remote pity the Scot studied the distraught man. Obviously, Purline hovered on the edge of complete madness. Durran's voice was gentle. "One suggestion. Go to a man of God. Confess all. Then you might come to peace with yourself. Although you're not a Catholic, if you should meet a priest on your journey east, talk to him. They are men of rare understanding and compassion. It would help."

Hope flashed across Purline's face. "Mr. Durran, you may have hit on it! I understand that church—although I've always despised its paganism—is experienced in exorcism. They could drive this specter, this demon, away from me. Yes, when I return to Montreal I shall adopt the Catholic faith. I may take a Frenchwoman as wife, and it would be best if I do become a Catholic." He shuddered. "I shall never enter that accursed cabin again. I will have my books, my records, and my clothes moved to that empty cabin opposite the stable." Springing to his feet, he extended a big hand to Durran. "You've been of great help to me. I'll not forget it, and I also know I can count on your discretion in this matter."

After a moment, Durran took the factor's hand. Purline clasped the Scot's hand firmly and looked directly into his eyes. "Mr. Durran," he said hesitantly, "even if what you

345

heard of my past did contain some truth, would you censor me for it?"

"All of us meet our Pass of Hajarial, and until we do meet it we can't tell what our own actions will be. Nay, I don't sit in judgment, General Purline."

Jerking his head in mute agreement, Purline left. Dishing out some of the savory mixture from the stewpot, Durran carried it to the table. He sliced off a thick chunk of bread and smeared jam on it. That poor devil of a Purline, he thought, pursued by the blood on his own conscience and still convinced it was a ghost. Anyway, it looked as though a rabid Anglican was going to convert to Catholicism for an odd reason. As he wiped out his bowl, he wondered what the other people at the fort would think about the general's sudden shift from his own comfortable quarters to the dingy little cabin opposite the stable.

As it worked out, the inhabitants paid no attention to Purline's move. Some things are much more horrible than even a ghost. Death comes in many guises, and in a short time it would walk again in the valley of the Nechako. This time its face would be a singularly terrifying one.

27

After he picked his mail up at the store, Laurie took it directly to his cabin. The place was deserted, and he remembered that Rowan had taken the children to the woods for the day. Wise Rowan—she must have spotted the mail canoe. What hell that arrival had meant to her through the years, and yet never once by even a look or a word had she reproached him.

Sitting down at his desk, he started to go through the stack. The packages, books, and London newspapers he put to one side. He riffled quickly through the letters. As usual there were three fat ones from Judith Hatch. He put these aside to read last. There were a number of other letters from England. Two were from old friends, one from his cousin Edward. Laurie picked up another English letter and frowned. It was from his family solicitor, Josiah Cavendish, who had been not only his father's legal adviser but also a close friend. Laurie thought the last letter was from Ashbury until he saw the seal and the small, crabbed writing. He tapped a finger against Hatch's seals. Wonders never ceased. Faithful Ashbury had neglected to write, but Charlie Hatch had.

Picking up the letter from Josiah Cavendish, Laurie hesitated and then set it aside. He slit open the one from Charlie Hatch. His eyes widened. Hatch's writing was unsteady, and the page was blotched with spots that might have been tears. He read the first two lines and chuckled grimly. The man was getting old and with age was beginning to repent his sins. If Hatch kept on like this he'd probably become a reformed sinner, and the villain might even try to buy his way into heaven. Then Laurie's eyes scanned the next few lines; he sobered, his breath quickened, and his mouth tightened.

"My years are heavy on me," Hatch had written, "and with them comes punishment for my sins. Before it is too late, I must atone. Your solicitor, Josiah Cavendish, will have a letter in this post to bring the sad news of the tragic accident that has bereaved both of us. My little Esmie, Ashbury, Mildred, and Miss Grace are dead. They perished in a boating accident, and it was only by the mercy of God that Chris was not with them. He and Judith were supposed to be in the boat too, but at the last minute, Chris did some small thing that annoyed his mother, and Esmie ordered him to remain behind as punishment. Luckily, Judith elected to remain with the boy, and both Chris and my wife were witnesses to what happened."

Laurie closed his eyes. Thank God his son was safe. Esmie's petulance had saved the child's life. He continued reading. "I've called this an accident, Laurie, but to you I must tell the truth. Judith saw it all, but she had presence of mind enough to pull Chris against her breast so he only saw the boat upset. It was cold-blooded murder. Miss Grace was the only person in the boat who could swim, and she deliberately upset it. When it was overturned and the other three were helplessly floundering in the water, Miss Grace strongly stroked her way over to Esmie. At first, Judith hoped she meant to save our daughter, but she clasped her arms around Esmie and pulled her under. The only people who know the truth are Judith, and I, now you."

Laurie groaned. Charlie Hatch had explained haltingly of Miss Grace's motive for the mass murders. Esmie had finally tired of her companion and had taken a younger, prettier lover. With deliberate cruelty she had kept Miss Grace on for a time, but the day before the boating trip Esmie had given the woman her discharge. Miss Grace had taken revenge. Rather than live without Esmie, she had chosen to die and take her lover with her. And with them had died Ashbury and Mildred.

His eyes flew down the uneven lines to the last paragraph. "There is no longer any reason for you staying in exile, my boy. As Mr. Cavendish will tell you, you're Ashbury's heir. Ashbury, by shrewd investment with me, had been able to amass a considerable fortune as well as enlarge the estate and renovate your old home, Woodbyne Hall. There's also a townhouse in Mayfair, very much like and very close to the one where you lived for the first year of your marriage. I urge you to return. Little Chris is now thirteen and much in need of a father. With Ashbury dead, I know not where to turn. Despite the good works I have done in recent years, my past still follows me, and there's no way I can act as proper guardian to a boy of his class. I know how you feel about me, and I admit I richly deserve it, but for your son's sake I humbly beg you to come home."

So blotched were the last few words that all Laurie could make out was the signature. He sat staring at the small objects on his desk. His hand moved out and touched the silver frame of his father's picture, the cold metal of the old decanter. There wasn't a speck of dust on any of the objects. Rowan carefully cleaned the desk and kept all his souvenirs spotless. *Rowan.* What was he to do? His eyes strayed to the etching of his home, that gracious old house among the lime trees. England! A land of small fields and fragrant gardens, a land of old trees, of gentle springs, of gray fogs. A land of dear memories. He pictured himself at Woodbyne Hall, at a townhouse in Mayfair, teaching his son to hunt, to shoot. He saw himself choosing schools for Chris, having the boy with him at Christmas, celebrating the boy's birthday.

Laurie stared around the cabin, and never had it looked as crude, as primitive as it did at that moment. The colored cottons around the sleeping cubicles were no match for hangings of velvet and brocade. The tiny gleams of silver on his desk brought memories of huge sideboards blazing with fine silver, china, crystal. On a planked floor were native rugs, lovingly woven by Rowan, but nothing like the soft tints of old Persian rugs on polished oak floors. His eyes wandered to the fireplace and the ancient pot dangling from the tripod over a heap of gray ashes. He had forgotten what it was like to live in a house where you didn't sleep, cook, and eat in one room. He sniffed. The cabin held pungent odors drifting from the lean-to, smells of fish and meat in brine, of pressed cakes of berries, of dried pumpkin and wild onion.

The smell of their daily lives had worked right into the logs of the cabin. He could distinguish the lingering stench of sodden buckskins that had been dried near the fire, the pungent tang of heavy winter furs, the reek of moccasins, the iron cold of December, and the sweaty heat of August. If he wished, he could return to a land where the only smells in bedchambers were of fine ladies' scent, of English soap, of linen stored in dried rose petals and lavender.

But—Rowan. Rowan and his sons. Laurie stirred restlessly. He must talk this over with someone. But with whom? There was no use in going to General Purline. Laurie knew what his advice would be. He could almost hear the factor's voice. "Your choice is clear, Mr. Woodbyne," Purline would say. "You owe no debt to those *bois brûlés*. Your duty lies in England with your legal son." No, Purline hated Rowan. He was out. The O'Casey brothers? They were fine lads, full of laughter and jokes and love of life, but too young, too lighthearted.

Getting to his feet, he crammed the letters into his pocket. There was only one man whose judgment he could trust. When Laurie arrived at the store, he poked his head around the door and called to Tim O'Casey, "Seen George around?"

The other man grinned broadly. "The dear man went storming out of here a few minutes ago, raving about not being a father confessor. First the general went running into George's room as though something was chasing him. Then Jourdin came looking for George with a long face.

The last one was my brother. Mike's got a problem at home."

"Any idea where George went?"

Tim leaned both hands on the counter, and his grin widened. "Growled something about seeking peace on the lookout platform, but if you follow the dear man, my advice is to call up and get permission first. The Durran can be testy."

"You should know all about that, Tim. Still limp a little, don't you? Was George in his cups?"

"Not so I noticed. You may be safe. He wasn't wearing a kilt, and I didn't see his bagpipe."

Nodding his thanks, Laurie went down the steps and headed toward the gates. He saw Durran's chunky figure leaning against the palisade, his back to the square. Heeding Tim's advice, Laurie called up to the Scot. Bending over the edge of the platform, Durran morosely regarded the man below.

"George," Laurie called. "I have to talk to you."

The red head shook violently. "Fresh out of solutions, Laurie. I've had my fill of others' problems. No one seems to think I might have a few of my own."

"Look, I know we've drifted apart lately, but once we were friends. I'm asking as a friend."

Sighing, Durran jerked his head. "Come up, friend."

Laurie climbed the ladder and found Durran again leaning against the logs, gazing out over the river. He joined the Scot. From this vantage point they could see the entire expanse of the valley. A group of canoes had just pulled in to the landing, and the Indian paddlers were climbing out of them. Smoke curled from the fires in front of the summer lodges, and women bent over their cooking pots. Tapinawa was in deep conversation with old Tupa, and the Liar was slicing up a deer carcass while a number of other natives lounged around watching him. Tiny brown-skinned children played in the dust of the trail with a number of shaggy puppies. A puppy snapped at one of the children, and she went howling to her mother. Laurie stared at the familiar scene, but actually he was picturing

351

himself standing on the Embankment, looking across the Thames.

"Well," Durran said impatiently. "What is it? Do you want advice on whether to become factor or let me shoulder the load?"

"Nothing like that." Pulling the two letters from his pocket, Laurie held them out.

"Just tell me."

"This concerns Rowan and the boys."

Without a word, Durran took the letters. He read them slowly and methodically, absorbing every word. Then he pretended to reread them to give himself time to think. His mind whirled. The two paths foreseen by his grandmother years before were now clear. If Laurie returned to England, his own long wait would be over. Rowan would be left here with her sons, and where would she turn? Durran knew that Rowan was fond of him, that she trusted him. If Laurie deserted her, Rowan would finally be his. On the other hand, if Laurie decided to stay, Rowan would be lost to him forever.

Durran stole a look at the other man. Laurie's brown eyes were fixed dreamily on a point across the river; the breeze was ruffling his pale hair. Laurie's face was rich in male beauty, but there was little strength in it. He could easily be influenced. All I have to do, Durran thought, is say a few words. Tell him he has no choice, his only course is to go to his oldest son, go back to his own country. It was too easy! There was a trap here.

Then Durran saw the trap. He recalled the words he'd spoken only a short time before to Purline. Every man comes to the Pass of Hajarial. As Purline had come to his, so George Durran had now reached his. A few words to Laurie, and he would be gone. Rowan would be his, but what would the price be? Loss of honor is the price, Durran decided grimly, and the knowledge that I robbed this woman of the man she loves, robbed her sons of their father.

Durran's mouth hardened, and he handed back the letters. "What do you want of me?"

"Can't you see?" Laurie spun around to face him. "I'm pulled in two! Chris on one hand, Rowan and the boys on the other."

Durran asked bluntly, "Where does your duty lie?"

"With Chris. He's alone. Ashbury is dead."

"Are there no others to care for him? Have you no blood kin to raise the lad?"

Guiltily Laurie thought, Many. Aloud he admitted, "I've cousins. There's one—Edward Woodbyne. Edward would gladly act as guardian. But George, I haven't seen my son since he was a tiny baby. Chris needs a father."

"So do Seamus and Martin. What about your other choice?"

"To stay here with my family. Stay in a cabin built of logs surrounded by wilderness, a cabin stinking of wood-smoke and wild meat and wet buckskins. Frying with heat in the summer, freezing with cold in the winter. Living, cooking, sleeping in a one-room hovel. A filthy country! That's my other choice."

"And the woman in that cabin?"

"A wonderful woman. We've been together eleven years. She's made me happy, and without her I doubt I could have made it. But Rowan will understand. Her own father left her mother and took his child with him."

"Aye, I've heard the tale. Eamon Malone died a miserable death from drink in an alehouse on the docks of Montreal. The fool left the one person he needed."

Crossing his arms on the hot logs, Laurie lowered his head to them. He mumbled, "I'll never find another woman like her. I know that. But there's a call, a call of blood, of memories, of country. Tell me, George, in my place—what would you do?"

"In your place?" Durran smiled without mirth. "How would a poor Scots lad know? You've a title waiting, a son, an estate. Fine food and wine and clothes. What waits for me? A few relatives I don't even know, a bare craggy land, the sight of Ben Venue over Loch Katrine. I love my land and always will, but Scotland I'll never see again. I lived there barely sixteen years; here I've lived

353

my life. This is *my* country." Durran moved his shoulders. His thin shirt stuck to his back, and sweat was pouring down his armpits. The day was hot, the August heat striking cruelly down upon them, but it was more than heat that made him sweat. How hard it was not to interfere. Durran took a deep breath. "You named two choices. There's a third, lad."

Lifting his head, Laurie stared at the other man. "What?"

"Do both. Go back to your land and take Rowan and your sons with you. Marry the lass and adopt the boys."

For an instant Laurie's expression radiated hope, and then, slowly, he shook his head. "Take Seamus and Rowan away from the land they love, the life they love? Take them like wild animals to be caged in a zoo, stared at as though they're in a zoo?" He gave a harsh, brittle laugh. "Have you looked at Seamus lately? Seen his coloring and size? The way he's growing up sounds like the description of those Sioux warriors. Can you imagine a full-grown Seamus in London?"

"The Sioux are handsome and proud. So is Seamus. Rowan's skin is as white as yours."

"When she loses her tan—yes. But again, think of her. Her eyes, her cheekbones, the way she moves. We couldn't conceal their ancestry."

"Would you want to?"

Laurie moved restlessly. "Don't look at me like that! I'm thinking of them, what they'd endure. They'd be outcasts, objects of curiosity, targets of ignorance. Because of them, so would young Chris."

"And you."

"And me!" Savagely, Laurie turned on Durran. "You've heard the names. Squaw man! A Woodbyne gone native!"

"Calm down." Durran tugged at his bristling red beard. "Sort your thoughts out. I noticed one thing. You haven't mentioned Martin."

"For a good reason, George. I'm not leaving him behind. I'm going to adopt Martin, and I'm taking him with me. Except for the setting of his eyes he looks enough like Chris to be a twin. Martin will be accepted. The two boys can grow up together."

"So," the other man said evenly, "you'll take the son who can pass as white. I've a hunch you don't know Rowan very well after all."

"What do you mean?"

Durran didn't answer that question. He asked one of his own. "Have you talked with the lass about this?"

"She's in the woods with the boys. I haven't had a chance."

"Then go home and wait for her. Talk to the one you should discuss this with."

Durran was urging the other man toward the ladder, but Laurie hung back. "Please," he pleaded, "give me some advice, George. Even a hint."

"Aye, here's a hint. If you're not off this platform immediately, you're going down the same way the O'Casey lad did."

Laurie didn't argue. He backed away from the rage in Durran's face. When his blond head disappeared over the platform edge, Durran sank down heavily in the shade the palisade cast. Drawing his knees up, he rested his head against them. I'd like to break every bone in his useless body, the Scot thought. He's not worth her little finger. But the lass loves him, loves every useless bone in his useless body. Laurie Woodbyne has all the wealth of the world in that cabin with him and doesn't have sense enough to know it. All he can do is complain about the smells from the foods the poor lass breaks her back to bring home. Durran cursed helplessly.

After a time he calmed down and waited patiently. He didn't see Rowan and the children when they returned to the fort at dusk, but he heard them. He heard Martin's high-pitched voice, the sound of Nicko's bark, and the rich tones of Rowan's laugh. They passed through the gateway. Then Durran pulled himself up, climbed down the ladder, and, closing the gates, barred them securely against the night. The heat from the day lingered for hours in the fort. In that dark, sweltering heat the people in the fort turned and tossed on rumpled beds.

Death came that hot night. It came unwittingly and in the name of mercy when it was carried into one of the lodges outside the palisade.

28

When Rowan and the two boys entered their cabin that evening, no lamps had been lit, nor had Laurie kindled a fire to cook supper. She could make out his shadowy form hunched beside the cold hearth, his head propped up on a hand. Checking a lamp, she lit it and placed it on the table. On the desk was a pile of her husband's letters and packages, but none of them seemed to have been opened.

Sending the boys to wash, Rowan quickly prepared a cold supper. Then she retired to the sleeping alcove, washed herself, and brushed out her hair. On impulse, she opened her chest and removed the black silk shirt and ruffled blouse that Sister Gabriel had stitched for her many years before. Both garments were mended, and the lace on the shirtwaist had yellowed, but she pinned her cameo brooch at the neck and pulled back her hair into a large, loose bun on the nape of her neck.

Martin and Seamus ate their suppers hungrily, but Rowan only picked at her own plate. She touched Laurie's shoulder and pointed at the table, but he shook his head. After she'd piled up the dishes, she sent the boys to bed. Seamus made no protest, but Martin, as usual, was difficult. His mother was firm. "Off you go," she said. "It's been a long day, and you're tired. You'll be asleep in no time."

By the time the cabin was tidied, both boys were sound asleep. For a time she stood over their bed, gazing down at them. She pulled a sheet over them, touched the blond head with gentle fingers, and caressed Seamus's firm cheek. Pulling the curtains closed, she started to fold some garments and put them in a woven basket.

For the first time since they'd entered the cabin, Laurie spoke. "Are you going out?"

"I'm taking some of Martin's outgrown clothes over to Middy. They're about the right size for her twins."

"That can wait. Sit down, Rowan."

She glanced again at the mail on the desk and put the basket aside. Sitting opposite her husband, she waited, her hands loosely folded in her lap. He pulled a couple of rumpled papers from his shirt pocket. "These came today. My wife is dead. A boating accident. My brother and his wife died too."

"Your son?"

"Chris is safe. He wasn't with them."

"Should I offer condolences?"

His lips twisted, and he held up one of the letters. She had a glimpse of a large red seal. "I'm not quite the hypocrite Charlie Hatch is. Not yet, anyway. I can't pretend grief. I hardly knew Mildred, and what I did know about her I didn't like. Ashbury and I were virtually strangers. As for Esmie . . . well, I told you I left England to get away from her." Pulling himself to his feet, he walked over to the desk, put the letters on it, and picked up the silver decanter. He turned it in his hands and then placed it on Rowan's lap. "Ever taken a close look at this?"

"Many times." She turned it around, looking at the engraving. "I don't understand the words, but this"—she pointed at an etched design—"this is your family crest, isn't it?"

"Yes, and above the crest is our family motto. In Latin, and only one word. *Invincible*." He laughed, but it was only a sound. "Perhaps at one time the Woodbynes earned that motto, but my grandfather was a realist and had the words written on the other side. He said they fitted Woodbynes better."

Moving the decanter around, she studied the lines of strangely formed letters. "What do they mean?"

"The three Graces' names in Greek. Aglaia—splendor,

Euphrosyne—mirth, and Thalia—abundance. The Graces were supposed to confer on human beings grace, beauty, charm, and, if they were fortunate, joy. As you notice, grandfather didn't mention anything about strength or invincibility."

Carefully, she set the decanter on the hearthrug at her feet. "You're going back to England," she said slowly.

He sank back into his chair and looked at her miserably. "I need your help, Rowan. I don't know what to do."

"You're Sir Laurence now, aren't you?"

"Yes."

She pointed at one of the pictures in the silver frames. "I suppose that belongs to you now."

"Woodbyne Hall is mine. My brother's entire estate is mine."

"What do you want from me?"

"Help. I went to George for advice and . . ."

"What did he say?"

"That it's my decision." His mouth twisted. "Then he threatened to throw me off the lookout platform. Fine friend!"

She looked down at her folded hands. "The best you'll ever have."

Jumping to his feet, he started to stride up and down. One hand wrenched at his hair. "What am I to do? I'm pulled two ways, Rowan. Chris needs me. He's all alone now, but there're the boys and you. Rowan . . . for God's sake, don't just sit there. Say something!"

She lifted her eyes to his flushed face. "I know what you want to hear. Your grandfather was right. You've beauty and charm and grace, but you're weak. You want to lean on my strength. You want me to tell you that you must go, that you must desert your sons and me. George was right. This decision you must make yourself, Laurie. No one can make it for you."

He stared at her. How impassive she is, he thought; she has the same expression that Marinska always had. He

359

cleared his throat. "I'll provide for you. Not much of my pay has been spent, and I'll have it turned over to you. You can live in comfort." Kneeling, he gathered her hands into his. "Rowan," he whispered, "I never lied to you. I never promised I'd stay forever."

She was as still and hard as a marble statue. "I made a vow. I vowed our marriage would last to my death or yours. Certainly, you're free to go, free to take another wife. But you're my husband, and I'll never be free."

"I release you from your vow!"

"You can't. It wasn't made to you. It was made to God."

He let her hands go. His brow was beaded with sweat. "Release me."

"No."

"Your mother let your father go."

"I'm not my mother. Perhaps I'm not as noble as she is, as self-sacrificing. Aluski had the power to hold Eamon Malone by force. If I'd been her I'd have kept him."

He stared up at her. Angry color flooded over his throat, mantled his cheeks. "You've grown hard, Rowan, but I can be hard too. You're forcing me to decide. Very well, I will. But I warn you—if I go, Martin goes with me."

"Martin."

"I'll adopt him and take him to England."

"You're using my own son to threaten me with."

"Either you release me and tell me to go, or I take Martin."

Her tilted eyes bored into his. "Martin looks like you, he even acts like you. But I won't see him become like *you.* I'll make a man of him. He stays with me."

"There's no way you can stop me." He added, with calculated cruelty, "A *bois brûlée* has no rights."

He jumped up and she slowly rose. "I'll see him dead first."

George Durran had told him he didn't really know this woman. Now Laurie agreed. Her face was implacable, and so was her voice. He remembered her hand reaching for her rifle when Charlie had been so badly mangled by the bear. He remembered her putting the barrel against the dog's head, her finger steady on the trigger. She meant exactly what she said. His eyes dropped. "He's your son," he muttered. "Keep him."

Without a word, she circled around him and went in to the alcove. In a few minutes the curtains parted and she stepped out again. She'd changed her clothes. She wore her buckskin skirt and shirt, and her hair was in braids. Picking up the decanter, she handed it to him. Then she took her rifle down from the wall and slung it over her back. With her hand on the doorknob, she turned.

"Make up your mind, Laurie, but remember one thing. This is a big country, and big men are needed to challenge it. Perhaps you aren't big enough."

As she opened the door, he cried, "Where are you going?"

She made no answer. Behind her the door swung closed.

Laurie never knew where she spent that night. George Durran did. He found her when he went through the store on his way to his rooms. She was stretched out on the narrow bench where years before Dutchy had taken naps. Going to his rooms, he brought back a pillow and a light blanket. Lifting her head carefully, he eased the pillow under it. Then he covered her with the blanket.

Standing over her, he remembered the first time he'd seen her. Her black hair had been resting against a pillow then too. Her short, stubby black lashes had made crescents over high cheekbones. Then she had opened those eyes, gazed at him, and turned to a man with silver-gilt hair. Rowan had changed in the past eleven years. Then her face had been that of a girl, soft and full. Now it was a woman's face, with wonderful stark planes. Faint lines marred the amber skin near her eyes; other lines were traced around her mouth. If possible, she was even lovelier than she had been as a girl. There was strength in

361

that face now—the fear, the softness, were gone. With those bones she'd be lovely when she was an old woman.

He put out a hand to touch her, drew it back, and sighed. Then he checked the lamp, turned the wick down, and slowly made his way down the hall to his own room.

29

Durran tried not to awaken Rowan when he left his quarters in the early hours, but as he tiptoed past the bench she raised her head. "No need to be quiet, George. I've been awake for a while."

He smiled down at her. "Did you rest well?"

"Much better than I expected to." She touched the blanket. "You covered me."

"It got cool later. No need for you to get up yet. Dawn hasn't broken."

"Why are you up this early?"

"Duty calls." He held up a bulging leather bag. "Old Tupa sent a message by the man on watch. Says a family was carried in last night to the lodges. Some of the Indians found them on the trail. Asked me to come down and doctor them."

She pushed the blanket back. "I'll walk down with you. Maybe I can help."

He stood back while she straightened her clothes, pulled the braids down into place, and picked up her rifle. Outside the store, the air still held the night chill, and they both shivered. "Never mind," Durran told her. "Later in the day when we're boiling under the sun we'll recall how good it was to feel cold." He darted a glance at her profile. "I suppose you know Laurie's news from home."

"That's why I was sleeping in the store."

"Martin?"

"Martin stays with me."

He asked hesitantly, "Has Laurie decided yet?"

"I imagine his decision was made when he read those letters." She squeezed his arm and tried to smile. "You've helped me so many times, George, but this time there's nothing anyone can do. It's up to Laurie."

They'd reached the gates, and Durran handed Rowan his bag while he lifted down the heavy bar. Stepping backwards, he called up, "Jourdin, Rowan and I are going down to the lodges. Better get down here and bar the gates."

A sleepy voice answered from the darkness over their heads. As they stepped out of the fort, Jourdin leaned over the palisade. "What takes you down there so early, *mes amis?*"

"A family came in last night, and all of them are sick," Durran called back.

A shadowy hunched form was waiting for them. After a moment Rowan recognized the wizened face of Tupa. "Good," the woman mumbled. "Come. Follow Tupa."

They followed her along the winding trail through the lodges. All was silent, and Rowan could smell the mingled odors of rawhide, freshly butchered meat, and smoke from the dying fires. One of the scrawny dogs ran up, his lips pulled back in a snarl. Casually, Tupa lifted a moccasin and kicked him in the belly. "Down there," she grunted, pointing at the end of a ladder protruding from the central hole in one of the underground lodges.

Durran peered down the hole. "Why the devil did you put sick people in one of these sweltering holes, Tupa?"

"Best," she said laconically. "Watch step."

Durran climbed down behind the old woman, and then Rowan carefully felt her way down. Partway down the ladder, the stench rose to meet her. Gagging, she forced herself down the last few rungs. At the foot of the ladder, on a flat stone, a small fire burned sulkily, and the place was dimly lighted by rags dipped in grease and set afire. It was a large lodge, and against the wall she could see numerous pallets arranged. Only four of them were occupied. Rowan tugged at Durran's sleeve. "What's that horrible smell?"

He turned grim eyes on her. "Let's have a look."

Tupa was waiting beside the pallets. Durran snapped, "Get some light over here."

As soon as the old woman brought two of the burning rags, he bent over the pallets. "The woman's dead," he said. "And so are these two children."

"Man soon be," Tupa said.

Rowan moved in beside Durran, and her eyes widened with horror. All four of the Indians were stripped from the waist down. They sprawled in contorted positions, their knees drawn up to their bellies. Their bodies were skin and bone, their noses stood out sharply, their lips were dark brown. They lay in pools of their own wastes, oozing graying paste and feces. Their heads were rimmed with puddles of watery vomit.

Durran took the man's cheek between two strong fingers and pinched. When he released his grip, the marks were still indented. He straightened. "He's a goner, too." His eyes sought Tupa. "You know what this is?" When her grizzled head jerked, he demanded, "Why did you summon me? Three were dead, and you knew the man was dying."

The old crone mumbled something, and Rowan asked the Scot, "What's she saying?"

"She says this way we have to help." Savagely, he turned on the Indian. "I'd have come to help anyway, but Rowan . . . Tupa, how could you?"

She lifted her face so the light caught it, and the toothless mouth moved. "Didn't know Rowan come. Have to have help."

Although she already suspected the answer, Rowan asked, "What did they die of?"

Durran's answer was in one word. *"Omikewin."*

"Plague?"

"Cholera."

She buried her face in her hands. "God help us."

"He'd better." Durran led her away from the pallets

and their grisly burdens. "Have you ever been in contact with this before? Have you ever had it?"

Numbly, she stared up at him. "Years ago there was an epidemic in Montreal. The sisters turned the convent into a hospital. I was too young to do much nursing, but I was in and out of the wards, carrying water, emptying slop pails. I didn't get it."

"So little is known about cholera, but I've noticed a few people have a natural immunity. Others . . . my whole family died of cholera. My granny couldn't save them, but I had it too and she managed to pull me through. Since then I've doctored people with it a number of times. It's possible we're both safe." Still holding Rowan's arm, he headed toward the ladder. "We can't do anything here. Let's get out and do some thinking."

The three of them climbed out of the pesthole as quickly as they could. At the top of the ladder, Rowan gulped deep breaths of clean air. Durrán was standing facing east, his eyes fixed on the first glimmers of dawn. His face was drawn with anxiety.

She went to him. "What are we going to do, George? The fort, the children—"

"The fort!" He set off at a run. Several yards from the log wall, he cupped his hands around his mouth and shouted, "Jourdin."

A rumpled head rose over the palisade. "That you, M. Durran?"

"Have the gates been opened for anyone since we left?"

"No."

"Keep them barred, no one in or out. Get the general up there, and better get the O'Casey boys and Mr. Woodbyne too. Hurry."

The head jerked and was gone. Durran felt Rowan's hand on his arm. Absently, he patted it. "Got to think. Can't let this hit the fort." He spun around. Tupa stood a few feet behind them, her hands folded under her blanket. "Tupa, how many people came into contact with those sick people?"

"Huh?"

"How many people carried them into the lodge?"

She held up both hands. *"Keepoh."*

"Ten," he muttered. "Was anyone else near them?"

"Many come down into lodge. See could help. Many come, women, braves."

He cursed. "You knew what it was. Why did you let them go down?"

"Wanted see if help. Tupa didn't know first. Later knew. Too late."

He threw up his hands. "Then we're going to have to hold them there. If they scatter, they could take infection with them."

Rowan had regained her composure. "Wouldn't it be better to let them go?" she suggested. "They might have a better chance in the forest. If we keep them boxed up at the lodges, the cholera will spread like a forest fire."

He regarded her bleakly. "If we let them go, do you think they'll stay in the forest? They'll head back to their own villages, to other forts. With them they'll take infection. The deadliest killer of all will ravage this land!" He looked into her eyes. "Can you kill a man?"

"If it's necessary."

"It may be. The natives may panic. Keep your rifle handy."

A hail from the fort sounded over them, and they both turned and lifted their heads. There was more light now, and they could see a number of heads poking over the palisade. Rowan saw Laurie's blond hair, still rumpled from bed, and beside him the factor's clipped dark head.

"What's wrong, Mr. Durran?" Purline called.

"We've four corpses in the lodges, sir. Cholera."

Rowan contemptuously waited for Purline's reaction to the dreaded word. A coward, she thought. Now he'll panic, he'll break into pieces. He surprised her. "Locals?" he asked calmly.

"Strangers. They were brought in last night." Durran swung on Tupa. "Was that after the gates were closed for the night?" When she nodded, he called, "They weren't in the fort, general. None of the other natives had been in since either. The gates were locked, and Tupa threw a stone at the palisade and had the watch give me the message."

Laurie leaned further over the log wall. "Rowan! Get in here."

Durran swiveled his head. "She can't come in. She's been down in the lodge where the bodies are. She may be infected. But Rowan tells me she was around cholera patients in Montreal. She may be immune, and I'm sure I am."

Purline took over. "What can we do to help, Mr. Durran?"

"We need supplies. Laudanum, sulphur, cloths, food. We need men. Find out if anyone in there has been around cholera before or has had it. I need men with guns. The Indians may panic, and we can't let this spread."

The big head nodded. "You'll have it. I'll send a runner to the Nor'westers' fort. Have them send medicines and any men who will come."

"Opium," Durran shouted. "Was there any opium in that last shipment?"

"A small amount."

"We need it, and ask the other factor if he has any."

"I will, Mr. Durran. Anything else?"

"Except for the men to help us, everyone else stays put. Pile the supplies outside the gates and we'll get them. Keep some sulphur and start burning it. Be careful of water. The men carrying it must avoid the lodge area. Boil it before drinking. Understand?"

Purline lifted his arm. "Completely. When will you tell the natives?"

"Now. Get those men out here as fast as you can."

"God be with you, Mr. Durran."

Swinging around, Durran started back to the lodges with Rowan by his side, her strides as long as his. She pulled her rifle from her shoulder and held it across her breast. She thought she heard Laurie calling her name, and there seemed to be a struggle among the men on the platform. She took one look over her shoulder and then walked on.

On the platform the O'Casey brothers were fighting to restrain Laurie. Purline was trying to reason with him. "Kindly control yourself, Mr. Woodbyne. No purpose is served by losing your head."

"That's my wife out there," Laurie panted.

"You heard Mr. Durran. She's been infected. She can't return. You've two sons. Do you want to watch them die of plague?"

Laurie ceased struggling and hung limply in the powerful arms of Tim and Mike.

"That's better," Purline said. "We must all work together. Mr. Durran needs me to back him if those savages are to be controlled. Call everyone in the fort together."

In a short time the general was standing on the steps of the store, and in the square below him, all the inhabitants of the fort were gathered. He began to concisely sum up the situation. Among his listeners, faces drained of color and hands knotted into fists. As he spoke he looked them over. The voyageurs stood to one side, smoking their short pipes. Laurie stood alone, but near him were the O'Casey boys and their families. Tapinawa and a group of hunters mingled with the cooper, the smith, the carpenter, and their women and children.

"Now," Purline concluded, "you all grasp the situation. Any questions?"

Chichi stepped forward. "What are the chances of keeping sickness out of the fort?"

"A good one. Mr. Durran acted with a cool head and with speed. The infected natives didn't enter the fort. If the sickness can be contained to the lodges we may be safe. We must help Mr. Durran as much as we can."

As Purline spoke, a small, tousled form hurtled across the square to Laurie. "Where's mommy?" Martin wailed.

Picking the boy up, Laurie hugged him to his breast. "Mommy's gone to help George, son."

Seamus had followed his brother. He moved up to Laurie and looked into his father's eyes. "I belong with them. Let me go."

Freeing a hand, Laurie stretched it toward Seamus, but the boy dodged back. "You can't go with them," he told his son.

Purline lifted a commanding hand. "We need volunteers. Have any of you been exposed to, or had, cholera?"

Jourdin stepped forward, and Louis Grand followed him. After a moment two other voyageurs, Pierre and Emile, joined them.

"Good. Anyone else?"

Grunting, Tapinawa moved up beside the voyageurs. One of the hunters followed him. Purline counted. "Six. Take your rifles and join Mr. Durran immediately." He swung on Jacques. "As soon as these men clear the gates, get them barred again. No one in, no one out. Anyone who tries to climb the palisade is to be shot. Understand?"

Feet shuffled and heads nodded. Then the six men went for their weapons.

Putting Martin down, Laurie patted his shoulder. "I have to help the general now, son. That will help George and your mother." Laurie followed Purline into the store.

Martin stood alone, looking after his father, tears trickling forlornly down his cheeks. Seamus took a few steps and put an arm around the shorter boy's slight shoulders. Martin's wet eyes gazed up at him. "Mommy's gone and so is daddy," he sobbed. "I'm all alone."

"Dry your eyes and be a man," Seamus told him sternly. His voice softened, and he said, "You're not alone. I'll look after you."

Turning the young boy toward their cabin, Seamus led his brother home.

When they got back to the lodges, Durran and Rowan found only a few squaws up, squatting before their cooking fires. In front of one of the bigger structures were a couple of hide drums. Durran pounded on one and watched the doors of the lodges, but it was going to take more than a drum roll to rouse the sleeping natives. Pulling a cart over to the lodge, he pushed it against the log wall and beckoned to Rowan and Tupa. "One of you stand on each side. Tupa, I want you to help us, not hinder. Back me up with your people. Rowan, fire a shot; that should bring them on the run."

She held the rifle out to him. "Do you want this?"

He gave her a crooked grin. "I should be the one handling it, lass, but I'm a lousy shot, and we could have a running target. Remember, if I tell you, you must shoot—not to wound, but to kill. Can you do it?"

Nodding, she turned the barrel toward the sky and pulled the trigger. As the reverberations died away, the Indian men and children tumbled from their lodges. Durran shouted in the trading dialect, "Gather round." He sprang up on the cart and faced the crowd. "You all know about the sick family found on the trail and brought here last night. Well, they're dead, and that's why we're here. Ten of you carried them, and many of the rest of you went down into the winter lodge to see them. It's possible you've caught their sickness, and it's a bad one."

While he paused to consider how to name that sickness without starting a panic, old Tupa decided to take a hand. *Omikewin!* she shrieked in her cracked voice.

The ranks of people swayed as though they'd been struck. That dreadful word resounded like their death knell. A young man, dressed only in a breechcloth, pushed his way forward. One arm, twisted and withered, hung uselessly at his side. Turning to face the natives, he held up his sound hand and shouted, "Hear me. Listen to Goraldi! We must all leave here. We must scatter to the four winds. If we don't, we'll die!"

Durran roared over the man's head. "You must listen to me. This man gives bad advice. Our only chance is to stay here, to fight this together. Do you want to take this sickness back to your tribes? Do you want to spread the plague the length and breadth of this land?" He looked

371

grimly down at Tupa. "You started this. See what you can do with them."

She jumped up beside him on the cart. "Listen Tupa. Durran straight with us always. Nurse our sick. Birth our young. Listen Durran!"

Some of the Indians had started to edge away. Now they halted and turned toward Durran again. "Hear me," he pleaded. "Medicines are being sent from the fort. Men are coming to help. You all know Rowan and me. We're staying right here with you. We'll save as many as we can. Here you have a chance. If you leave with this sickness, who will care for you on the trails?"

Swinging around, Goraldi glared up at the Scot. "I go. No man keeps me here. I not stay and die!"

Catching his eyes, Durran held them. "Try and leave and I promise you will die. Men are coming with rifles. They'll patrol this area. Anyone who tries to leave will be shot. We'll not allow you to spread this plague."

"Not me." Goraldi spat on the ground, and his sound hand gripped the hilt of the knife at his waist. "I go before men come." He turned on the other Indians. "Any with sense follow Goraldi. Come!"

He sprang away like a deer, running fleetly toward the distant forest. A woman ran after him, and then two men followed. A group of children straggled after them, and the rest of the natives streamed away from the lodge area. Grabbing Tupa, Durran pulled her down from the cart with him. He hoisted Rowan up. "Kill the leader," he ordered.

She raised her rifle, sighted it on Goraldi's bronze back, and pulled the trigger. Even after the bullet plowed into him, he kept running. Suddenly he stopped, threw up his sound arm, and collapsed full length on the grass. In long strides, Durran reached the young man's side. The rest of the Indians faltered, slowed, and gathered around. Durran bent over Goraldi. "Dead," he said. He looked up at the circle of dark faces, searching for hostility, but they only looked dazed. Grimly, he said, "Goraldi brought this on himself. You all heard me warn him. Make up your own minds. Go back to the lodges or join this man."

Some of the natives stared at Durran's implacable face, others at the dead man on the ground; some turned to look back at Rowan, still standing on the cart, her rifle trained in their direction. A woman turned, took a child's hand, and started to trudge back to the lodges. The rest of the Indians slowly followed her. As Durran retraced his steps, he heard a shout. Jourdin and five other men came running from the direction of the fort. All of them carried rifles.

Jourdin shouted, "Trouble? We heard shots."

Durran pointed to Goraldi's sprawled body. "Tried to cut and run. If we'd let him go, the rest of the natives would have been out of here in minutes. A damn shame—the boy was out of his mind with fear."

"Had to be done," Jourdin panted. "You do it?"

"I wish I had," Durran said bitterly, "but I couldn't hit a moose at ten paces. No, I forced Rowan to kill him." He looked over at her. She was perched on the cart, her rifle leaning against it, her head in her hands. He touched her shoulder, and she lifted a face drawn with horror. "I'm sorry," he muttered. "And I fault Laurie for the way he treats you."

She got unsteadily to her feet and picked up her rifle. "We couldn't let him go."

He shook his red head, sighed, and said, "We'd better get to work." He touched the rifle butt. "Put it away. The killer we face requires other weapons."

She lifted her chin. "Tell us what we must do."

Durran called to the men from the fort, and when they'd gathered around him, he told them what to do. The fight against *omikewin* began.

30

The war against *omikewin* was waged on two fronts, and both were commanded by able leaders. In the days following the discovery of plague, Ezra Purline finally earned the title he had adopted. He proved he was a Purline and the descendant of generations of generals. Coolly and methodically, he rallied the people in the fort and put them to work. It was far from easy work, for as well as feeding themselves they now had the populace of the lodges to provision. Hunters were sent out accompanied by a couple of armed voyageurs. The hunters were fairly reliable, but Purline suspected that, spurred by fear of the pestilence, they might break and make a run for it. The voyageurs took no part in the actual hunting. Their job was to bring the hunters back, and this they did. The water carriers and wood details also had armed guards, and lookouts patrolled the platform day and night watching the palisade carefully.

The women of the fort were put to work cooking and preparing cloths and bandages. The men hauled wood, water, and food, and each morning outside the gates a pile of provisions awaited the men from the lodges. Sweltering August heat pressed down over the valley, making the log structures bake ovens. Burning sulphur mingled with the smoke from cookfires, and at times even breathing was difficult.

Purline set an example himself. No longer was he immaculately garbed. In rough clothes he pushed and hauled beside the men, struggling with heavy pots and loads of wood and water. Every evening at sundown he mounted the platform to speak with George Durran.

The work at the lodges started within minutes of Goraldi's death. Durran found twelve natives, seven women and five men, who had been previously involved in cholera epidemics, and these he pressed into service as nurses. The men from the fort, led by Jourdin, Rowan, the twelve natives, and Durran, numbered twenty, and the Scot sensed that once the sickness began these might be all who could be counted on. In the meantime he drove every able-bodied man and woman to make preparations. Two of the big lodges standing opposite each other were evacuated and made into hospitals. One was to be for men and boys, the other for women and girls. Rush mats were made ready and laid side by side in rows, shelves were built for the small store of medicines, barrels were placed in corners for water, and Durran had larger openings cut into the walls for ventilation. While this was being done, men dug latrine trenches behind both of the hospital lodges, and large mounds of lime ash were dumped into place beside them. Between the lodges and the edge of the forest, a huge pit was dug, and wood was hauled to stand in orderly rows beside it. As soon as it was ready a fire was kindled, and the bodies of the first four plague victims and that of Goraldi were burned. Durran asked for a horse and wagon, and Purline sent them out from the fort.

When the preparations were finished, they waited. After the second day, Rowan began to feel a faint stirring of hope. The natives seemed much the same as they always had been. They went about their chores, the women squatted in front of their lodges cooking and working at leather and bead work, the men played their favorite gambling games, the children tumbled and frolicked in the dust, and mangy dogs prowled around, cringing away from well-aimed kicks. As she watched the familiar scene the third morning, Rowan said to Jourdin, "Perhaps no one is infected. Maybe it was only the four they brought in."

He rubbed his scarred brow. "It could be that the saints have decided to spare us."

They weren't to be spared. A short time later a tiny girl who had been leaning listlessly against a lodge wall watching her friends at play stumbled to her knees and began to vomit. Her mother came running and scooped the child up in strong arms. "She all right," the woman told Rowan. "Eat too much. Fanai all right."

Durran was beside them. Gently he touched the child's leg, and she whimpered with pain. He detached Fanai from her mother's clinging arms and handed the little girl to Rowan. "Your first patient," he said grimly.

By noon, when the sun was high in a cloudless sky, they had fifteen patients. Some were brought in supported by relatives, others fell in the dust of the trail and were carried to the hospital lodges. For the first few hours the patients were able to make their way to the latrine behind the lodges, but that phase quickly passed. All the victims craved water but as soon as they drank would spout it back in surges of vomit. Their flesh appeared to melt from their bones, turn to fluids, and be expelled from their bodies from every orifice. The nurses cut off all the clothing below the waists and worked tirelessly mopping up the loose stools and vomit, replacing the soiled mats, bringing water to people who couldn't retain it. Fires were kindled, and the filthy mats and cloths were burned.

Rowan worked night and day, snatching brief periods for rest and quick meals. She couldn't believe the speed of the killer that was loose among them. A strong woman was brought in, a woman with firm flesh and a hard muscular frame, and within hours her skin hung like a sack over her bones; cramps racked her, working up from the legs, knotting her thighs, twisting the swollen belly, and then attacking her throat. In the agonized face her nose jutted, needle-thin and sharp, her bronze skin wrinkled and became the color of lead, her lips darkened to brown. Finally her eyeballs rolled up, a massive convulsion seized her, and Rowan pinched her cheek. The marks remained deeply indented. Rowan pulled herself to her feet. It was over; in a few minutes the woman was dead.

Durran went from one hospital lodge to the other, carefully measuring out the small stock of laudanum and the even smaller stock of opium. Rowan questioned him. "Will these help?"

"My granny used them. Pure opium is best. It helps retain fluids. It's dangerous, but sometimes it saves. But we have so little—so little of anything."

Cholera proved to be a strange, whimsical selector of victims. A young girl named Weskia was carried in by her husband early one morning. She was heavy with child and was far from robust. The girl fought the cholera and not only lived but later bore a healthy child. On the pallet beside Weskia was a squaw in her prime, a massive, healthy woman. This woman died in four days.

Twice a day the wagon would rattle up the trail and halt in front of the hospital lodges. Contorted bodies would be carried out and piled like cordwood on the wagon bed. Then the horse would be turned and the dreadful load pulled to the burning pit. At first, relatives of the dead followed the death wagon, screaming and wailing in anguish, but gradually little attention was paid to the wagon. Apathy fell over the people; even the fear of death became less. Horror, pain, bereavement became familiar, as familiar as the stench that surrounded them. The nurses tied dampened cloths over their nostrils and mouths trying to avoid that stench, but no cloth ever invented could prevent it. The smells of fluids gushing from the patients' bodies, the fumes of burning sulphur, the smoke drifting from fires consuming sodden mats and filthy cloths, the effluvium of smoldering flesh from the burning pit, worked right into the nurses' skin, their hair, their very beings. The nurses were as filthy as their patients. There was no time for proper washing, no time for a change of clothes, no time for anything except their work.

Two weeks after the cholera had been discovered, the twenty nurses were stumbling and dazed, half-sick and hopeless. They forced themselves on, no longer conscious of smells or sounds, hardened to the dead and dying, going through the motions of saving those they could. From the platform at Fort Purline, Laurie and the O'Casey brothers looked down with pitying eyes, and the men would swear. They'd curse the plague, they'd curse themselves because they couldn't help more, they'd curse the Nor'westers for not responding to their call for help.

They shouldn't have cursed the men from the Nor'westers' fort. They hadn't been idle. One of the native children brought the news. The boy ran up to Durran and tugged at his sleeve. *"Keetsi keechp?"* Durran asked impatiently.

The boy told him what he wanted. "Canoes," he babbled. "Two."

"Rowan!" Durran shouted and ran toward the landing. Rowan was at his heels. "It has to be the Nor'westers," he called over his shoulder. "Purline's posted men up and down the river to stop anyone else."

They reached the landing as the lead canoe swung into position and the men disembarked. Rowan's eyes widened. There were eleven men, five in the first canoe and six in the second. The canoes were heavily loaded with cases, bags, and bales, but the man walking to meet them was the reason for her amazement. He was tall and rapier-thin. He wore a velvet coat, an embroidered waistcoat, and a pearl-gray stock. His shirt was ruffled and trimmed with lace, and he brandished a lace-trimmed handkerchief. From this luxurious scrap of cloth came a rich perfume. He bowed, and the grace of that motion in that valley of death was ludicrous.

He spoke English, and the musical lilt of his native tongue lent it beauty. "Chevalier Maurice Keronet, at your service, sir."

"Durran," the Scot grunted.

"Ah, yes. M. Durran. We've never met, but I've heard much of you."

Durran was no more impressed by the chevalier than Rowan was. With dismay he eyed the man. Keronet was

378

handsome in a satanic way which he appeared deliberately to exploit. Dark gleaming hair marched back from a deep widow's peak, his eyes were wine-dark and heavily lashed, and he'd cultivated a hairline moustache and a carefully trimmed Vandyke beard. They've sent us a dancing master, Durran thought disgustedly, a perfumed fop. His disgust showed in his voice. "Have you any experience with this?" One hand waved in an expressive gesture.

Keronet took a delicate sniff of the foul air, and the wine-dark eyes sparkled with ironic amusement. "Many times, *mon ami*. Now, to details. Have you managed to contain the pestilence?"

"We have."

"You're certain?"

"We took a head count as soon as it was discovered. They're all either there"—he jerked his red head at the lodges—"or there." He pointed at the column of greasy smoke drifting from the burning pit.

"Hmm, burning the corpses. A wise idea. Unpleasant, admittedly, but necessary. What are the numbers?"

"Head count of two hundred and seventeen. So far ninety-three stricken." Durran's mouth twisted. "Forty-eight dead so far."

"A good average. You've done well." Keronet waved the scented scrap before his nose. "Beastly odor, but one gets used to it in time." He turned to his men. "Unload the canoes and transport the goods to the settlement." He spun gracefully back to Rowan and Durran. "Your companion, Mr. Durran?"

"Rowan. Her husband and children are in the fort. So far we've managed to keep it out of there."

Keronet bowed gallantly to Rowan, and instantly she was conscious of her own appearance. A soiled cotton dress clung stickily to her body; her hair was bound back under a piece of ragged cloth. She was filthy and smelled like the lodge she worked in. Keronet didn't show distaste by even a flicker of an eye. "Enchanted, madame," he assured her. Then he was all business. "We must have accommodations. Can you provide these?"

Durran jerked his shaggy head. "I'll have mat tents erected. One for you, a larger one for your men. How about medicinal supplies?"

"As much as we had, I brought. A good amount of laudanum and—"

"Opium, we need it badly."

The other man sighed. "Only a small amount." He snapped his fingers at a man bearing a wooden case. "Careful, Gagnon, that is my vintage wine." He fingered his neat, pointed beard. "M. Durran, you will show the way, please."

As they led the way back to the lodges, Rowan whispered to Durran, "He'll be worse than useless. He'll only be in the way."

Turning a gaunt, exhausted face to her, Durran said slowly, "It looks that way, lass, but remember, he's a Nor'wester and Nor'westers are men."

Durran proved to be correct. Keronet's beautiful manners and foppish dress concealed the real man. Actually he was rapier-thin, rapier-tough, and rapier-valiant. An hour later, when he stepped from his hastily erected tent, he looked a different person. He wore buckskin pants, a thin cotton shirt with the sleeves rolled past his elbows, and over his mouth and beard he'd stretched a dampened, perfumed mask of cotton.

Through the mask, his voice was muffled. "M. Durran, you and Madame Rowan will take a brief rest from your duties." He pushed two tall, slim bottles into Durran's hands. "I even give you some of my delightful wine. Take clean clothes and food and leave this area for a time. Find a higher place to camp, above this abominable stench, and clean yourselves, eat, sleep. In three days return."

"We can't," Durran protested. "We're needed here."

Keronet raised a dark eyebrow. "You're all reeling with fatigue. A short time and we'll have the nurses as patients. My men and I will cope. When you return rested, we'll take our turn. Then we'll relieve you. To save lives we must first make sure we're strong enough to do it. You understand, *mon ami?*"

"The voyageurs and our Indian helpers?"

"They will be sent for rest. With them I'll send a keg of high wine. Go now, wash from yourselves the smell of this pesthole."

Durran nodded. Keronet was right. None of the original group of workers could go any further without rest. Durran and Rowan took packs and headed off toward the creek. They followed its banks until they were high above the valley, high above the fort and the lodges. There they made camp. They didn't bother with a shelter. Durran cut fragrant cedar and fir boughs, and Rowan spread clean blankets over them. They shed their foul clothes and plunged into the clear, cool water.

For modesty's sake Rowan wore a cotton shift, but there was no modesty once it was wet. As she soaped herself and scrubbed her hair and scalp, it clung to her body like a second skin. Durran's tired eyes didn't turn her way as he washed. It wasn't lack of desire that kept his gaze from her; it was fear. She was so thin he knew he'd see, outlined against wet cotton, the sharp ridges of her rib cage, the prominent bones of arms, hips, thighs. God protect her, he thought. The plague might not kill her, but she is so tired, so weak, that exhaustion might.

After they'd bathed they sprawled on the springy beds and slept. The hot breeze dried their bodies and hair, dried the cotton shift that Rowan wore. Toward evening they roused, ate some cold food, and slept again. For two days they were content to wash, to eat, to rest, and to breathe deeply of the clean odors of soap, fragrant evergreens, grass, and wildflowers. They seldom spoke; they lived in silent, warm, gratifying comradeship.

Their strength returned, and with it some words came. Unease came with it. Once more they were conscious of each other. On the third morning, Durran started to pack the blankets up. "Time to return," he told her. "Let's circle the fort and look down from the hill."

They trudged through the woods behind the fort,

mounted the foot of the mountain, and came out on the clearing high above the river, where the burial ground was located. They peered down into the valley. A scum of smoke from fires blanketed the lodge area, but they could see across the Nechako to the dense woods on the far bank. Turning her back on the valley, Rowan wandered among the wooden crosses. "Strange," she told her companion, "this is the first time I've been here since Marinska and I . . . since after the massacre."

"You feared to come?"

"The graves. The way we had to dig them, and they were so . . . so raw. Now grass and flowers have grown on them and the crosses—" Stooping, she looked at a cross. "Beau must have done this. He was clever at carving."

"Aye, Beau carved all of them."

She read the words on one cross. "Cherishin, known as Little Moccasins, and the Honorable Robert Henry Holden." With tender fingers she touched the cross. "I never knew Little Moccasins's real name, and I didn't know that Bobby was the Honorable Robert."

"Third son of a lord, Rowan."

"Strange bedfellows," she mused.

"No more strange than this grave, Armand Petier, who was a villain, Louis Lapointe, who was a fool, and Portelance, who was a fine man."

Sinking down at the foot of another grave, she rubbed her hand over the crisp grass. "It's so peaceful now."

"No matter the way of the death, peace does come."

She stared at the cross. "I don't know how Nell Burns Purline can rest at peace. Nell had none in her life, and her death was dreadful." She lifted puzzled eyes to Durran. "Marinska told me the Sioux chief said he was giving Nell mercy. He said he would give none to her husband. Yet he killed Nell and allowed General Purline to live."

With a big hand, Durran cupped a tiny white flower growing on Nell Purline's grave. "The Sioux chief sounds like a wise man. Death would be more merciful than the life that tortured man must live."

"You sound as though you pity him."

"I do."

Anger flared in her eyes. "How can you?"

"No matter what face Purline presents to the world, he must live with himself. That isn't easy, lass." He cast a sidelong look at her face. "You judge too quickly. Have you judged your husband?"

"I have."

"And?"

"He's weak."

"Aye, he's weak."

She turned on him. "And you'd find excuses for Laurie, too. What are you, George Durran? Always goading, goading . . . never really saying anything." She flung back her head, and her hair, thick and loose, streamed out behind her. "For a time I didn't know Laurie, but I loved him. Now I know him. I still love him, but I don't like him. What do you want me to do, make it easy for him? Tell him to go home, forget me, forget our sons?"

He combed blunt fingers through his red beard. "What am I?" he said slowly. "An observer, Rowan, a man with little life of his own who watches other people's. No one wants a mere observer. They want me to tell them what to think, what to do, what not to do. Like you, Rowan. Right now you're waiting for me to give you advice, to tell you to let Laurie go, or how to keep him."

"No!" She sprang to her feet. "A few weeks ago, yes. I'll admit that's what I wanted. Not now."

"Why not?"

She pointed down to the smoke-blanketed lodges. "Because of that. I've watched children and adults die. I've watched people who hunger for life lose it in the most horrible, humiliating way a person could die." She took a deep breath. "When Laurie first told me, I thought if he left me I *would* die, I'd have no desire to live without him. I was mistaken. If he leaves, the children and I will go on. Life is too precious to give up. We'll live, we'll survive without him." She brushed her hand across her eyes and then said soberly, "We must return to the lodges."

He started down the hill. "Yes, we're needed."

As she followed the Scot, she glanced toward the fort. A tiny figure was standing on the lookout platform. She saw sunlight glinting on silver-gilt hair. She thought, Laurie—I wonder what he's thinking?

She didn't wonder long. They moved from the sweet, clear air into the lower valley, and as the smoke and stench closed around her, her thoughts returned to the lodges full of sick and dying people.

In the men's hospital lodge, Durran found one of their own men stretched out on a stinking pallet. He knelt beside Louis Grand's contorted form. Sadly he gazed at the voyageur. Already the nose had sharpened, and it jutted from the lead-colored face. "Why?" Durran asked gently.

Louis Grand made the only sound he'd been able to utter since his throat had been pierced—a grunt. Lifting the man's head, Durran gave him a little water. "You never had cholera, did you?" Louis Grand's shaggy head moved sideways in a no. "Why did you volunteer?"

A thin hand moved and touched the throat. Then Durran understood. This poor devil had possessed only one valuable gift—his silver voice. Like the legless voyageur who had begged for death many years before, Louis Grand had no desire to live without his voice. The following morning Durran carried the voyageur's wasted body out and placed it on the death cart. He stood back and watched the voyageur carried away to the burning pit. For an instant it seemed Durran could hear the echo of rich male voices lifted, one tenor soaring true and sweet above the others.

"Roulez, roulant, ma boule roulante," Durran whispered. Then he went back to work.

It was soon found that Keronet's idea of giving leave to the two groups of workers, although sound in theory, couldn't be put into practice. The influx of patients picked up, and it took the combined efforts of all the workers to tend them. When he could, Keronet would single out a couple of the most exhausted of the nurses and send them away from the lodges for at least a day.

Rowan and Durran both marveled at the man they had at first sight condemned as a perfumed fop. The chevalier was indomitable. He was a more able doctor than even Durran was, and he was everywhere. He dashed from one hospital lodge to the other, dosing the patients, tending them, offering suggestions for their care to the nurses. He was in and out of the other lodges, examining the natives, trying to catch the disease in its earliest stage. He was often seen kneeling in the dust of the trail, a number of children around him, joking with them and watching keenly for the first sign of the plague. Keronet fought cholera with every scrap of knowledge he possessed, with every ounce of strength in his wiry frame. His attitude was much different from the rest of the workers'. Durran, Rowan, the voyageurs, and their Indian assistants worked hard, but they feared the enemy, they feared its hideous face, its unbelievable malignancy. Keronet went for the jugular with the deftness, the sureness, of a man engaged in a titanic struggle with an old and known enemy. Keronet was so vital a force that it was some time before George Durran realized that although the chevalier had sent everyone else for rest, he had taken no leave himself.

One morning Durran met him as Keronet stepped from the men's hospital lodge. He took a close look at the satanically good-looking face, and then he stopped the other man. The Frenchman's face was drawn, and even thinner, dark smudges circled his eyes, and he'd developed a nervous tic high on one cheek. "Maurice," Durran said sternly. "It's time for the doctor to prescribe for himself."

"I'm fine, *mon ami.* Be good enough to take your hand from my arm. A patient awaits me."

"I'll attend to the patient. You stressed our need for personal health. Would you kill yourself?"

Keronet's dark head drooped. "You're right, George, and Gagnon is as weary as I am. We'll both take a day."

"Two."

The look of ironic amusement glinted in Keronet's

wine-dark eyes. "The good Mr. Durran if necessary will enforce his order, won't he? Very well." He spun on his heel. "Gagnon," he called. "Pack clean clothes and provisions for two days. You and I are taking a holiday from death. Don't forget a couple of bottles of my precious wine."

Before he returned to work, Durran made sure that Keronet and Gagnon had left the lodges. In the men's hospital he found another of the Frenchman's devoted followers, an older man named Rivard, hard at work. Durran paused beside the other man to tell him that Keronet and Gagnon had left for a rest.

"That is good," Rivard said. "The chevalier was walking in his sleep."

Durran watched the man's big, deft hands. "You've been with him a long time, haven't you?"

"For years." Pulling himself to his feet, Rivard looked down at the boy on the pallet. "This one is nearly finished," he said mournfully. He glanced at the Scot. "You are curious about our leader, Mr. Durran?"

"Interested. He's an amazing man. He acts as though he's wrestling with the devil and is determined to win."

"And so he is—his own devil. Once the chevalier had a family. His wife was young and lovely, with hair the color of moonbeams, and his two little daughters were in the image of their mother. In Montreal within a week he lost all three of them."

"Cholera?"

"They died like this." Rivard pointed at the boy on the pallet. Although he'd just removed the soiled mats and mopped up the loose stools and grayish paste, already more foul matter was being squeezed inexorably from the child's contorted body. "Those three lovely females died a death that robbed them not only of life but of dignity and beauty. For a time I thought the chevalier would lose his mind. Perhaps he did. Anyway, he works madly to save those he can from the same disease."

Durran nodded and went to work. He fancied he was so hard now that no further death, after so many, could pierce his shell. He was wrong. A few days later one of his faithful Indian helpers, a huge man named Opectim, carried a tiny child into the hospital. Durran hurried to meet him. When he looked at the boy, he winced. The child couldn't have been over two.

"My son," Opectim grunted. "First my woman, then my girl children, now my only son. He mustn't die. My son mustn't die."

"We'll do our best," Durran told the distraught father.

Durran did everything in his power to save the child. He took a tiny piece of the precious opium and fed it to the baby with spoonfuls of broth, but the child couldn't retain it. He spewed it back in vomit. Durran was conscious of a dull pain in his heart, and he wondered if hearts could break. For weeks Opectim had worked at his side, a magnificent man, a tower of strength. The man had lost his entire family; now his son was dying. Opectim never left the baby's side. With agonized eyes, he watched cramps rack the tiny form, squeezing upwards from the legs through the little belly to the throat. When the last convulsion was over and the baby was limp, Opectim left the lodge without a word.

Moving like a sleepwalker, Durran wrapped the baby in a scrap of cloth and picked him up. Through fogs of fatigue, he could hear the death wagon rattling up the trail. He carried the tiny body to the door of the lodge and stepped out. Then he saw Opectim. In one huge hand he brandished a hatchet, and his face was twisted with hate. He'd gone raving mad.

"Murderer!" he shouted at Durran. "You're murdering us! You forced us to stay here to watch us die. You kill women and children and babies. Now you die!"

Durran watched the madman lunging at him, but he made no move. I welcome death, he thought, I can stand no more. Helplessly, Rowan watched from a distance, but Keronet stepped out of a lodge, leveled a silver-butted pistol, and shot the madman. Opectim fell in front of Durran, the hatchet slashing into the earth at the Scot's feet.

Keronet was at Durran's side, taking the little body from his arms. He waited until two of the voyageurs picked up Opectim's massive body and put it on the wagon bed, and then he tenderly placed the child across the father's chest. The chevalier patted Durran's shoulder. "A close shave, *mon ami*."

"I can't thank you," Durran said dully.

"You would prefer to be on that wagon yourself, to be out of it. It's never that easy. We need you."

"And Opectim?"

"His family had perished. Perhaps he is lucky."

Rowan came running up. Tears were wearing clean trails through the dirt on her thin cheeks. Throwing her arms around Durran, she buried her face against his shoulder. Keronet patted her arm and said softly, "Easy, *mes amis,* it's nearly over."

Durran spoke across the woman's head. "What do you mean?"

"There was only one new case yesterday—that baby boy of Opectim's. Haven't you noticed? The wind has shifted. The weather has changed. We had a light frost last night."

Raising a ravaged face, Rowan gazed around. It was the first time she'd actually seen her surroundings in days. She noticed the air was cooler, that a few of the trees near the riverbank were changing color. "It's September," she said slowly. "Do you think the epidemic is over?"

Keronet nodded his dark head. "It's run its course. We still have patients; a few more may die, but the rest will live. I've kept careful count. So far, out of two hundred and seventeen we've lost eighty-four. We've done well. We've deprived cholera of many of his victims."

Durran's arms tightened around Rowan's thin body. "I pray God you're right, Maurice."

Keronet shook a fist at his invisible foe. "You're licked, you demon, you scourge from hell! We've licked you!"

388

31

Laurie Woodbyne had witnessed Opectim's attack on Durran. He was on the lookout platform peering down at the lodge area, and the wind had shifted, blowing the smoke temporarily away. He clung to the palisade so hard that the rough logs bruised his hands as he watched Durran step from the hospital lodge, a bundle cradled in his arms, to be faced by the huge Indian and his hatchet. Helpless, Laurie saw Durran standing there, making no effort to protect himself as the native lunged at him. Laurie breathed a sigh of relief when Keronet shot the berserk man down, but then his eyes widened as he saw his wife throw herself into Durran's arms. Durran was still holding her against his body when smoke swirled up and Laurie could see no more.

His thoughts were whirling, and he felt a violent surge of emotion. As often as he could he'd made his way up there to try and catch a glimpse of Rowan. He saw her the day she left the lodges with George Durran, packs on both their backs, their legs moving slowly and wearily. Laurie saw them the day they returned from the hill where the burial ground was. He watched her long legs flashing, her black hair streaming loosely over her shoulders, as she followed Durran down the hill. What had they been doing all that time alone? he wondered. Was it possible he was jealous of Durran? Jealous of a woman he'd decided to discard? His mind was made up, and in the spring, with the brigade of canoes going eastward, he'd leave. Laurie had always suspected that the Scot was in love with Rowan, and that could be an answer. Durran would be happy to take Rowan as wife, delighted to raise the two boys. Then he could leave Fort Purline with a clear conscience, knowing his family was in Durran's capable hands. Perhaps when the plague was over and they returned to the fort, Rowan would move into Durran's quarters. Laurie knew that once he told her his decision she'd no longer live with him. His problem was solved.

Laurie's brows drew together in a frown. Then why did he feel so upset? He remembered what Rowan had said—that she would always be his wife, wouldn't be free to take another man—and suddenly he felt better. He cursed under his breath, and self-disgust overwhelmed him. He was a proper cad! A dog in the manger. Willing to desert the woman who'd been his wife for over eleven years and unwilling to think of her in another man's arms, in another man's bed.

Pushing away from the palisade, he slowly made his way down the ladder and headed toward his cabin. When he got there he found that Seamus had cooked supper for Martin and himself and bedded the younger boy down. Seamus was cleaning up the kitchen. As his father entered, Seamus lifted his dark eyes and nodded toward a pot standing on the hearthstone. "There's your supper, father. It's still hot."

Shaking his head, Laurie slumped down on a chair. "What have you and Martin been doing today?"

"Hauling wood. Martin can't do much, but he's trying."

For the first time in weeks Laurie looked closely at his older son. The boy was growing in stature. He'll be much taller than me, Laurie thought. Seamus was also extremely handsome. "You work too hard, boy."

Seamus shrugged broad shoulders. "We all do. You do too. Did you see mother from the platform?"

"For a few minutes."

"How did she look?"

"It was hard to tell. All the people down there are so thin, so haggard-looking." Reaching for the brandy bottle, Laurie splashed some in a cup. "You miss her."

"So does Martin. Don't you?"

"Of course."

"It could kill her," the boy muttered.

"George told us there's no chance of her getting cholera."

"I wasn't thinking of cholera. I was thinking of too much work . . . and heartbreak."

Laurie stared at his son. How grown-up he was, and how he kept his thoughts concealed. The boy had worked like a slave since his mother had left. Seamus took care of the cabin, cooked the food, looked after Martin, and also managed to do a man's work on the wood and water details. The boy put away the last dish and reached for a light coat. "Where are you off to?"

Seamus opened the door. "Going to the O'Caseys for a while. Better eat something before you go to bed." He looked back over his shoulder, glanced at his father's face and then at the cup in his hand. Without another word he left.

Laurie put the brandy down untouched. That look . . . was it contempt he'd seen in the boy's eyes? What did the boy expect of him? Did Seamus want him to lunge out of the fort, race down to the lodges, and die? George Durran was the boy's hero and he was down there, but Durran was immune. He wasn't. He'd never been near cholera in his life. As Purline had repeatedly assured him, he was needed here. Silly lad. Seamus must be at the stage where he expected heroics.

Impatiently, Laurie jumped up and strode over to his desk. Sitting down, he fiddled idly with the small objects on it. He touched the decanter, a picture frame, and then pulled open the drawer and found the two letters from London, tattered now from reading and rereading. Somehow they no longer brought the full, rich feeling of pleasure they originally had. Digging around in the drawer, he found the sheaf of drawings that Judith had sent him over the years. He looked at them one by one. Chris at two, when he was five, another drawn when he was eight, and, in the latest one, the boy as a stripling of

391

thirteen. Chris looked much as Laurie had at the same age, much like his grandfather and namesake, Sir Christopher. Laurie looked closely at the last sketch. There was one difference. Chris's full lips were exactly like Esmie's. Was that a hint of her petulance in the boy's expression? Laurie vainly tried to recapture the baby he'd held in his arms in the nursery of the tall house in Mayfair. He tried to remember that warm little body hugged to his breast and failed. Finally he admitted that the tall boy in the last sketch was a stranger.

Putting the sketches down, he leaned his head back and closed his eyes. He was using Chris as an excuse. The boy didn't need him, didn't even know the man who'd fathered him. Edward could look after Chris, and the boy had Judith Hatch. Laurie thought wearily, I'm thirty-eight; by the time I'm in my mid-forties, Chris will be leaving me as I left my own father. What will my life in England be? A round of empty pleasure in London, a lonely aging existence in Essex, a procession of doxies like Lila Lansom. I suppose I could marry again; I'll certainly be an eligible widower. Whom will I marry? Some blue-eyed, fair-haired girl with soft, useless hands could be my wife. I could choose a girl this time from an impeccable background, a lady. A perfumed beauty who wouldn't know how to draw a fowl let alone gut a moose. How would that lady measure up to the woman I've had? How could she ever take the place of Rowan? Now, there's a woman! A woman who can hunt, fish, save her children from a massacre, bury the mutilated dead. Rowan could kill a man if she had to; she could use gentle, strong hands to nurse plague victims.

His eyes snapped open. He stared at his father's pictured features, and it seemed a tiny, sardonic smile hovered around Sir Christopher's painted mouth.

"Why, I love the woman," Laurie said aloud. "I've always loved her. God's teeth, I'm a ruddy fool! No wonder I saw contempt in Seamus's eyes. He must know . . . or suspect . . . what's been going on. He sees a fool of a father who would desert a woman like that, who would desert sons like Martin and him." Again, Laurie saw Rowan in Durran's arms, her head pressed against his shoulder. "No way, Durran. She's mine!"

Pulling open a drawer, he selected several sheets of paper, uncapped his inkwell, and picked up a quill. He bent over the desk and wrote for almost two hours. When he'd finished he held a stick of red sealing wax to the candle, dripped it carefully on the paper, pressed his seal down, and piled up four letters. Sitting back in his chair, he waited.

When Seamus eased open the door and tiptoed into the cabin, Laurie was still waiting. The boy was startled. "I thought you'd be in bed, father."

"Come here," his father ordered. Looking into his son's dark face, he thought, How like Rowan this lad is—the same hair, the same cheekbones, the same steady gaze. Laurie said awkwardly, "I know I have no claim on your affection, and that's my fault, not yours. I've never been a father to you, and I can't make promises about the future." His mouth twisted wryly. "Your mother's much better at keeping promises than I am. But we both love her, and I feel I can ask your help."

"What do you want?"

"A number of things. First, there are four letters here. One is to be given to General Purline; the other three go in the mail pouch."

"I'll see to it."

"Next thing." Laurie took a deep breath. "If anything should happen to me, I'd like to know you'll look after Martin and your mother."

"You don't have to ask that."

"No, I don't." Laurie's fingertips touched the pile of letters. "I've taken care of your mother financially and made arrangements for my own affairs in England. Now the third part, and this will be difficult. I want you to act as decoy."

"When?"

"Early tomorrow morning, just after dawn." It was only later that Laurie realized Seamus's question had been

393

about the time, not the reason. "This is what I want you to do."

Laurie explained carefully, and when he had finished his son nodded. The boy stuck his hand out, an adult gesture, but his quivering lips and suddenly damp eyes betrayed his true age. "I'd like to shake your hand, father."

Getting to his feet, Laurie took the hand in his own. He felt the boy's warm, young strength, and he thought, I may feel pride again but I doubt it could ever equal this moment.

Without another word, they went to bed. Laurie stretched out in the wide bed that had been so empty without Rowan's silken body, and he slept. He slept a dreamless, contented sleep. It was Seamus who was awake that night, staring wide-eyed at the tracery of shadows across the rough, beamed ceiling.

The next morning, as the sky lightened across the Nechako, Seamus was on the lookout platform in animated conversation with the two voyageurs on watch. From the shadowed square, Laurie watched until the boy managed to maneuver the men so their backs were to the fort. He darted across the square, circled the cooper's shop, and emerged in the narrow area between the log buildings and the palisade.

It was still pitch dark there, and he fumbled along the ground until his hands touched the ladder he'd taken from the carpenter's shop earlier. Propping it against the palisade, he heaved the ladder up, grunted, and thrust it across the tops of the uneven logs. He swiftly mounted it. Balancing himself on the narrow ledge, he tried to lower the ladder on the outside of the palisade. It dangled from his hands, nearly pulling his arms from their sockets. He swore under his breath. The damn ladder was too short; it would never reach the ground. Tugging it back, he tried to lower it on the inside of the palisade, but it fell to the ground with a dull thud. He clung to the logs, holding his breath, but there was no stirring in the fort below him.

There was nothing he could do but jump for it. He hauled himself to the top of the palisade and looked down. It seemed a long way. He swung his body forward, still clinging to the top of the palisade, closed his eyes tightly, and released his grip. He hit the ground rolling and continued to roll down a steep slope. A tree trunk checked him, and his body thumped against it. For moments he sprawled there, his chest heaving, getting his breath back. Pulling himself to his feet, he found his shirt sleeve had been ripped and his arm was grazed. The shoulder he'd landed on felt bruised, but he was all right.

Hugging the shadow of the palisade, he crept along toward the front of the fort. Climbing out of the fort wasn't the toughest part. There was no real cover between the gates, and the lodge area. The men on the platform could spot him, and if they did he might be overtaken and hauled back to the fort.

Cautiously, he stuck his head around the corner, peering up toward the platform. From that point he couldn't see the voyageurs, but he could hear the rumble of their deep voices, Seamus's higher one, and then a burst of laughter. He stepped out further and craned his neck. He had a clever son. Seamus had now managed to get both the men to turn their backs to the river.

Laurie raced toward the lodges. Keep it up, Seamus, he said under his breath; keep them occupied. It was getting lighter. He could distinguish the colors of the trees along the river. He didn't dare look back. If the voyageurs spotted him now he'd have to outrun them.

It wasn't one of the men from the fort who saw Laurie first. It was Rivard. The Nor'wester stepped from his lodge rubbing sleep from his eyes, glanced toward the fort, and saw a slender figure with light hair running straight at him. He gave a shout, and the voyageurs and Indians came tumbling out of the lodges.

Rowan was the first one to reach Rivard. She'd been up all night with her patients, and she was so exhausted that for moments the figure coming toward them was merely a blur. Then her eyes widened, and she shouted, "Go back, Laurie!"

Keronet appeared beside her. The black waves of his hair were mussed and tangled. *"Sacrebleu,* man!" he roared. "Back to the fort."

Durran came running up. Cupping his mouth with both hands, he called, "Laurie, the plague is over. Don't come further. We don't need help now."

The blond head shook, and Laurie steadily approached. As the distance between them narrowed, Rowan stepped forward and pleaded. "Laurie, I release you. You're free. You can go home."

This time he did answer. "I am home."

Swinging on Durran, Keronet growled, "This man is as mad as Opectim."

Durran said nothing. He watched as Laurie reached Rowan and threw his arms around her. She tried to turn her head away, but he grasped her chin and forced her face up. With deliberation he pressed his lips to hers. Then he lifted his head, looked into Durran's eyes, and said, "I love her."

"Mad," Keronet raged. "The man has lost his mind."

"No, he's found it," Durran told him. "Laurie's reached his own Pass of Hajarial."

Turning to face the Scot, Keronet looked keenly at him. "It occurs to me that you may be a bit mad too. All of us down here would now have the plague if we were going to get it. But him . . . it's suicide." He paused and then asked, "Tell me, *mon ami,* what is this Pass of— what did you call it?"

"The Pass of Hajarial."

"Where is that?"

"Not where. Not really a place but a . . ." Durran searched for words and couldn't find them. He said haltingly, "I don't think I have to explain. I think you've met yours. Aye, I think you have."

Wine-dark eyes met the Scot's. "It's possible I have, George."

Both men turned. Laurie was leading Rowan toward

them. She stumbled, and he put his arm around her thin waist. He looked at Keronet and then at Durran. "I've touched her," he said evenly. "You can't send me back now."

With a sense of sad recognition, Keronet eyed Laurie's silver-gilt hair, the beauty of his fine features. "No," he said. "Now you must stay."

32

Keronet's assessment of the plague had been accurate. No further patients were brought to the hospital lodges. Three of those already there died—a man and two women—but the rest were soon on the mend.

There was still work to do, and Keronet drove them into it. Mopping up, he called it, a necessary precaution in the aftermath of an epidemic. The lodges were dismantled and mat tents put up to house the Indians. The death wagon now didn't haul bodies but transported poles and logs to be burned in the pit. After that was done, lime ash was strewn over the surface of the burning pit, and the voyageurs started to shovel earth back into it. The latrine trenches behind both hospitals were strewn with more lime ash and covered thickly with piles of earth and stone. Gradually the fires used for burning offal and sulphur died out, and the air became sweet and clean again. Autumn came early that year, and every morning the ground was covered with light films of frost. The trees flamed with gold and crimson and yellow, and the wind whistling down from the mountain peaks held the frigid hint of an early winter.

Among the plague fighters there was an unvoiced agreement to keep Laurie Woodbyne away from the more infected area of the lodges. He wasn't allowed near the burning pit or the latrines. Excuses were made so he didn't enter either of the hospital lodges. Keronet assigned him to the wood detail and sent him as often as possible into the forest. He also put Laurie in charge of the men bringing down the provisions that still were piled daily by the fort gates.

Many pairs of concerned eyes watched Laurie. A week after he'd made his successful bid to join his wife, Durran anxiously questioned Keronet. "What do you think, Maurice? Has he a chance?"

Bleakly, Keronet watched Laurie's slender figure as he unloaded wood. "By now, *mon ami,* you know cholera as well as I do. It's a strange disease. It can hit a family, take several members of that family, and for some unknown reason the rest don't get it. It's possible that Laurie won't get it. I've been watching him, and there's no sign yet. I still can't understand why he came down here. You told the factor the evening before Laurie made a break for it that the plague was past."

"General Purline had no chance to tell Laurie. He must have made up his mind, and that was it."

Keronet was still watching Laurie. "Pray God he doesn't get it. That wife of his—such a beautiful, gallant woman. They make a striking couple. She's so dark and he's so fair. Once I knew someone with hair the same shade as his."

Yes, Durran thought, you knew three people—a woman and two little girls with hair the color of moonbeams. Aloud he said, "Rowan needs a rest. Why don't we send the two of them away for a few days?"

Keronet snapped his fingers. "A fine idea." He called, "Laurie, come here a minute."

Wiping his hands down his shirt, Laurie joined them. He looked inquiringly at the chevalier. Keronet said solemnly, "Your wife is in need of a rest. George and I both find it hard to handle Rowan. Could you persuade her to go away with you for a couple of days?"

"Aren't we needed here?"

"We can spare you. The work load is lighter. This is merely a precautionary period before we enter the fort. Look around you."

Laurie glanced around. Life at the lodges seemed back to normal. The women were going about their usual work, the men sprawled inside the tent flaps playing interminable games of hand and la-hal, and two tiny children raced past chasing a puppy. "I'll speak to Rowan," Laurie told them.

Rowan didn't hesitate or waste a moment in leaving the lodges. Quickly, she gathered together clean clothes, soap, some food, and blankets and packed them. In less than an hour they were walking toward the creek. "Where shall we camp?" she asked.

"Our island, Rowan. The Ile Ste. Anne."

She winced as she thought of the night she'd waited in front of the cave while Martha and the children slept a drugged sleep. Laurie recalled only the good parts on that island, the days of lovemaking and joy in the early months of their marriage. She forced herself to sound gay. "The very place. There's a canoe in the willows and—"

"Rowan." He whirled on her, anger striking sparks from his brown eyes. "Don't humor me as though I'm a child. Do you think I'm completely stupid? All of you—Keronet, Durran, the voyageurs—have been looking after me as though I'm a half-wit. Giving me easy jobs, trying to keep me clear of the patients—" Breaking off, he muttered, "You all think I'm a damn fool. Breaking out of the fort to be a hero when all I am is an extra burden."

She touched his arm. "You didn't know the plague was waning." She raised her deeply circled, exhausted eyes. "I don't think you're a fool. I think you're . . . invincible."

He put an arm around her and pulled her close to his side. "You're the only one who counts."

They located the canoe and paddled to the tiny island. There they rested, bathed, ate hearty meals, and, in the depth of the cave, made love. At the end of the second day, as they lay in each other's arms in the friendly darkness of the cave, Laurie nuzzled his lips against her throat. "You're so thin, Rowan—a rack of bones with skin drawn over it."

"I'll fill out." Her hand groped out and stroked the thick hair back from his brow. "We have to go back tomorrow."

"Hmm."

"We haven't really talked. Why did you come down from the fort?"

"I told you. I love you. After eleven years I suddenly realized I love you." His arms tightened around her. "And I saw Seamus, really saw our son, and he made me ashamed. He's so like you, such a fine boy, and all these years I've . . . but it's not too late. I'll make it up to him and to you."

With a fingertip, she traced the lines of his mouth. "Chris?"

"Chris will be fine. I sent letters to England, and my cousin Edward and Judith Hatch will look after him."

"Are you sure? Are you sure you won't regret—"

He closed her lips with his own. Later, he said dreamily, "We're going to have a wonderful life . . . you, the boys, me."

"Will we stay on here?"

"For a time. The general is leaving next spring to be the chief agent in Montreal. I'll be factor here, and we'll move into the Purline cabin. It's bigger, and the boys will have more room. In a few years, I'm taking all of you to Lower Canada. The boys should go to school."

"You and I?"

"We'll buy a tract of land, and I'll build you a house. A real house, Rowan. One with a parlor and a separate kitchen and a big bedroom with a feather bed. You'll have a hired girl and you'll never have to work hard again. You'll have clothes, silks and velvets and—"

"It sounds wonderful." Her fingers moved down over his throat. She could feel the hard muscles across his shoulders. She whispered, "Do you remember our first winter when we'd lie on the bearskin before the fire and you'd make up poems?"

"Terrible poems."

"They were mine. I remember one. 'Oh Rowan, my tree of delight—' "

" '—with crowns of blossoms sweet and white.' Yes, I remember."

She sighed. "How happy we were."

"No. How happy we *are*. How happy we'll always be."

She held him fiercely to her breast. Long after he'd fallen asleep she held him and she thought, I don't want a big house and silks and velvets. All I want is you, all I've ever wanted was you.

The following morning they started back to the lodges. Laurie was in high spirits. He'd eaten a hearty breakfast, taken a last plunge in the cool water, and as they walked, he hummed. "Let's take the long way back," he suggested. "Go around the fort and down the hill. Like you and George did."

"You saw us, Laurie. Were you spying?"

"I certainly was. As often as I could I'd hang over the palisade watching for you."

They entered the forest, and tall trees closed in over their heads, dry leaves crackled under their feet. For a time, Laurie strode ahead, and then he fell back beside Rowan. She glanced at him. The warm color had seeped away under his tan, and his hand rubbed his stomach.

"Do you feel all right?" she asked.

"A bit queasy." He grinned down at her. "You're too good a cook. Think I ate too much breakfast."

A short time later he stopped, braced an arm against the trunk of a cedar, and mumbled, "Go on ahead. I'll catch up."

She walked on, and behind her she could hear sounds. He was being sick. Her hands clenched until her nails drew blood from her palms. Laurie, when he caught up to her, was still cheerful. "That feels better."

For a time she had hope, but before they reached the foot of the mountain he'd vomited twice more. Now his face was bloodless, and he walked with difficulty. By the time they reached the burial ground, Rowan had shouldered the heavy pack and Laurie was leaning on her. "You'd better wait here," she panted. "Sit down in the shade."

As she eased him down, he groaned with pain. "Cramps in my legs."

She touched his bright hair. "Rest. I'll get help."

She started to run down the hill. After a few yards she paused and threw the pack down. Then she ran like a deer. Gagnon was the first one she saw, and she shouted, "Get a litter and some men. In the burial ground. Laurie."

He jerked his head and took off. Durran and Keronet, with Rivard at their heels, ran to meet her. "Laurie," she called. "Vomiting and cramps in his legs."

"*Mon Dieu*," Keronet muttered. Shading his eyes with one fine hand, he looked up the slope. Then he straightened his shoulders and bellowed at Gagnon. "Hurry. As fast as you can."

"Not the hospital lodge," Rowan panted. "Bring him to my tent."

Without slowing, she ran the length of the winding trail, her moccasins raising clouds of dust, children and dogs scampering out of her way. She entered her tent and started to gather her possessions together. Piling them in a corner, she hastily made up a bed of clean mats. Taking a water ewer to the barrel, she filled it with cool water. By the time the men arrived with the litter, all was prepared. Durran and Keronet were already waiting in the tent when Rivard and Gagnon carried Laurie in. Behind them Jourdin, Pierre, and Emile crowded in.

Keronet knelt beside the sick man. "Look at the number of nurses you have," he said lightly. "You're a lucky man, Laurie."

"Very lucky," Laurie said grimly. "I've cholera, haven't I?"

Keronet dropped all pretense. "You have cholera, but we've caught it in the first stage. And, God knows, we know a great deal about the scourge."

Rowan swayed. Durran moved closer to support her, but she pulled herself away from him and stood erectly, her chin lifted. Keronet looked up at her. "Get some warm broth, Rowan. Rivard, go to my tent and get that last piece of opium—"

"Opium!" Durran gasped.

The chevalier's white teeth glinted as he smiled. "I've been hoarding a morsel. Only a few grains, but it might make the difference."

All their faces brightened, and Rowan and Rivard hurried from the tent. Laurie's head was rolling from side to side. "Water," he pleaded.

Lifting his head, Keronet held a cup to his lips. "Only a few sips."

Laurie gulped the water, and the chevalier pulled the cup back. Then Laurie pushed himself up on an elbow, and vomit gushed from his mouth. "Ugly," he moaned as Keronet wiped the foulness from his face. "An ugly way to die."

Keronet touched the silver-gilt hair. "Don't speak of dying."

Blindly, Durran headed out of the tent. Crossing the trail, he squatted in the shade of another tent. Old Tupa wandered up to him. "He got *omikewin*?" she asked.

"Go away," Durran grated. "Get the hell away from here."

With a kind of hatred he looked around. Dirty savages, he thought, bringing this filthy kind of death. He saw people who'd had the plague and recovered, and he resented them. They turned bewildered eyes on the gaunt, wild, hate-filled face of the man who'd nursed them. Durran was aware of Rowan passing, going into her tent, of Rivard hurrying by. He sat there, sinking deeper and deeper into hatred and despair. Durran had no idea how long he sat there, and then a hand touched his shoulder and he looked up into Keronet's compassionate face.

"The filthy bastards," Durran groaned. "They killed Louis Grand . . . now Laurie."

"So, George, you find scapegoats to hate, to blame. How many of *them* died? I'll tell you. Exactly eighty-seven. The people you're glaring at have lost brothers, sisters, wives, children. Many of them worked as hard as we did nursing the sick, burning the dead. Now, because your friend has cholera, you fasten the guilt." He threw his head back. "Put the guilt where it should be. Hate the disease itself. Hate the scourge from hell we know so little about. Hate our own lack of knowledge, but don't, *mon ami*, hate its innocent victims."

Durran rubbed his brow. "I know. It's just that . . . You're right, Maurice. Aye, it's not these poor devils." He pulled himself up. "How is he?"

"I gave him a few sips of broth and opium. He couldn't keep it down."

"The flux, has it started?"

The Frenchman nodded. "But no blood in the stools yet. If he could just keep some opium down. We'll try later."

All that day they tried. Tiny sips of the precious fluid were spooned into the sick man's mouth, and he struggled to swallow it, to keep it down. Their own throats ached in sympathy as the cords in Laurie's neck stood out tautly, trying to hold back, to retain the fluid. Then his mouth would contort, his chest heave, and involuntarily he'd spew it back up. They worked tirelessly, lifting him to remove the soiled mats, wiping up pools of fluid, sponging his lower body and his face. Men came and went, but Rowan never left Laurie's side. Several times Keronet tried to force her to rest, but she shook her head, never taking her eyes from her husband's face. The light faded, and Jourdin brought lamps. Through the night hours they fought the killer.

Toward dawn Rowan rose stiffly and beckoned to Keronet. He followed her out into the chill darkness. She had to clear her throat before she could speak. "Tell me," she said.

"He's strong, Rowan, a strong, fairly young—"

"The truth, Maurice. I've seen men younger and stronger than Laurie die."

He tried to find words. None came. He told her the truth. "I don't know. The progress is very fast. He's weakening."

Her nails bit into his arm so painfully that he winced. "He can't die. I can't let him die. I almost lost him. I can't lose him, Maurice, not this way."

He couldn't see her face, but what he heard in her voice brought tears to his eyes. He caressed the fingers biting into his arm. "I know."

She slapped his hand away. "How could you know how *I* feel?" she shrieked.

Grabbing her shoulders, he shook her. "Do you think you're the only one who has ever watched the one they love die of this horror? Do you think no one else has seen a beautiful face fall into wrinkles and hollows, a beloved body pull up like a knot of twisted wood?" He shook her harder. "Well, do you?"

She started to cry, and he gathered her against his hard chest as though she were a child. He smoothed the hair back from her face. "Easy, easy, Rowan. He still lives. There's a chance. Now, go rest. That's an order."

From then on Rowan obeyed him docilely. When Keronet told her to rest, she went to his tent and stretched out. The hours blurred into days. Durran did none of the nursing. Once in a while he'd step into the tent, gaze helplessly down at the contorted form on the pallet, and then quietly leave. Each evening toward sunset he'd make his way up to the fort to report to General Purline. Most of the men gathered on the platform to hear how Laurie was. Seamus always was at the factor's side, but Martin never was there. Durran guessed that Seamus was shielding the younger boy. All he could tell them was that Laurie still lived, still was fighting the disease.

For five nights Durran went to the fort to report Laurie's condition. The sixth evening, as he returned to the lodges, he began to stagger. His knees folded under him, and he sank down on the grass. Rolling over on his back, he watched the last light from the sunset throwing its glorious oranges, reds, and violets upwards to the lower edges of a massive bank of gray clouds. Rain, Durran thought drearily. By morning it would be raining. His thoughts turned to Laurie. He was amazed at the fight that Laurie was putting up. He knew the man was fighting for Rowan, for his sons, for his own right to live. Durran sensed it was a losing battle. Laurie's nose had sharpened, standing starkly out from his face. His skin was dull gray, wrinkling, the flesh caving in around the eyes, the mouth. The smooth cap of pale hair lay limply against his skull now, as sere and bleached as straw.

I wanted Rowan, Durran thought, wanted her as much as a man could ever want anything. I've coveted her for years and waited for Laurie to desert her, for something to happen so she would be mine. But not this way. Let him live, Durran prayed, let Laurie live. Let him live for Rowan. I'll go lonely to my grave, but spare him.

The prayers for Laurie Woodbyne were unanswered. Shortly before six the next morning, he died. As he went into the last convulsion, the rain started—a hard, cold torrent of rain bouncing off the hard-beaten dirt of the trail, turning the dust to oozing mud, pelting against the stretched hides and woven mats of the flimsy shelters.

Rowan's eyes remained fixed on the dead face. She made a gesture, and the men filed silently out of the tent to stand in the rain and wait. They waited for an hour before the tent flap was pushed aside and she stepped out. She held her rifle, and she pointed it directly at Durran's chest. "You're not going to burn him," she said quietly.

Durran stepped forward. "Put that down, Rowan."

Her finger tightened on the trigger. "He's not to be burned. I won't let him suffer this . . . this final indignity. I've washed him and wrapped him in blankets. If you don't bury him, I'll kill you."

Keronet stepped to the Scot's side. "Rivard and Gagnon have gone to dig a grave. George said you'd want it beside the grave of a woman called Nell Purline." He moved closer to her. "Give me the rifle."

She gave it to him. Emile and Jourdin carried the litter, and Rowan walked beside it. Behind them Keronet and Durran came, then all the voyageurs and many of the Indians. The grave had been dug, and already rain had turned the soil to soupy mud. Rowan stood while they lowered the blanket-covered form into it. She stood beside it while they shoveled soil in great, moist masses back into it. Sinking to her knees, she bowed her head while Chevalier Maurice Keronet prayed. Durran bent and touched her shoulder. She was squeezing a ball of mud in her hand. It oozed clammily out between her fingers. She lifted glazed eyes to Durran's face. "It's so raw, isn't it? But grass will grow, and there'll be flowers. Will there be a cross?"

"Yes," he told her hoarsely, "there'll be a cross. I'll carve one."

Wind buffeted them, driving icy rain against their faces. Water streamed down Rowan's cheeks, but it was rain, not tears. Then she sighed and collapsed across the muddy grave. Durran tried to lift her, but his knees buckled and he sank weakly down beside her. Jourdin carried her down the hill. Behind him Durran staggered, supported by Gagnon and Emile. The rest of the men straggled along after them.

For a time Keronet stood alone by the grave. Water streamed down his face, and not all of it was rain. The chevalier wept for Laurie, for Rowan, and for a lovely girl with hair the color of moonbeams who had died long before.

A few days later a forlorn procession straggled back to the fort. For the first time in almost two months the gates stood open, and the people of the fort gathered inside the gates to watch their comrades come home.

In shocked silence they saw Rowan, in Rivard's arms, carried past them. Her face was a mask of despair, and although she was conscious she appeared to see no one. Durran staggered in, his arms around two voyageurs' shoulders. Then the others came, shuffling along like old men.

General Purline's eyes moved down that stumbling line, and then his hand snapped to his beaver hat in a military salute. There was nothing military about the people he saluted, and yet the gesture didn't appear ludicrous. For they were soldiers, soldiers who had battled the enemy. Some battles they had won, some they had lost, but the war against cholera could never end in a decisive victory.

Hand stretched out to the survivors, hands trying to convey comfort. Rowan felt hands touching her arms, her shoulders, but for her there was no comfort. Her bed was ready, and a fire blazed on her own hearth. She was placed on that bed, covered warmly, and left alone. She didn't care. There was no comfort. Seamus and Martin came to her. Martin threw himself down beside her; his head burrowed against her shoulder, his tears wetting and warming her.

Seamus stood over her, and his eyes were dry. "He knew, mother," Seamus told her. "He knew he might die. He had to go. He was a man."

Then she felt a measure of comfort. After a time she slept.

33

As though to make amends for the early, hard winter, the spring of '28 came early. By the first day of April the ice and snow were gone, the river was running clear, and the trees surrounding Fort Purline were putting out tender leaf buds.

In the burial ground, sheltered from the north by a stand of tall cedars, it was warm and pleasant. Lemon-yellow sunlight washed the sunken plots and wooden crosses. The mellow light gleamed from Rowan's dark hair. She sat beside her husband's grave with the skirts of her silk dress carefully spread out around her. The silk was close to the color of her eyes, and the material and the frosty lace at the throat were gifts from Chevalier Maurice Keronet. At Christmas he'd made the trek from the Nor'westers' fort by dog team, and the sled had been laden with presents. He'd obviously enjoyed his role of Father Christmas and had happily passed out wine to the men and trinkets to their women. For Rowan he had a lavishly wrapped parcel containing the dress length, satin slippers, and a flask of French cologne.

As she touched the silk of the skirt, she smiled at the memory of the donor of the gift. Her tilted eyes wandered down to the landing. It was a beehive of activity. The flotilla of canoes was to leave the following morning, and the crafts were surrounded by laboring men. Chichi was overseeing the loading of his canoe, and a short distance away Jourdin, now also a steersman, was hovering over his.

A travois drawn by a shaggy pony was bringing down more bales. Rowan could see Seamus driving the horse while Martin perched among the bales. The figure of General Purline loomed head and shoulders over the other men. From this distance, with sunlight glinting from his tall beaver hat, snowy linen, and the gold head of his cane, Ezra Purline looked the same as he had the first time she'd seen him. At closer range the changes in the man were startling. Since the cholera epidemic he'd aged visibly. His wide shoulders had sagged, his face was furrowed and care-worn, and his clothes looked too large for him, as though through the winter months he'd shrunk. Rowan no longer hated the factor; Purline was too pathetic to rouse such a strong emotion. On many winter nights he'd wakened the entire fort with screams. Once he'd run out into the snow-covered square clad only in a nightshirt. The O'Casey brothers, with that gentleness big men are capable of, appointed themselves his guardian angels. Often one of them would sleep in Purline's small cabin to keep the tormented man company. The brothers' duties would be over the next day. General Purline was leaving with the flotilla to take up his new position in Montreal.

In a few days only a handful of the original inhabitants would be left at the fort. Jourdin would come back, and Four-Finger Jacques was remaining. Tapinawa was still sleeping in the stable, but the old man was crippled with rheumatism. Most of the time he sat against the wall of the stable smoking his pipe, his rheumy eyes watching the activity in the square. George Durran was also leaving. He'd refused the position of factor, and three new men from Fort Timberline had arrived. The oldest of them, an Englishman named Grant, would be the new factor.

Rowan sighed. Many of the people she'd known and loved rested in the graves that surrounded her. Laurie's grave was still raw, but the soil had been neatly raked over the plot, and there was a faint green haze of grass already growing on it. In a couple of months it would be covered with the same rich mantle that carpeted the older

411

graves. At the head of his grave was a beautifully carved and polished cross. George had brought all his skill to bear on it, and the letters were perfectly formed. Rowan didn't have to turn her head to read the words. They were clear in her mind—*Sir Laurence Woodbyne, 1779—1827.* Under the dates one word was carved—*Invincible.*

Although Rowan had requested the word, she wondered how apt it was. How invincible had Laurie really been? She sensed that his sudden decision to join her during the epidemic had been largely emotional. She also sensed that if he'd lived he would have kept his word and remained with her, but . . . in the long years of exile would his first enthusiasm have turned to resignation, would his ardor and love have been gradually replaced by resentment? She'd never know now. All she had was the memory that he had come, had declared his love. It was all she had—it had to be enough.

Lifting her head, she looked down at the landing. She could see Durran talking to Purline. The factor lifted his cane and pointed toward the hill. Durran turned away from the river and started the long walk up to her. He wore a cotton shirt with gaudy purple stripes that contrasted violently with the red of his hair and his neatly trimmed beard. As he drew closer, she thought how he'd aged. His thick mane of hair was graying at the temples, and there were white strands through the fiery beard. The wrinkles near his eyes and around his mouth were deeper, but his walk was still youthful. Coming over the hill, he dropped down at her side. "Whew." He pulled a handkerchief from his pocket and wiped his face. "Warm for April."

"Have you come to say good-bye?"

Instead of answering the question, he asked one of his own. "When do you plan to leave?"

"In a week. As soon as I can hire a few more men to handle the canoe."

"You still plan to head west, then?"

"Yes. I'm going to locate the Chilcotins." She pleated the silk in her lap, noticing how white her hand was against the blue material Her tan was gone, but a few weeks of sun and she'd be as brown as ever. She met Durran's eyes. "I started out to find my mother years ago. Now I'm going to."

He glanced at the grave they sat beside. "Have you stopped blaming me for Laurie's death?"

"You knew?"

"Aye. I was the one you pointed the rifle at, and you've done everything to stay clear of me since."

"It was mad, George. Even at the time I knew it was mad. I think I must have been unbalanced for a time. I had to find someone to blame."

He rubbed his brow. "How well I know. I was the same, only I put the blame on the poor Indians. Maurice set me straight. Have you found peace, lass?"

"Does anyone ever find peace? Look at the general."

"He still flees from the ghost of his wife."

She asked hesitantly, "Do you think Nell *is* haunting him?"

"Nay, and neither do you. He flees from memories. But there's hope even for Ezra Purline. He plans to become a Catholic and find someone to exorcise his demon."

The breeze had worked a tendril of hair loose from the bun, and Rowan felt it tickling her neck. She tucked it back in place. "Do you think a priest can actually help the man?"

Durran shrugged. "Perhaps. If Purline believes the demon has been exorcised it probably will be, but that's his problem, and he's more than earned it. Now, about our problems. Will you stay on with your mother's people?"

"No. I only want to see her and have the boys see that side of their heritage."

"Where will you go from there?"

"East, to Lower Canada. The boys must go to school."

He waved a hand toward the river, up toward the mountain peaks. "Will you ever turn your face westward again?"

She took a deep breath, a breath rich with the odors of

413

spring, the indescribably vibrant air alive with the awakening of land and vegetation. "I suppose I'll have to. I think this land will draw me back. I know it will draw Seamus."

"Martin?"

"I can't tell about Martin. He may want to go to England, to seek out his father's family, to meet his half-brother. What about you?"

The wrinkles around his eyes deepened as he smiled. "In the end I'll travel east myself, for a time. Probably take a tract of land and farm. But I'll come back. This land draws me too. That new fort at the coast—"

"Fort Langley?"

"Aye. They say the weather is more clement there, a gentler climate. I may go there."

"To work at the fort?"

"Nay, I'll take up a homestead near it and live out my days."

Rowan dropped her eyes from his face to the purple stripes on his broad chest. "I must be honest with you, George. I know how you feel about me."

"How long have you known?" he asked gently.

"Since that day I was caught in the storm and you hauled my snowshoes off and lectured me."

Leaning over, he cupped her chin in his hand and lifted her face until their eyes met. "Aye, I love you. I've always loved you. Now I'll ask you. Have you any feeling for me?"

"Of course. I respect you, I'm fond of you, and I've come to depend on you, perhaps too much."

"That would do for a start."

She moved away from his hand. Her own hand brushed the soil on the grave. "I loved Laurie, George. I still love him. I don't think I'll ever love again. Not like that."

"I don't expect the kind of love you gave Laurie, Rowan. But you've a big heart. There's room in it for many loves."

The skin between her dark brows wrinkled in thought. "Someone else once said that to me. Who was it? Oh yes,

414

it was Martha MacLeod. When I asked her if she'd loved Nell's father, she said yes, but there was room in her heart for more than one love. I don't know if there's room in mine. And we'll have no time to find out. I'm heading west, and you're going east with the flotilla tomorrow."

"Who told you that?"

She stared at him. "You turned down the job as factor. I assumed—"

"You assumed wrong."

"Are you staying on here?"

"Nay, I'm coming with you. Did you think I'd let you set off into the wilderness with two lads and some Indian paddlers?"

"I have Seamus. He handles a rifle as well as I do."

"He's a fine lad, but he's only a boy, too young to have to take the part of a man. You need a man to protect you."

She laughed softly. "I'm no longer afraid, George. Do you really think any man would try to lay hands on me now?"

He looked at her, at her strong slender body, at her capable hands. She was still beautiful, but it wasn't the soft, helpless beauty that would tempt men to try and take her by force. The man who tried to molest this woman would have to be foolish. He told her quietly, "There are other dangers besides men, Rowan. There are wild beasts, sickness, wild water, possibly forest fires. It never does to underestimate this land. I'll take you to your mother's people, and then I'll take you to Lower Canada. I won't press you for what you're unwilling to give. I won't press you for marriage or for anything else. I'll simply accompany you and the boys."

She took his hand. "I'd be glad of that company, and so would the boys. I'd like you to come, but I can offer you nothing. I can give no promise or even any hope."

He pulled her to her feet, and his hand dropped away from her. "I ask for neither, lass."

Turning away from him, she started down the hill. He watched the silk of her full skirt billowing around her, he

415

heard the rustle of the silk as she moved away from him. Then he raised his eyes and looked across the Nechako at the mountains etched against the pale blue of the spring sky. His eyes glazed, as his grandmother's had when she'd parted the veil between the past and the future. If he did see anything, it seemed he liked what he saw. His lips parted in a contented smile. He was still smiling when he followed Rowan down the hill toward Fort Purline.